Streams of Mercy

Books by Lauraine Snelling

An Untamed Heart

SONG OF BLESSING

To Everything a Season   *Streams of Mercy*
A Harvest of Hope

RED RIVER OF THE NORTH

An Untamed Land   *The Reapers' Song*
A New Day Rising   *Tender Mercies*
A Land to Call Home   *Blessing in Disguise*

RETURN TO RED RIVER

A Dream to Follow   *More Than a Dream*
Believing the Dream

DAUGHTERS OF BLESSING

A Promise for Ellie   *A Touch of Grace*
Sophie's Dilemma   *Rebecca's Reward*

HOME TO BLESSING

A Measure of Mercy   *A Heart for Home*
No Distance Too Far

WILD WEST WIND

Valley of Dreams   *A Place to Belong*
Whispers in the Wind

DAKOTAH TREASURES

Ruby   *Opal*
Pearl   *Amethyst*

SECRET REFUGE

Daughter of Twin Oaks   *The Long Way Home*
Sisters of the Confederacy   *A Secret Refuge 3-in-1*

SONG OF BLESSING • BOOK 3

Streams of Mercy

LAURAINE SNELLING

BETHANYHOUSE
a division of Baker Publishing Group
Minneapolis, Minnesota

© 2015 by Lauraine Snelling

Published by Bethany House Publishers
11400 Hampshire Avenue South
Bloomington, Minnesota 55438
www.bethanyhouse.com

Bethany House Publishers is a division of
Baker Publishing Group, Grand Rapids, Michigan

Printed in the United States of America

Library of Congress Cataloging-in-Publication Data
Snelling, Lauraine.
    Streams of mercy / Lauraine Snelling.
        pages ; cm. — (Song of Blessing ; 3)
    Summary: "A recent widow from Norway settles with her children in the
early 1900s community of Blessing, North Dakota, where her growing friendships with two men in the community bring her to a challenging choice"—
Provided by publisher.
    ISBN 978-0-7642-1730-2 (hardcover : acid-free paper)
    ISBN 978-0-7642-1106-5 (softcover)
    ISBN 978-0-7642-1731-9 (large-print : softcover)
    1. Widows—Fiction. 2. Mate selection—Fiction. 3. Man-woman relation-
ships—Fiction. 4. Triangles (Interpersonal relations)—Fiction. I. Title.
PS3569.N39S77 2015
813'.54—dc23   2015015379

Scripture quotations are taken from the King James Version of the Bible.

Cover design by Jennifer Parker and Paul Higdon

Author is represented by Books & Such Literary Agency

15 16 17 18 19 20 21   7 6 5 4 3 2 1

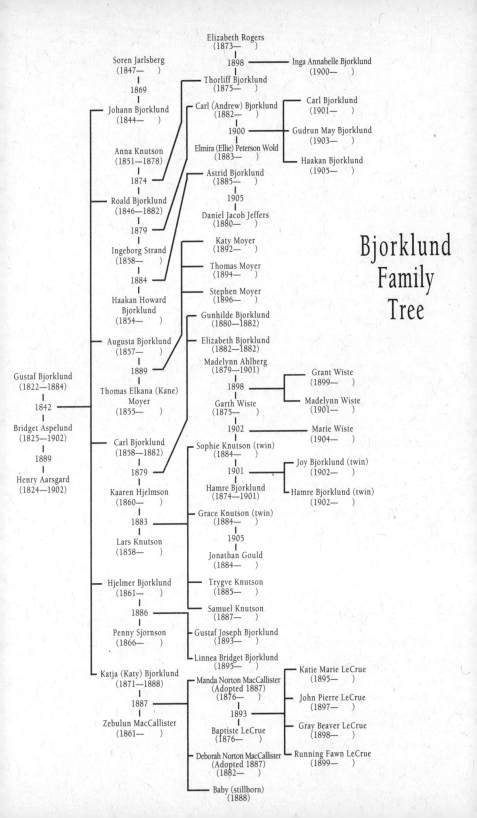

CHAPTER 1

APRIL 1907

Tears again.

Ingeborg awoke. A dream. It had been a dream. She could almost vow Haakan had been right there with her. She wasn't sure if the tears were sorrow or joy, but her eyes felt as though a dust storm had just blown through. Dreams and weeping attacks came less often now that more time had passed since Haakan went home to heaven. The rattle of the grate at the kitchen stove made her smile. Who got there first this morning? Freda or Manny? The two seemed to have an undeclared contest going as to who would start the kitchen stove. Now that he could walk without a cane, even though he limped, Manny had a new zest for living.

Ingeborg stared up at the dimness that was

the ceiling. She should get up, but today she'd rather huddle back down under the covers, where she could not see her breath on the air, not that she could in the predawn darkness anyway. The light under her door beckoned. She reached for her robe at the same moment as she threw back the covers and slid her feet into the moccasins she kept right by her bed. Every morning she thanked her Lord for Metiz, who had made the moccasins those years ago and, like the moccasins, had helped her friends in myriad ways to adapt to life on the prairie.

That thought led to Metiz' grandson, Baptiste LeCrue, who had married Manda and moved to Montana, where her adopted father, Zeb MacCallister, had gone after his wife, Katy Bjorklund, died in childbirth. Later Baptiste and Manda had moved south to Wyoming. She hadn't heard from any of them in a long time. Perhaps today would be a good day to write to them, as well as to her family in Norway and perhaps even to Augusta, Roald's sister, who had settled with her husband, Kane Moyer, on a ranch in South Dakota. Winter, even with spring almost here, was always a good time for writing letters.

When she opened the door to the kitchen, she could feel the warmth flowing out from the stove. "You are down already. Good morning, Freda. Has Manny gone to the barn?"

"Ja. That young whippersnapper came

down to the kitchen before I did and got the stove going. He sure takes his responsibilities seriously. Not that anyone said he had to start the stove."

"He is growing up so fast."

"Sure is. His pant legs are too short already. Good thing you put a deep hem in them." Freda glanced up at the clock just as Emmy came down the stairs. "Morning, Miss Sunshine."

That was some change since when Emmy first came to live with Ingeborg. Freda's attitude toward the little Indian girl had changed over time, from only accepting her at first to liking and now loving her.

Emmy was indeed family now, and Manny was too. To Ingeborg they'd been her family since the day they'd arrived, whether they knew it or not. God had strange ways of giving her more children, but she never questioned the gifts. How Haakan would delight in watching Manny grow up into the farmer Haakan dreamed he might become. He had taught Manny how to use a knife for carving, and now Manny kept the box for kindling stocked as he carved both useful spoons and ladles and something he wasn't showing her.

"Grandma, can Inga come home with me from school and spend the night?"

"As long as her mother and father agree, I see no problem."

"Good. May I call her and tell her?"

Ingeborg hid a smile. Emmy asking to use the telephone? Would wonders never cease? "Of course." She watched as Emmy pulled the little stool Haakan had made for the grandchildren under the oak box attached to the wall and wired into the restored telephone service.

Slowly but surely the town was recovering from the explosion of the grain elevator a year and a half ago now. The bank had been rebuilt, the post office and telephone building as well. All the people who used to live in Tent Town now had homes of some kind, either in the apartment house or sharing one of the other houses. The boardinghouse remained full of mostly single men, including Dr. Jason W. Commons, who was their newest intern from the hospital in Chicago, and also the two student nurses, Abigail and Sandra, who had arrived in August.

She half listened to Emmy's conversation while she stirred the oatmeal bubbling on the stove. Freda had laid pieces of salt pork in the heavy black skillet to fry and then would pour beaten eggs into it. She checked the oven, where sourdough biscuits were rising nicely. Freda had made the dough the night before, left it to rise overnight, and rolled out biscuits first thing. Manny loved biscuits of all kinds, from the ones with added cheese to the cinnamon-sugar-topped ones and everything in between.

Speaking of Manny, that was Manny

outside the back door, stomping snow off his boots. Ingeborg could easily tell; one stomp was louder than the other. Manny's one leg, which had been not only broken but also shortened, was weaker than his other one. He burst in on a wave of cold.

Emmy pushed the stool back where it belonged and went to the cupboard to start setting the table. She glanced down at Ingeborg's feet as she passed. "You have Metiz' moccasins on."

"They are my winter slippers. Can you still wear the ones I gave you?"

"My feet are too big."

"We'll go look in the box when you get home from school." Ingeborg kept a box full of children's clothing that had been outgrown by other children but was good enough to use again. Emmy and Inga loved to search the box and try clothes on. Now they passed Emmy's outgrown things that weren't complete rags to Inga or to the boxes the ladies of the church kept available for the immigrant children, or anyone else in need.

"Are you going to quilting today?" Freda asked as they waited for Manny to finish washing his hands and sit down.

"I am and I am hoping you will too."

"I have some things I am working on here, and that is the only time I have alone it seems." She looked to Manny. "We have another order for cheese and we are nearly out of crates. Could you work on that when you get home?"

"Sure. Last time I checked you still had plenty." Manny had taken over the job of nailing crates together for shipping the cheese. That was something he'd started doing while his broken leg was healing, and now he took it as a point of pride that he kept ahead of Freda.

Patches barked, making the two young ones leap to their feet, bundle up in coats from the coat tree, grab books and lunch pails, and head for the door. Samuel Knutson drove a wagon with a big box on it to protect the children from the weather. When the snow fell last fall, they replaced the wheels with sledge runners. Ingeborg hoped they would be able to put the wheels back on in the next week or two. Samuel first loaded students from the deaf school taught by Grace Knutson Gould, one of Samuel's older twin sisters. The children in the deaf school attended the regular school as soon as they learned sign language, a fine arrangement. Manny waved and Emmy blew Ingeborg a kiss, as she so often did.

"Whew," Freda commented, making a joke out of wiping her brow. "How John Solberg corrals all that energy at the school and still loves his job, I'll never understand."

"It is easier on him now that Father Devlin teaches at the high school. Or rather, *Mr.* Devlin." Ingeborg picked up her dishes and, like the others had, placed them in the steaming dishpan on the stove.

Freda waved a hand. "You go on and get ready. I'll take care of things here. Are you taking the sewing machine?"

"Planning on it. Why? Did you want to use it?"

"If you don't mind."

"Not at all. There's plenty of other sewing to do at church without this machine along. I hope Miriam can come today."

"Will you try to talk with Hildegunn?"

Ingeborg shook her head. "She just freezes me out. I don't know if she talks to anyone anymore." Ever since her husband, Anner, left Blessing several months ago, she had withdrawn more and more. Since she was the postmistress, no one else knew if she heard from her husband unless she volunteered the information. As far as Ingeborg knew, Hildegunn had received very few letters. She nearly asked Gerald one day but hated gossip almost as much as Reverend Solberg did, and that would be borderline.

"Is Kaaren picking you up?"

"Ja." Ingeborg took out the bread knife and started slicing one of the loaves she had baked the day before. Once the bread was sliced, she started on a block of cheese from the icebox she now kept in the pantry, blocking the window, cooled by the frigid air.

"Who is bringing the soup today?" Freda took over stirring the oatmeal.

"Mrs. Magrun and Anji Moen." Ingeborg stood erect and stretched her back. "How is the supply of sheep fodder—have you noticed?"

"Down. When you bought those sheep, I thought it was a good idea. Now, I'm not so sure. No milk, no meat, no wool. Just more and more hay and grain disappearing. And that ram? No use at all." Freda gave the oatmeal one more stir and dragged it aside.

"To everything a season."

"Oh, I know, but . . . "

Ingeborg smiled. "Have you forgotten what lambing is like?"

"Ja. Lots of work in the middle of the night. Never a nice convenient time. And shearing. Uff da."

"Maybe I'll ask Thorliff if he sees any ads for fodder. He gets papers from other towns. Someone might have spare. And possibly even for sheep. I have been thinking we might get a few more. We can always use the wool. I've not done any spinning for ages. And I would like to hang a couple of hindquarters in the haymow for fenalar. We've not had that for a long time." Ingeborg smiled to herself. Since fenalar was brined and dried lamb or mutton, not smoked, the summer heat in the rafters of the haymow would do a fine job of drying the meat.

Freda nodded. "That does sound good, all right. So does salted and dried fish. We didn't do any of that last summer either."

"We never caught more than we ate. Besides, we get fresh fish from the fish house." Manny had been joining Trygve and some others down on the frozen river, fishing through a hole cut in the ice. Cold weather didn't stop her fishermen.

Ingeborg had her baskets of dinner contributions and sewing things ready when Patches announced that Kaaren had arrived. Waving as she went out the door, Ingeborg shivered when the north wind hit her as she made her way to the sleigh. She set her baskets in the back seat and climbed into the front beside Kaaren, tucking the heavy robe around their legs. "Sure feels like snow to me," she said in greeting.

"I know. The clouds look it too." Kaaren waited until Ingeborg was settled and flipped the lines to move the horse forward. "I remembered to bring the horse blanket this time. We should have built a long shed to protect the horses, you know."

"Should have built lots of things, but an addition to the schoolhouse or a new one needs to top the list. How is Jonathan coming with the plans for the deaf school?"

"He and Grace have big dreams. I have trouble looking beyond the cost. But we've had to turn away too many people who need our help, and that is not good either. We have four bunk beds to a room now, and we might have to start eating in shifts. It's a good thing I've been able to hire two women who once lived in Tent Town to work in the kitchen. Their English is improving all the time, so life is easier for Ilse. Whoever dreamed that my little school would grow this big?"

"God did and does. I think Grace is right. You should go back to New York and visit the school where she taught."

"Uff da, now you sound like her and Jonathan. As long as they are knowledgeable, why should I have to put up with that terrible long train ride? Besides, who would run the school if we both left?"

"Ilse, of course." Ingeborg tightened the scarf around her neck and over her hat. Although it was her habit to wear a hat to church, no matter the purpose, she should have abandoned it for the warmth of a heavy wool scarf and a shawl. Or a knitted stocking hat. Now, wouldn't that draw attention and probably chuckles. The first to comment on anything was always Hildegunn, and critically too.

Ingeborg thought about that for a moment. "Why is it that we women continue to wear hats like we do in the middle of the winter, and why have we allowed Hildegunn to be our dictator of what is proper?"

"Style? Fashion? Habit? How should I

know? Regarding Hildegunn, because it is easier to give in than to argue. Your question makes me think of Inga."

"The bottomless question pit?"

Kaaren grinned and continued. "She asked why God made some people deaf."

"And you said?"

"I asked her what she thought, and she said it was so they would learn to listen to Jesus in their hearts better."

Ingeborg felt her jaw drop. "She didn't. I mean . . ."

"I know. I just smiled and nodded, because I could not think of an appropriate response."

"You need to tell that to Thorliff and Elizabeth."

"I plan to." Kaaren turned the horse to the hitching rack on the south side of the church, where several others were already waiting. Together the two women climbed down, threw the heavy blanket over the horse, and after tying a lead over the rail, fetched their baskets from the back of the sleigh. Kaaren paused. "Are you all right?"

"Only a twinge. I have decided that God wants me to kill her with kindness."

"Kill?" Kaaren could arch her eyebrows very effectively.

"My translation." Fighting to keep herself calm and thinking kind thoughts, Ingeborg led the way up the three steps. That time she was frozen in the wagon, unable to move, because of confronting Hildegunn, still caused twinges in spite of the months in between.

Warmth and laughter greeted them as they pulled open the heavy carved doors given to the church in memory of Haakan. He had started carving them before he got so weak, and Thomas Devlin, along with Manny and a couple of others, had finished the job. The doors had been installed on the anniversary of Haakan's death in August.

Hildegunn must not be here again, Ingeborg thought as she walked down the stairs. Too much frivolity going on. *Ingeborg Bjorklund, what happened to your resolution to think kind thoughts?* Sometimes her inner voice could be sarcastic too.

Anji Moen smiled at them both as she took the food baskets from them and carried them to the table. "Coffee will be ready in a few minutes."

Anji seemed so much older than Ingeborg remembered her to be, and sadder. Anji had grown up in Blessing, and after Thorliff went away to college, she had met a journalist from Norway. After they married, they divided their time between Norway and North Dakota. Ivar already had two daughters and together they had four more children. Last fall, a year or so after he died, she and her four children returned to Blessing to be closer to her brothers and sisters, leaving her husband's daughters with his family in Norway.

With a smile Rebecca took their sewing baskets over to the sorting table.

Usually Hildegunn came early and fixed the coffee. If one or the other of them failed at their duties, she'd be huffing and slinging criticism as if they had committed a major sin. Ingeborg flinched inside but managed to smile on the outside. At least she hoped she did. She unlooped her scarf and laid coat and scarf on the coat mound on one table. Kaaren nudged her and smiled.

"All will be well," she whispered.

Ingeborg inhaled and breathed out slowly. "Ja, all will be well." So often through the years she had said that to others. She believed it bone deep, but it was easy to forget, and everyone needed reminding.

"I am sorry to be late," Hildegunn said as she came rushing down the stairs.

Ingeborg flinched in spite of herself. The desire to leave immediately blew through her mind. She turned. Hildegunn had apologized. Say something!

"You are just in time so we can start the meeting. Welcome, everyone," she said, raising her voice. "Will you please get your coffee and take a chair so we can begin?"

Ingeborg glanced up to find Hildegunn staring at her. *Haunted* was the only word she could think of to describe the look in her eyes. *Move!* the voice in her head commanded in no uncertain terms. So she did. "Here, let me help you with that." She took Hildegunn's basket to set on the table. "It's so terribly cold with that wind. Did you walk over?" Smiling over her shoulder, she saw Hildegunn close her eyes for just a moment. Surely those were tears she had blinked back. *O Lord God, give me the right words.*

"How else would I get here?" Hildegunn shook her head as she laid her coat on the mound. "Some of us do not have a team and sleigh, you know."

"I'll get your coffee." Choosing to ignore the barb was definitely heavenly grace. It would be so easy to snap back. "I'll set it on the table."

As the fifteen women took their places in the circle of chairs, the hubbub calmed to a murmur. Kaaren patiently waited, her smile intact.

Ingeborg felt like she was off in a corner observing, even though she was sitting next to Anji with Rebecca on the other side.

Across the circle Amelia Jeffers smiled at Anji with a bit of a wave. "How are the children? Did your youngest get over the croup?"

"Ja, thanks to Astrid and the syrup Ingeborg has been making for so many years. I couldn't find anything like it in Norway."

"I know. Metiz taught me the basis and I added more ingredients."

Anji smiled. "Speaking of Metiz makes me think of my mother. Coming back here has made me think of her even more."

"You are the picture of her in those early years. Agnes Baard was the best friend anyone could have." Ingeborg squeezed Anji's hand. "I'm glad you are back here for always."

"My, how our group has grown," Sophie said as she took the chair beyond Rebecca. "We should be able to accomplish great things."

"Uh-oh. Something gives me a feeling we are about to—"

"Let us pray." Kaaren bowed her head and the others followed her actions.

Ingeborg settled herself, but her mind wanted to follow that conversation.

"Lord God, thank you for bringing us together to praise you this morning and to do your will. You promised to be right here with us, and we count on your presence to teach us, to mold us always into your family so that we may obey your command to love one another even as you have loved us. Father, we confess that we stray so easily from your Word. Controlling our minds and tongues is an ever-present duty, so please fill us with your spirit of love today and every day. Guide us on your path, we pray in Jesus' precious name." They all joined together on the amen.

She raised her head and smiled around the group. "Thank you for braving the cold.

Yesterday I thought spring was almost here, but winter is surely blowing back today. We have a lot to accomplish, but let's start with the Word. Penny, would you read our verses for today?"

Penny opened her Bible and stood. "Our lesson today is from First John 4, starting with verse 7: 'Beloved, let us love one another: for love is of God. . . .'"

Love. There it was again. Love for all, and that included Hildegunn. The Bible did not make easy demands.

Kaaren thanked her and nodded. "For those of you who are working so hard to learn English, Amelia, could you please simplify the first three verses?"

Ingeborg glanced across the circle when she heard a tongue clicking. Sure enough, Hildegunn was making her disapproval known.

Shades of Anner Valders. And it was so sad. Anner had considered anyone who did not speak fluent Norwegian to be a foreigner, including any Indians who might have lived in the Dakotas for centuries before Norwegians ever arrived. But he had mysteriously disappeared several months ago after losing his position at the bank because of his mistreatment of an immigrant. Packed a carpetbag and got on the train. Ingeborg had wondered once if Hildegunn actually had a problem with foreigners moving to Blessing or if she was simply parroting her husband's opinion. Apparently it had become her opinion as well.

Amelia stood and repeated the verses slowly and clearly, then reworded them.

Several of the women smiled and nodded.

"Thank you, Amelia. Hopefully one of things we are doing here today is showing God's love for each other and those who are blessed by our quilts and our sewing. Let's get through our business as quickly as possible so that we can get to work. Hildegunn, will you read the letter we received from the tribal agency where we sent the girls' clothes we sewed?"

Hildegunn nodded and unfolded the piece of paper.

> *"Dear Women of the Lutheran Church in Blessing, North Dakota,*
> *Thank you for sending the warm dresses to our schoolgirls. For many who are new here, that was the first time they had something brand new of their own. They loved the bright colors, and thank you for putting deep hems in the skirts, as they are growing so fast."*

Hildegunn folded the paper. "They thanked us for the quilts we sent earlier too."

"Thank you, Hildegunn. Sophie, you had something you wanted to say?"

"I do." She paused while the whistle of

the incoming train made it hard to hear, then continued. "I've been talking with doctors Elizabeth and Astrid, and they said that they could use more gowns at the hospital. We had sewed a stack of them before, and they are hoping we will do so again. As some of the sheets and bedding begin to wear out, they will give us the holey ones to use to create new gowns. The fabric, of course, is usually still pretty good around the edges. Are we willing to do that for them?"

"What about the quilts we have already started? Shouldn't we finish those first?" Rebecca asked. "I think some of our towns-people still do not have warm enough bedding."

"If only we had more wool batts."

"I raised many sheep in Latvia, before we came in America," one of the women said. "I make quilt battings out of the locks and thribs; you know, the short, coarse wool."

Ingeborg nodded. "I purchased some sheep last fall when they were cheap and plan on buying more sheep if I can find them without going too far. Perhaps others might consider that too. I haven't done any spinning for so long, and I miss it."

"Oh, ja." Mrs. Juris, the woman who had just spoken, nodded. "I too. Spinning is so peaceful, relaxing. I help you?"

"Ja. Perhaps others too?"

Another woman raised her hand. "I too."

Kaaren interrupted. "Let us continue that discussion later. In the meantime, Penny, how many batts do you have in stock?"

"None, but I have some on order."

Heavy footsteps caught their attention. They all looked at the stairs.

Anner Valders! The prodigal banker. Many gasped; others whispered. After all these months of silent absence, Anner Valders!

He came sweeping into the room, as imperious as ever. He didn't even bother to take his hat off. He stared at his wife, no hint of a smile or a glance for any of the others, no word about where he had been all those months. "Mrs. Valders, come now! We are leaving."

"But—"

"Now!" He barked the order and headed back up the stairs.

Ingeborg and Kaaren stared at each other, dumbstruck, then watched as Hildegunn stood, crossed to the pile of coats and hats, and picked hers up, sliding her arms into the sleeves as she mounted the stairs. Hildegunn Valders disappeared.

CHAPTER 2

I think we should have built a bigger house. Or at least a bigger kitchen."

Miriam watched Trygve Knutson's face as he glanced around the kitchen that was not even a year old yet. He wasn't teasing.

They were sitting with their morning coffee at the kitchen table. He had added two new leaves so that all six of them could sit down for a meal together, since they did not have a table and chairs in the dining room yet. It so filled the kitchen, one could hardly get around. He wagged his head. "I should have built a huge kitchen like Tante Ingeborg's."

Sitting across from him, Mrs. Trygve Knutson grinned. "You forget that my family lived in a Chicago tenement that probably could have fit within this room. This is a huge house, and I love every bit of it. And the builder too."

He laid his hand over hers as they smiled at each other across the huge table.

"There they are, at the moony stuff again," Este, Miriam's fifteen-year-old brother, announced over his shoulder as her siblings all charged into the room to eat before they headed for school. He'd recently shot up several inches, growing from an undersized boy to a tall and lanky young man. He folded himself up like a carpenter's rule and perched at the end of the table.

Mercy, seventeen, had helped make breakfast before she went up to dress for school, a privilege now that they lived in Blessing. When she walked in with a blue ribbon holding her hair back, Este grinned at her.

"You look really pretty in that dress," Joy, the second to youngest at age twelve, said with a smile.

"I like the blue ribbon." Miriam set bowls of oatmeal on the table. No one in their family had been able to afford ribbons for a long time, so to see her sister in a blue dress with a matching ribbon made her smile all the way through. "Mercy, please bring the bowl of biscuits from up on the warming shelf."

"I am." Mercy patted Truth, their littlest sister at age ten, on the shoulder as she set the bowl on the table. "I'll finish your dress tonight, so you will have something new too."

"Will everyone please sit down so we can have grace?" Trygve asked, the twinkle still in his eyes.

Miriam felt her heart flip, sending a flutter clear to the top of her head. His smile always managed to do that to her, and instead of getting better, it was getting worse. And to think she tried to fend off her very persistent husband all those months before he finally convinced her that she could finish nurses' training, marry him, and take care of her family all at the same time, or close to it. She brushed a hand over his shoulder on her way to her chair. Since she was off duty today, she could take time to enjoy this meal with them. The one thing she loved almost as much as Trygve and her brothers and sisters was her career as a nurse. It paid very little, but it was so rewarding.

"That wind sure is cold this morning," Este said in between bites. "The chickens are all fluffed up." It was his chore to feed the chickens that Miriam and Trygve had received as a wedding present.

"Wind here comes right down from the North Pole—no hills in the way, and probably hardly any fences to slow it down." Trygve buttered and spread jam on a biscuit. "Sure wish we could convince Tonio to get out here. Daniel said he has room for one more in the training session for the machinists." Her brother, staying behind in Chicago, was so stubborn. Wonder where he got that?

"He didn't answer my letter yet either." Mercy shook her head.

"Tonio doesn't like to write letters much." Joy picked up her bowl and put it in the steaming dishpan on the stove. "We need to leave in the next couple of minutes. We do not want to be late." She went to the coat hooks that lined the hall and carried all the coats and scarves into the kitchen.

After she kissed them out the door, Miriam brought the coffeepot to the table and poured them each another cup. "How come you're still sitting here? Is your crew not working today?" Trygve had taken over one of the construction crews working on the last of the three houses built for the immigrants.

"I have to go over the shipment coming in on the train." He smiled at her. "It sure quieted down in here. What are you doing today?"

"I am going to work on the dresses I'm sewing for Joy and Mercy. Keeping them a surprise is a lot harder than I thought it would be."

The telephone on the wall by the doorway to the hall jangled their ring, so she went to answer it. Having telephone service back in town after the explosion was still a treat.

"Miriam, this is Deborah. You know that young woman you admitted last night?"

"Yes, of course."

"I'm afraid it is pneumonia."

"I figured."

"You were right. She had a rough night. Do we have any contact information for her family?"

"I wrote out everything we know."

"I saw your notes, but there is so little. I was just hoping there was more information. Was there any mention of a husband?"

Miriam tipped her head back to think. "A man brought her in and left immediately. He went out the door before I realized he was leaving. Other than that, no, I don't think so. Why?"

"Older man, younger, what?"

She shrugged, even though Nurse Deborah couldn't see her. "He was all bundled up. You know how chilly it was."

"Well, I think she might be pregnant, and I thought someone else might know more."

Miriam bit her lip. "I know she is emaciated and dehydrated. I started pushing fluids. Do you need me to come in?"

"No, you need your days off. I'll talk with you later."

Miriam hung the earpiece back on the hook and turned to find Trygve shrugging into his coat.

"Everything all right?" He reached for his hat.

"I have no idea." Briefly she told him what she'd learned.

"Thorliff knows all the farmers in the area. Talk to him. What did you say her name was?"

"I have no idea." Miriam picked up the remaining cups and plates and slid them into the steaming water. "Now my curiosity is in full raging force. Looks like a mystery here." Actually it sounded more like something they might have seen in Chicago rather than here in quiet North Dakota. Young women often turned up on the doorstep there without much help or family history. But then perhaps she was borrowing trouble, something Ingeborg kept warning her not to do.

After saying good-bye to Trygve and finishing the dishes, she brought a venison haunch from the icebox and put it in a big roasting pan. She chopped some onions, added salt and pepper, and added some steaming water from the teakettle before sliding the whole thing into the oven. Bless Este's heart. He had also filled the woodbox. Humming a hymn from the Sunday service a couple days ago, she set her kitchen back to rights, lowered the damper so the roast would cook slowly all day, and headed to the sewing room upstairs. It was a good thing Trygve had gone ahead with the two-story house from Sears instead of the story and a half he'd originally planned. And here he thought it was already too small.

Just thinking about him made her smile. She realized she was smiling a lot these days. She set the flat irons on the stove to heat and fetched the ironing board to have it ready when she needed to press her seams flat. She looked fondly at her sewing machine, a wedding present from her dear husband. One time she must have mentioned how she loved sewing on Ingeborg's sewing machine, and when she returned from Chicago, she found it set up right in front of the window, exactly where she would have wanted it.

She lifted down the royal-blue serge out of the box she kept up on the shelf in the closet, along with the other dresses she was making. Since she could only sew on her days off, she wanted to make good use of her time. She'd never sewn pin tucks on a machine, but it went well. If only her mother had had such a fine machine. Of course that thought triggered others, and one tear opened the dam for more. She dug her handkerchief out of her apron pocket and mopped her eyes quickly so as not to drip on the dress.

On Sunday, when she'd been talking with Ingeborg and Kaaren after church, she could tell Ingeborg had been crying during the service. "Some days are still just harder than others, and church seems to be where I cry the most easily," Ingeborg had said.

"I thought the tears would be gone by now.

After all, it's been well over a year since my mother died." Miriam sniffed when Kaaren put an arm around her shoulders.

"I found myself crying the other day for no reason, or so it seemed." Kaaren slid her arm through Miriam's. "And then I started a mental list of all those who have gone on before me and I realized I was grieving that winter when Carl and our two little girls died."

Ingeborg had nodded. "I still call that time the Black Pit. I do not want to ever go that way again. Sometimes, like after Haakan died, it would be so easy to get sucked back in, but I keep thanking God that He keeps me from the edge." Ingeborg wore a faraway look. "This winter has been hard. Sometimes I still miss him so much."

"But you keep on going. I have a feeling most of us have no idea how hard it's been. You always seem so at peace."

"Peace and pain can visit at the same time."

Miriam brought herself back to the present and, pinning the pieces of the rounded collar together, set her feet on the treadle, and the machine began stitching evenly around the collar. She clipped the seam, rolled the collar to the right side, and finger-pressed the edges. Digging into the box where she kept trims, she pulled out a narrow band of white lace and, easing around the corners, stitched it to the collar. Then needing to press that, she started on the sleeves. She had learned to get as many pieces as possible ready for the irons, since the sewing room was upstairs and the stove downstairs. At least this way, she could shut off the room if she needed to hide things. The problem was her sisters liked to use the machine too. That was why she had to hide any presents she was making.

When she had the sleeves ready to press, along with the bodice, she gathered her pieces and started for the stairs.

"Miriam, you home?" Trygve must have come home for something.

"Coming right down. Add some wood to the stove, would you please?" She heard the clang of the lids being lifted off just as her foot hit the floor. Surely it wasn't dinner time already. "Are you all right?" She entered the kitchen and stopped. Her mouth dropped open, but she could say nothing.

Tonio!

She threw herself at the young man standing by the stove. "Tonio!"

He grabbed her and hugged like he'd never let go. "Did I surprise you?"

"Surprise doesn't begin to cover it." She tried to sniff back the tears and failed utterly. Sobbing into his jacket front, she blubbered, "I'm so glad you are here. I was getting worried— you didn't write—and we didn't know . . ." She smacked his upper arm. "Wait until the others

see you! They are going to . . . to . . ." She shook
her head and stepped back to wipe her eyes. "I
am so glad to see you."

"Could have fooled me." Trygve set the lids
back in place. "Are you hungry?"

Tonio stepped back. "Starved. I didn't have
any more money to buy food. I brought what
I could with me."

"What happened to your job?"

"They changed foremen, and the new one
wanted his own guys on the crew, so they asked
if I wanted to go work down on the steamships,
but I decided it was time to come west. You
all sounded far too happy in your letters, and
I was sick and tired of being all by myself in
Chicago."

"You could have gone to work at the hospital."

"I know. I thought of talking to them, and
then I just wanted to see you all. I've never lived
alone before, and I didn't like it at all. I even
moved to a smaller flat, but . . ." He shook his
head. "Besides all that, one man came in drunk
to work and fell down, and his load knocked me
over. We could have been really hurt. I was so
mad at him that I could have kicked him when
he was moaning on the ground. What a fool."

Miriam slid his jacket off and took it to the
hooks by the door. "You go wash, and I'll get
you something to eat. The bathroom is that
way. Do you have a suitcase?" She glanced at

the clock and then at her husband. "I know it's a bit early, but do you want dinner now too?"

"Why not. What are we having?"

"The leftover soup, and I'll fry a couple of cheese sandwiches. The venison roast is for tonight." She eyed the box and carpetbag by the door. "That's it?"

"You all took most of the other stuff." He headed out the arched door to the hall. "I gave the rest away."

"Smart man." Trygve picked up the box and bag. "I'll take these upstairs. Wait until Este finds out he has a roommate now."

"Wait until the girls see who is here. We have to hide him." Somehow a grin had found its way to her face and just kept stretching her cheeks. Her family was all together again. Her mother must be dancing in heaven to know her children were safe and out of that horrid tenement. When the two men returned to the kitchen, she handed them each a cup of hot coffee and pointed toward the table. "The rest will be ready in a minute."

"Cream? Sugar?" Trygve asked.

"I could try it, I suppose. We never had that choice."

Trygve fetched the cream pitcher from the icebox and set it next to the sugar bowl. Then he grabbed a teaspoon from the pint jar next to the butter dish. He lifted the lid to the cookie jar. "Ingeborg has been here."

"No, Mercy baked those yesterday after school. We do know how to cook and bake here too, you know." She loved coming home from work to the fragrance of cookies baking. It reminded her of her months of living with the Jeffers family, where Mrs. Jeffers made sure her cookie jar was always full. Hospitality was one of the things she had learned early in Blessing. The coffeepot was always on, and no matter where you went, cookies or cake or some other treat would appear as if by magic. Ingeborg Bjorklund made the best bread and the best cheese. Amelia Jeffers had the corner on roses and lemonade. Rebecca Valders could be counted on for sodas and ice cream all summer long and into the fall. And Miriam's now mother-in-law, Kaaren Knutson, made sure meat appeared in their icebox.

With the soup steaming in the bowls and the golden sandwiches on a plate beside, she grabbed the coffeepot and, after refilling the cups, took her place at the table so Trygve could say grace.

"I didn't know you even knew how to do all this." Tonio's eyes twinkled. "You were always at the hospital."

"Only those last two years."

"But you worked there before that."

Trygve cleared his throat, one eyebrow arched, and said the Norwegian grace she was still trying to learn. They all said amen, and she watched as her brother took a bite of sandwich and dug into the soup.

"We have plenty, Tonio. And there is no hurry, at least not today."

"So what do you want to do?" Trygve asked. "You can go back to school if you'd like, or you can join a construction crew, or you can talk to Daniel about the training he is running at the machinery plant."

"You have a machinery plant here?"

"We do. They produce seed drills and adapters farmers can attach to their own machinery. I have a feeling that Daniel has something else he is planning. That's why the training."

"Is there pay while in training?"

"I guess I don't know. He hired experienced men at first to work all the machinery needed to make the drills, but he is constantly looking ahead and coming up with new plans."

"He inherited his father's skills at inventing too, so who knows what all he will come up with." Miriam sighed and just sat watching her brother eat, her smile still firmly affixed. "I think you are going to like it here, dear brother. I know I do, and now the others do too. Wait until you hear them rave about the school here and how nice the people are. How about after we eat I take you on a tour about town?"

"I have a feeling I won't have to worry about getting lost."

"Not until a blizzard hits." Trygve lifted his bowl in a plea for more.

"Oh, sorry. Of course." Miriam refilled all three of their bowls. As she set the bowls back down, she smiled at her husband. "I think tonight you should take Tonio over and introduce him to the cows and the milking."

"Oh you do, do you?" Trygve turned back to Tonio, who looked between the two, as if trying to figure out the joke. "I think we'll save that for another day." Trygve shoved back his chair. "I need to get to work, so I'll see you tonight after your big tour. But you better be careful, Miriam, when you show him around. You know how fast news travels in Blessing. If you really want to surprise the others, that is."

Miriam nodded. "Good point. Did you sleep on the train?"

"Not much."

"Then perhaps you would like to take a hot bath and sleep for a while."

"I saw the bathtub. Do you have hot water here too?"

"We do. Trygve made sure we have a good stove and indoor plumbing with a hot water heater, and he even wired our house so when electricity comes to Blessing, we will be ready."

"It's all so hard to believe. And going back to something you said earlier—could I really go back to school if I wanted?"

Trygve shrugged into his coat. "You could.

Or there might even be people here who would have evening classes for you if you would rather work with Daniel during the day. I'll talk to him and you can meet him in the morning." He kissed his wife good-bye and headed out the door.

"Pinch me. I think I must be dreaming." Miriam held out her arm, but Tonio waved her away.

"A real bath. I saw the tub. Have I ever washed in a tub that big?"

"Not to my knowledge, but we don't have enough hot water to fill that tub to the brim."

"It would slosh over then." Tonio leaned over and kissed her cheek. "Thank you for a full stomach right now, and whatever you have in the oven smells mighty good for supper. Let's forgo the tour today. I want to surprise the others."

Miriam nodded and watched her brother leave the room. Tonio was here to stay—like the rest of them. Surely Mum and Da were celebrating too—if people in heaven really could know what was happening to their loved ones on earth. Perhaps she should ask Reverend Solberg or Father Devlin. Could be an interesting discussion. Now she was feeling a bit like Trygve's niece, little Inga of the inquisitive mind.

CHAPTER 3

And how be ye on this fine day?" Thomas Devlin sounded as cheerful as ever.

"Cold, like everyone else. I am convinced that the north wind is colder in North Dakota than it is in Norway." Anji unwrapped her scarf, but when she started to shrug out of her wool coat, he stepped behind her to help her. Having a man help her off with her coat was something she had missed after her husband died. Ivar had always had such genteel manners. She rubbed her hands together. "So my class is ready?"

"They are indeed."

Anji had agreed to teach a class on Norwegian history on Wednesdays starting the first of the year, followed by a class on the Norwegian language. Since not everyone in the high school had learned Norwegian as a child, her class was quite a mixture. The beginners were learning the language, and the others were improving their language skills and their grammar.

He opened the door into the classroom and then closed it behind her.

"Gud dag."

"Gud dag," her ten students replied.

"Everyone talks about the Vikings and their raids. No wonder; it's exciting! However, let's start with what happened in Norway *after* the Vikings. Then when we look at the Viking period, from 793 to 1066, you will see not only the impact they made on all of Europe, but also how Europe changed the Norse." She stepped to the blackboard and wrote the years upon it.

By the time the class ended, the discussion on the role Norway played in world trade, and especially in inland Europe, was only half finished. Anji smiled at her students. "We'll continue during our next class. Thank you. I am really enjoying teaching you this. You are splendid students."

"Did you have a class like this when you were our age?" one of her students asked.

"No. I learned most of Norwegian history from my husband. He loved history, and for years he wrote about the immigrants coming to America and how their lives changed. He made sure I had books to read, and he loved to tell the ancient stories, especially of the

Vikings. We have much to look forward to here."

The bell rang and, at her nod, everyone stood up for their break.

She had known very little about Blessing's schools when she arrived, other than to get her children enrolled, and now here she was teaching! America was indeed a land of opportunity. She was teaching at the high school level, and she also learned in passing that Thomas Devlin now taught reading, writing, and arithmetic in the grade school—in addition to teaching Latin, world history, and advanced math at the high school—so that Reverend Solberg, who used to teach the smaller children, could spend full time on his duties as the growing school's principal.

A few minutes later her pupils gathered for their language class. After introducing the vocabulary words and common phrases for the day, explaining their meaning, and having everyone repeat them after her, she walked around the room, pointing to the windows, the door, the furniture, even to clothes they were wearing. She said the word, singular and plural, and then drilled them as fast as they could respond. It became a game of sorts, a competition. Door! Shirt! Shoe! Window! The last part of class time the students paired up, one who spoke Norwegian at home and one or two who didn't, and practiced bits of conversation.

She spoke only Norwegian during the last

part of the class when they were practicing. Just before the bell was to ring, she smiled at everyone. "You are learning so quickly, I am really proud of you. Tusen takk. Ha det; vi snakkes." *Thank you very much. Good-bye. Talk to you later.* This was great fun!

After the last classes of the day, the three teachers met in the office before leaving for their homes.

"Well, Mrs. Moen, it sounded like your students are not only progressing but also having a good time at it," Reverend Solberg said with a wide smile.

Anji rolled her eyes. "Mrs. Moen?"

"That is who you are here, whether I taught you as Anji Baard or not."

"Did you ever dream that your early students would return to teach here?"

"I guess every teacher hopes for that. Thorliff has taught a few classes on journalism. Sophie did one on Seattle and the fishing and lumbering. Fishing and lumbering are both foreign concepts to some of the children. Grace, of course, teaches sign language, and Astrid speaks on hygiene and answers medical kinds of questions. So actually my former students get put to work a lot. But you, teaching a formal ongoing class like this, is a first."

"I am honored. And now that all the children are home, I need to get back to help Rebecca." Anji stood.

Since Anji and her children lived with Rebecca and Gerald, whose house was one of the first ones repaired after the devastating fire, the place was plenty full when all the school-children came home.

"I'll walk you home." Thomas Devlin fetched her coat and held it for her. "See you tomorrow, John. I shut the dampers on the stoves."

"Thanks. I have some more to do here. Tomorrow we need to talk about building a storage shed to free up that extra room. Storage is a poor use to make of class space." He waved them out the door.

Anji walked close to Mr. Devlin on the downwind side. It was not much protection against the cold, but any little bit helped. "How is your woodworking class going? Ingeborg said Manny has to tell her all about it when he gets home."

"Ah, 'tis a rare pleasure. Grace's idea to combine hearing and deaf students is working well."

Anji frowned. "But you don't sign yet, at least not fluently. How do you instruct the deaf students?"

"Just as I instruct the hearing students— by showing them how to do it. Wood and tools speak the same language in the doing. Haakan got Manny started well with whittling and carving, and now the students are each constructing a workbench, using only pegs, no metal. And the older boys are learning mortise and tenon. I think next we'll do a general class project building the bookcases for the classroom that will be in the new wing of the deaf school."

Even though her cheeks stung from the wind in spite of her long wool scarf, Anji enjoyed the Wednesday walks with this man, short though they were. "Have you ever thought of teaching them to repair broken things?"

He stopped and stared at her, nodding all the while. "Now that be a very fine idea. I will ask Kaaren if she has anything needing repair. Put the lads to work on it."

"Folks around here are so handy, there might not be a lot."

"True."

She studied him for a moment. The jovial face seemed to carry some secret woe. "Some people address you as Father Devlin. You're certain you are not a Catholic?"

He cackled. "Absolutely. I not be so sure the Mother Church would have me. Nae, I be Anglican by ordination, and wild hare by nature. I'm not practicing as a priest at the moment, except on those rare occasions, of course, when a priest be needed." He kicked the slushy snow off his boots at the house steps and followed her up to the porch.

"Won't you come in?"

"Thankee, but not today. I promised Maisie Landsverk I would fix the drain in the boardinghouse kitchen. Mrs. Sam also has need of me, and she makes the best apple fritters I've ever met."

"Then I shall see you Sunday."

"There be a gathering at Thorliff's on Saturday. I shall go. Would ye join me?"

"That sounds like fun. I would love to." The last gathering at Thorliff's had gone from games into a sing-along with Elizabeth playing the piano. She watched her escort stop halfway down the short walk and turn to wave at her. She waved back.

What a fine man. It was a shame she wasn't on the lookout for another man. *Anji!* She chided herself as she turned and entered the house to hear children's laughter, including the chortles of her youngest, Annika, and Mark, Rebecca's tot, who at fifteen months was trying to run after the others. She hung up her outer clothes and peeked into the hall, where Benny was giving the two little ones rides on his wagon—Benny's wheels, as they all called the low cart that had made him mobile since the amputation of his legs. Out in public he usually used his wooden artificial legs. Around the house, he frequently used his strong arms to simply drag his stump legs along.

"Ma!" shrieked Annika, waving her arms. "Look at me!"

"I see you." She crossed to the stairs and sat down on the third step. Annika and Mark raced each other, Annika falling into her arms first. Coming home to a welcome like this always made going out easier. She sat the two little ones on either side of her and hugged eight-year-old Gilbert next. He looked so much like his father, she wondered at times if she had had anything to do with creating him. His grandmother, Eunice, in Norway had shown her pictures of Ivar at this age, sitting on a settee, wearing a much embroidered and tucked pants and a shirt in a light color, with blond ringlets. Eunice said he too had been a happy child.

"I got a hundred on my spelling paper today," Melissa announced. She was almost ten and was Anji's sober child, always taking her responsibilities seriously. She had inherited her father's curls too, although this last year hers had become dark honey. "Benny did too."

"I almost missed one." Benny sat on his cart, leg stumps resting on the floor. He shook his head. "Arithmetic is always easier." He cocked his head. "How come you don't teach in our room?"

Annika wiggled to be let down; she had sat still for about as long as she could. Anji dropped a kiss on the top of her head as she ran off. Little Mark reached up his arms. Sitting in a lap was his favorite place, no matter whose. Since his mother was busy, Anji was happy to accommodate him.

"I'm putting the coffee on," Rebecca called from the kitchen. "Pie and cookies will be out in a minute."

Benny and Lissa, as they usually called her, grinned at each other and headed for the kitchen. The others followed, like lemmings after the Pied Piper.

Mark popped his thumb in his mouth and leaned against her chest, heaving a contented sigh. Anji cuddled him close, rocking gently, listening to the ruckus going on in the kitchen as the others clambered up on the chairs around the table, Joseph telling Gilbert to wait his turn. In Norway the children had been confined to the nursery, allowed downstairs with the adults only at certain times. That was the way of the wealthier society, but not the way Anji wanted to raise her children. Ivar's daughters by his first marriage had grown up with that and fitted into it quite comfortably, which was why she had agreed with their grandmother to leave them there. Life was comfortable for them there, but Blessing was home to her, with its energy and exuberance and its casual, easygoing approach to life. Mr. and Mrs. Moen had not been pleased with her decision. She regretted that, but not enough to remain in the stiff, strictured culture of Old Norway.

"Coffee's on."

"Cookie?" Mark squirmed to be let down, so Anji stood and swept him up in her arms. He probably would not allow himself to be carried much longer. She jiggled him on her hip, making him giggle. In the kitchen she set him in his high chair and helped settle Annika in hers. What a handful! Seven children, all ten or under, Benny and Melissa being the same age.

Rebecca turned from sliding the cookies from the pan onto a rack and then to a plate. With her baby, Agnes, sleeping in the sling she wore tied around her neck, leaving her hands free to do all the daily chores, she grinned at Anji. She nodded toward the two pies on the counter. "I made extra dough just for this."

"You are such a wise woman. You must take after our mother."

Rebecca set the plate on the table and watched as Melissa finished filling the glasses with milk. "Now pass the plate—carefully." As always, whether she was standing or sitting, her body swayed, keeping the infant content. Then she brought two full coffee cups to the table and sat down with a sigh.

"Tired?"

"Ja. So how were your classes and how come Mr. Devlin didn't come in?"

"I so enjoy teaching those students, and Mr. Devlin had something to repair at the board-inghouse. He is looking for broken things that can be fixed so he can train his woodworking group in both building and repair."

"There might be things over at the other house. With Anner gone so long, Hildegunn let things slide somewhat."

Anji reached for the milk. "Has anyone heard from either of them?"

"Not that I know of." She mentally counted back. "But then they left only three days ago."

"Do you think they'll be back?"

Rebecca snorted. "Not if he has his way."

"I felt so sorry for her, dragged off like that." Anji grabbed for a glass of milk that was bumped by the passing plate. "Uff da!"

"Hildegunn was pretty strict with the children, almost harsh, but Benny melted their hearts, even Anner's, from the first."

"When are Grandma and Grandpa coming back?" he asked from the other end of the table.

"I have no idea. Do you have homework tonight?"

"Ja and Lissa does too."

"Not me," Joseph said, teasing the other two.

"Good. Then you can read to the smaller ones." Rebecca bobbed her head.

At the sound of boots kicking against the steps, all eyes swiveled to the door.

"Uncle Gerald's home!" Joseph bailed off his chair before anyone could even say a word and threw open the door, letting in a blast of cold air.

"Shut the door. You want to freeze us out?" Rebecca turned away so the draft wouldn't hit the baby in the sling, who at the shout was now making waking noises.

Gerald came through the door, and Joseph slammed it behind him. "The temperature is dropping even more." He slapped his gloved hands together and headed for the kitchen stove. "You'd have thought I walked a mile rather than two blocks." He patted his adopted son on the shoulder as he passed him. "Did you save me a cookie?"

Benny shook his head. "We ate them all."

"And your mother didn't save me even one?"

Benny shrugged. "But we didn't eat the pie."

"I should hope not." He kissed Rebecca on the cheek. "Toby is coming over tonight to talk about something. He didn't say specifically what, but it sounded like something was on his mind. I told him to come for supper."

"Of course. It'll be ready in about an hour."

"I told him five thirty." After warming his hands, he hung his coat and hat on the rack by the door.

Anji rose and poured him a cup of coffee. "To help warm you. Has the wind died down?"

"Not much."

"Uncle Gerald, Benny got a hundred on his spelling," Joseph said with a wide smile. "He doesn't like spelling much."

"I know. Good for you, Benny. I think you will have a surprise in the next day or so."

"Really? What?" His whole face lit up.

"If I tell you then it won't be a surprise." Gerald had yet to leave his position by the stove. "Sure smells good in here."

"Pa-a." Benny scrunched his face. "Can I ask a question? Does Ma know?"

Gerald glanced at his wife, his forehead wrinkling. "Ah, no, I don't think so."

"Aunty Rebecca knows everything," Lissa tartly informed Benny.

"Okay, you children go put your toys away. Lissa, you set the table, and I'll go feed the baby. You want to get supper on the table, Anji?"

"Of course." She well knew that if little Agnes was not fed before supper, she would make her ma's meal miserable. Patience did not seem to be part of her makeup. Anji studied Gerald, wondering what was going on. It had to be something momentous.

She started slicing bread and checked the roast in the oven. The meat looked to be getting dry, so she added some water from the teakettle steaming on the back of the stove. Potatoes, turnips, and carrots surrounded the well-done meat, but when she forked a carrot, she knew it would be a while longer until supper. "Lissa, set a place for Onkel Toby." Leaving Lissa to her work, she checked the hall and stairs. "Gilbert, no toys on the stairs. You know that."

"Not even a book?"

"No. You can take that and sit down with the little ones in the parlor."

"I brought the paper," Gerald said as he sank into the leather rocker by the parlor stove. "Looks like we need some wood in here." He stared at Gilbert. "Isn't keeping the box full your job?"

"Yes, sir." He grabbed the leather carrier and headed for the back porch.

"Sorry. I should have reminded him."

"No, Anji. He and Benny are old enough to remember their chores."

She nodded. True, but chores had never been part of their lives before they returned to Blessing. In Norway the servants did the menial tasks. Life certainly was different here.

He asked, "Have you ever considered writing some articles for the paper?"

"Perhaps, but Thorliff seems to be doing fine."

"Well, I know you were looking for something else to do besides teaching . . ."

"I helped Ivar with his articles for the last couple of years. I guess it's something to think about."

"I know. That's what made me think of it. The series Thorliff ran at Christmas about all the nationalities here in Blessing now was really popular."

A crash from the kitchen made her charge into that room. "What happened?"

Lissa clutched her hand. "I dropped the pitcher and cut my hand." Tears welled. "I'm sorry."

Milk was spreading across the floor, the pieces of glass glittering like ice on a lake.

Anji grabbed a towel and wrapped it around her daughter's hand.

"It was an accident," Lissa said.

"Of course."

"Will Tante Rebecca be angry and yell at me?"

"No, she won't yell." Not like the children's nurse in Norway who did not tolerate mistakes or accidents. Anji gathered her daughter to her side and tightened the towel to stop the bleeding. "You sit in the chair and keep this tight while I mop up the mess."

"Do you need me?" Rebecca called. "We'll be done here soon."

"No, you finish." Anji picked up the big pieces of glass to put into the dustpan before dumping it in the trash, then started mopping the remaining mess. Gerald had come into the kitchen, and the other children were gathered at the door.

"You all stay out of here," Gerald said as he peeled back the towel. "Uh-oh. Looks like a bad one." He pressed on Melissa's wrist artery. "I think we are due for a run to the hospital. How did this happen?"

"The handle broke off and I tried to catch it all and . . ." She sniffed. "It hurts."

"I'm sure it does. Anji, leave that and call the hospital. This is mighty deep, and there might be glass in it." He wrapped the towel even tighter and kept his fingers on the artery. "Joseph, go get Lissa's coat and scarf. Benny, bring the blanket from the parlor."

Just then the door opened and Toby came in. "Good grief, it looks like a battlefield in here. How can I help?"

"We're taking her to the hospital."

Anji set the receiver back on the hook. "They are calling Astrid and will be ready."

"Wrap her up well, and we'll take her and Anji on the toboggan."

Within minutes Toby was pulling the toboggan with Anji holding her thumb on her daughter's wrist and cuddling her in the blanket. The wind blasted them, throwing ice bits into the air. Lamplight from the houses marked the way, with the boardinghouse looming in the darkness. The wind howled around the corners of the houses, fighting to rip the blanket off Anji and her sniffing daughter. Not a night fit for man nor beast, that was for sure. And here two days earlier, the Chinook wind was blowing and they thought spring had arrived.

CHAPTER 4

Astrid met them at the door, still in her heavy coat and scarf, which she unwrapped as she led the way. "Bring her right in here."

"We're all set up." Miriam turned from setting out the instruments tray.

Toby lifted Lissa up onto the table. "There you go."

"Thank you," she said, along with a sniff.

Astrid scrubbed her hands at the sink. "Please tell me what happened."

Anji recounted the accident and finished with, "So we've kept pressure on the wrist to stop the bleeding."

"Have you let it up?" Astrid peeled back the towel and motioned Anji to release the pressure. "Ah, good." Bright red blood hovered near the surface but did not well over. "You've cleaned it?"

"But there might be glass in it," Toby said from by the doorway.

"There was broken glass and milk all over the floor." Melissa sniffed again. "It really hurts."

"I'm sure it does. You are one brave girl." Astrid carefully probed the wound, watching Melissa's face to see if she flinched more. "Okay, we'll clean this up as soon as some pain medicine can take effect." She nodded to Miriam, who poured some syrup into a spoon and held it for Lissa, who wrinkled her nose.

"Just swallow quickly. There is honey with it, so it won't taste too bitter. It is a salicylic acid mixture that tastes awful but does the job."

Lissa looked at her mor, who nodded. She clenched her eyes and opened her mouth. A smile tried to come out, but a hiccup hid it. Miriam held a glass of water and Lissa drank some.

"Now, you think about pleasant things— summer things. Let's get your coat off, and you can lie back on the table. Your mor will stay right here with you while we clean this out and sew it up."

"Sew me? Like my embroidery?"

"Well, sort of. But we'll only need three or four tiny stitches."

"Stick a needle in me?"

"That's what sewing is. But see, I'm dabbing a bit of a chemical called Stovaine. It's brand new, and it kills the pain right at the spot."

Within a couple of minutes, Lissa's eyelids drooped and she did not seem to be thinking of summer things, or anything. Astrid wondered if the Stovaine and the salicylic acid had interacted; some of the new medical compounds did that.

"You close this," Astrid said to Miriam when she finished inspecting the wound and stepped back. "Miriam is a better seamstress than I am." When the stitches were in place and the wound wrapped, Astrid smiled at Anji. "It was a clean cut; glass is good at that. Keep it dry and watch it. If it starts bleeding, bring her back in immediately."

Miriam helped her sit up.

Astrid asked, "How old are you?"

"Almost ten."

"Good. You are clear-headed and responsive." If there was an interaction, it was certainly mild.

"You should see her mothering Annika, and she adores Rebecca's little ones." Anji sighed. "I am so glad you have the hospital here now. What a relief to not have to stitch that myself, like our mothers used to."

"Mor sutured many a wound. So many limbs and lives she saved."

"You know, I remember those early days, and I would not want to go back." Anji helped Lissa put her coat back on.

Astrid looked to Toby. "You're planning on taking them back on the toboggan?" At his nod, she grinned at Anji. "Some people will do anything to get a toboggan ride."

The child pouted. "I didn't want to."

"You might fix a sling tomorrow to help keep from bumping it. You'll be famous at school with your hand all bandaged."

"She can go?" Anji asked.

"If she feels like it. That will probably depend on whether she can get some good sleep tonight." Astrid saw them out the door and watched as Toby settled them back on the toboggan, tucking another blanket around them. "Now, that is one fine man. It's a shame he hasn't found a wife yet."

Beside her, Miriam grinned. "I saw him making eyes at Gretchen. You know how many of your student nurses end up marrying here in Blessing."

"You, for instance." Astrid chuckled. "Hmm. I wonder what we can do to encourage that. Let's have Gretchen clean up this mess, and I want you to check on our mystery patient with me. She's been here what? Four days now? And we still have no idea who she is."

"She still doesn't speak, but then for a bit, I wasn't sure if she was going to pull through.

Have you talked with Thorliff yet? To see if any of the area farmers know anything about her?"

"I mentioned it. He didn't have any information." Together they entered the room and stood by the bed, Astrid's hand going immediately to check the pulse. "Have we gotten her to eat?"

"Some, but not enough."

"Bring her soup and warm milk every two hours. Feed her if necessary. I think we need to bring Mor in on this. She can get a stone to talk."

Miriam nodded.

"How old do you think she is?"

"Maybe seventeen or eighteen. I think she understands Norwegian, but I'm not sure how much English."

But when Astrid asked the girl her name in Norwegian, she did not respond either.

"A puzzle, that's for sure. If there is nothing else, I'll be at home. Thank you, Miriam. You did a fine job." Astrid stopped by her office to pick up her coat and scarf. "Call me if you need anything."

"Will Dr. Elizabeth be in tomorrow?"

"Ja, she insisted. And I'm sure Mor will come too."

"Oh, did you hear the news?"

"What?"

"Dr. Deming and Vera are expecting a baby."

"How wonderful."

The two had been married the summer before at Vera's family home in Chicago, then returned to Blessing. Theirs was one of the houses finished last fall, and while Dr. Deming still helped with some of the boardinghouse construction, his dental practice was growing as he became known beyond the borders of Blessing. The nearest dentists were in Grafton or Grand Forks. Vera worked part time at the hospital too.

Bits of snow and ice needled what bare skin was visible as Astrid went from a fast walk to a trot. And to think the fickle weather had teased them with a touch of warmth before winter blasted back. The thought of spring put a bounce in her step as she mounted the stairs to the porch.

"I'm home," she called as she closed the door behind her.

"I'm in the kitchen," answered Amelia.

"Is your son back yet?"

"No. I'll put the coffee on in a minute."

"How about tea for me?" Astrid hung her garments on the rack by the door and inhaled an unusual smell. "What are you doing?"

"Making candles." Amelia smiled from her position beside the stove reservoir where she dipped a rod with four candles tied to it in a kettle of melted wax, then hung the rod on hooks beneath the shelf and retrieved another. "Third dip. They're coming along."

Astrid inhaled. "What fragrance did you put in?"

"Roses and some mint. A little bit of mint oil goes a long way. It takes a lot of rose petals to make the oil strong enough. I didn't get much of that made last summer. I just wanted to use up the remaining beeswax. After all, we'll have more this summer."

Astrid leaned over the kettle and inhaled. "That hand lotion you made last summer still smells good. You and Mor come up with the nicest things that smell good." She moved the teakettle to the hottest spot and added wood to the firebox. "Do you want some tea too?"

"Of course. These will need to hang awhile before I dip them again. I added rose petals to the teapot too. How is little Melissa?"

"Not so little anymore, but it was a clean cut, no glass in it, and it didn't look to have severed any nerves. That was my big concern." She heard boots kicking against the steps, announcing Daniel's arrival, and reached for a third cup.

"Why didn't you call me?" Dr. Jason Commons asked with a slight bite to his tone the next morning. "I was on call, after all." Dr. Commons had come to them last August as the first intern from the doctors in training at the hospital in Chicago. As it was with the nurses, the hospital in Blessing would now be a training ground for doctors in training.

Astrid clamped her teeth together to keep from saying what she actually thought. No one wanted to work with this man because of his supercilious attitude, which was evident right now. It was time to talk with him again, a job both she and Elizabeth disliked. They had even discussed shooing him back to Chicago, but Ingeborg had reminded them that God had a purpose in sending the young man to Blessing. He was a pain, though. He had an over-developed case of real-doctors-are-male, so he didn't care to be working under two female doctors. And on top of that, Dr. Astrid was younger than he, which made him even more uncomfortable.

"I'm not sure why I was called instead, but probably because Mr. Valders asked for me."

"And you had Nurse Knutson close. But that still is no excuse for not calling a medical doctor."

"Please follow me." Astrid turned and headed for her office. The nursing desk was not a place for a discussion like this. *Lord, give me the best words, not the words beating through my head.* How to get this young man to work as part of the team. She'd heard rumors that he was rude, especially to the two student nurses, but she'd found Miriam gritting her teeth one day too. She and Elizabeth should both be at this discussion, but Elizabeth had been up half the night with baby Roald, so Astrid told her to stay home.

She held the door to her office open for him and motioned him to the chair beside her desk, then closed the door, careful to not let it slam.

"Dr. Commons, it appears to me that you don't really care for women in the medical professions." Might as well hit the problem head on.

"Ah." He stared down at his hands, then looked up at her. "Everyone knows that this is a profession where men excel."

"And what gives you that perception?" She kept her voice even and tone mild.

"I know you and Dr. Elizabeth managed to get through medical school, but . . ."

Keep calm! She took in a deep breath. "Here in Blessing and at the Morganstein Hospital, we believe a person's gender has nothing to do with his or her ability to make a fine doctor. I am not sure how you got this far in your schooling in Chicago with your beliefs, but here we work as a team, with everyone learning all they can and taking responsibility for what they do. We train both nurses and doctors and have trained women to be nurses on the Rosebud Indian Reservation. I'm sure you knew or at least knew of Dr. Red Hawk, who has returned to help his people."

She waited for his response. At a barely

perceptible nod, she continued. "We do the best we can with our limited resources, grateful for our partnership with Chicago. We ascribe to the Golden Rule: Do unto others as you would have them do unto you, and we expect you to do the same. You are here to practice medicine, to learn all you can. Agreed?"

"Yes." He continued to look down, obviously not wanting to meet her gaze. She studied his reddening ears as she spoke. "I know your father is a physician too, correct?"

Another nod.

"Are you planning to join his practice on your graduation?"

He shrugged.

The urge to shake him blew on by. "You have a choice, Dr. Commons. You can remain here and get all the medical training we have to offer—excellent training in a small-town medical practice—as long as you agree to work as part of a team, accepting the full value of all those working on this staff and treating them accordingly and with respect. Or you may return to Chicago on the next train." She did not add "*with your tail between your legs*," but she thought it. Letting the silence stretch, she studied the top of his head as he studied his hands.

"I hope I have made myself clear?"

"Yes, Doctor." His slight emphasis on the title made her want to send him off. How would they get through to him?

"You will be on call for the rest of this weekend and through Monday. And I will leave instructions to that end. We will be having a staff meeting on Monday. That includes all doctors and nurses. I hope I do not hear any further murmurs of rudeness."

"What time?"

"After the morning shift change. We will be finished in an hour so those just getting off duty can head for bed. Any questions?"

He shook his head. "May I leave now?"

"Yes. You are on duty now?"

"Yes."

"Would you please assess the woman in room two?"

"The one who wants to die?"

That gave her pause. "Why do you say that?"

"She doesn't want to eat, refuses to communicate, and—"

"Are you sure she isn't just too weak to eat?"

"Her vitals seem stable. A bit thready but not something to be concerned about."

"And what kind of treatment do you recommend?"

"Send her home."

"Do you know her history?"

"A man brought her in, diagnosis possible pneumonia. Her lungs are clearing, her temperature has returned to near normal, she is pregnant."

"And her name?"

"Unknown."

"Address?"

He shrugged. "Nothing on the chart."

"So where would we send her?"

"Surely there is someone who knows of her. If she stays here, who is going to pay her bill?"

"Ignore that part."

"But if someone brought her in, someone knows her or about her, and . . ."

Astrid waited, watching his reactions.

He straightened. "And how would we find that person is your next question, right? And I have no answer for that, since you have no police to assist you."

"But why police? We have no certainty of wrongdoing."

"He deserted her, dumped her like a bag of garbage."

"True. But at least he brought her here. He could have just left her out in the snow." She waited again. "Well, I am asking you to examine her again and see if we can ascertain anything else. Our job is to save her life and that of her baby. And hopefully, give her back a life along with it."

"Then we'd better force-feed her." He stood and turned to exit the door.

"Have you ever attempted to feed someone who is unresponsive?" Astrid stood.

"That is a nurse's . . ." He caught himself. "No."

She motioned him through the door. "What do you suggest feeding her?"

"Warm beef or chicken broth, and then hopefully graduate to soft or finely chopped food." The two walked across the hall to room two. They paused in the doorway to watch Miriam giving the patient a sponge bath, all the while talking softly in hopes of getting a response.

She glanced up. "I will be finished in about five minutes."

"Are you using the lotion Ingeborg left?"

Astrid looked to Dr. Commons. "We care for the whole patient. The lotion also helps prevent bed sores." She turned to Miriam. "When you are finished here, please come to my office." Pausing again, she looked to the young man beside her. "And you will implement the treatment you decide to use and then explain what you expect to all of us. Correct?"

His jaw tightened, he took in a breath, and he nodded. "Of course."

O Lord, if his staying is your will, please give us all the grace we need to accomplish your plan. Whatever that might be. She made a mental note to herself. *Get the prayers focusing on Dr. Commons and the situation here.*

CHAPTER 5

W hat do you suppose Toby wants to talk with us about?"

Rebecca turned to Gerald. "Well, I'm sure I have no idea, but supper will be ready when he gets here." By the time Toby got back from the hospital last night with Melissa and Anji, Rebecca had already served supper to the rest of the family and they had postponed their discussion for a day.

"Toby usually just comes over, not official like this."

Rebecca turned from sliding a pan of biscuits in the oven. "I made his favorite, so that should put him in a good mood, not that he is ever in a bad mood." She laid her hot pads up on the stove warming shelf and looked to her husband. Gerald was leaning against the doorjamb, hands in his pockets.

Anji reached up for the plates so that Lissa could set the table. Her hand was still wrapped with bandages, but she wasn't in pain today.

Anji's thoughts went to the strange situation with Toby and Gerald's parents. Toby Valders had always lived with his mother and father, taking care to see the house was maintained, sometimes trying to be a calming agent when one of them was irate, which was often. He'd not been successful at that venture in the last years. When Anner insisted Hildegunn leave with him, Toby had continued as usual, both he and Gerald as confused at their actions as everyone else.

"Do you suppose he heard from your mother?"

"Possibly. It would be helpful if someone did. I mean it seems a shame that all that house is not being used. Not with this housing shortage." Gerald shook his head and sighed. He turned at the sound of Benny's wheels on the hall floor and the giggles preceding him. "Here they come. Be prepared."

Benny sat with Annika and Swen in front of him and Joseph pushing. Annika waved her arms at her mother when they stormed into the kitchen.

"Uh-oh. Here comes the Benny Express." Gerald smiled down at his oldest son. "I bet you are all starving."

"Yep." Benny grinned up at him. "Delivering the little ones."

"Oh, they have trouble walking now?"

"Ride. Benny, ride." Annika lifted her arms to her mother and Anji swooped her up while Gerald grabbed Swen and spun around with him in his arms.

Swen had the most infectious giggle, and within moments the kitchen walls bulged from the laughter.

"How are we supposed to get food on the table with all the children underfoot?" Rebecca raised her hands in mock surrender. "Guess there will be no supper tonight."

"No supper?" a familiar voice came from the doorway. "Oh no!"

"Uncle Toby!" The children shouted together and headed for the man who had just come through the back door and was hanging his coat by the door.

"Help! I'm being attacked!"

"Serves you right. Take your admirers into the parlor so we can get supper on the table." Rebecca motioned down the hall with a nod.

"Sorry. We are being banished." He grabbed the rope to Benny's wheels and away they went, everyone trying to tell him something important at the same time.

Shaking her head, Lissa looked up at her mother. "I think they like Onkel Toby."

"I think you are right." Anji looked over the table. "What are we missing?"

"Milk. I can't carry the pitcher yet."

"Sorry, I'll get that. How does your hand feel?"

"Thumpy, but it doesn't hurt."

Anji filled the glasses on the table, many only halfway for the younger ones. She set the cream pitcher next to the sugar bowl with a teaspoon already in it. For some strange reason, lately she had decided she liked her coffee better with the addition of cream and a little sugar. Her mother and father would surely roll over in their graves if they knew what she was doing.

"We can eat as soon as the biscuits are done. Gerald, will you please supervise the hand-washing, and then we can sit down." Getting everyone in their right place, including two high chairs and a small box for another, sometimes took some doing.

After all were seated and grace said, Anji set the platter of biscuits next to Rebecca and took her own seat next to almost-four-year-old, towheaded Annika, who needed a box on her chair to get her to a comfortable height. Had the Valders grandparents been in attendance, the children would have been silent at the table, but Onkel Toby was often at their table and enjoyed getting them talking—and laughing.

Toby looked across at Anji. "Seems to me

I see you and Thomas Devlin together a lot lately."

She nodded. "He's become a good friend."

At the wiggle of his eyebrows, she could feel warmth start up her neck. Perhaps she should rethink her plan to go with him to Thorliff's gathering tonight. Toby wasn't the first to inquire if there was more to their friendship than they were revealing. Since Mr. Devlin was still an Anglican priest, Anji hadn't given the possibility much thought. Now, if he chose to remain here in Blessing as a teacher and give up the priesthood . . . She banished that thought before it could grow. However, he most certainly was an entertaining friend.

When they'd finished the meal, with only one glass tipped over and that almost empty, the children were sent to the living room, where Lissa and Benny would read aloud. The two women cleared the table and did the dishes. After refilling coffee cups, they sat down at the table, and the three adults looked to Toby, who was drawing a letter out of his pocket.

"This came today, and I figured we should make some decisions right away."

"The letter is from?"

"Mor and Far."

"Well, I'll be . . ." Gerald shook his head. "Took them long enough. Are they coming back?"

"Doesn't sound like it." Toby pulled the

kerosene lamp closer so he could read more easily. "Dear Toby and Gerald . . ." He looked up. "Mor's handwriting." He returned to the page.

> *"I am sorry to have left everything in such disarray, but I was given no choice. We are settled now, and Mr. Valders has a job at a local bank."*

"Where are they?" Gerald asked.

"I have no idea, other than the postmark that is so blurred because it got wet that I can hardly read it."

"No return address?"

"No, none."

Gerald and Rebecca exchanged puzzled looks. "Go on."

> *"Mr. Valders has decided that if you boys want to keep the house, that is fine with us, but if you choose to sell it, please send us the proceeds. I pray all is well with you and your families. Greet the others from me.*
> *"Sincerely,*
> *Mrs. Hildegunn*
> *Valders"*

"Wait. Our own mother signed it Mrs. Hildegunn Valders?" Gerald stared at his brother.

"Ja, if this isn't the strangest letter, I don't know what would be." Toby held the paper up for them all to see. "That's it." He handed Gerald the envelope. "See what I mean?" Picking up his coffee cup, he sipped and shook his head. "I personally think Far has gone over the edge. I thought that when he stormed out of town, and when he returned like he did, I was sure of it. It could even be that he dictated this letter. It sounds more like him than her." He laid the paper in the middle of the table. "So, the way I see it, we need to decide what to do."

Gerald shrugged. "What is there to decide? We have a house, and you need a place to live, so it is yours."

"But that house is far bigger than this one, and you have a growing family. You would be much more comfortable there. We would just exchange."

"But this one is set up for Benny."

"He goes up and down the stairs here, so he could do the same there, and we could build a ramp outside like we did here. Granted, this house is closer to the soda shop, but not that much."

Gerald studied his wife, who was looking troubled. "What do you think?"

"I think I would rather stay here." She frowned. "True, the other house is bigger, but . . ." They all waited for her to continue. She chewed her bottom lip. "I . . . I don't like that house as much." She stared down at her hands, clenched in her lap.

Anji watched her baby sister struggle with trying to figure out an answer. "Do you have to decide all this tonight?"

Both men shrugged. "There is a third possibility to consider—well, actually several others. We could sell it and bank the money until we have an address to send it to. I'm sure there are plenty of people who would love to purchase it. Another idea would be for Anji to move into the house."

"But you live there." Anji blinked. "Besides, I . . . uh . . . I don't have the money to buy that house."

"I didn't say *buy* it. You are family, after all. You wouldn't need to buy it."

"But what if . . ." She paused and shook her head.

"What if what?" Rebecca asked.

"Well, what if your folks come back and get really angry and . . ."

"The letter leaves the decisions all in our hands. There is no way we can send them the money or anything else, since we have no idea where they are. What we decide is what happens. Besides . . ." Toby grinned at Anji, an eyebrow raised. "You could marry me, and then we'd both have a place to live, and no one would be able to gossip."

"You aren't serious. You're like my brother."

"But we really are not related."

"And I have four children."

"All of whom call me Onkel Toby and are already family."

Anji had never been one to sputter. She calmly made decisions and acted upon them. But this—this crazy idea . . . "Surely you—you don't mean this."

"Toby, quit teasing her." Rebecca rolled her eyes and shook her head. But then she grinned at Anji. "You know that really might be a good way to solve several problems. Maybe we could kill two birds with one stone."

"An apt description, my dear." Gerald patted her hand and gave his brother one of those looks of big brother exasperation. "I think we've talked about this as far as we can for now."

Lissa appeared in the kitchen doorway. "Mark is crying. I changed him but he wants you, Tante Rebecca."

"I'll be right there. Takk." Rebecca stood. "I suggest we think on this, pray on this, and then decide. In the meantime, we go on as we are." She left to take care of her crying son.

"I'll put the children to bed. Do you want more coffee first?" Anji looked to each of the men, who shook their heads. "Good night, then, Toby." As she left the room, Toby's offhand remark ate at her mind. Surely he wasn't serious. Of course anyone in Blessing would say Toby was a very good candidate for marriage. In fact, she'd heard some of the others wondering why he hadn't married yet. Not that there were a great number of eligible women. When it came right down to it, there were more men in town who needed wives than women who needed husbands.

As she tucked her children into bed and listened to their prayers, she prayed right along with them, but this time her prayer was for wisdom. Yes, she would like to marry again, someday. Immediately Thomas Devlin strode through her mind; she always enjoyed the way he made her laugh. There had been a serious lack of laughter when in the presence of the elder Moens. Proper. Everything had to be proper. If she heard that word once, she'd heard it a thousand times. One had to act and be proper, according to the expectations of society.

Her children had blossomed since moving back to Blessing too. Lissa had gone from sober to sunny. She gazed down at her two boys already asleep in their bed. Joseph had spent the summer out on the farm and grew from sickly to robust, his funny sense of humor making others laugh. She kissed his forehead and then Gilbert's. They both looked so much like the pictures she had seen of his father when he was young. Like his father, Gilbert was more serious. He loved reading and learning, although he often confused his two languages. Bilingual was not a bad trait, as Ivar had so often told her. Seeing her sons so peaceful brought back memories of their father. He had gone against the social customs of the day and spent a lot of time with his children. His desire was to create in them a love of learning and the importance of reading. His love of words and story was one of the reasons she had fallen in love with him in the beginning.

All those years ago, when she had still been recovering from her years of loving Thorliff but sending him on his way to a life apart from her, she knew she'd done what was best for him, but . . . She shook off the memories. Had that been the best for her? She bent over and kissed her sons again. These children she and Ivar had been given were worth any of the heartbreak she had endured. "Thank you, Lord," she whispered as she left the room. She owed her Norway family another letter. Best get to it.

Back in the parlor, where a big grate brought up the heat from the good wood furnace in the cellar, she joined Rebecca and Gerald. He sat in his wing-back chair reading the newspaper and Rebecca in her rocking chair was hemming a dress for Lissa.

"I thought to do that next." Anji now had her little maple lap desk tucked under one arm.

Rebecca smiled at her. "You look to be ready for writing letters, and I love hemming. Good thing we can pass your Lissa's clothes on to someone else. She has grown so fast. Now that I can hem diapers on the machine, this is good."

She smoothed the daisy-sprigged garment with one hand. "And besides, it reminds me spring and summer haven't completely deserted us."

Anji reminded her, "We always get at least one more blizzard after a warm spell."

Rebecca nodded and returned to her task. "It seems winter always tries to stay around. Perhaps he wants to feel some of the spring warmth too."

Anji rolled her eyes. Leave it to her fanciful baby sister. Although referring to the accomplished young woman across the floor grate from her as her baby sister was almost a joke. "I saw you had your soda recipes out. Thinking ahead?"

"Yes. As much as we all love coffee, I'm thinking of using coffee both in a soda and in ice cream. I was over at the soda shop the other day, and it sure needs cleaning up."

"At least we got the mouse and rat traps set last fall." Gerald flipped one side of the newspaper over so he could see his wife. "They sure like to move into an empty building. And here I thought I'd gotten all their possible entrances repaired."

"I know. The last times I checked, there were no dead bodies."

Anji set her lap desk up in her lap and uncorked the ink bottle. Pencil would be much easier, but ink was mandatory for this correspondence. She also used her better paper.

Switching her mind to Norwegian, she dipped her pen in the ink.

She didn't want to open the letter with *Mor.* Too casual. She'd better stay with formal.

> *Dear Mrs. Moen,*
> *Thank you for the recent letter. I was glad to hear your winter was not terribly severe either. While we have had a lot of snow, the blizzards have been fewer. Now as the melt starts, we pray it will continue slowly enough to not cause flooding. Our Red River has such a propensity for overflowing its banks, due to the northward flow that ends in a lake that takes longer to thaw.*
> *The children are well and Melissa is outgrowing all her dresses.*

Anji paused. Should she say that or would it be interpreted as complaining? Or a suggestion that they were in need? Why did even letter-writing feel like she was walking a tightrope? Perhaps she needed another time with Ingeborg, who had come to take the place of her own mother through the years. But she knew what Ingeborg would say, only because she'd said it before. *"Pray for those who spitefully use you and trust that God will take care of this too. He can see across the ocean, you know."*

She heaved a sigh and went back to her letter. What to say?

Melissa, Gilbert, and Joseph are doing well in school. I so appreciate that the children in Blessing also learn to speak in sign language due to the deaf school here in town. The other day Melissa asked if one could sign in Norwegian. I said we should look into that. I am sure that in spite of the fact that it is called American Sign Language, other countries must be doing so also. Is that anything about which you might have information?

Joseph can already read. Both he and Gilbert look just like the pictures you showed me of Ivar when he was this age. Joseph has many of his far's traits too, being of a more sober mien than the others. He learns so quickly.

Annika is the little mother to Rebecca's baby Agnes. She does not have any opportunity to misbehave, Annika makes sure of that. I am always amazed at how different each child is.

I am happy to hear how well the older girls are doing. I am sorry they will not be coming to see us this summer, but I understand that there are plenty of events happening there that they would not want to miss. Their far would be so proud of them. I am including Lissa's letters to her sisters.

> *Sincerely,*
> *Anji Baard Moen*

There, that is done for a few more months. While she had originally thought she would write monthly, quarterly seemed to be what was happening. She knew she would receive a letter back rather quickly asking when she was planning to return to Norway. Ivar had asked her more than once before he died to make sure she brought the children back to Norway, if not every year, at least every other year. Just the thought of making that trip again tied her stomach in a tangle of knots.

CHAPTER 6

Why was it that she always forgot from one spring to the next how the thawing ground turned into mud that could stop a train? Black, thick mud that stuck to anything that moved and weighted it to a stop unless scraped off. That included boots, wheels, horse hooves. Even the cat had to clean her paws of Red River mud.

"I sure am grateful the dangers of flood have passed," Freda said by the back door as she scraped her boots at the scrubber and jack combined. "The cheese house is now clean and ready for us to begin another season." As soon as the pasture was high enough for grazing, thus bringing up the milk production and the cream content, they would start making cheese again.

"We do have some left for us to eat, don't we?" Ingeborg asked as she turned from kneading the dough for bread. "Since it's Saturday, I thought to fancy the rolls up a little and put grated cheese in them for supper tonight."

"Of course. You think I want to lose my head?"

Was that a twinkle she saw in Freda's usually stoic face? What was this world coming to? Ingeborg returned to her kneading. The cat sat in the kitchen window. Ingeborg had given up and put the sprouting seeds in the other windows after the cat took over that one. She had barely caught the tray as it started to fall one day. This year she was trying something new: starting seeds in eggshell halves filled with soil she had saved in the cellar over the winter so she could get seeds started earlier. That was her bid for a warm spring.

It was finally warming too. Ten days ago, blizzard-like winds and cold; now, balmy days. And her letters were all written, including a nice long one to Augusta. It really must be spring.

"Grandma, there are two new calves in the barn!" Inga, with Carl hot on her heels, burst through the kitchen door.

"And another cow in a calving stall. Pa says her calf will come soon." Five-and-a-half-year-old Carl looked from Ingeborg to the oven. "Are the cookies ready yet?"

"Where's Emmy?" She pointed to the plate on the counter. "Help yourself."

Inga propped herself at the table on her elbows and watched the kneading. "She's helping Benny clean his wheels. Manny was going to pull his wheels with Joker, but Onkel Andrew said the horse hooves would mud up too. Are you going to make cinnamon rolls?"

"No, not today. We are about out of bread."

"Fry bread?"

"Now, why would I want to do that?"

Carl joined her. "'Cause your grandchildren need fried bread. It's been forever since we had any."

"That's 'cause only Grandma makes it."

Ingeborg felt her inside smile bloom on her face and expand as she heard the thump of crutches on the porch floor. Ever since Benny had learned to use the artificial legs Manny and Trygve created for him, his strange gait had a sound all its own.

"Wait. I'll get the door." Manny's voice cracked in the middle.

Inga and Carl looked at each other and giggled.

"Uff da," Emmy said when she came through the door. "That mud."

Ingeborg rolled her lips together. The *uff da* from the little Indian girl always made her chuckle, but only inside so as not to hurt her feelings. "How did you get out here, Benny?"

"Manny rode me piggyback." He grinned up at his friend, who had grown three inches since last summer. "We stayed on the sod."

"Did you know the grass is greening up so fast, Pa said you could see it happen? I tried to watch, but I didn't see it get greener." Carl wore a puzzled look. After all, his pa never made mistakes.

"Ah, Carl, that's just a saying. During the summer they say the same thing about how fast corn grows."

"But Pa said . . ." He shook his head, lips turned down.

"Don't worry about it. Grown-ups say things that don't make sense to kids." Inga shook her head too. "They are strange that way."

Ingeborg swallowed not only a chuckle but an out-and-out laugh. How did God happen to send her two such literal thinkers? Inga had a mind like none she had known before. And for Carl, if Pa said something, it was gospel truth. He did not understand teasing, at least not from his pa. She needed to remind Andrew of that. Figures of speech were an unknown language to his son. She formed the dough into a round and plunked it back in the crockery bowl to sit on the warming shelf to rise.

"Uff da," Freda muttered with a grin only for Ingeborg. She got nearly as big a chuckle out of the children as she did, but chuckling was not as near the surface for Freda as it was for Ingeborg.

"Grandma, are we going to have tea?" This was new from Emmy too. As if this last winter she had figured out she really was one of Ingeborg's grandchildren, and that was a mighty good thing.

"I think we could do that. Would you like to pour some hot water into the teapot? Manny, could you please reach the tea tin down? Inga, you fix the cookie plate, and Carl, you and Benny set the table." This hadn't been on her list of things to do today, but the way these children were growing up, she'd figured out she'd better take every advantage.

"While Manny and the boys clean out the chicken house, could we sew?" Inga asked as she brought the cookie tins out of the pantry.

"I thought you were going to help in the chicken house."

Inga made a horrible face. "It stinks bad. I'd clean all the calf pens, but I can clean out the nests and put in new straw."

Carl gave her a disgusted look. "We got pigpens to clean too."

Freda moved the steaming teakettle off the hottest part of the stove. "Spring cleaning starts in the house next week too."

"Spring cleaning in the houses, spring cleaning in the barns. I'd rather go fishing."

"The fish aren't biting yet," Benny said,

joining the conversation. "Sure was cold out ice fishing this winter." He pulled out a chair and sat down, leaning over to rub his legs around the harness they had created to hold his artificial legs in place.

"Hurting?" Ingeborg asked.

"Some, but no sores."

Astrid had impressed on him the seriousness of watching that sores didn't develop on the stumps of his legs, and he was wise enough to pay attention. Benny was another unusual child who called her *Grandma*, like the others did. He referred to Hildegunn as Grandmother Valders. One day he had asked Ingeborg about his other grandmother. Was she coming back?

Ingeborg often wondered the same thing. Hildegunn was often on her mind, and she knew all she could do was pray for her.

They all took chairs at the table, and Emmy poured the tea. They passed around the sugar bowl and commenced to clean off the cookie plate, the cocoa cookies disappearing first, then the gingerbread men, only because they were larger. Ingeborg basked in delight. Ah, the need to hear the laughter of children.

As they were finishing their tea and cookies, Ingeborg announced, "We have to work fast. Easter is just around the corner, and we want to be done by then. So I have an idea. How about all of you go out to spring clean? You boys clean out the chicken house while the girls clean out the calf pens. Then you girls clean out the nest boxes and spread the clean straw while you boys start on the sheep pens. I think Andrew has the manure spreader by the chicken house. Wheelbarrow the manure up in it. Then we will have dinner, and the girls and I will sew, and you boys can—"

"Sweep out the haymow."

"Good and then I will make fried bread for a treat."

"And syrup?" Carl asked.

"Definitely syrup."

Freda exhaled with relief when the whirlwind of energy exited with the laughing children.

Sometime later, Andrew appeared. "Thanks, Mor. They were a great help." He stopped at the mat by the door. "That chicken house has never been cleaned so fast in all its years. You should have seen Benny cleaning out the nest boxes. I would not have suggested he do that. He just took over. I think he was really pleased that he could work with the others."

"Will you have dinner with us?"

"No, thanks. I told Ellie I'd be back for dinner."

"Then I'll send a loaf of bread home with Carl later this afternoon."

"You know we never turn down a loaf of your bread. Good thing we had two wheelbarrows. The girls got one of the calf pens done.

You should have seen them moving those calves from pen to pen. We let the older ones out in the small pen since we can let the animals out at least part of the day now. The cows are all sunning themselves on the south side of the barn."

"I am sure I will hear all about it."

"You will. Here they come. Oh, and I told them to put part of the sweepings from the haymow in the chicken house. The chickens will appreciate scratching around in that."

"I'm putting basins out for them to scrub before they come in." Freda rolled her eyes. "Never did like manure stink."

"Good and remind them to take their boots off at the door."

As they were all finishing their fried bread and syrup, Inga propped both elbows on the table with her chin in her hands. "I sure do like Saturdays when we can all come to your house, Grandma. It's more like summer."

Carl shook his head. "I like snow, but not so much the mud."

Emmy smiled at Ingeborg. "We saw little violets blooming on the south side of the chicken house."

"Already?" Freda almost smiled.

"Do you want me to pick you one? There were only two so far." Inga dunked the last of her bread in the syrup.

"Takk, but no. There will be more soon. Why, the snowbanks aren't even gone yet." Ingeborg smiled inside and out. Spears of grass so green they glimmered, tiny violets, all the harbingers of spring, sometimes sprouting up right at the edge of the retreating snow turned slush.

"We better get going, Benny, so I can get back for milking."

"I'll pull his wheels," Inga offered.

After hugs all around, cookies tucked into pockets, Ingeborg with Emmy at her side waved the others off. Carl trudged home across the field while the others took the lane, with Benny riding piggyback on Manny, his crutches on the wagon that Inga was pulling.

"I'm surprised you didn't go along."

Emmy looked up with a smile that was always at the ready these days. "I want to finish my skirt. I was thinking . . ."

"Ja, about what?"

"I want to make a tunic out of one of the deer hides and do the beading on it, like the one that is too small."

"We can't sew that on the machine, at least I don't think we can."

"I know. It will take me a long time, but . . ." She paused, her forehead furrowed.

Ingeborg waited, knowing this meant Emmy was thinking hard. She put an arm around the girl's shoulders and Emmy shifted even closer. *Ah, Lord, thank you for this daughter you gave me.*

"I don't want to forget my people. I want to do the things my mother would have taught me."

"I think that is a very good idea. I have a suggestion. What if you made moccasins first? That would go a lot faster."

"I could make a pair for Inga too."

"That you could."

"You still wear the ones Metiz made for you."

"I know. And we still have the rabbit fur mittens she made. They don't wear out. I've thought of sewing new soles on my moccasins before they wear out. Should we do this together?"

Emmy beamed up at her. "I'll ask Trygve and Andrew if they have any hides." She giggled. "But don't tell Inga. I want to surprise her."

"A birthday present, or maybe Christmas?"

"Maybe, or maybe just because she's my best friend." They turned back into the house. "I'll go feed the chickens and check for more eggs."

The frost during the night made getting to church easier in the morning. They settled into the pews as usual, Emmy on one side and

Manny on the other side, Thorliff and family in front of her, one-and-a-half-year-old Roald on his shoulder, waving with one hand, his other fist in his slobbery mouth. Since he had learned to walk, he was harder to hold on to. With Elizabeth at the piano, Ingeborg almost offered to take her little grandson, but it was good for Thorliff to have him. Emmy hid her face and giggle in Ingeborg's upper arm. Roald made the girls laugh all the time.

By the end of the service, Roald had finally fallen asleep, until they rose for the benediction and he saw his mother, letting out a crow of delight that made those around them try not to laugh out loud.

"Thank you, Roald," Reverend Solberg said as he raised his arms to give the benediction. "The Lord bless thee and keep thee, the Lord look with favor upon thee and give thee his peace. In the name of the Father, and of the Son, and of the Holy Spirit." Everyone joined the amen, Elizabeth and Jonathan played a duet, and the congregation rose to make their way out the doors, where Solberg greeted them all.

"Never a dull moment, is there?" Thorliff asked his mor.

"At least he wasn't crying." The baby had done that more than once too. She reached for him and Roald came to her immediately, patting her cheeks and beaming at her.

Halfway down the aisle, Ingeborg kissed the baby cheeks. *And to think I didn't think of Haakan even once or cry. Thank you, Lord.*

Pastor Solberg came to dinner at Ingeborg's that afternoon, although Mary Martha and his children had been invited to another get-together in town. When all the family had left after enjoying Sunday dinner, Pastor Solberg stayed behind at Ingeborg's request.

"I've been thinking," she said, her rocking chair singing a slow tune.

"I am not surprised. Winter and the coming of spring are always good times for thinking. I know this has been a hard winter for you."

"It caught me by surprise. I thought I would be more accustomed to Haakan's leaving by now, but I think I missed him more this winter than the last, the first after he went on to heaven. I know the number of days is the same and this was even a milder winter than last, but the days just seemed darker, or the nights longer, or something."

"Perhaps last winter you were still numb, but you have not seemed terribly sad or depressed."

"I know. I haven't been. That's why this is so puzzling to me. I keep looking in the Word, and God speaks to me through it, over and over. Ah, so many promises, and I treasure them.

Perhaps that's the reason I've needed the dark, to drive me to His Word."

"The pit?"

"No, that was last winter. I call it the fear of the pit time. But just dark." She rocked, her head resting against the back of the rocker. She felt a smile begin somewhere inside where smiles are born. "Is that why we need the dark and hard times, to make us draw closer to Him?"

"Ja, that is true. Hard lessons to learn, but—"

"But we need to learn them." It was not a question. The rocker sang along with the snap and crackle of the logs in the stove. "I know clear down to my bones that He is always with me, and I think that I am finally understanding that when I can't sense Him near, it isn't that He has left me alone."

"No. He never does. He promises over and over to never leave us nor forsake us. I believe that with everything that I am."

"I always thought that the hard places would get fewer, or at least not as painful, as we get older."

"I think as we draw closer to Him, He keeps training us up in even more ways, so that we are prepared to do what He has put us on earth to do."

"Do you ever wonder?" She paused, searching for words. "I mean, is there really more for us to do?"

"After all this town has been through these last two years, you think you've not been doing His will in all the love and prayers and healing you help bring about? Look around you, Ingeborg. You are raising two children He has given you. All the people who come here for love and a listening ear. All the prayers you have prayed for those around you. Your grandchildren like nothing better than to come to Grandma's house. And the young woman from the hospital. You were right there with your hands and your prayers. When you fret that you may not be doing enough, remember where that kind of thought comes from—the enemy, who always comes to lie, steal, and kill. Trust that God will always guide you in the right direction."

Ingeborg sighed. "I do trust, most of the time. It is so easy to let my mind get away from me."

"Ah, Ingeborg, it is just a good thing He knows us so well and loves us anyway. We all struggle with trusting and praising Him in all things. But He won the war."

"Ja, He did. But these skirmishes sure can be painful."

His smile warmed her heart as always. "Ja, but we get stronger."

I sure hope so, she thought, rocking. *I truly hope so. No, I trust so. Go away, worm of doubt.*

CHAPTER 7

What are we going to do with her?" Astrid looked from Elizabeth to head nurse Deborah MacCallister, and Miriam and Ingeborg, who had just been giving their patient one of her combination conversation, muscle work, and prayer times. They were gathered in Astrid's office at the hospital.

"The more difficult question is how do we help her want to live?" Ingeborg picked up her knitting.

"You'd think she'd want to live for her baby's sake." Deborah studied the chart Miriam passed her. "We've done all we can for the pneumonia. I mean, even though she still coughs a lot, she has not run a temperature for the last twenty-four hours, and thanks to the percussive thumping, her lungs are clearing.

We've force-fed her, but she is still not eating enough for that baby too."

Astrid shook her head. "Thorliff has had no success with finding out who brought her in, so where did she live and who with? We have absolutely no history. How far did that man travel to bring her here? And why didn't he take her to Grafton or Grand Forks?"

"Why do we keep thinking she came from south of here? To the north and northwest, we have more small towns with no medical help." Elizabeth reached for the chart. "As you said, we've done all that we can do. Ingeborg, you said she could come to your house, but I hate to burden you with another patient. Do we have anyone else willing to take her in? She should be strong enough soon to be a help around the house."

Astrid nodded. "If we could figure out how to communicate with her."

Elizabeth passed the chart to Ingeborg. "Has she said a word?"

All of them shook their heads.

"Can she speak?"

Leaning over, Ingeborg put the chart on Astrid's desk. "She understands Norwegian. When I ask her to move her legs or arms, she can do that. When she opens her eyes, she is following me. She does not seem to be afraid of me any longer." She picked up her knitting again. Her needles kept up their soft clicking as she spoke. "But she does not respond to a direct question, and yet she can hear. So is this non-response by choice or . . . ?"

"And that is the question. Can fear make someone go mute or was she already mute or . . . ?" Astrid tongued a canker sore on the inside of her cheek. "When Reverend Solberg went into her room, she was all right, but when Thorliff tried to ask her questions, had she been able, she would have pushed herself right through the bed or the wall. She shook for an hour after he left."

"So it seems a man was cruel to her."

"But not a minister. She trusted him. Or at least was not afraid of him."

"I think my house is the best idea. I speak Norwegian and no men live there, though she will have to get used to Trygve and the others. Once she settles in and gets stronger, we will be able to figure this out." Ingeborg nodded at Astrid and the others. "To me, this just seems the best plan for now." She tipped her head slightly to the side. "And maybe having the children around will be a good thing too."

Astrid rolled her eyes. Leave it to her mor. "Let's go lay this out before her and see how she reacts. I guess what bothers me the most is that we have no history. I mean, what if . . ."

Ingeborg spoke gently. "We need not fear any what ifs. We have all prayed about this. Has anyone else come up with a plan?" She waited.

No one said anything.

Ingeborg put her knitting aside. "For some reason, God brought this woman to us to be cared for. All the while I have been praying God's will be done. He knows who she is, and I trust we will learn what she needs in good time."

While the others returned to their jobs, she, along with Astrid and Elizabeth, returned to private room two.

"Let me be the observer, and I will take notes," Elizabeth said.

"Good idea," Astrid commented before taking a deep breath and leading the way into the room.

The mysterious young woman was sleeping, so Ingeborg touched her shoulder and smiled when her eyes flew open, fear leaping out. But she relaxed when she saw who it was.

Ingeborg spoke in Norwegian. "I know you can understand me, so please nod and answer my questions. All right?"

The woman blinked and dipped her chin, keeping her gaze on Ingeborg until Astrid picked up her hand, holding on when she tried to jerk it out.

"This is my daughter, Dr. Astrid, and this is my daughter-in-law, Dr. Elizabeth. Our last names are the same: Bjorklund. Do you remember that?"

Astrid would have missed the nod had she not been watching.

"You have been very sick with pneumonia, but you are getting better every day. Ja?"

Another slight nod.

"Do you know you are with child?"

The woman clamped her eyes shut and started to shake again.

Ingeborg smoothed her hair back and laid a hand on her shoulder. "I know this should not be, but we have to be realistic. Am I right that you are not married and this pregnancy is not your fault?"

Tears leaked from under the clamped shut eyes and ran down the girl's cheeks. They'd referred to her as a woman, but they had no idea how old she was. She covered her face with both hands and shuddered with the force of her sobs.

Astrid muttered, "I'd say that was a yes."

Ingeborg handed her a muslin square to wipe her tears and blow her nose as the sobs let up. "We will take care of you. You do not need to be afraid. No one will hurt you here."

Astrid watched the tears run down her mor's cheeks and mopped at the ones on her own. Such terror. No one should be like this.

"Ah, dear one, as soon as you are strong enough, I am going to take you to my house. You are now a member of my family, and you need not be afraid. No one will come for you. I am going to call you Clara until you can tell me your real name. *Clara* means clear and bright, and your future is clear and bright. So, Clara, one of the nurses is going to bring you soup and bread with cheese that came from my cheese house. I will stay with you while you eat. No, do not shake your head. You will eat and get strong, and you now have a new life in Blessing, North Dakota, where you will be known as Clara Bjorklund for as long as you so desire."

"We will help you sit up." Astrid smiled as she and Elizabeth moved to the head of the bed and lifted as Ingeborg stacked pillows behind their patient. "There now. The tray will be here in a few minutes. You will eat, right?"

Clara heaved a sigh and let her head fall back against the pillows. She nodded, as if she had no more will to fight them.

"Good." Astrid patted the hand now lying flat on the bedclothes. "Takk. We just want to help you. And I have always wanted a sister named Clara."

Clara's eyes opened wide, and she stared at Astrid, then flashed a look to Ingeborg, who was nodding and smiling.

"Ja, that is so." Ingeborg sat in the chair beside the bed and picked up her knitting again. "Do you know how to knit?"

Astrid and Elizabeth left the room and, after giving orders to one of the new student nurses, retreated to the office.

"I could quite cheerfully shoot the man who

did this to her." Elizabeth sank into one of the chairs by the office door. "It would probably be better if Thorliff gave up his search as to where she came from. Let her just have a new life and not bring up the old unless she volunteers more information."

"I have no trouble with that. Other than my curiosity is in rampage mode. The line that keeps going through my mind is 'one of the least of these.'"

"As in 'What you have done unto the least of these, you have done so unto me'? A paraphrase, but you get the gist."

"Ja, that one." Astrid propped her head up on her hands, elbows on her desk. "Have you noticed how many people who have come to Blessing seem to fit into that category, at least until they've been here a while? Emmy, Manny, some of our immigrants, so many of our deaf students, our Indian nurses . . ."

"Thorliff told me about Gerald and Toby all those years ago."

"I forgot about them. But Deborah would have been one too. She and Manda."

"All those years ago when everyone got together and named their little town Blessing. Who would have dreamed of all this ahead?" Elizabeth commented.

"God did."

"Ja, God did. And to think I did not really want to come here. I thought I would be a doctor in Minnesota. Until Thorliff came into my life."

"As Mor says so often, God does good work when we let Him."

"Dr. Astrid, we have a patient waiting," Miriam said after tapping at the door.

"I'm going on home, then," Elizabeth said. "Remember, you have tomorrow off. Thelma will do just fine with Roald. He needs to learn that I am not always there."

"If you insist."

"I'll check in on Clara before I leave." Elizabeth slid her notes into her bag. "I'll rewrite these to make some sense for the records."

Astrid checked to make sure she had her stethoscope in her apron pocket and headed for the examining room. *Lord, please give me the same wisdom you give my mother. Thank you for blessing our hospital the way you do, and help us especially with Clara. You know I would like to get even with whoever abused her, but as Mor would say, vengeance is yours, not ours. But if there is a special place in hell for a man like that, please see to it.* She tapped on the door and entered the examining room to see Johnny Solberg sitting on the table with a foot so swollen he couldn't wear a shoe.

"What happened?" Astrid asked him as she rolled up his pant leg.

He looked to his mother, Mary Martha Solberg, who was sitting in the chair by the door. She shook her head. "You tell her."

"I, um, we were playing soccer and I, um, accidentally hit the tree."

Astrid gave him a questioning look. "You kicked the tree?"

"Well, Gunner and I were scrambling for the ball, and I kicked at it but he kicked it first and I hit the tree instead." He scrunched his face and tried to pull back when she, trying to be as gentle as possible, probed the foot. "Oww."

"Sorry, Johnny, but I have to see if any bones are broken. When did this happen?"

"Yesterday after school."

"Why did you not come in then?"

"He tried to hide it, but when he couldn't walk this morning, I packed some ice around it, which I would have done last night had I known about it." Mary Martha glared at her son. "Last night he said he didn't feel well and just wanted to go to bed, so I thought he was coming down with something and didn't bother to look at his foot, which was under the covers."

"I see." Astrid shook her head. "Until we get this swelling down, I can't tell anything. Let's get you in a bed, and we'll get your foot elevated and iced and see what happens. Can you bend your ankle?" He did with a groan. "Move your toes?" This time he clamped his jaw tight and his face paled.

"Let's hope it is just a sprain and bruised. I'll call the nurses to get a bed set up and in the meantime, we'll give you some pain medicine." She looked to his mother. "You'll want to bring him some nightclothes. We're going to have to open that pant leg to get it over his foot. You wait here, and I'll be right back." Outside the door, it was all she could do to keep from laughing. Not that the injury was funny, but what a story.

She explained to Miriam and the student nurse what they would do and stopped in Clara's room to see if her mother was still there. When they said she'd gone home, she asked Deborah to call Ingeborg and ask if someone could bring in Manny's crutches when they came to town. No rush. Johnny would be off that foot for a couple of days at least. If only they had one of those wonderful new inventions, the x-ray machine. Oh to be able to see those bones without having to cut the foot open. What a shame it would be if the bones were broken and she was not able to set them correctly.

That night at the supper table she told them about Johnny kicking the tree. "Talk about a crazy accident."

"Well, at least he'll still be able to play the guitar." Astrid's husband, Daniel, tried to keep back a snort.

"I'd be careful not to laugh if I were you," his mother, Amelia, admonished. "I seem to remember a few *accidents* that were more than strange at our house too."

"Like the time I got my tongue stuck in that bottle?"

Astrid's mouth fell open. "You did what?"

Amelia scowled. "I had to break the bottle, and I was scared to pieces it might slash his tongue to bits."

"May I ask why you . . ."

The scowl did not soften. "He said it was an experiment. His father said he understood since he was of an experiential nature also."

"You couldn't get any oil . . . ?"

"We tried everything."

"I see." Astrid cocked an eyebrow. "Remind me when we have children not to tell them things like that, just in case they might want to try it."

But Amelia was not done with the conversation. "Remember when your pa said don't put your tongue on the pump handle in the winter, and you did, and we had to pour warm water over the handle for what seemed like hours to get your tongue loose?"

"I've always wondered why he said that. I never would have thought to do such a thing." Daniel shrugged. "I asked him once, and he never answered."

Astrid giggled. "I wonder how much of his tongue was left on the pump handle when he was a boy."

"Ma, would you please pour some coffee in her cup and stuff a piece of cake in her mouth?" Daniel nodded toward his wife, who by this time had progressed from a giggle to an out-and-out laugh.

Amelia was smirking too. "So, Johnny Solberg. What will you do for him?"

"Get the swelling down first and pray there are no broken bones. There are so many small bones in a foot, one or more could easily be shattered. I'd rather not have to open the foot and look for bone fragments. That tree is kind of hard on our kids. Inga fell out of it and broke her arm. Another child fell into it and had a mild concussion, and now Johnny with his foot."

Daniel was nodding thoughtfully. "I was thinking the other day that we ought to build some swings for the school. That and some monkey bars. Give them some other things to play on during recess."

"The women would say build another school first."

"Somehow I can't see the two competing, at least in scope. I think I'll talk with my class at the machine shop. Let them design it and see if something new comes of it. I sent them out to talk with the farmers about what might be a helpful addition to their machinery. That Tonio is one sharp young man. I've been meaning to mention that to Miriam Knutson."

"Her other brother and sisters are doing well in school too. Their mother and father raised a fine brood in spite of the father's death and the ensuing poverty. They are really hard workers, all of them." Astrid caught a yawn but Daniel noticed anyway.

"You're not planning on going back to the hospital, are you?"

"No, I'm going to bed. I've felt really good for the last few months and now I'm feeling really tired again. Hope I am not coming down with something."

CHAPTER 8

Four days later, the nurses and Astrid helped Clara into the lightweight buggy, and Ingeborg drove her out to the farm. On the way she pointed out the buildings of Blessing, including who lived in which house. Patches yipped a greeting soon after they turned into the lane. At least the west wind had helped dry out the mud so that when she drove on the shoulder of the lane, they didn't sink deep. She caught an almost smile on her patient's face. Ah. So she liked dogs.

"His name is Patches and if you give him a bit of cheese, you will be his friend forever." She continued to speak Norwegian, wishing she had an idea of what was going on in that mind so hidden by the lack of speech. "Freda is my cousin. She lives with me and helps here each day. And she handles the cheese making. I've told you about Manny and Emmy, and while Manny is getting tall enough to look like a man, he is still a fourteen-year-old boy. Well, almost fifteen. You must not be afraid of him. In fact, out here there is no one to fear. You are now a member of our family, and we take care of each other. The children will be home from school in an hour or so, but I would like to get you settled so you can rest a bit. Between you and me and Freda, we will get you up the steps to the porch."

They'd been walking her for the last two days at the hospital, and while Thorliff and Daniel had both volunteered to help, Ingeborg had turned down the offers. She could have called Reverend Solberg, but he was teaching school and she did not want to bother him. She whoa'd the horse at the back gate, watched her patient's reaction to Freda coming out the door, and stepped down to the ground. "You wait for us to help you, all right? Clara, please nod so I know you understand."

Clara's chin jerked, but the fear had returned to her eyes, and she was shaking again.

Freda tied the horse to the post and waited for Ingeborg.

"Slow but sure," Ingeborg whispered with her back to Clara. "I'm not sure, I've ever seen anyone this fearful. Let's get her into the house."

"I made up that cot in the parlor like you said. You don't think she can climb the stairs?"

"These four will be hard enough. She did remarkably well once we got her up, but she's as weak as a baby bird."

Together they helped Clara down, keeping the blanket wrapped around her shoulders. With her between them and each with an arm about Clara's bone-thin body, they made it to the bottom of the porch stairs before they paused.

"Can you lift your feet up for each step?" The nod accompanied a shudder. Her fingers dug into Ingeborg's. "Good. Here we go. I'll step first." Feeling as if she were talking to a toddler, Ingeborg put one foot on the bottom step and lifted at the same time as Freda. By the time they reached the porch floor, they were all panting.

"We made it. Let's sit her on the bench." With Clara huddled on the bench by the railing, Ingeborg looked over the young woman's head at Freda. They both rolled their eyes and sucked in a breath. "Kitchen chair next."

"By the stove. We have to get her warmed up."

While Clara was shaking, Ingeborg wasn't sure if it was from cold or fear.

Patches parked himself right in front of Clara and whimpered, staring at her, his head slightly cocked to one side. Clara reached out one shaking hand and laid it on the dog's head, earning her a quick lick on the wrist.

"I've never seen him act like this, Clara. It's as if he knows you. Good dog, Patches."

Clara flashed her a look that, had it been words, would have been a poem.

"You have had a dog before?"

A nod.

"In North Dakota?"

A sharp shake of her head.

"At home in Norway?"

Clara moved her hand gently to massage the dog's ears.

"Time to get moving again." Freda gripped Clara's hand and elbow. They lifted her to standing, crossed the porch, and then Freda pushed the door open.

"You've been baking bread." Ingeborg inhaled the yeasty fragrance and glanced at Clara, whose eyes were closed but her chest moved with the deep breaths. "Smells good, doesn't it?"

This time the nod was full-headed, and another breath brought on a smile.

Why did such a simple thing as a smile make Ingeborg want to dance across the floor? *Tusen takk, Lord God. There is hope, not that I truly doubted, but takk and takk again.* "Freda will cut you a slice of bread as soon as it is cooled enough. Along with a slab of cheese and some of that chicken soup ready in the pot to the back of the stove. How does that sound?"

"I planned on fixing dumplings for supper, but we can have some soup in the meantime." Freda moved a chair nearer the stove, and they sat Clara down on it. Then before doing anything else, Freda opened the oven to check on the bread. "Pretty near done. I'll take your coat and hang it up."

Clara clutched her lapels, shaking her head.

"You take it off when you get warm enough, then." Freda took Ingeborg's coat and scarf and hung them alongside her own on the pegs by the door.

Ingeborg lifted a lid to check on the fire, then set it to the side to put more wood in the firebox. Even the rattle of the lids sounded friendly. Leaning over, she tucked the blanket back in around Clara, glancing down at her moccasin-clad feet. Ingeborg's moccasins showed their age, but at least the girl's feet were dry. Whoever had left her at the hospital had not even brought her shoes.

She glanced back at her charge and recognized her eyes were drifting closed and her head drooping forward. "Freda, help me." Together they lifted Clara to her feet, walked her to the cot near the parlor stove and, after sitting her down, removed coat and moccasins and helped her lie down. Clara was asleep before they got the covers pulled up.

Ingeborg puffed out a breath. "Scared me for a moment. I thought she might fall off the chair." She heaved another sigh. "I wish I had some kind of bell here so she could call for help."

"Are there any cowbells down at the barn? I know, sleigh bells."

"Good idea. While you get the bread out, I'll walk down to the barn and see what I can find." Ingeborg snagged a shawl off the pegs and threw it around her shoulders as she headed out into the sunshine. The sun had looked deceptively warm from the inside of the house. She hoped spring was finally there to stay. Now that it was late April, it was unlikely they'd get another blizzard.

She thought back to Easter. For the first time they'd had a trumpet heralding the day along with the other instruments. The *alleluia*s soared even more than usual. She murmured the greeting again. "Christ is risen. He is risen indeed." Her "Tussen takk, Lord" danced with the sunbeams.

With Patches trotting beside her, she picked up her pace. Rather than searching for a cowbell, she would grab one of the short lengths of harness leather with a couple of bells attached. The men had let the cows out into the small field right behind the barn. She could hear them gathered in the sunshine, snorting, moving around a bit, chewing their cuds. Hay had been spread out there instead of tossed into their stanchions.

"I know how you all feel," Ingeborg said. "I need the sun on my face too." She pulled open the door and stepped into the dimness. Someone should wash the windows so more light could come in. Barns had different smells in different seasons. Today, used bedding dominated, even though they cleaned the gutters every day and hauled the manure out to the pile. Since the harnesses were hung by the grain bins, oats and corn blended with dust, lending an overlay. Two cats wound around her legs, suggesting that perhaps it was milking time. Studying the harnesses hung from racks on the wall, she located a couple of leather straps with bells on them. At Christmastime they attached them to the harnesses for the joyous bells of Christmas. She unhooked one and, making sure the barn door was fully closed, returned to the house.

"Uff da," she said as she came through the kitchen door. "That barn sure does need spring too. I think you notice the smell more when the cows aren't in there."

"They'd better enjoy the reprieve. I have a feeling another storm is on the way."

"There are no black clouds in the north or west." Ingeborg hung up her shawl and stopped at the kitchen sink to wash the dust off the bells. "The bread perfume met me halfway up from the barn. The men are right when they say bread calls them." She glanced over at the loaves of bread lying on their sides, covered by a clean dish towel.

"We need to churn tomorrow—we're almost out of butter." Freda stirred the chicken soup and moved it back to the coolest corner of the stove. "The kids should be home any time now. I'll go warn them to be quiet as soon as Patches announces them."

The words were no more out of her mouth than Patches barked his welcome-home bark as he charged down the lane.

"I warned Clara that Manny is tall but is still only a boy, not a man to be feared."

"You better not tell Manny you said that. He is convinced he is a man by now." Freda hustled out the front door to shush the two climbing out of the bus wagon driven by Samuel. The wagon looked like a large outhouse on wheels, or in this case, on iron-rimmed sledges, four runners in place of four wheels. It slid over the mud almost as easily as over snow. The horses' hooves were not as fortunate.

Ingeborg had explained to Emmy and Manny that a new girl—she was far too young to call a woman—would be coming to live with them, that she couldn't speak, and that she was terrified of men. Grateful that Inga had not been there to grill her on all the whys and what fors, she set the cookie jar on the table and checked the teakettle to see how close it was to steaming.

She had to give it to Freda. The children came inside more quietly than usual.

"She is here?" Manny did manage to whisper as the two followed Freda into the kitchen. They set their lunch pails on the counter by the sink and hung up their coats and hats. "Can I go upstairs?"

"She's exhausted, so she should sleep hard for a while. Just be as quiet as you can."

"She can't be 'fraid of me." He rolled his eyes. "I wouldn't hurt her."

Emmy jabbed her elbow at his ribs. "Be nice."

"I am being nice." He snagged a cookie from the jar on the table and managed to get up the stairs without a sound.

"No wonder he's such a good hunter. He even missed the creaky stairs." In the last year, Freda had finally come to accept Manny and appreciate him for who he was now, not who he had been when he first arrived with his bank-robbing brothers. The scum left him behind with a badly broken leg. They didn't get far before they were caught, but Manny was in the hospital in surgery by that time. While Manny still limped because one leg was shorter than the other, he could bring in game when they needed meat. Emmy wore a deerskin coat with the hair side in, one that would be passed down when she outgrew it, not worn out. Manny had bagged the deer.

"Is she better?" Emmy asked, motioning to the parlor.

"She's terribly weak, but we got her in the house and to bed."

"And she doesn't talk at all? Not even little words?"

"That's right."

"Not like she can't hear? You know, not deaf?"

"Ja."

"Can she sign?" Emmy signed the words as she spoke them. Like all the other children, Emmy had learned sign language in school so that everyone could communicate with the students at Kaaren's school for the deaf.

"I don't think so." Ingeborg shook her head. "She doesn't."

"We'll teach her!"

"She only understands Norwegian."

"I speak some."

"I know." *Mostly the phrase* uff da, *but you are learning well, little one.* Ingeborg studied Emmy, who stared back at her, dark eyes lacking their normal sparkle, concern visible instead. Emmy took other people's pain very seriously, seeking ways to help with wisdom beyond her years. "She will do well here." Ingeborg cupped the girl's cheek in her hands. "Oh, my child, I love you so."

Emmy slipped both arms around her waist and laid her check against Ingeborg's chest.

They held each other close for comfort time, then Emmy leaned back to see her grandmother's face. "We'll make her good again."

"Ja, we will." Wiping the ever-near tears from her cheeks, Ingeborg nodded. "We will love her well."

"Why doesn't she talk?"

"I don't know. It could be she was born that way, or she got sick and it took her voice, or—or sometimes when something terrible happens, people lose the ability to speak. Perhaps one day, when she learns to sign, she'll be able to tell us, or we may never know. But God will give her new life here, with us."

Manny returned to the kitchen as silently as he'd left. "She doesn't look very old."

"I don't think she is, maybe seventeen or eighteen I'd guess, or perhaps even younger." And she's going to have a baby. We will have another baby in this house. *Dare I think, Lord, of this little one as a great-grandchild?* She smiled to herself. Grandchildren, great-grandchildren. God certainly was answering her prayers in strange and wonderful ways. Through the years she had often questioned Him about not giving her and Haakan more children. Thorliff was the son of Roald and his first wife, but Haakan had mostly raised him. Andrew was born to Ingeborg and Roald, and Astrid was the only child she and Haakan had had together. For a long time she did not understand why, until she learned that men could become impotent after suffering with mumps. She still remembered how sick Haakan had been and how his face looked more like a pumpkin than her dear husband, due to the swelling.

"Grandma." Emmy returned from changing her clothes. "I'll go gather the eggs and feed the chickens. Are you going to take eggs in to Garrisons'? We have plenty."

"Good idea. Please fix a basket. We'll have extra butter to take too. I'll take them to town in the morning."

As the two went out the door, Manny called back, "I'll be down cleaning the barn."

Freda shook her head. "Never thought I'd hear that boy volunteering to clean the barn or do any other farm work."

"I know. Haakan would be so proud of him." Ingeborg sniffed. "I sure hope those in heaven can see what is going on here on earth. In this case, I'm sure he is bragging up a storm."

Patches' barking alerted them that someone was coming up the lane. When the bark changed to a welcome, they knew it was family. Thorliff tied up his horse at the fence and, after petting the dog, mounted the stairs to the back porch. When he stepped into the kitchen, he smiled at his mother. "I knew you had baked bread today. Almost called to make sure but brought out your mail and Tante Kaaren's. Do you need anything to go to town?"

"Do you have time for coffee?" Freda pulled the pot forward to heat.

"I'll stop on my way back from Kaaren's. Bread and cheese too?"

Ingeborg and Freda glanced at each other and shook their heads as the door closed behind him. "Some things never change."

"That man can smell fresh bread clear from town." Freda pulled the knife from the drawer and started slicing the bread.

Ingeborg picked up the mail that Thorliff had laid on the table. "We finally have a letter from Norway." She slit open the envelope and read through it quickly, then smiled at Freda. "Three people would like to come—two men and a woman. No relatives, but I know their families."

"It took them long enough to decide."

Ingeborg read her the letter. "Do you know those families?"

"Ja. They're good workers. The family owned a store north of Valdrez. The two boys worked for my onkel sometimes on the fishing boat. I'm surprised they want to come here to farm."

"Boats." Ingeborg shook her head while she folded the letter to put back in the envelope. "Sophie and her first husband ran off to Seattle. He drowned when a fishing boat went down. I've never had a desire to get back on a boat after we came over those long years ago.

That was a terribly hard voyage. I'll give this to Thorliff." She slit open another envelope. "Well, look at this." She sat down at the table. "From Augusta, Roald's oldest sister, who is in South Dakota."

Dear Ingeborg,

I must apologize for the long times between my letters. I promised myself I would not wait to write until we had bad news to tell. I so often think of you, burying two husbands. I don't know what I would do without Kane. I see that he is slowing down some, but I would not dare to mention it. He was thrown by one of the younger horses in the fall, and getting back in the saddle took some time. We are still raising beef, along with hay and some grains, mostly for cattle feed. The boys, Thomas and Stephen, are taking over more of the work now that they are growing, and Frank, a nephew of Kane's who loves ranching too, came to live with us last year. Katy and Lissa are such a help in the house now, although Katy would prefer working with the horses. Lissa is only nine, but already she wants to teach school. It is hard to believe our children have grown up so quickly.

We are looking forward to spring. The

winter has been hard, with a lot of sickness going around. Am I getting old that I am more aware of that? Our pastor died of pneumonia this winter, and we have yet to find a new one. We are learning that not too many want to come out here on the northern plains and shepherd three small churches.

I am still hoping that we can come to visit you one of these days, since I never made it to Blessing. God most certainly does work in strange ways, His wonders to perform. This winter I slipped on the ice and had to stay off my foot for several weeks, so that gave me more time to think on the years gone by.

I pray all is well with you and yours, and I hope you do not copy me and write so seldom.

> *From a distant*
> *family member,*
> *Augusta Bjorklund*
> *Moyer*

She handed the letters to Thorliff when he came in. "You can read these at home if you'd like. You still have time for coffee, right?"

"Ja, I will take time. The Norway letter—someone is coming?"

Ingeborg nodded, cocked her head while

she listened, and headed for the parlor. Sure enough, Clara was awake and shaking hard enough to make the cot rattle. "Shh, all is well. Thorliff, my son, brought the mail and is having coffee." While she spoke, Ingeborg leaned over to take her patient's hands in hers. "Settle down. You are safe here, I promise. You need not be afraid. I am going to bring you some bread and cheese. I think you can eat that without needing to sit up." She felt like she was calming one of the animals that could not talk back. But the fear that slowly leaked out of Clara's eyes near to broke her heart. How horrible to be so terrified. "I'll be right back. Soon you'll be strong enough to join us at the table and enjoy a real meal for a change." She gently stroked Clara's hair back from her face. "You are safe here, Clara. Always."

CHAPTER 9

Ye're an excellent teacher. Have ye considered going to school and becoming a certified teacher?" Thomas Devlin smiled at Anji.

"Thank you. But how would I leave the children behind and go to college?"

"Ah, true. But perhaps there be other ways. Mayhap an examination ye might take, a proficiency test. That used to be the way it was done."

Anji studied the man leaning against the doorjamb of her classroom. The final bell had dismissed the students, but she had decided to spend some time correcting papers. She had required her students to write a few paragraphs about their families in Norwegian. With their limited vocabulary, they had struggled. Some had dropped in an English word when they were stumped, others had left a blank space.

"Besides, I do not really want to teach full time. I need to take care of my little ones." By *little ones*, she meant Rebecca's as well as her own. Anji made herself look back down at her papers. Thomas Devlin was mighty easy to look at. And to talk with. Laugh with. She'd come to look forward to their walks back to the house she shared with her sister and family. Soon Rebecca would be opening the Blessing Soda Shoppe for the season, and Anji knew she'd be needed to help there too.

"Will ye be ready to leave soon?"

"Ja, I am ready any time." She started to gather her papers.

Reverend Solberg appeared at the door. "Thomas, could I talk with you before you go?"

"Of course." Devlin smiled at her. "Be right back." The man had a devastating smile.

"I'll continue with what I am doing, then." She listened to their shoes tap as they went down the hall to the principal's office. The high school was not connected to the grade school, but the area separating them became a mud wallow in the spring. Right now snow was still banked in the corners with mud in the middle. Four classrooms, a library that had only a few books and some storage, and the principal's office made up the high school. Returning to her papers, Anji caught herself shaking her head at times.

Her students spoke better Norwegian than they wrote. She'd just finished, stacked the papers, and put them in the desk drawer to hand back the next day when Devlin stopped at the door again.

Anji gathered her bag, and by the time she walked to the coat pegs by the door, he was holding her coat for her. He rested his hands on her shoulders for a fraction of a minute, but still, the heat of his hands warmed her shoulders. Being treated with such care was easy to get used to. Those little gallantries were some of the many things she'd been missing since Ivar died. "Thank you," she said over her shoulder with a smile. Looking up into his twinkling blue eyes made her catch her breath. *Stop this,* she ordered herself as they made their way to the front door. *Thomas Devlin is a friend, a delightful friend, but that is all. Besides, you know he's unavailable.* Since when had her mind gone veering off in a romantic direction? It had not been two years yet since Ivar had died. So technically she was still in mourning, even though she had put off her widow's weeds before she arrived back in North Dakota. Had she remained in Norway, that would not have been permitted. The thought of Ivar drenched her eyes. Grief was strange, attacking at odd moments, then running off again as if gleeful at the misery left behind. She dabbed at her eyes as she stepped through the door.

"Are you all right?" he asked, being too perceptive for her comfort.

After sniffing and forcing a nod, Anji paused on the south-facing steps and lifted her face to the sun. "Feel that. Still warm this late in the day."

"According to John, we can expect another storm any day."

"I know, the better reason to absorb as much of the sun as possible. I wonder what it would be like to live someplace where there was no snow in the winter." She stepped down and nearly stumbled on the uneven ground. He took her arm and tucked it through his.

"The better to keep you safe."

"Takk. This reminds me of how we used to go skating on a manmade pond out to Ingeborg's. Oh my, the good times we had."

"They don't do that anymore?"

"Not since we all grew up. We need to start the tradition again for the children."

"It would be easy to make a pond by the hospital." Thomas nodded, obviously thinking hard. "Do people often skate down on the river?"

"It all depends on how smooth the ice is. When the wind blows while the river is freezing, it creates ice drifts. Too rough for skating."

"Doesn't seem to stop the ice fishermen."

"Did you go ice fishing this winter?"

"No thanks. In the summer you fight

mosquitoes, and in the winter the cold wind. Fishing around here separates the men from the boys."

"And the boys being the intrepid fishermen?"

"Right ye are, lass. But then, I've never cared much for fishing anyway, after me experience out on Lake Superior. Now, that was a real experience. 'Twas a fine morning when I went out on a fishing boat with a captain and two crew. They netted fish, and I helped haul in the full nets. But a storm came rampaging out of the north, and when those waves came up, I was sure we were going down. Meself? I don't have a big desire to repeat the experience."

"You might try it here—no boats, no real waves, and—"

"And no fish?"

"Not true. We have perch, bass, and a northern pike or a muskie now and then. They taste mighty good, especially when Ingeborg does the fish frying. Sometimes they land catfish too. Fresh fish, right out of the river. I remember as a child I would go there with my brothers and Thorliff, and even Trygve, who was younger than the rest of us. Ingeborg loves to fish and would hunt more if propriety didn't frown upon a woman using a rifle." She paused. "Back in the early days Ingeborg wore pants, but after she married Haakan, she gave them up for him. I guess the men's pants embarrassed him."

Devlin looked down at her with a sly grin. "Would ye have worn pants?"

"If I were forced to do all that Ingeborg did—breaking sod, seeding, harvesting—I believe I would have. Milking cows would be far easier in pants too. In fact, all farm work would be easier. Gardening too." They stopped when they reached the bottom of the porch. "Would you like to come in for coffee?"

"I think not today, but thank ye. Perhaps next time."

She stopped on the porch and watched him stride down the walk to the gate, where he turned to smile at her and touch the brim of his hat.

"That is one fine man," Rebecca said when Anji came through the door.

She paused as she hung up her coat and scarf and unpinned her hat to set it up on the shelf. "He is that."

"I think he is sweet on you."

"Nonsense. You know he is a priest—Reverend Solberg says that when he first came to Blessing he was wearing a clerical collar, though he does not wear one now."

Rebecca snorted. "But not like priests in Norway, who do not marry. He's a different sort. I forget the name, but he can marry and have dozens of children. Why, even John Wesley's father was a priest."

Anji's heart gave a little bigger jump. Not

unavailable after all? She hoped it didn't show on her face. "We are just friends walking back together from our place of employment." She stopped at the stove to rub her hands together over the heat. "I asked him in for coffee but he declined."

"Hmm." Rebecca gave her older sister a raised-eyebrow look.

"Don't you go all *hmm* on me. Besides, technically I am still a widow, and you know the codicil in Ivar's will. All funds will stop if I marry again. And I cannot raise the children on the small sum I receive for teaching."

"Except for funds to return the children to Norway for visits," Rebecca said. "Mrs. Moen has a rather diabolical streak, it seems to me." She raised her hands. "I know, I know. Primogeniture is still the law there. But for the here and now, she is not making your life a whole lot easier, like she should."

Anji knew she could not let her mind loose on the subject of her mother-in-law, so she chose to ignore her sister's jibe. "What shift is Gerald on?"

"He'll be home for supper at five thirty and then go back to work on his proposal for more services and schedules. For some silly reason he says he can't get any work done here."

A shriek from the parlor and Lissa charged into the kitchen. "Mor, Joseph pushed Swen down, and he is crying."

"And you are being a tattletale. Tell him to come in here."

"It was an accident," Joseph said, running in to glare at Lissa. Swen followed him in.

"If you can't get along, you'll have to each stand in a corner. Now apologize."

Joseph almost rolled his eyes. "I'm sorry." Fortunately, Anji had not insisted on sincerity.

"Me too." Swen looked up at his aunt. "Can we go now?"

"Yes, you may." She put the emphasis on the *may*. Now both boys did the eye roll, then turned and darted out of the kitchen. "I really didn't mean to," Joseph threw over his shoulder.

Anji and Rebecca gave each other mother looks and half shrugged. "Uff da."

"I'll be glad when spring comes to stay and they can be outside all the time again. I know I say this every winter, but by the time spring finally does decide to stay, I am chomping at the bit like a horse at the starting gate. I know the mud causes havoc for the farmers and anyone who has to drive a buggy or wagon. Or tries moving in it for any reason. Remember how Far used to come in and grumble about the cursed mud?"

"And Mor would say, 'Remember, that cursed mud grows the finest wheat, corn, whatever we plant in it.'" Anji stared out the window. "Even after all these years, sometimes I miss her so I just ache."

"Ingeborg says the same thing at times. They were such good friends."

"Good friends like that don't happen all the time," Anji said. "They saw through a lot of hardships together. Who would you say is your best friend?"

"Besides you?"

"Ja. I'm your sister."

"But still my best friend. I guess Astrid would be, but she is so busy, she doesn't have time to spend with me." She paused and studied the kettle she was stirring. "The four of us were so close, Astrid, Sophie, Grace, and I, and now, even though we live in the same small town, we are all so busy we rarely have a party or any kind of get-together with just the four of us. We need to do one again."

"I'll take care of the children."

"Takk." Nodding while she thought aloud, Rebecca continued. "I'm going to mention this to Sophie. She's the best for getting things done." She grinned at her sister. "Something to look forward to."

"Will you call her or go see her?"

Rebecca shrugged, her eyebrows going up to match her shoulders. "Why?"

"I just think you should call her before you forget."

"Why?"

"Because once the land dries out, every minute gets spent in the garden, readying the soda shop, getting the house readied for summer, all those yearly things. You need to get together sooner rather than later." She held up her hands, flat palms out. "I know. It seems strange but just a feeling I have."

"Feeling about what?"

"Mor, I'm hungry." Swen stared up Rebecca.

"Supper will be ready in just a few minutes. Tell Gilbert it's his turn to set the table. You can help too."

After they'd eaten their whirlwind supper and the kitchen was cleaned up, Anji sat down in the parlor with the children on either side of her to read their nightly story. She took Gerald's place on the evenings he had to work. She opened at the bookmarked place and, laying it open on her lap, clasped her hands, leaning forward. "Who can tell me what happened last night?" Swapping a smile with Lissa, she let the younger ones answer. Joseph had already finished reading the book to himself, since he was so impatient to know what happened next. "Good." She let Annika climb into her lap and started to read. Joseph was nodding off, draped against her, so she was holding the book with one hand and using just the cramped fingers of her other to turn the pages, since the arm had long been asleep and now yielded pins and needles.

"And that is all for tonight."

"Just a few pages more?" Annika asked hopefully.

"No. Bedtime." Standing up with a child in her arms wasn't easy, nor was carrying him upstairs to bed. *Uff da*, she thought. *He is getting too big for this or I am getting too soft. I need the garden work as much as it needs me.* After tucking the children into bed, listening to prayers, and blowing out the lamps, she made her way back down to the kitchen, where Rebecca was talking on the telephone.

"How does a cup of tea sound?"

Rebecca nodded and held up one finger. Obviously she was talking with Sophie.

0"Snowing again." He hung his things by the door after a shake to dislodge the snow.

"Ugh. I was hoping we were done with winter." Rebecca rose to fetch another cup. "We're having tea, not coffee."

"Just so it is hot." He rubbed his hands together over the heat of the stove. "Toby is pushing for a decision on the house."

Rebecca shook her head. "I really don't want to move. We'd have to redo all the things for Benny, and this is closer to the soda shop."

"Not that much. And the house is larger. I mean, who knows how many children the Lord is going to bless us with."

"I know, but Anji already has four children."

"But what about Toby if I move there? A man and a woman not married—in one house?"

Anji shook her head as she spoke. "That will not do."

"So marry Toby."

She frowned at Gerald. "Convenient lodgings is hardly a reason to get married. Besides, he hasn't asked me and besides that, it would be like marrying my brother. No, that is not the solution."

"Toby said if you want the house, he will go live at the boardinghouse until his house is finished. We talked about finishing his kitchen and a bedroom; then he can live there while he finishes the remainder of the house."

"Are you two sure of this? After all, giving a house away . . ."

"We won't be giving it away. We'll keep it in our names, but you can live there. And no, you will not pay rent. It was a gift to us, so we can use it as a gift if we so desire."

"But . . ."

"No." He covered her hand on the table with his. "This is what it means to be family, at least here in Blessing, in our family. When would you like to move into your house?"

"We'll all help you clean it," Rebecca said with enthusiasm. "I'm sure the dust has seeped in and into everything. We can have a house-cleaning party, just like raising a barn."

Gerald shook his head. "Cleaning. I hadn't thought of that. We'll inspect the roof, though, and probably need to recaulk some places. Mor didn't do much to keep the place up, I'm afraid, and Toby is working. The kerosene barrel most likely needs filling, and we need to check if there is enough coal for the furnace. Not that you will need to use that a whole lot longer."

A house, a real house of my own again. I did not think that would happen. And it is even all furnished. Tomorrow she would go look at it with new eyes. It will no longer be Hildegunn's house, but Anji's house. *Thank you, Lord, for your provision.*

Oh, I do hope this is a wise move. As close as these houses are, I will truly be by myself. I've never lived by myself. Of course she would have the children, but she would be the lone adult. And it was a big, big house.

CHAPTER 10

Devlin, old top, you take such pride in the depth and breadth of your learning, but there is one huge gap where nearly all of your students are smarter than you are: courting.

He strolled casually along Ingeborg Bjorklund's lane with Anji at his side, returning her to her home. Should he take her hand as they moseyed along or was it too soon in the courtship? Perhaps he should have done so before now. Should he kiss her? If so, when? Does one pucker preparatory to kissing, or just let it unfold in some mysterious way? The only thing he knew for sure was that this woman had seized his heart and mind like no other woman had ever done.

Did he want to pursue a formal courtship?

Absolutely! Did he have the least notion how to go about it? Not a chance in Hades.

He was, he admitted to himself smugly, quite the one for conniving, however. He had dropped by Anji's early on Saturday, and she, her children, and he had all walked to the Knutsons' together. The evening was, as usual for Ingeborg and her clan, altogether delightful. Excellent food and drink, excellent conversation. Some of the talk was light and airy chat, some was very deep and instructive, such as his discussion with Reverend Solberg on the Synoptic Gospels. And John Solberg seemed to enjoy it just as much as he.

And then the conniving commenced.

As he felt certain she would, Anji said, "I have to take the little ones home. It's past their bedtime. But you can remain here and talk."

"Hmm. Melissa be ten and her best friend, Linnea, be twelve. Do ye think they could handle putting the wee ones to bed?"

"I suppose they could. . . ."

"Or. Mayhap Linnea's friend Rachel could also take part in this. At fourteen she's utterly convinced she's fully grown. I know. She be me pupil."

Anji laughed out loud. "What a great idea! I'll ask Lissa."

And therein lay the conniving. For Devlin knew before Melissa even picked up the phone to call Linnea that Linnea's friend Rachel would be amenable to the idea—he had already bribed Rachel with a silver dollar if she would help out. When Rachel exclaimed, "You're sweet on Mrs. Moen, aren't you!" he adjured her to keep silence, and she'd eagerly agreed. Such duplicity always comes to light eventually, but for a while, at least, Rachel would be his willing co-conspirator. And the prospect of more silver dollars in the offing didn't hurt either.

And so, thanks be to conniving, here they strolled, just the two of them.

Anji tilted her head up. "The moonlight is nearly bright enough to make out colors. These nights are so beautiful."

Impulsively, he scooped her hand into his. "Aye, beautiful indeed. And I enjoy the company of one who appreciates beauty as I do." He should release her hand. He did not. Neither did she pull it away. That simple, insignificant thing pleased him more than he could have imagined.

She looked at him. "How many languages do you speak?"

"English, Latin, and Gaelic. I read Greek—not modern Greek, the old Greek of the New Testament—but I do not speak it."

"Oh, of course. From seminary. And you grew up with Gaelic, I assume."

"Ye assume correctly. Gaelic is still common, particularly in the west of Ireland. Miriam Knutson also speaks Gaelic and Latin and, I believe, Italian. Speaking with her is the only Gaelic I've used for a decade. It is not easy to find Gaelic locally."

She laughed again. "I was thinking you might like some lessons in Norwegian, but I don't want to clutter up your mind too much."

He tilted his head slightly and said casually, "Hmm. Norwegian should be most handy around here—indeed, all across the northern plains." On the inside his heart was jumping up and down gleefully and clapping. What a brilliant opportunity to spend more time with this splendid lady! Brilliant! And it was all her idea. He was not pushing himself on her.

"I would be very happy to help you learn some."

"Ye're right. I should have at least a passing knowledge of Norwegian. Aye, I should like that." And his heart nearly turned inside out for joy. Was this what falling in love was like?

"You have a way with children, I was noticing. They love you."

"And yerself the same. Ye grew up with younger children 'round about to mind, I should think."

"I did. Did you?"

He smiled. "Thirteen in our family, not counting adults, and meself the next to eldest."

Again that tinkling laugh. "That'll do it."

Quickly, Devlin! Come up with another topic of conversation. Keep this going. And he could not. What a dolt! As a courting swain he was a complete loss.

And so they strolled along in silence, and that was almost as good. A few days ago, wind and frost as cold as death threatened to freeze every person in place who ventured out into it. Tonight, a remarkably warm breeze was pushing the clouds north.

"If this keeps up, the last remnants of snow will melt quickly," he said.

"Yes, and bring behind it even more mud," she replied. "True Dakota spring mud. Black and gooey to the extreme. There is nothing like it."

"I certainly be in a rush to see the snow leave. A harsh winter it's been."

"Yes, but not as bad as some years."

"Indeed. Ye would know. Ye grew up in this town."

She nodded. "And it wasn't half the size it is now. They've come such a long way."

Yes, and I built some of it. Devlin thought back briefly to his arrival. He made his living then as a carpenter and woodworker, working on housing for the influx of workmen and their families. Most of the work was ordinary, mundane. Putting up walls, framing doors and windows, installing stringers and siding, shingling roofs. Pleasant work. And fairly frequently, he could use his woodcarving skills. He almost got to carve gargoyles for the new post office, but Thorliff stopped him. Thorliff was afraid the town was not quite ready for gargoyles. So now the post office roof drained into drab, pedestrian tin flumes. Gutters.

"Do you ever do any hunting?" She was looking up at him again.

"In me youth, I went fowling with me uncle, but not much more than that. I have no hunting firearms. No firearms at all, actually." He smiled down at her. "What do ye wish hunted? I be fairly good with a club."

"I was just wondering. Benny says that Manny is a good hunter. Benny kind of idolizes Manny; Manny got him up riding on a horse, and he helps Benny when he needs it. He's a gentle boy."

"Manny is indeed. And he's developing into a fine woodworker. He says Haakan Bjorklund got him started and taught him how to keep his knife sharp."

She nodded, smiling. "I sometimes think Ingeborg takes in every stray in the county."

Silence closed in around them except for the squish of their footsteps. And then she said something that thrilled him. "I'm enjoying this pleasant walk home with you."

Lass, you could not possibly have said anything more wonderful.

They were approaching her house now, and that would be the end of this lovely evening. Was it too soon to offer a good-night kiss? How he wished he knew! At least he could kiss her knuckles. He was still holding her hand.

He was going to say something—he didn't know what exactly—when a distant noise made him stop to listen more carefully.

She must have heard it too. She was frowning. "What was that? It sounded like a clunk. The trash can lid. Maybe the children are throwing away garbage."

"Perhaps we best go see." He let go of her hand and walked smartly toward her house. The clunk happened again, and a child's voice yelped! A door slammed! Devlin broke into a run, heading around the house to the back, and Anji right beside him.

Dogs! Half a dozen at least, all sizes. And they were not friendly dogs. They wheeled and crouched to look at him, snarling, teeth bared as he came around the house. He snatched up the snow shovel beside the back door.

Which was the alpha? There! The lead dog was that nondescript gray one. She turned broadside to him, a bitch, probably the mama of at least some of them. Growling, she held her ground for a moment, but as he came directly at her with the shovel, singling her out, she turned and ran. He skidded to a halt and spun around a hundred eighty degrees. Sure enough, a male, probably one of her pups, was slinking in behind him. He swung. The shovel knocked the dog ten feet. The others ran off at full tilt and disappeared beyond the house. The dog he'd swatted found his feet and followed his pack mates, running three-legged.

"Lissa!" Anji barged in through her back door. "Lissa!"

"Ma! There's a pack of wild dogs out there!" Devlin jogged up onto the back stoop and went in, but he did not let go of the snow shovel. He slammed the door behind him.

Lissa was sobbing as she spoke, her words tumbling over one another. "I heard the garbage can and thought it was a raccoon, so I got the broom to chase it off. But when I opened the door, it was dogs! Nasty dogs! They started toward me, and I slammed the door."

Rachel and Linnea were standing beside her, frightened nearly to tears.

Anji wrapped her arms around Lissa. "It's all right now. You're safe. It's all right."

Devlin dropped down on one knee beside Lissa. "Ye did exactly right. And yer ma be correct. Ye're safe now."

Anji looked to be near tears too. "We've never had wild dogs up in the town, Thomas. What if the little children had been out there?"

He stood up. "The children at school have been talking about a pack of dogs—feral dogs— down by the river. I would guess these be the same. And if they're typical of loose packs, they hunt by night. The children should be safe enough by day, but ye might keep the wee bairns inside after dark. At least until we settle the business."

She nodded. "Would they attack farm animals? Dogs?"

"Aye, possibly. Is yer chicken coop sturdy?"

She smiled. "The chicken thieves around here are weasels and raccoons, and sometimes coyotes. So yes, it's sturdy."

"We ought to go home now," Rachel said timidly. "Uh, Mrs. Moen, can we borrow your broom?"

"Better'n that, ye may borrow her escort. I shall see ye safely home." He turned to Anji. "I shall return yer snow shovel tomorrow before church, though I doubt ye'll be needing it."

"Thank you, Thomas." Her beautiful blue eyes locked with his. "In spite of the dogs, it was a lovely evening."

"'Twas me great delight as well. Good evening, lady." Without really thinking about it, he took her hand in his and politely pecked her knuckles. He turned to Rachel and Linnea. "Ready, ladies?"

They grabbed their coats off the pegs and slipped into them quickly.

It was proper for the gentleman to open the door and stand aside to let the ladies precede him, but tonight Devlin would take some extra measures. He went out, stepped off the front porch, and stood for a moment listening and watching. He turned, the snow shovel across his shoulders, and smiled. "Shall we be off?"

They came down off the porch and walked beside him. Very close beside him.

Linnea wagged her head. "I was so scared when we heard the rubbish can clatter. But Lissa just grabbed up her broom and slammed out. I don't think Lissa is ever afraid of anything."

Rachel was still pressed very close. "Maybe she's brave because she's done so many things we haven't. Her pa died. That was really hard, she said, and then she sailed all the way here from Norway. She took the train too. I don't mean she sailed *all* the way."

"Mr. Devlin, you sailed across the ocean too." Linnea pressed just as close.

"I did. But I could not afford the fare, so I had to work my way across as a seaman. Most of the time I was down in the boiler room shoveling coal and tidying up. As I think on it, it may well be easier to cross the ocean with a job ye must do than having to simply sit idle for days on end."

Rachel nodded sagely. "I think I'd agree. We complain about chores around the house and washing dishes, but just having to sit idle would be worse."

Devlin chuckled. "I wager that will not stop ye from complaining when next ye're assigned duties."

Rachel giggled. "Of course not." She sobered. "I feel so sorry for Mrs. Moen. And Lissa. Lissa was telling us what her grandmother is like—the one in Norway. Very cold and formal, she says. And critical. And that's sad too. Lissa doesn't have anyone, you know, like Manny and Emmy have Mrs. Bjorklund, someone to lean on when you need someone. And Mrs. Moen doesn't really have anyone either. Lissa says the Baards are all right but not real close." She looked up at Devlin. "That's why I'm kind of hoping you and Mrs. Moen might, you know, warm up to each other."

"Thank ye, lass."

And, lass, ye'll never know how fervently I hope the same.

CHAPTER 11

"Please, Clara, just ring the bell, and I will come when you need help."

Clara sat on the edge of her cot, staring at her hands clenched together as if to keep them from flying apart, or perhaps praying desperately.

"If you understand me, please nod."

Shadowed by the veil of hair, Clara nodded.

Ingeborg placed her hands around Clara's, warm and comforting, then tightened slightly when Clara tried to draw away. This time, she did not jerk and freeze but heaved a sigh as she relaxed her hands. "Good. Very good." She wanted so to wrap her arms around this poor waif of a girl and rock her, let the healing flow through her arms and into the emaciated body and soul. *Thank you, Lord God, we are making progress.*

"Now, let's walk together around the house. You are gaining strength, and I think you will enjoy being in the kitchen with Freda and me." She tucked Clara's arm within her bent elbow, and they started off, stopping to look out the windows, Ingeborg explaining what they saw. The barn, the chicken house, the machine sheds, the cheese house, the deaf school, and the Knutson farm. Even though Ingeborg had explained everything before, she wasn't positive how much of the information Clara was absorbing, so she took care to repeat the information every couple of days.

"As I mentioned before, one of the things taught at that school is sign language so that deaf people can talk with their hands. Since I know you can hear but not speak, I am thinking you could learn to talk with us using sign language. Emmy and Inga—you've met our girls—" She waited for a nod. "Actually they are my grandchildren. Emmy and Manny live here, as you know, and Inga and the others live with their parents, my children. Next Sunday I am hoping they can all come for dinner after church." She could feel Clara pull back. "Now don't you go worrying. We can choose not to do that if it frightens you too much." They had arrived back at the kitchen table, and Ingeborg motioned to a chair. "You sit there, and I'll get the coffee heated up. Freda is out at the cheese house making sure all is ready for when we start making cheese again. Have you ever made cheese?"

A slight nod.

"In Norway?" Nod. "In America?"

Clara went rigid, as she did at any mention of America. She still collapsed in on herself at any mention of the place she had lived. Her gaze darted around the room like a wild animal trapped in a pen.

Ingeborg finished what she was doing. "Would you rather have coffee?" A nod. "Or tea?" A shrug. "Do you mean you don't like tea or have not had tea?" Puzzlement was easy to recognize. "All right. I will make tea the way the children like to drink it, and if you don't like it, that is not a problem. While that is heating, I'm going to cut some bread and cheese to go with our coffee or tea." She glanced up at the clock. "The children will be here in half an hour or so. When they come in the door, I want you to stay right there. Remember, Manny is a kind boy, and he would like to be able to help you too."

Clara darted a glance from her hands to the door, to her hands and to the arch to the parlor, where her cot was her safe haven.

Ingeborg pressed on. "Manny loves to help people. I know you could walk back to your bed by yourself now, but I'd like you to try to do what I am asking. I promise you that no one will hurt you here. You are safe." She reached over and brushed Clara's now clean but still unruly hair from her face. "All will be well. You are safe here."

One tear squeezed from Clara's right eye and meandered down her cheek to drop on Ingeborg's hand.

"Oh, my dear. You have been hurt so terribly, but that is over. Here you are safe."

Clara turned at the sound of boots on the porch, her eyes growing wider, her hands clamped on the chair seat until the knuckles turned white.

Freda stepped in the door. "Why, Clara, how good to see you out here. Welcome." She hung up her coat and scarf and then bent over to unlace her boots. "Look at my boots, and I already cleaned them on the scraper." She toed the boots off and slid her feet into a pair of moccasins that used to belong to Haakan. "Ah, both the coffeepot and the teakettle are steaming. Are we having a party?"

Clara stiffened again.·

"Now, now, just the three of us can be a party."

Ingeborg set the loaf of bread and wedge of cheese on the cutting board. "You fix this, and I'll make the tea. I thought we could have cookies too, if there are enough for Manny and Emmy."

"Bread and cheese for all, then."

Ingeborg measured the tea leaves and added them to the teapot, then poured in the hot water. "We'll let that sit a bit. Are you cold?" At Clara's nod, Ingeborg fetched a shawl off one of the pegs by the door and draped it around the girl's shoulders. "There now, better?"

With the food on the table, Freda and Ingeborg sat down. "Now, this is tea." She poured some in a cup. "Emmy likes hers with sugar and some milk." Ingeborg added the two and handed the cup to Clara. "Drink some. It is hot, but see how you like it."

Clara used both hands to bring the cup to her mouth. She swallowed, looked at Ingeborg, and sipped again, this time with a nod.

"Would you rather have coffee?" A slight shake of her head.

"Fine, then here." Freda passed the plate that held slices of bread and cheese.

Clara set her cup on the table and helped herself to one of each before passing the plate to Ingeborg.

Ingeborg tried to keep from smiling but failed—miserably. She felt like dancing around the room. Clara was sitting at her table, eating with obvious enjoyment, and drinking tea. *Thank you, Lord God, worker of miracles.*

Patches yipped and left the porch barking short, sharp barks.

Clara started to stand, frantically searching

for a place to hide or run to—Ingeborg wasn't sure which.

"Clara, listen to me." She spoke firmly and clearly. "Patches is announcing the children coming home from school. That is his family bark. When someone he doesn't know comes, you'll hear the difference in his bark. Just sit here and finish your bread and cheese. Manny and Emmy will come through that door, and they will be so happy to see you at the table." Slowly Clara sank back down, but when she reached for the bread, her hand was shaking so much she dropped it. Instead of reaching for it, she cowered back in her chair, her arms shielding her head.

Ingeborg and Freda stared at each other, Freda shaking her head.

"Clara, it is all right." Ingeborg put her hand on Clara's shoulder and kept it there. "We will just pick it up." While Ingeborg crooned, Freda did just that.

They heard the children shouting good-byes and boots clumping up the steps.

Clara grabbed Ingeborg's hand with both of hers, tears dripping off her jaw, and tried to disappear into the back of the chair.

Freda left them and stepped outside the door. Ingeborg could hear her admonishing the two to come in easy, Emmy first.

Ingeborg stroked Clara's head with her other hand and kept on murmuring mother sounds. *Lord, help her and give us wisdom to bring her into the light and love, both yours and ours.*

Emmy tiptoed into the house and stared at Ingeborg, who nodded. "Now Clara, you have met Emmy before. She has helped you eat a couple of times." She nodded to Emmy, who squatted down by the chair so Clara could see her. "Hello, Clara. I am glad to see you here at the table."

Clara raised her chin and slowly nodded. Studying Emmy, she nodded again.

Emmy smiled, her dark eyes gentle, her voice soft. "This is good. You will like living here. Grandma takes good care of everybody." She reached out and touched Clara's hand, then stood and turned to Freda. "Manny is coming now, Clara. He will not hurt you."

Freda ushered Manny in and closed the door behind him. He looked to Ingeborg for instructions, sadness in his eyes. When she nodded, he walked softly to the end of the table and stood there, his hands on the chair back.

"Clara, you've met Manasseh McCrary—Manny. When he came here, he had a badly broken leg and could only walk with crutches, but now he can walk well again."

"I limp some, but I'm getting stronger all the time. Grandma helped make me get all better." His soft Kentucky drawl and ready smile dared Clara to quit strangling Ingeborg's hand and greet him.

Eyes like saucers, she looked up at Ingeborg, who nodded, and back to Manny, who smiled and nodded. Slowly she released the pressure on Ingeborg's hand and slowed her breathing. Her nod was imperceptible but grew until her whole head moved. She looked from Emmy to Manny and back to Ingeborg.

O Lord, if only I knew what she was thinking, how to help her. Both Emmy and Manny are so good with the animals . . . will this be much different? A terrified girl or a terrified horse? As she watched, the other two pulled out their chairs and slid onto them, all the time reassuring Clara with smiles and nods.

"Would you like more tea, Clara?" Ingeborg asked. At the nod she refilled the cup. "Manny, Emmy, what would you like? Manny, yes I know, we have cookies for after the bread and cheese."

"Manny likes cookies best of all," Emmy said. "Someday maybe you and I can bake cookies. Do you know how?"

Clara nodded, again so slightly it would be easy to miss, but Emmy was watching carefully and sent her a sparkling smile. "Good. You just need to get better quick so we can do that."

"So, Manny, how did your test go?" Ingeborg asked when they were all eating.

"I missed two."

"Only two? On your spelling?"

"Yep. I got a hundred on my arithmetic."

He grinned at Ingeborg. "Mr. Devlin said I come a long way in a short time. He is helping me with reading. Today I read to the little kids."

"He did really good too. Inga said so." Emmy looked to Clara. "Can you read?"

Clara drooped, her head shaking.

"I couldn't read either when I came, but I learned." He grinned at Ingeborg. "Grandma even taught me to read in her Bible."

"Taught," Emmy said softly.

Manny rolled his eyes. "All right, *taught*. But I learnt it."

Emmy giggled. Ingeborg and Freda chuckled. Manny grinned. And Clara? Was that twitching in her cheeks the beginning of a smile? She reached for the last bit of her bread and cheese and washed it down with more tea.

Ingeborg felt like shouting from the rooftops. There was hope after all.

When Emmy came back down from changing her clothes, she stopped at Clara's chair. "Would you like me to help you back to your bed? You look pretty tired."

Clara nodded and, grasping the table, steadied herself as she stood. Emmy took her hand and together they walked back into the parlor and over to the cot. Clara sat down and slid off her slippers, then almost fell into the bed. Emmy pulled up the covers that had been folded at the bottom and tucked them around

Clara's shoulders. "You sleep now, and then we'll have supper."

Ingeborg watched from the doorway. It made sense, really. Emmy was small and therefore not so threatening. Also, the two called her *Grandma*, and that seemed to be a relief. Did Clara know what *grandma* meant? Did she understand some English? Was it possible to teach her both English and sign at the same time? How old was Clara? When would the baby be due? Where had she come from and who had treated her so horribly? Other questions filled her mind. Right now the job was to get her strong enough to be up and around and helping to grow a healthy baby. Would that baby have a chance after not having enough food for so long?

But as she had learned, the growing baby always took what it needed before the rest of the mother's body was nourished. Now it was up to them all to make up for this.

Time passed quickly, and it was finally evident that spring was there to stay. The mud dried back to the rich earth with seeds of all kinds bursting forth. A robin trilled his song one morning, announcing his return home. One morning Ingeborg brought Clara and Freda out on the porch to listen to the robin and watch him as he listened carefully, head cocked to the side, then drove his beak into the soil and came up with a curly fat worm. The worm disappeared in three gulps, and Ingeborg sighed in delight. Clara leaned her elbows on the porch rail and turned to look up toward another bird singing in the cottonwood tree that was just greening out, its leaves still only suggestions. Ingeborg followed her gaze.

"That's a goldfinch. They are some of the first birds to return. Manny tells me that further south, they stay around all winter. Soon we'll be hearing the meadowlarks heralding us from the fields." She closed her eyes and lifted her face to the sun. "I do so love the springtime." She glanced over to see Clara doing what she had done. The horrible black circles were fading from around her eyes, and surely her cheeks had filled out a slight bit. She now walked without assistance, and every day her naps were shorter. Once Ingeborg showed her how to card the last of their wool, the slap and brush sounds of the carding paddles came from the back porch on fine days, and the parlor or kitchen on others. Two lessons on the spinning wheel, and she left off sewing on the machine in the evenings and spun the carded wool into yarn instead. She had walked out to the garden with Ingeborg, and when Manny brought his horse, Joker, to the house, Clara wore a real smile. When Joker nuzzled her cheek, she shot Manny the biggest grin, wrapped her arms around the horse's neck, and leaned into his chest.

"You'll get all dirty," Manny said.

Clara shrugged and reached up to rub Joker's ears.

"He likes that. Wait till you see him when the carrots are ready. He'd run a country mile for carrots. Did you ever ride a horse?"

Clara nodded.

"In Norway?"

She nodded again.

"Clara, we got to get you signin' so's we can talk." He glanced up at the sun. "I better put him out in the pasture. It's about time to get to milkin'." Taking up the reins, he swung aboard and waved down at her. "'Bye."

She stepped back and waved too.

Ingeborg watched them from the porch, wishing she could have heard all of their conversation. Manny had no idea how much he had helped Clara already, mostly by being the gentle boy they had found under all that tough exterior he'd arrived with. And to see her delight in Joker. Clara had known horses in Norway, so she must have grown up on a farm. She knew her way around a kitchen, filling the woodbox, sweeping the floor, and washing the dishes, all jobs she had taken over.

Tonight they would start the sign-language learning.

After supper, when Emmy and Manny had finished their homework, the dishes were done, and Freda's sourdough was rising for pancakes in the morning, they gathered by Ingeborg's chair in the parlor. She pulled out a chart of the alphabet with the signs beside each letter. "This is what we will start with. Emmy, you form the signs when I say the letter. *A*." Emmy formed the sign. "Now, Clara, you make the sign also. *A*."

She handed Manny the book they were reading. "You read tonight while we work on the letters. We are on chapter thirty-nine." So while Manny read, asking for help when he couldn't figure out a word, the others worked on the letters. Freda sat next to the other lamp, mending socks with the wooden sock egg inside and her darning needle weaving a patch to fill in the hole.

When the telephone jangled, Ingeborg listened to make sure it was her ring, then went to answer it. "You all keep on as you are doing." She couldn't help but smile as she picked up the earpiece. "Hello."

"Mor, I'm just calling to find out how Clara is doing."

"Oh, Astrid, you won't believe this is the same person. Manny is reading aloud and Emmy is teaching Clara to sign. She might not be able to talk now, but she can communicate somewhat, and with sign she will be able to be part of the world."

"How is she doing with her terror of men?"

"She has accepted Manny, and now I think it is time she meet some of the men. I have asked John to come tomorrow and have dinner with us, since it is Saturday. Then I think either Lars or Trygve. She has watched them out the windows going back and forth to the barn, and yesterday Trygve came and dug out the straw stacked against the house. We'll go spread it over the garden tomorrow. She is used to working; she is not used to kindness. But we are working on that."

"Ah, Mor, I knew you would work miracles."

"Never think it is me. Only our God works the miracles. We get the privilege of being His hands here. Think of all the wounded He has brought to us here in Blessing."

"So true. Oh, by the way, have you heard from Anji and Rebecca?"

"No, what?"

"We're going to have a housecleaning on Monday, as many women as can come. Some men would be helpful too, I am sure. We're going to clean the Valders' house from top to bottom and Anji and her family will live there."

"What a wonderful idea. I will be there,

and perhaps Freda too, but I think it is too soon for Clara."

"Will we see you in church?"

"Ja, I will be there."

"Good, I'll talk to you then."

Ingeborg hung the earpiece back on the prong and paused in the archway to listen to the babble.

"The end." Manny closed the book. "I'm thirsty. How come readin' aloud makes me want to drink a gallon?"

"Good for you, Clara." Emmy looked up to see Ingeborg. "Come on, let's show Grandma."

Ingeborg nodded as Emmy showed off her pupil. "Well done." She reached out and patted Clara's shoulder, fully expecting the girl to withdraw. Instead, she tipped her head and laid her cheek against Ingeborg's hand. Her eyes said all the thanks that Ingeborg could ever need.

CHAPTER 12

I t doesn't feel right being here without Hilde-gunn," Anji said as she looked around inside the entryway.

"Not that we were ever invited when they lived here." Ingeborg shook her head.

"Really?" Anji welcomed them into the kitchen. The house cleaners were starting to gather to scrub the Valders' house from attic to cellar. "I know I was never invited, but I didn't think that applied to everyone. As soon as everybody is here, I'll let people choose where they want to work."

"We should start by taking all the curtains down and hauling the rugs out to the clothes-line to be beaten. Then, while the rugs are air-ing, we can wash and hang the curtains out." Ingeborg frowned as she looked around.

Sophie arrived next. "All the children who aren't old enough for school are invited to my house. Linnea says she will make them all dinner. I brought a hamburger and noodle hotdish." She planted her hands on ample hips—the leftovers from birthing babies. "You know, this is the first time I've seen the inside of this house."

Ingeborg smiled. "We were just commenting on that. Kaaren and I will start upstairs with the curtains. Thorliff said he'd have a crew here later to do the outside and carry out the rugs." She looked around the kitchen. "Looks like the walls need scrubbing in here too. Is there a bathroom?"

"No, but a hand pump in the kitchen. The outhouse is out back by the garden. We should have hot water shortly. I started the boiler." Anji pointed to the no-longer-shiny cast-iron stove. "I remember Mor polishing her stove. She was so proud of that stove with a big oven, a reservoir, and the warming shelf."

"Ja, for those of us who had cooked over a fireplace, those stoves were our greatest treasures. They came in on the train even before Penny's store." Kaaren wore a half smile— remembering. "We didn't have cookstoves until we built houses. There was no room in a soddy for such a big thing."

"The first one came to the boardinghouse. Remember? We all went to admire it and dream of owning one too." Ingeborg turned to greet Amelia Jeffers.

"Daniel said to tell you they'll be right over, and he is bringing his machine class over to help too." She glanced around the kitchen, up to the ceiling and the windows. "Well, it looks like we have our work cut out for us. Sophie, let's you and I start on the kitchen. Several of the other women are coming too. Mrs. Sam will be sending over dinner so we can get done in one day. Anji, what will it feel like having your own home again?"

"You have no idea. I never dreamed I'd have one this big. I loved my house when I lived here, but the family house in Norway . . ." She shook her head. "Let's just say I am glad to be home."

As the women scattered to their stations, several others arrived and were set to other rooms.

In the parlor, Anji eyed the oak rolltop desk in the corner, collecting dust like everything else. Shaking her head, she returned to the kitchen and picked up the telephone earpiece. "Can you get Gerald Valders for me, please." While waiting, she took the dustcloth from her pocket and dusted the top and down the sides of the wall-hung instrument. Had Hildegunn not cleaned in a long time, or could things really get this bad so soon? "Gerald, we are cleaning in the parlor. What do you want us to do with

your father's desk? Clean it out or leave it be?"
She heard his sigh and knew he didn't really
want to even look in it. And yet as the elder
of the two sons, he should. So she suggested,
"Would you like me to take everything out of
it and put the papers all in a box for you to go
through later?"

"Thank you. That would be ideal. Perhaps
Toby and I can take an evening and get through
it all."

"How about I do the same with all we find?"

"Good. Toby said he'd be working on the
outside. I would, but I need to fill in here today."

Anji hooked the earpiece back on the prong.
She should be the one to do this chore, much
as she hated to. Returning to the parlor, where
Kaaren was just handing the heavy drapes
down to Ingeborg, she hurried over to assist.
"Shouldn't you let the younger women do the
stepladder part?"

"Uff da. And take all the fun out of it?"
Kaaren blinked and wrinkled her nose, then
sneezed hard, another and a third, earning a
Bless you for each. "If we do nothing more
today than get all the dust out of here, we'll
have accomplished miracles."

"I think we should beat these like we do
the rugs."

"Do I have to put them back up?" Anji
asked. "They make it so dark in here."

"Anji, this is your house now. You can do

whatever you want. To tell you the truth, I hate to block any light out, although they do help keep the house warmer in the winter."

"Fine. Let us wash them and hang the lace ones back up and pack the heavy ones away until winter." Feeling like she had just made the first move to make this her house, Anji returned to the formidable desk. She tucked her fingers under the lip of the rolltop and lifted. "It's locked. Where do you suppose Anner would have kept the key?"

"On his keychain." Kaaren felt along under the flat front drawer. "Nothing."

Anji got down on her hands and knees and inspected the underside of all the surfaces. "Nothing." She felt under the bottom drawers and under the rolling chair.

Ingeborg came in. "Think like Anner." She tried to see behind it. Between the three of them, they pulled the desk away from the wall. "About anything could be buried in the dust and cobwebs."

Kaaren returned with a broom and swept both the back of the desk and the wall. A dull clunk caught their attention, and Anji dropped to her knees, fingers sifting through the mess on the floor. "Here!" She polished the key on her apron, then held it up, all the while getting to her feet again. *We did it, ha!* Now, why did she feel she was outsmarting Anner Valders? After all, he had run the bank.

She slid the key into the lock and turned. A click and the spring to the rolltop released. At the same time, all the drawers could now be opened too.

"I'll go find you a box. Any idea where that might be?" Kaaren and Ingeborg bundled up the curtains and headed for the kitchen.

Amelia pointed out the back door. "They are washing curtains on the porch. Two young men are beating rugs on the clothesline, and Thorliff said to tell you Astrid is sending over two of the nursing students, and Thelma is sending coffee and cookies with them. She figures we must be due for some food by now."

Anji giggled. "Thelma always thinks someone is running out of food."

Mary Martha Solberg, with a basket hooked over her arm, a broom and mop over her shoulder, hustled up the steps. "Sorry I am late. Where do you want me?"

"Set your basket on the table with the others and join Anji in the parlor. I imagine we ought to clean the ashes out of that stove too."

When the telephone rang the Valders' rings, Ingeborg answered, since she was closest. "Oh, Thelma, of course. Ja, we have a coffeepot on the stove and . . ." She glanced out the window. "Looks like the men started a fire, and there's a pot of water heating on that too. Bring another broom if you can. And stove black. We need stove polish. Ja, I think everyone is ready for coffee." She hung up, shaking her head. "She's bringing cinnamon buns too. Uff da. We suffer so when we get together."

"No one can work on an empty stomach. That is Thelma's motto, you know that."

"Call everyone in," Thelma said a bit later after she spread the buns and cookies out on the rewashed table. "Glad I didn't get here earlier. Good thing we have so many hands helping. This place is a mess!"

When Ingeborg and Kaaren rolled their eyes, Anji glanced at them and started to giggle. The giggle ran around the room, leaping over chuckles and landing as full-blown laughter. "A mess!" someone else said. "A terrible mess."

"What's so funny?" Thorliff asked as he came in the door. That made people laugh even more.

"I bet this is the most laughter this house has heard in all its life," Sophie said.

"And that is downright sad," Kaaren said. "Anji, dear, we are blessing your house with laughter, and I pray these walls will ring with joy and laughter the rest of the years."

In a short time, everyone returned to their work, and the house seemed to come alive as they stripped away the accumulation of dust, cobwebs, and spider and rodent droppings. By the end of the day the windows sparkled, the floors shone with wax, the woodwork had been washed and waxed, and soon the beds were made with clean sheets and blankets, rugs returned to the floors, and curtains rehung. What a huge task—done! The outside of the house glowed too, after a fashion, with the repairs and sweeping. They threw their dirty water on the fire outside and tipped over the tubs to drain dry.

"This house needs a blessing," Thomas Devlin announced. He and Reverend Solberg and some others had come to help after they were done with work.

Solberg nodded. "I agree. I'll go get my Bible." He paused and looked to Anji. "Unless you'd rather wait until Sunday after church, and we'll all come over?"

"No, thank you. Let's do it now. Drive away any ghosts or . . ." She shivered just a bit. "This is a cold house. Don't you feel it?"

"I'll be right back."

Devlin dug down in the woodbox. "A good fire will help."

Anji went to stand by Ingeborg, her hands cupped around her elbows. "I know this is a strange thought, but Ingeborg, I feel this house needs something."

"Besides love and laughter?"

Anji nodded. "And light?"

"And singing. I don't imagine there has ever been much singing here. Say, will you answer a question I've been wondering about? I thought Toby lived here."

"Yes, Toby slept here. Maybe he made coffee, but I think he had most of his meals at the boardinghouse. Or with Gerald and Rebecca. We fed him a lot." Anji paused. "I should ask him." She shook her head. "No, like Mor used to say, '*Better to let sleeping dogs lie.*' But his plan now is to live at the boardinghouse while he finishes his house." She removed a shiny clean chimney off the kerosene lamp and, borrowing a tinder stick from the stove, lit the lamp and set back the chimney. "There now, that helps."

"Do ye want me to start the parlor stove burning too?" Thomas Devlin asked. "Get the heat going up to the bedrooms?"

"Thank you. That would be nice. We're having supper at Rebecca's."

"I think we need to give you a housewarming." Ingeborg and Kaaren nodded at the same time. "All food things. The cellar is empty, and there's not much in the cupboards either. No wonder Toby never cooked here."

Reverend Solberg came in through the back door. "Gather everyone who's still here together." As the room filled he raised his hands. "Let us sing together, 'There Shall Be Showers of Blessing.'"

"'There shall be showers of blessing; this is the promise of love.'" As she sang, Anji looked around at her friends, relatives, and neighbors, all their voices raised in the hymn. Kaaren took one of her hands and Ingeborg the other. When they finished the song, Reverend Solberg said, "Let us pray." When the rustling ceased, his calm voice spread peace among them all. "Lord God, creator of our universe, of our land, of this home, of each of us, we thank you for all the myriad blessings you so freely pour out upon us, our homes, our families, our friends, and neighbors. Father, this house is yours, this family is yours, and you have brought them back to Blessing to be part of us all. Remove from this place all animosity, all strife, all hard and hurt feelings. Take away the dark and fill it with your most glorious light. Bring joy, peace, contentment, and above all, love to reign here today, tomorrow, and always. You, O Lord, are head of this family. Keep them safe and secure in the shadow of your mighty wings. In Jesus' name we pray, amen."

Kaaren started the next song. "'Blest be the tie that binds our hearts in Christian love. . . .'" By three notes into it, the others had joined in and followed Reverend Solberg into the parlor. At the end of the verse, he lifted his arms again.

"Lord, bring love and laughter into this room. May all who come into this house be blessed by the love here, the gifts of your Holy Ghost. Let sun flood this room and every other room in this house, that the darkness may be driven away and light remain and grow anew. That everyone always feels welcome here, that children play and study, that your purpose and plan for this house, this family, may come to pass. In your holy name, amen."

Kaaren started verse two. "Before our Father's throne . . ."

Back in the kitchen, Reverend Solberg announced, "Let us close in the way Jesus taught us to pray. 'Our Father . . .'"

At the amen, a silence, this one warm and comforting, settled around them all.

"Thank you, Reverend Solberg. That was perfect." Anji could feel tears prickling at the backs of her eyes. She sniffed and felt a warm presence close behind her. Thomas Devlin, adding his own comfort. Yes. To her amazement she could feel his presence. "Thank you, everyone, for all the work you have done here. This is so far beyond what I could have dreamed. In fact, I dreaded cleaning this place, but now . . ." She looked up at the ceiling, at the shiny cupboards, the gleaming stove. "This is a home, our home. Thank you."

She hugged and thanked everyone as they picked up their tools and buckets and headed for home. Now it was only she, Thomas, and Toby.

"We'll be back to dig up your garden later," Toby said, then leaned closer. "This house has never felt this good. Bless you, sister."

"Toby, I shouldn't ask, but why was it in such a state? I would think Hildegunn was a good housekeeper."

He pressed his lips together for a moment. "For months after Far went away, Mor did nothing but sit up in her room and write letters. She even put ads in newspapers. The letters always came back marked *Addressee unknown.* She eventually quit trying. When she went out into public, she was the usual Hildegunn. Here in the house she sat with her drapes closed. I offered many times to clean the place up, but she'd say, '*No, no, don't. I'll get to it.*'" He shrugged. "So I didn't. It was her house, after all."

"Oh, Toby, that is so sad."

"She was a miserably unhappy woman. I can only hope and pray that since Far came back and got her, she is happier now." Then he took her hand. "Come on. Rebecca has supper ready, and then we'll bring your clothes over."

"Right. Tomorrow we will really move in." Stepping out on the back porch, she looked to the west and caught her breath. "Oh, look at the sunset." Banners of every shade from lemon to crimson, fiery pink to purple, blazed across the sky. Even the clouds to the east were tinted in shades of pink-trimmed light gray. Anji felt her smile widen. The glorious sunset truly blessed the house cleaning, her new home. All these people—family, friends, and all around good folk. Yes, returning to Blessing had been a wise move, even if her mother-in-law was still upset with her. And that was stating it mildly.

Toby tugged on her hand. "Come on. I don't want Rebecca mad at me when, for a change, it's not my fault. Thomas, grab her other hand and let's go."

"You are coming too?" Anji asked Thomas.

"Yes, I was invited."

"Good." She jumped the bottom step. "Oh, did anyone bank that fire?"

"Not me. Don't worry, we can start it again. And it's not so cold tonight. Spring might really be here to stay." Toby waved to Gilbert, who was standing on the back steps of Rebecca's house, and yelled, "We're coming. Your mother was dawdling."

"I couldn't just run off and leave all those people without a thank-you, now could I?" Somehow her hands were still clasped in the men's. She felt like a little girl running off to play with her friends. The house was clean, even the beds all made. Now to move their belongings over and make it their home. *Oh, Ivar, how you would enjoy this.* He had loved living in Blessing too. The way he had decided to move back to Norway, perhaps he had an idea he was not going to get well again. He'd never mentioned that, but he always wanted to please both his mother and his wife. And himself.

⁓

"I think we need to have a housewarming," Rebecca said later when supper was finished and the adults were sitting around the table, enjoying a last cup of coffee.

Gerald frowned. "But why? The house has all the furniture it needs, plus bedding and kitchen things."

"All but food," Toby said.

Anji nodded. "That's what Kaaren said too. You'd better talk with her. I've already started a list to give to Penny. She said since she couldn't come today, she wanted to give me some staples."

Gerald smiled. "Leave it to Penny. Did you really get it all done?"

"No. I never got back to the rolltop desk, and there are some drawers in the kitchen that still need to be sorted. And the cellar. But that will be easy to clean. There is nothing down there but empty canning jars and odd stuff. I don't think the attic was swept either. They did kill a couple of mice, though. As soon as I can get some traps, I'll set them."

"We have some you can have. What you need is a good mouser cat."

"Won't Lissa be thrilled with that! She's always wanted a cat." *But her grandmother Moen didn't like dirty animals in the house.*

"I'll find you one," Toby said, picking up the last of the crumbs of the cake with the tines of his fork. "Rebecca, what about you? Should I find two?"

"You might ask at the farms round about.

They always have batches of kittens in the barns."

She and the children would sleep in their new house tonight, a strange house, but tomorrow they would bring over all their belongings and make it theirs. It would not be strange for long.

Later, when her children were tucked into their new beds, Anji readied herself, washing her face at the bowl behind the screen. She'd carried up the warm water and hummed while she slid her nightdress over her head. She blew out the kerosene lamp and climbed into bed, the sheets fragrant with fresh air. The quilt had been aired too. As she lay back against the down pillows, the dust beaten out of them too, she gave a sigh of delight. "Lord, thank you for this lovely clean house. Please drive the sadness away and fill our house with love. Thank you—" She stopped. Was that footsteps she heard?

"Ma?" A voice quivered, and a little body threw itself onto the bed, quickly followed by two more. Lissa paused in the doorway.

"The little ones are scared." Her voice shook just the littlest bit.

"Come on in. This bed is big enough for us all, at least for tonight."

"The house is . . . is noisy." Joseph snuggled into her side.

Gilbert lifted the covers and scooted under them.

Anji made sure everyone had covers, then laid back down herself. "Now, no kicking, you hear? Or you'll be back in your own bed before you know it."

Within moments the three younger children were breathing softly. She reached across Joseph and took Gilbert's hand. "'Night, Gilly." She'd not used that old nickname for years. Funny how it had slipped out. *Lord, bless us all and good night.*

CHAPTER 13

Sometimes spring creeps in, hesitant like a shy kitten. Other years spring throws open the doors and blows the trumpets, heralding her arrival. This year started out like the first, the fierce growl of winter sending the kitten back into hiding. But once spring pounced back again, she stayed. The mud finally dried up, the river that threatened to flood slid back into its banks, and the migrating waterfowl filled the sky with the wild free song of honking geese and calling ducks. The meadowlarks sang their way back north and the chickadees of winter headed to their summer home.

"Can you hear them all?" Ingeborg asked as she, with Freda and Clara, raked the newly tilled and disked garden to ready it for planting. The potatoes would go in first, a good part of the garden—Ingeborg had insisted they plant half an acre into potatoes. Today they would also plant lettuce, peas, and a few other early crops. The remaining space would go to corn, to be planted as soon as the threat of frost had abated.

"You mean the birds?"

"Ja. How I would love to go hunt geese again."

"Better not to." Freda attacked a clump of black dirt that had dried rock hard. "I think Manny and Trygve will be going tonight."

"We need an abundance of goose down. One can never have enough for feather beds and pillows."

"Smoked goose never goes to waste." It seemed that Freda almost smiled.

Clara wielded a hoe and rake with some enthusiasm, often raising her face to the sky, as if desperate for the warmth. Although she still tired easily, she was learning to sign and to write letters on a slate, as if starved for the knowledge. She would point to something, such as the twine wrapped around a stick that they used to mark the rows in the garden. She carried a small slate in a big pocket that Ingeborg had sewed onto her apron. Ingeborg would identify the object in English, sign it for her, and write it on her slate. The many times a day she did thusly slowed her down considerably, but seeing smiles come to Clara's face made all the delays well worthwhile.

Ingeborg's sewing machine had become Clara's best friend. In the evenings when the children were doing their homework and Ingeborg was reading aloud, Clara sewed quilt blocks together, all straight seams so that when the quilters got together, they would have more tops to back and tie.

"Did you ever have a sewing machine before?"

Clara shook her head and pantomimed hand sewing with needle and thread. She had caught up on the household's mending too, since that was something she could do while still recovering.

Easter was well behind them, and now they found themselves nearly to mid-May. Spring was passing so quickly! Ingeborg nearly wore out a fingernail brush. You cannot knead bread with grit under your fingernails! But most of the planting, and most of the bread, happened anyway.

The Friday sunrise caught her breath. Sunrises and sunsets, God sandwiching her days between glorious color and infinite moments of peace. Coffee cup in her hands, Ingeborg leaned against the turned post on the porch and watched the world blend from one color to another. As the beauty faded, she looked toward the corral where the sheep were bleating to be released to pasture. They'd lined up at the gate where Manny let them out to get a drink and graze their way out to pasture. They had fifteen lambs, as four ewes had twins this year. Last year's crop was mostly ewe lambs, and they had butchered all the males in the fall. By next fall she would need to borrow a different ram so that there would be no inbreeding. As Haakan had warned her, raising sheep was more than seeing the lambs leaping and playing in the pasture. Manny had stepped into the life of sheepherder, along with making the crates to ship cheese and anything else he was asked to do or could see that needed doing.

And to think Anner Valders had wanted him jailed along with his brothers. That led her to thoughts of Hildegunn. Where were they and how were they? *Lord, you know you promise to keep your eyes on the sparrows, so I know you are watching over them. Please bring Anner to his senses and back into closeness with you. As John said, "Power corrupts" and we gave him that power. Please protect Hildegunn.* She sipped her coffee. Now, where had that idea come from?

Down at the barn, the men were loading the wagon to truck the milk cans up to the springhouse to be run through the separator, and there the cream and milk would cool. They needed to churn butter today, so the older cream would come up to the house. With this milking there should be enough cream to start the first batch of cheese. Freda would be pleased.

"Breakfast, Grandma." How Emmy could walk the porch without making the boards squeak was another one of those mysteries.

Ingeborg reached out an arm and gathered the little girl close. "Takk. You should have come to see the sunrise."

Emmy leaned her head against Ingeborg's apron. "I like spring. One more week and school will be out."

"Do you ever wonder about your people?"

"Ja, at times. At bedtime I pray for them. Someday I want to go visit."

"Ja, we will do that when you tell me you must. God will lead us."

"Can we sew dresses for them again?"

"We can. As soon as we get the garden planted."

"Good." She took Ingeborg's hand. "In summer Inga can come here more."

"And we'll go fishing after the school party."

The two made their way around the porch that wrapped three sides of the house to the back and into the kitchen. Clara flashed them a smile and picked up the pot to refill Ingeborg's coffee.

Another reason to rejoice: Clara busy and smiling and gaining enough weight to have lost her gaunt look. While she would never be a beauty, the smile overrode any plainness.

Even her hair, while thin, no longer hung in limp strands. She wore it braided and tied the two braids together with one of the ribbons Ingeborg insisted she have, at the nape of her neck. She signed "Sit down, please," and Ingeborg did so with a smile to Freda.

A week later at breakfast, Ingeborg announced that sheep shearing would start the next day. She looked to Clara. "Trygve and Thorliff will be here to shear the sheep, with Manny helping. They should get done in one day. Have you ever seen sheep sheared, Clara?"

She shrugged and shook her head, looking puzzled.

"We cut off their wool so they can grow more. The wool in one piece is called a fleece, which we wash and dry, and that is what you have been carding. We have eleven ewes now, and some neighbors are bringing their sheep here. Our barn makes a good shearing floor. We will card some of the fleece into batting for quilts. That's what we did with most of the wool from last year. The rest we spin into yarn. One of these days when we have a lot of shanks of yarn, we'll have a dying day. While you can buy many of the dyes now, I like to use some of the natural things too. Onion skins make a nice yellow, and dark blue comes from indigo."

Clara picked up her carding paddles and

began the back and forth motion. When all the hairs lay in the same direction, she rolled them up and laid the roll in the basket.

Ingeborg watched her. *Reverent* was a word that came to mind. Clara did so many things with that same sense of awe. What had her life been that such simple things were not part of it? *Lord, please fill me with your love and wisdom for this young woman you have brought into our house. I take so many things for granted, and perhaps you are showing me not only new things but the value of what I have. I get the feeling I am rich beyond measure, and I don't even know it.*

Manny blew through the door, washed at the sink, and headed upstairs to change out of his overalls into pants for school. Emmy had insisted he not go to school in chores clothes. Back at the table, Clara set a plate of bacon, fried eggs, and fried cornmeal mush in front of him.

"We have big tests today and Monday."

"Are you ready for them?"

"I guess so. I've never studied so hard in my life."

"You didn't used to go to school." Always practical Emmy.

"Maybe this is why." He wolfed down the meal. As he cleared his plate, Clara set a second with a smaller serving on the table and patted his shoulder.

Ingeborg and Freda swapped looks of

astonishment. Clara had voluntarily touched Manny.

Patches barked a family welcome, and heavy boots scraped on the porch. "Anyone home?" It was Trygve's way of letting Clara know who was there. While she stiffened, she did not run to hide in Ingeborg's bedroom. They had put away her cot, and she had slept with Ingeborg for a few days, until the stairs were no longer a problem. Now that she could handle the stairs, she had a room upstairs.

Trygve stopped inside the open door, being careful to keep the screen door from slamming. "Good morning, Clara." She nodded and jumped up to get the coffeepot.

"Have you eaten yet?" Freda asked.

"Ja, we ate early since Miriam is on the day shift." He eyed the platter of fried cornmeal mush. "Unless you've got extra of that."

"Figures." Freda handed him a plate off the warming shelf.

Manny and Emmy grabbed their lunch pails and headed out the door, throwing good-byes over their shoulders. They greeted someone else, and boots again sounded on the steps.

By the time Lars came in the door, Clara had disappeared into the bedroom.

"I thought you already ate." He greeted his son and looked to Ingeborg, shaking his head. "You'd think he was still growing."

"I am." Trygve patted his middle. "Besides

Freda makes the best fried cornmeal mush of anyone." He looked to Freda. "What do you do that makes it different?"

"Cracklings."

"You still have some left since last fall's butchering?"

"Not much."

"I heard you were going hunting tonight," Lars said to his son as he accepted the cup of coffee and sat down.

"Me and Manny. Do you want to come?"

"No, but Samuel does." He smiled at Freda, who set a cinnamon roll in front of him.

"How come he got one of those and I didn't?" Trygve looked longingly at the warm roll sitting in front of his father.

"You asked for fried mush. Besides, this is the last one."

Lars nudged his son. "Sometimes there are privileges for being the elder." He glanced around the kitchen and raised an eyebrow with his voice lowered. "Clara?"

Ingeborg nodded to the bedroom. "She's getting better and braver all the time."

"And Thorliff never found out where she came from?"

"No and perhaps that is just as well. At least that's what I remind myself."

Lars sipped his coffee. "How old is she?"

"Sixteen. She came from Norway two years ago, but she will not answer any of my questions about her life in America. Or about Norway either. It's like she has closed the door on anything that happened before she woke up in the hospital."

"I stopped by to ask if you want more help with the shearing tomorrow. I've got some extra time now that the machinery is all in order."

"Far, shearing sheep is a young man's job." Trygve looked to Ingeborg rather than his pa. "I'll be training Manny."

"Is that a challenge?"

"Why, not at all, just a fact." He pushed his plate away and picked up his coffee cup.

"And what time do you plan to start the shearing?"

"Right after breakfast." Ingeborg crossed to the bedroom door and found Clara sitting on the bed. "I think you should come out and meet Lars Knutson, Trygve's father and Kaaren's husband. He is safe." She held out her hand, praying all the while. Clara closed her eyes and stood, head down. She sniffed and let out a slow breath before sliding her hand into Ingeborg's.

Ingeborg led the way back to the kitchen and stopped at the end of the table. "Lars, I want you to meet Clara. She is unable to speak, so she is learning sign and English at the same time. Clara, this is Mr. Knutson."

Clara lifted her chin to look from Trygve, who smiled at her, to Lars, whose smile looked so like that of his son. She nodded, very slightly, but a nod nevertheless. And she did not run back to the bedroom to hide. Her hand clutched Ingeborg's so hard she almost winced.

"It looks like both of these men will be shearing sheep tomorrow, along with Manny. I thought you might like to come watch so you can learn all about sheep shearing."

"Maybe next year you can help us," Trygve said, his smile again seeming to calm her. "I know you like to go watch the sheep."

Ingeborg could feel the pressure relax on her hand. *Thank you, Lord. We are moving forward.*

The next morning the cows were milked and let out to the pasture that was now fully green. The sheep baahed *You forgot us,* confused when Manny did not let them out too. As soon as breakfast was finished, everyone gathered down at the sheep corral. Lars and Trygve teased back and forth about who was best. Manny held a pair of newly oiled and sharpened shears in his hand, squeezing them, watching the blades open and shut.

Ingeborg and Freda had a table set up for the fleece.

The sheep milled in a tight knot, all bunched in the shed, their lambs now corralled off and bleating for their mothers. Emmy and Clara waited outside the corral, watching every move.

"Okay, Manny, and anyone who needs a refresher, gather round." Trygve grinned at his far and Thorliff. "You old-timers might pay close attention too, as I demonstrate how to shear a sheep."

He strolled over to the bunch, grabbed a sheep by the neck and, with a smooth move, flipped the sheep up to sitting on her rump, her legs jutting out straight ahead, her belly exposed. He braced her tightly between his knees. Both hands free now, he sank his shears into the fleece and started clipping. The fleece began to fall away in one matted piece, as more and more of the sheep was converted from a wooly gray blob to a naked white goat-like animal. Within a couple of minutes, it was done. He tipped her forward, back on her feet, and off she trotted to where Emmy and Clara opened the gate and let her through, then released her lamb from the other pen.

Trygve rolled up the fleece and laid it on the table. "Any questions?"

"Can I watch a couple more?" Manny asked.

"As you wish. Thorliff, Far, you ready?" The three strode toward the sheep. Thorliff missed his first catch. Lars caught his and dumped her on her rump. Seemingly without hurry he snipped and clipped, bending low over the beast to reach the back and odd spots. When he let her go, Manny came and scooped up the fleece, rolling it as he went to Ingeborg.

By that time Thorliff had caught his and was clipping away. Trygve caught his second, and the routine was established through the next six sheep. "You ready now, Manny?"

"I . . . uh . . . yes, sir. First I got to catch one, right?" He moved gently into the sheep flock, grabbed one, and dumped her butt down. "Easy, girl, we'll get this done nice and easy." He pulled the shears out of his back pocket and clipped exactly as Trygve had done, but a lot more slowly and carefully.

"You need to get closer to the skin," Trygve said, watching closely. "But you don't want to nick her skin either. Flies find bloody spots faster than we can. You're doing fine."

Manny nodded, talking to the ewe the whole time and, when done, tipped her onto her feet and watched her trot off.

Ingeborg threw the latest fleece across the table. "I have some salve for the one you just nicked, Lars. If you can catch her again, we'll smear it on."

"I shouldn't have let her go. Sorry."

Clara reached for the ewe as she came toward the gate and caught her around the neck.

"Grandma, we have her," Emmy called. "Clara caught her, but we don't have any wool to hang on to now." Together the two girls wedged the ewe between them and the corral fence while Ingeborg brought over the salve and smeared it over the wound.

"We'll doctor her again tonight after they come into the corral. You can let her through now." She turned to Clara, speaking Norwegian as usual. "That was quick thinking. Takk."

Clara beamed back at her, nodded, then signed "Welcome."

Freda returned to the house and brought back a jug of water, along with a bowl of cookies.

"What? No coffee?" Thorliff wiped his forehead with the shirt on his arm, his leather gloves protecting his hands.

"Be grateful for water." Freda handed him the cup. "You can dump this over your head too if it will help."

"What are the scores?" Trygve asked after drinking one cup dry and pouring another.

Ingeborg read from the slate. "Thorliff, four; Lars, five; Trygve, five; and Manny, two."

"Even up. And we're over half done." Lars poked his son.

"I had to train the new guy." Trygve winked at Manny, who grinned back.

"All right, push on through now, and we'll be done before dinner." All three men and the boy grabbed a sheep and set to the shearing. Lars was the first to release his and grab for another. Ingeborg fetched his fleece and laid it on the table. Quickly, she and Freda ran their hands over the wool, picking out the brush stems, grasses, dried manure, whatever had lodged in the fleece and would not easily wash out. Trygve was only seconds behind.

"I'm not cut out for shearing sheep," Thorliff said, deadpanning his own pun.

Ingeborg chuckled. "Remember Sheep that first year we homesteaded? That's what you named her, Sheep."

"I do. She lasted a good long time." He rubbed his back and returned to the dwindling flock. "I'd rather milk that cranky ewe than shear these stinky sheep."

Manny grabbed the final ewe, Trygve having just snagged the ram. They clipped away with Lars and the others cheering them on. Manny finished only seconds behind Trygve and the two shook hands as the animals scampered over to the gate. With all the ewes and lambs together, most of the lambs began nursing as soon as their mothers paused long enough.

"The tally is . . ." Ingeborg dragged out the announcement. "Manny, three; Thorliff, four; Lars, six; and Trygve six. I declare a draw. Neither the older nor the younger has won. We all won, because the sheep are sheared. And all before dinner."

"Dinner will be a bit late." Freda and Ingeborg piled the fleeces on the wagon, and everyone helped carry them up to the house to stack on the porch.

At the house, Freda said, "Clara, you take a water jug around; Emmy, you get water from the reservoir so they can wash up on the back porch; and Ingeborg and I will get dinner on the table."

"You keep pushing her out there, don't you?" Ingeborg whispered with a smile.

"I do. And she keeps trying. She has come a long way."

"And yet she has even further to go. What will become of her?" Ingeborg shook her head.

Freda shrugged. "How many times do you say, 'God knows, and He is the one in charge.' Why would it be any different with this one?"

CHAPTER 14

The picnic is at noon and the awards and games after," Manny said as he and Emmy both grinned at Ingeborg.

"I will be there. The beans are baking and the cakes are ready."

Emmy looked to Clara. "Will you come too?"

Clara shook her head, her eyes suddenly full of fear. She looked frantically to Ingeborg, who smiled back. "You don't have to go, but we would like you to. There are many good people in Blessing who would like to welcome you. Soon you'll be coming to church with us too. And quilting. You are part of a much larger family than you realize."

Emmy patted her hand. "People are good

here. You do not have to be afraid." She glanced up at the clock. "Got to leave."

Manny mopped up the last of the eggs with his toast and drained his cup. "Thank you for breakfast." He grinned at Freda and Ingeborg. "I'll get to cutting pieces for the cheese crates when I get home."

Emmy asked, "Can Inga come home with us?"

"We'll see."

At Patches' welcome bark, the two flew out the door.

Clara got up to clear the table, as she had taken over doing the dishes. While she had regained some weight, her arms and legs were still sticklike, and the baby rounded her out like a ball in front.

"We need to sew you some summer shifts with pleats on the sides," Ingeborg said. "The one you are wearing is about to split."

Clara nodded and pointed to herself with a quick flick of her wrist.

"What color would you like?"

Clara paused, her eyes widening, along with a smile that was coming more frequently all the time. She walked over to the windowsill that held a pink geranium with a white eye, along with tomato and cabbage starts, and fingered the blossom.

"That is pink." Ingeborg signed pink and said it in both English and Norwegian. Clara signed the *p* and *i* and frowned when Ingeborg shook her head. She signed the four letters back. Clara nodded and copied her exactly. Then added "Thank you."

"As soon as you finish the dishes, you can come help us plant the garden. Hopefully we can get it done before the picnic."

Clara pointed to the plants in the window.

"Ja, we plant the cabbages, and we'll plant the tomatoes and put jars over them to protect them from the cold nights."

Freda checked on the beans that had been in the oven all night and were again bubbling and filling the kitchen with the fragrance.

Out in the garden both Ingeborg and Freda set to work with hoes, hacking out the weeds that always grew faster than the vegetables. The carrots and lettuce were up, as were the peas and beets. They mounded more soil around the thriving potato plants. A meadowlark trilled for them from the far fence posts, and swooping swallows were bringing mud from the riverbank to build their nests under the eaves of all the buildings. A pair of bluebirds had taken over the birdhouse, making Ingeborg wish they had more birdhouses to put up. "Perhaps Manny would like to build us some birdhouses."

"The robins are nesting in the lilacs. Inga will be happy to see that."

Ingeborg shaded her eyes with her hand to look out across the fields. They had finally dried enough that the plowing and discing were nearly finished. Now the seeding could begin, the wheat fields first, then the oats. This year she had requested a field of flax, partly because she loved the blue blossoms and partly because flax was a profitable crop—not only the seeds but the stalks, since a mill she had heard about in Grand Forks now processed flax for weaving linen thread.

She blinked back the tears that leaped into her eyes. Haakan had so loved spring planting time. Every day he'd go out and squeeze a handful of dirt from various fields, always anxious for the land to get dry enough to plant again. The cornfield would be the last planted, since sprouting corn was the most vulnerable to frost. Haakan was never happier than when he was harnessing up the horses to the plows. Now they used horses for sowing and both horses and steam donkey engines for reaping. Progress.

Trygve and Thorliff had teased Haakan about getting one of those fancy new steam tractors to take the place of horses. Haakan, usually fairly progressive, snorted, *"Show me a steam tractor that produces a new baby tractor every spring, and I'll consider it."*

∾

Anji hustled Gilbert and Joseph out the door. "I'll be there for the picnic, most likely to help set up. Make sure you have your books to turn in."

Lissa stopped on the front porch. "Benny isn't here yet." She had taken over helping pull Benny on his wheels to school. While he used the new crutches within the buildings, he needed to build up more strength to navigate the distance to the schoolhouse. Sometimes Gilbert helped her pull, especially if there were mud puddles.

Anji watched from the screen door that had just been put back up, the storm door retired to the cellar for the summer. She breathed in the cool, fresh air that carried the birdsong straight to her heart. Gratitude welled and made her sniff. She was back home in North Dakota, in Blessing, where she was born and raised. Norway was gloriously beautiful outside of the cities, but the Moen family lived on the fringes of Oslo, far more city than country. Sometimes she missed the mountains and the skiing, but nothing could compete with the heady birthing of spring here at home.

She waved to the children as they made their way to school, swept the black dirt off the porch steps, and returned to preparing certificates for her students. One for the greatest improvement, another for the best accent, and a third for writing and spelling. She really had enjoyed teaching the Norwegian language. Over the summer she hoped her mother-in-law would send the box of Norwegian books she had requested—most of them Ivar's books but some with children's stories, along with some textbooks.

She hummed a Norwegian folk song as she cleaned up the kitchen, the song that her classes would sing at the program during the picnic. Johnny Solberg would accompany them with his guitar. He and the hostler's daughter, Leanne, would play a duet and sing, with her on the piano. Both of them were becoming very accomplished.

Anji put all her things in two baskets and telephoned Rebecca to see how she could help there. Between them, they got the baby ready, dug out the other wagon, and plopped Mark and Agnes in the wagon along with the baskets, and set out for the school. Like most of the other fathers, Gerald would come at noon.

The older boys had already set up all the tables, so the women spread tablecloths and arranged the dishes as they came in. Since so many of the Blessing families had children at school, most of the businesses had shut their doors with their signs saying *Closed noon to three*. Everyone brought chairs or quilts to sit on, and a few minutes later, Reverend Solberg raised his hands for quiet.

He motioned to the schoolchildren gathered together and invited everyone to stand and join in singing a favorite song. "'God bless America, land that I love . . .'" After they finished, Reverend Solberg said, "Let us pray. Lord God, we thank you for this beautiful day, for the end of our school year, and for all these families who made sure their children received good educations. Thank you for our teachers, for books, for music, and for these children who have worked hard to learn so much. Thank you for this food and for all those who have prepared it." A motion with one hand and the pupils harmonized on the amen. All the adults joined too.

Anji sighed. "That surely is what singing will be like in heaven."

Ingeborg squeezed her hand. "You are so very right."

For a change, all the students were permitted to go through the lines on each side of the table and fill their plates first, followed by their families, everyone laughing and teasing.

Anji glanced over her shoulder, and sure enough, Thomas Devlin was smiling at her. She felt a tingle in her back and realized she felt like smiling even more now that he was there.

"And ye have your certificates ready?" he asked, his smile sneaking around her heart.

"Just finished them. And you?"

"Last night. There were many. More perfect attendance than I expected. I was hoping for everyone to get one, but apparently life does not work out that way. When is Rebecca planning to open the soda shop?"

"We got it all cleaned up and ready, so I guess it depends on the weather."

"Speaking of which, we could surely use a good soaking shower." They took their filled plates and sat down on the schoolhouse steps, along with Kaaren and Lars.

Anji asked, "Did you get the seeding all finished?"

Lars scowled. "Not yet. Some of the lower fields are still too wet from the last of the snow, so a late start for those. It would be good if the rain held off until the wheat was in."

"How does one determine 'too wet' anyway?" Thomas wondered aloud. "Obviously there be methods other than simply staring at the ground." He attacked his beans with gusto.

Lars chuckled. "Pick up a handful of dirt." He held out his cupped hand with imaginary dirt. "Squeeze it tight and open your hand. If the soil stays in one thick lump, it's too wet. If the lump breaks up into two or three pieces, it's just right. If it crumbles, it's too dry. If you work the ground when it's too wet, you destroy its texture and the plants have to struggle to survive."

"Ah." Thomas nodded sagely. "Interesting. In Ireland we have no such thing as too dry, and in Chicago we had scant need of soil. And yet the gardens could use a shower, I understand."

"Shower wouldn't hurt, but heavy rain for

a day or two would slow us down again. We just thank the good Lord for seeds to plant and good land to plant them in." And Lars seemed to enjoy the beans just as much.

Solberg moved from group to group, welcoming everyone and reminding them that there was plenty of food left. The program would begin at one o'clock sharp and last for an hour, and then the games would begin.

The program started with the choir singing "Children of Our God and King" followed by "Going to Jerusalem Just Like John." The little ones sang "Old MacDonald Had a Farm" so that all the smaller children could join in on the animal sounds, then "She'll be Coming 'Round the Mountain," with everyone, from the youngest to the oldest, singing the responses. Chuckles and giggles finished off the rendition.

Next it was time for Anji's class to sing the Norwegian folk song they had practiced, accompanied by Johnny Solberg on the guitar. And the final musical presentation was the beautiful duet done by Johnny and Leanne. After the applause died down, Reverend Solberg stood behind the music stand with a stack of certificates to hand out, starting with perfect attendance. He signed the names for the four students from the deaf school, and Grace signed the entire program for all those who could not hear.

"Only in Blessing," Sophie murmured to Kaaren as they all paid attention.

"Ja. Here our students are always part of the community, not set apart like at some other schools." Grace both signed and spoke her comments, as usual. She was always mindful of practicing speaking so that her voice would continue to improve, even though she was totally deaf herself. Her husband, Jonathan Gould, always watched her with such pride that Anji wanted to hug him. Even though she was two years younger than Sophie and Grace, they had all grown up together, more like a group of sisters than merely friends.

When Reverend Solberg called Manny's name for the student who had made the greatest progress for the year, Ingeborg clapped till her hands hurt, Benny whooped from his wheels, and someone else whistled.

"You've done well, Manny McCrary," Reverend Solberg said with his warm smile. "I'm glad you stayed at it."

"Me too, sir." Manny's face looked hot enough to start a fire. He looked for Ingeborg and grinned at her before sitting down.

When all the certificates were handed out, Thomas Devlin raised his arms. "Let the games begin." There were gunnysack races, three-legged races, spoon and egg races, races for speed, and races for precision. Then there were jump-rope contests and the final event—a tug

209

of war. They divided the teams up as evenly as possible and drew a line in the grass. Whichever team dragged the other across the line would win.

While the events were happening, some of the men were cranking away at the ice cream makers. The winning team would get to have ice cream first.

Thomas Devlin coached the blue team and John Solberg the red. All those not making ice cream lined the tug-of-war ground, cheering their team. Back and forth it went, with the bigger boys on the knotted ends of the thick rope. Slowly Devlin's blue team dragged the little kids over the line, then the larger, with girls and boys pulling for all they were worth, until finally the red team's end man fell. Benny declared the blue team the winners, but both teams were panting so hard, they could barely stand. Everyone applauded and shouted for their team. One little girl on the red team started crying until her ma wrapped her arms around her and comforted her.

"Ice cream is ready," Thorliff shouted. "Blue line comes in first, then the red, and then everyone else. We have plenty for all."

When the picnic had finally come to an end, Emmy, Manny, and Inga climbed into the wagon with Ingeborg, with Manny driving and waving as they left.

Anji and her four took one wagon, while Rebecca and Gerald pulled Benny's wagon with him holding his little brother, Mark. Swen rode on Gerald's shoulders, and Rebecca carried the sleeping baby Agnes in a sling. Thomas Devlin walked with them. "So, Benny, what was the best part of the day?"

"No more school till September. Now we can go fishing and I get to ride Joker again and . . ." He paused for dramatic effect. "I get to stay out at the farm sometimes." He looked to Rebecca. "And Ma said I can help in the soda shop. Pa built me a stool so I can make sodas too."

"I shall be yer first customer. Strawberry be me favorite."

"Ma has been making new flavors. Pa said coffee is the best of all."

"Coffee-flavored sodas?" He looked to Anji, who nodded.

"They are very good. Rebecca made some coffee-flavored ice cream too, sometimes with chocolate sauce in it."

"It's best with cookies. Ma breaks cookies up and mixes them with ice cream."

"Come now, Benny, ye must be teasing me."

"No, really, Mr. Devlin. We've got the best ice cream and soda shop anywhere."

"Well, let's see . . . we have the best cheese anywhere, Ingeborg makes the best bread, and Amelia Jeffers grows the most beautiful roses . . ."

"Our flour mill makes the best flour."

"And our deaf school gives the best training anywhere. Grace said so."

"A lot of bests for such a small town." Devlin glanced to Anji. "Wouldn't ye say?"

"Yes, I would. Would you like to join us for supper? It won't be the best anywhere, but you won't go home hungry." Anji glanced at her daughter, who was nodding vigorously. "And there is the possibility of a checkers tournament afterward."

Benny bounced in his wagon. "I'm the champion so far."

Gerald shook his head. "As one who was trounced repeatedly, you might not want to challenge him."

"Really!" Devlin slanted his eyes to Benny. "Ye think ye can beat me?"

"I can try real hard." Benny stared right back at him.

"Maybe the tournament will have to start while supper is getting ready," Rebecca said with a smile for her husband. "You can help us so you needn't feel so bad."

They all trooped into Rebecca's house and within minutes, two checkers boards were set up. Melissa sat at one with her onkel Gerald and Benny sat at the other with Thomas Devlin. Two of the little ones fell asleep on a folded blanket behind the stove. As soon as the stove heated, Rebecca brought a kettle of soup from the icebox and set it to heat while Anji got out the flour and other ingredients for biscuits.

"King me." They heard Benny's voice from the parlor and swapped looks, along with the shaking of heads.

"Do they ever play checkers at school?"

"Sometimes, when the weather is really bad. I know Thomas was teaching the older students to play chess. But near as I can tell, there is a big difference between the two games. Ivar used to play chess."

"I like dominoes better. Remember when we used to play dominoes? You taught me how, and Sophie and that Ecklund girl from down by the river did not like to lose so they wouldn't play with us anymore?"

Anji nodded. "That seems a lifetime ago."

"It was. I remember the year we got the dominoes game. Far made it for us all. I wish I had that set, but it is out at the farm. That's where Benny learned to play so well."

Anji grinned at Rebecca when they heard "King me" again.

That night, after supper and after Benny had won one game and Thomas had won one, with Gerald and Lissa splitting the other board,

Anji took her children back to their new house, Thomas walking with them.

"Ah, Benny. That lad has a mind like a bear trap. He never forgets anything."

"Amazing, isn't it? And to think when he came here, he could barely read or do numbers. John Solberg recognized it before anyone else did. Benny has a problem with his legs, but he can outthink anyone in our school. He wins spelling contests, geography contests, and as you know, John is coaching him in higher math."

"And to think he was an urchin off the streets of Chicago." Devlin smiled at Anji. "I best be getting on home. Thank ye for the evening." He held the door open for her and the children. "See ye in church on Sunday?"

"Unless you are brave enough to come for supper tomorrow night?"

"'Twould be me pleasure. I never look a gift meal in the mouth. I might have a surprise for ye as well."

"Ma-a-a!"

"Coming." She smiled at him over her shoulder.

"Ma, Gilbert won't do what I tell him."

Thomas tipped his cap. "'Night."

Rebecca had hinted that Thomas wanted to court Anji. Perhaps she was right. But wasn't it too soon to be thinking of another man? There was a slight war going on between her mind and her feelings.

CHAPTER 15

What is so rare as a day in June?

Ingeborg had read that line in a book about the Fireside Poets long years ago—some of the first literature in English she'd ever read. And it was so true! There was nothing as charming and invigorating as a fair day in June. She walked from her stove to the kitchen window to look out at pure delight: June! The fresh grass, the trees newly leafed out and their treetops dancing in a light breeze, the baby elephant pulling on the lowest cottonwood limbs with its trunk, the spring flowers, the lambs gamboling out in the—

Her brain stopped thinking. Stopped completely. She gaped. An elephant. Her cottonwoods. Elephant. In her yard. The baby turned its back on the cottonwoods and walked over to the flowers. Its trunk reached out—

Ingeborg dashed to the door and ran outside waving her arms. "No! No! You must not eat my flowers! Go back to . . ." To where? An elephant! "To somewhere! Go!"

The baby looked at her for a moment, not fearfully, just cautiously, then ambled off toward the garden out back.

Ingeborg seized up her skirts and ran faster than she had run in years. "No! You must not eat the lettuce! No!"

As Ingeborg rounded the corner of the house, Freda came running out the back door with a broom. "Go away, you little beast! Eat someone else's garden!" She swung her broom as she approached the elephant, and it got the message. It flung its trunk up, flicked its ridiculous little rope tail, and shuffled off toward front yard. Were it a horse, you would call its gait a flatfooted walk, always with two feet on the ground. It actually traveled mighty fast.

My flowers! Ingeborg reversed direction and ran around to the front.

But the baby elephant had apparently forgotten about flowers. Its wallowing shuffle carried it out the lane and off toward town, those silly ears flapping, its trunk waving from side to side. Freda had stopped, but Ingeborg kept running. She had to know what was going on. An elephant!

The elephant did not seem to get winded at all, but Ingeborg was huffing and gasping. She slowed to a fast walk. The little elephant was headed toward the mill. Good! Let it eat grain, not Ingeborg's new garden.

What was this? A train was parked behind the mill. She could not see the locomotive and tender, but she could see the caboose and seven or eight of the cars. The cars were painted bright red with yellow trim. As she got closer, she could read the ornate lettering on their sides: *Stetler and Sons Traveling Circus.*

A circus! In Blessing! Well, that would explain the elephant.

A man standing near the caboose cried out, "Look! Here she comes! She's back!" He was waving toward either the elephant or Ingeborg.

"Get Violet!" someone else shouted.

Ingeborg was so winded now she staggered. She stumbled to a hasty walk to the mill and out behind it. She was sweating and her lungs hurt.

Thorliff laughed. Thorliff! He was behind the mill talking to a dapper gentleman in a bowler hat and lace ascot tie. "Mor, did you just chase that elephant back here?"

She was too breathless to answer.

He turned, still chuckling, to the man. "Mr. Stetler, I probably owe you an apology. When you sent your people off looking for the elephant, I should have simply told you to go straight to my mother's house. Every hungry stray in the state ends up on my mother's doorstep." He held out a hand to Ingeborg. "Mother, I present Owen Stetler, the owner and manager of this circus. Mr. Stetler, my mother, Ingeborg Bjorklund."

"Charmed, Mrs. Bjorklund!" The man tipped his bowler. "Thank you for returning our errant baby."

Up by the tender an elephant trumpeted. Ingeborg watched amazed as the mother elephant—that was obvious—greeted her baby and the baby pressed in against its mother. Their trunks touched and entwined. Even elephants knew mother love!

She asked, "When did it wander off?"

"We were just talking about that," Thorliff replied. "You know the pack of feral dogs down by the river. I was talking to Sophie a few days ago. She thought raccoons or something were raiding her garbage cans at night, but when she heard them and ran out with a lantern, it was dogs."

"And they raided Anji's too. So they're coming up into town now." Ingeborg frowned. "That's not good."

"And becoming bolder and more aggressive. That's not good either."

"When we're going to be in one place for a few days, we bring the animals off the train, corral them in a field or something," Mr. Stetler explained. "Let them run around a little." He smiled slightly. "Not our lion, of course, or the chimpanzee. But the horses, elephants, goats. The bison. We had let Violet down the ramp and her—"

"Violet is the mama elephant," Thorliff added.

"Yes. Her baby came down behind her. We chained her up, as we always do, but we didn't have to chain the baby. Her name is Fluff, incidentally, because of that down on top of her head when she was born."

"Fluff." Ingeborg wagged her head. This was getting weirder and weirder.

"We'll probably change the name. We didn't expect any problems. Baby elephants never wander away from their mothers. Never. Suddenly here were these dogs, and some of them were big. Violet was chained and couldn't do much. They menaced the baby and she took off running. Then the goats jumped the fence of their enclosure and chased the dogs—protecting Fluff, I suppose." He looked very tired.

"And it wasn't even sunrise yet." Thorliff looked rather tired as well. "The goats drove the dogs away, and Owen here sent his animal keepers off in all directions trying to find Fluff."

Ingeborg was still sweaty, but at least she'd gotten her breath back.

Mr. Stetler said, "We will only let the

animals out during the day now, of course, and keep them in and protected at night."

"I feel so bad that this happened in Blessing." Thorliff studied the ground. "It's not that kind of a town."

Mr. Stetler laid a hand on Thorliff's shoulder. "And they're not your dogs. Most towns have a pack of strays. You needn't apologize."

"It's wonderful to have the circus visit, though." Ingeborg straightened. "I had no idea you'd be here. I haven't seen posters or anything."

"This is not a scheduled stop. We heard you have a fine hospital and several of our troupe are quite ill—a strange disease of some sort. We canceled our next engagement and came here so they can be looked at and treated."

Ingeborg frowned. "There are bigger hospitals in bigger towns."

"But not hospitals with the reputation yours has. Two of our jugglers and several of our children are extremely ill. We fear for their lives. We have heard that if anyone can save them, your facility can."

"That is flattering." Ingeborg didn't have to think very long. "Mr. Stetler, it was my pleasure to meet you. Now, if you will excuse me."

Mr. Stetler tipped his hat again and smiled.

She turned and headed for the hospital, at a fast walk. She'd done enough running for the day. A mysterious illness that was too strange for larger hospitals to tackle? What was going on here? This was just as weird as an elephant in her yard.

When she arrived at the hospital, she went directly to the examining rooms. No one there. She tried the private room. A man with a nasty cough lay on the table with two student nurses hovering over him. Was his skin really bluish, or was he someone from the circus's freak show who was naturally that blue? One of the nurses dabbed at his brow with a wet compress as the other applied carbolic acid to a large open sore on his leg.

He was having difficulty breathing. He gasped, "I'm cold."

Abigail, at his head, said, "I'll bring you another blanket." She hurried off.

Ingeborg stepped up to the woman working on the leg. "That is an ugly lesion." It was the size of a silver dime and deep enough to expose muscle tissue. It was surrounded by a wider circle of sloughed outer skin, revealing the bright pink of the skin layer below.

Gasping, he groaned and jerked his leg.

"I'm sorry, sir, but it is infected," Sandra told him. "We have to clean it out. I'm very sorry I'm hurting you, but this must be done."

"No. No more." He seemed to be sinking into a restless sleep. He murmured, "I can't breathe. I can't juggle." His gasps were getting louder, coming more frequently. "I can't juggle. I'm done now."

"What does Astrid say?" Ingeborg asked.

"She says she's never seen this before."

"Neither have I."

Abigail returned and tucked an additional blanket around the poor fellow. She picked up a clean dressing from the tray and held it close to the man's leg, ready to cover the wound as soon as Sandra was ready.

Ingeborg turned away and headed down to Astrid's office. She rapped lightly and opened the door. There sat Deborah, Miriam, Astrid, Elizabeth, and Dr. Commons, the resident intern.

Astrid was on the telephone. "Yes, I know he is in lecture. I need him. Is Dr. Brokaw available?" Pause. "It is an acute emergency. We have people dying here." Another long pause. "I'll wait." With her phone at her ear she stared blankly at Ingeborg.

She hasn't even noticed me. Please, God, help us here. Help us!

Astrid scowled. "No, we need it now. Right now. Very well. I'll be waiting." She reached up to the wall, stretching, and cradled the phone. "Dr. Brokaw cannot be found, and Dr. Monroe is in lecture. The receptionist promises that the first one she finds will call me."

Dr. Commons nodded. "Dr. Brokaw is a

contagious disease specialist, and Dr. Monroe treats primarily lungs and hearts."

Miriam looked grim and drawn. "They start with a fever, a sore, raspy throat, and a cough. Then they develop difficulty swallowing and breathing. Mr. Morris, the juggler in our private room, turned blue before they brought him in. His heartbeat is irregular."

"I saw the open sore."

Miriam nodded. "Now he has trouble controlling his right arm. A juggler needs very precise control. I'm afraid he will just give up if he can't use the arm."

Elizabeth looked just as grim. "They brought in a small child, a darling boy. He said his neck hurt, and then he said he was very tired. He fell asleep soon after he came in and did not awaken. He just faded away. We wrapped the poor little body in a sheet and returned him to his mother. Now she has a sore throat. He was not much older than Roald. Ingeborg, I'm terrified! What is this thing?"

"I am going to check on Mr. Morris. Mrs. Bjorklund, please take my chair." Miriam left, closing the door behind her.

"Mr. Morris. The juggler." Ingeborg crossed to Miriam's vacated chair and sat down. She also felt very discouraged and weary. Probably the hard run following the elephant had something to do with it. Probably also was the fact that she had not eaten yet.

Elizabeth really was terrified. It showed in her face. "Astrid, we should have sent that train on down the track. We have just exposed this whole town to a disease about which we know nothing. Nothing! Not even how to ease its symptoms."

Astrid stared at her. "Are you saying turn away people who desperately need medical care?"

Elizabeth was almost shouting. "Medical intervention! Medicine that will help them. We don't have that! We can't help them, but they can devastate us!"

The phone rang. Astrid grabbed the receiver off the hook. She listened for a moment. "Oh, thank God!"

Ingeborg listened closely, but she could not hear the voice on the other end. Astrid was nodding, grunting, saying an occasional yes. Whoever was on the other end had gone into some sort of lengthy discourse.

Was Elizabeth right? Was this the one time they would be wise to refuse the urge to help, to send desperate people to some other town? She had certainly made an excellent case for doing that. Ingeborg had no idea what to do, even which way to start moving. Elizabeth and Astrid, well-trained doctors, were flummoxed. Miriam had no idea, and she grew up in the big city.

A sudden heavy pall of gloom dropped

down on Ingeborg, turning her whole world dark. What if little Inga got sick, or Emmy? Manny was doing so fine, growing in wisdom. What if he succumbed? Innocent children, cut short? *O God, no!* But everyone in Blessing was suddenly vulnerable, exposed to a hideous danger that no one could control.

O God, please, no, no, no!

"Yes!" Astrid said to the telephone receiver. "Oh yes! I agree. Thank you." She listened. "Yes, we'll do that. Thank you!" She hung up and flopped into her chair.

"Well?" Elizabeth was on the edge of her seat.

"That was Dr. Brokaw. He says the symptoms suggest diphtheria. Doctors managed about twenty years ago to isolate and identify the bacterium that causes it. They have developed an antitoxin to counteract it, an antidote, but you have to administer it before the symptoms appear."

"What good is that?!" Elizabeth sat back.

"It keeps the person who receives it from developing the disease. He is sending a shipment of the antitoxin to us as quickly as possible."

Deborah asked, "But what can we do for the sick people?"

"He explained about intubation, which is inserting a breathing tube put down the throat of a person who cannot breathe well. You have to sedate the patient first, of course. The tube lets air past the tonsils, which develop a thick membrane that blocks air passage. Dr. Brokaw is sending us a supply of the correct size of stiff rubber tubing. Both things should be on the train tomorrow. We'll get them the next day."

Astrid sank back, looking very tired. "Dr. Brokaw also told me this. Do you remember in the news that President Cleveland's daughter—the former president, you know, Grover Cleveland—his daughter, Ruth, died a couple years ago? What started out looking like a sore throat and tonsillitis turned out to be diphtheria."

Elizabeth looked stricken. "Astrid, I remember that. She was dead in less than a week."

Ingeborg's whole soul seemed to just shrivel up. "How can you tell a diphtheria case from a simple sore throat?"

Astrid studied her desktop for a moment. "We all know Mr. Morris's symptoms. But they are apparently advanced. Every sore throat that comes in, we must immediately examine the tonsils using a tongue depressor. If you see any gray substance starting to grow on the tonsils, put the person in quarantine. Also, Dr. Brokaw said if a child—or an adult too, I assume—has a strangely swollen neck, that is a sure sign. He called it 'bull neck' because it looks like the overly thick neck of a herd bull."

Ingeborg was also staring at Astrid's desk. "The disease is easily communicable, right?"

"Right. Unless you've had the antitoxin to counteract it."

She nodded. "If more people in the circus get sick, we won't have room for them here. If the disease spreads into the community, we won't have room for our own. We should somehow set up a ward or facility on the train and go to them rather than having them come to us."

Deborah nodded enthusiastically. "Good thinking, Ingeborg. I agree. We might even set up a facility in town, at the school or boarding-house, if some of our people get sick."

Elizabeth hopped to her feet and crossed to the bookshelf. She ran a finger along the book spines and pulled out a massive tome. She sat down, plopped it in her lap, and consulted the index. "Diphtheria. Diphtheria. Here." She opened the book and flipped several pages. She read for a moment with her lips pressed into a tight line. "It mentions fatigue, headache, and a foul nasal discharge. Does Mr. Morris have those?"

Astrid picked up a chart on her desk and scanned it. "They are not recorded here. That doesn't mean he doesn't have those, of course, just that he didn't mention them and we didn't notice them."

Ingeborg couldn't think. This was just too much. "I suggest one thing, though."

Inga! Emmy! Manny! All the other innocent children.

"Let's keep all the children home, in their respective homes, to protect them. How long is the incubation period—the time from when you get the germs until the first symptoms show up?"

Elizabeth paused, then read, "'Symptoms appear two to seven days following exposure.'"

Astrid nodded. "Mor, with school out, we need to contact the families. Reverend Solberg knows all the families and can get the word out quickly. I think keeping the children close to home for a week or so is better than taking risks. Also, let's ask him if we can set up the school rooms as an infirmary. If this diphtheria becomes an epidemic, we will need a central place to house and care for the sick."

"I will." At last. Something to do about this horror. Ingeborg stood up.

Miriam appeared in the doorway. She looked drained, stricken. "Mr. Morris, the juggler, has died."

CHAPTER 16

W e need to go from house to house and tell everyone to stay away from the train, and tell children to remain at home." Reverend Solberg looked ten years older. He sat in the spare chair in Thorliff's office, his long legs stretched out in front of him.

"I'll get some flyers printed so we can post them." The circles under Thorliff's eyes, he knew, spoke of lack of sleep even more than the stoop to his shoulders did. He looked to John Solberg. "Don't you think God is letting down on protecting us?"

Solberg smiled gently with a heavy tinge of sadness. "I know it seems that way, but we must trust Him. He promised He is right here with us."

"With three dead already? And yes, those

are all people from the train, but the antitoxin will not arrive until the day after tomorrow, and we already have people here exposed."

"We've kept the exposure to a minimum, thanks to the wisdom of our doctors."

Thorliff nodded. "At least we have tried to. I'd better get this set so we can get them out. Thomas, would you be willing to help me?"

Off in the corner leaning against the wall, the cheerful Irishman grinned. "Aye! I feared ye'd never ask."

Thorliff smiled in spite of himself. "John, you can pick up the flyers in about an hour. We all better be praying for protection for everyone." He didn't add *if God is listening*, but he thought it. Last year the grain elevator blew up, and now half the town could die. God may not have turned His back, but was He listening? Thorliff was not convinced. He was pretty certain God had at least lost His happy smile. That was for sure.

With a nod, Reverend Solberg put on his hat, said good-bye, and left.

Devlin flopped into the chair the reverend had vacated. "Ye might start, I suggest, by allowing only people who are immune to venture near the train and mill."

"How do we know who's immune?"

"People who have survived diphtheria—'tis no death sentence, I assure ye—and once ye've had it ye cannot fall ill with it again."

Thorliff grunted. "Where did you hear that?"

"From yer darlin' wife, who read it aloud from a book."

Thorliff thought about this a moment. "What if someone decides not to take that advice—to stay away from the train? I wonder if there is some way to force them to obey the edict. We've never bothered too much with ordinances in this town. People are generally quite thoughtful and kind. But what if?"

Devlin frowned at the desk in thought.

Thorliff picked up the phone and cranked it. "Hello, Gerald. Thorliff. Can you connect me to Charlie Becker up in Grafton?" He listened. "Of course." He cupped his hand over the mouthpiece and explained, "Charlie Becker is the new sheriff in Grafton. Used to be Clyde Meeker, but he moved to Minneapolis. Clyde hauled our bank robbers off to jail a while back. But Charlie will know what's legal and what's not."

It took Gerald several minutes, but the sheriff's jovial voice finally boomed. "Thorliff! Good to hear from you. How's it going out there in the woolly farmland?"

"Not good. We have a circus train parked behind the mill with a number of sick people. Diphth—"

The jovial voice turned startled. "They surely didn't stop there in Blessing! Those . . ."

and he used a word Thorliff had not heard for years. And it wasn't Norwegian.

Thomas surely heard the sheriff's voice, because he was frowning, leaning forward attentively.

"What are you saying?" Thorliff's spirit thudded.

"Plague train! They stopped here wanting to use our medical facilities, and we chased them away. Drove 'em off, and good riddance. I called around and learned that a couple other towns chased them away too. I'm really sorry Blessing didn't, Bjorklund."

We were such fools! God, why did you not warn us? Thorliff sighed heavily. "You turned them away. What legal precept was that? I mean, what legal basis did you have?"

"Bjorklund, I'm sworn to protect the citizens, and the citizens' lives were at stake. I didn't need any legal basis. I did it."

"But we need some sort of legal basis here, I think."

"You're right. You gotta elect yourselves a village constable to handle this sort of thing."

They chatted a few more minutes as the sheriff asked about Miriam, Elizabeth, and Astrid. Finally he hung up.

Devlin sat back. "Well, that explains much."

"Too much." Thorliff's heart ached. If only they had known . . . "I suggest we put a line on the flyer that if anyone has had diphtheria before, we need their help in caring for the sick."

"Good idea."

Thorliff crossed to the door and propped it open to get some air moving through the building. "This heat sure isn't helping any."

Together they wrote and designed the flyer. Thorliff set the type, and Thomas ran the printer. He held up the first sheet for their fast edit and mutual approval and then cranked out the printed flyers. They handed them out, and within an hour most of the people in town had received the paper. Copies were posted in all the public places.

Thorliff kept busy, refusing to allow the bone-wracking fear to take over. Elizabeth had gone out to the train. He'd not asked her if she'd had the disease as a child or received the antitoxin while in Chicago. But as far as he could figure, they might not have had the antidote yet when she received her medical training there. And she never had regained her full strength after the birth of Roald. Lack of knowledge was a strong part of that fear. So far all they knew was that diphtheria was most deadly to small children and older people with infirmities.

He started calling around. He learned that Miriam and her family had been exposed and had light cases. Mrs. Geddick remembered having croup, at least. Mr. Sidorov said he had lost two brothers and a sister but had lived through it. Reverend Solberg wasn't sure if he'd had croup or diphtheria. Both of the student nurses had been inoculated when they went into the nursing program. Those who had grown up in Blessing and came from Norway were the vulnerable ones.

Everything hinged on the arrival of the antitoxin. And nothing could bring it faster than the train.

Thorliff went in search of his wife and Astrid at the hospital.

The door was blocked with a sign saying *No admittance. Call for assistance.* Head nurse Deborah MacCallister saw him standing there and came to speak to him through the door.

"How can I help you, Thorliff?"

"What is happening here?"

"Another of the circus children died, and we are hoping to get supplies in time to save the others. Astrid has done two tracheotomies. Everything here has to be boiled with carbolic acid. It's a good thing we only had three patients here before this hit. Elizabeth did an inspection of the circus train and told them what they must do to try to save other lives. There are too many more sick people out there. They are setting up an infirmary tent behind the mill."

"Thomas Devlin is immune. I suggest you put him in charge of helping those on the train and don't allow any more into the hospital."

"That's what Dr. Elizabeth wanted to

do—isolate them somewhere else—but we can't just let people die without help."

He told her about the flyers and what they were doing, but he did not mention Stetler's perfidy. He handed her the list of people they knew were immune. "I've asked them to come help as we need them. How are you staffwise?"

"Everyone is exhausted, but Mrs. Geddick just keeps cooking. Keeping ahead of the sheets and bedding to wash is impossible. Miriam's sisters and eldest brother are here helping with laundry and meals, but the youngest two were born after their family had it."

"We've sent some of the men over to the cemetery to dig graves." Thorliff rubbed his forehead. "And we thought we had a pretty good emergency plan for here."

"I have to go. I'm needed."

"Thank you." He headed back to the newspaper office to start a special edition of the paper. And answer the telephone.

"Thorliff," Sophie called from outside the door.

"Come on in." He hoped he smiled at her, but by this time he was not sure.

"Do you suppose anyone who came in on the train that dropped off the circus train could have caught diphtheria from being on the same train?"

"You'd have to ask Astrid or Elizabeth about that, but from what I know, it is not likely."

"If someone brings it into the boarding-house . . ." She shook her head. "We should never have let that circus train stop here."

"We had no idea what they were carrying. All the owner said was he had some sick people aboard. He failed to mention he had two dead bodies."

"News travels fast here in Blessing, and I tell you, people are already close to panic. Perhaps we should just send them on their way."

He stared at her. Sophie glared back at him. "So you want us to reload the sick and dying onto the train and expect another town to take them in?" All the while he was shaking his head. "Sophie, we have to deal with things the way they are. As long as none of your boarders were involved when the train stopped and you don't go near the hospital, you and your family should be safe."

"In an article I read, they burned the bodies and all the clothes, everything that touched the sick person."

"True, but boiling with carbolic acid works the same, and those at the hospital are doing their best to contain it."

"But what if their best isn't good enough? What if . . . what if the disease is carried on the breeze? What about the bodies they are going to bury? Maybe burning them would be better."

Thorliff tipped his head from side to side, trying to stretch out his shoulders and neck.

"You are asking questions that God alone knows the answers to. Now go back to the boardinghouse, warn everyone, and make sure your children stay home. We'll post quarantine signs if we know of a house and family that have been infected. The antitoxin should be here the day after tomorrow."

"Are they sending enough for the whole town?"

"I have no idea."

"What if someone has already been exposed? Will the inoculation stop the disease?"

"Sophie, I am not a medical doctor. I don't have all the answers." He raised a hand. "And before you ask, yes, Elizabeth has been exposed, as have all the others working at the hospital. Only God knows tomorrow." He knew he was quoting Reverend Solberg, because right now he wasn't sure if he trusted God to protect them or not. Or to heal those who were ill.

She asked, "Do you know when Hjelmer will be back in town?"

"No, and don't go ask Penny. Use the telephone."

Sophie glared. "You needn't be condescending. I have every right to be concerned."

"Don't we all?" He didn't tell her that Elizabeth had been home to sleep beside him before they learned the true diagnosis. She'd held her children. Could that bring it to them also? He watched the screen door slam behind her and ran his fingers through his hair. The headache did not want to go away. If only he and the others had not answered the call when their wives asked them for help in transporting patients from the train to the hospital.

The stench on that train should have scared them away right from the beginning.

Every time he closed his eyes, the horror of it blasted him again. Two or three dead bodies, people coughing and choking, children crying, some fighting to breathe, others lying in their bunks turning blue. The quarters so close, a narrow aisle between rows of bunk beds, some holding two sick ones. The lanterns hanging from the ceiling cast more shadows than light, like ghostly figures reaching to strangle the suffering. He had to step outside before he vomited. He'd never smelled anything like that, not even years earlier when they had to burn all the cloven-hoofed animals due to the hoof and mouth disease that had come in from the south. He could still see his pa crying as they shot all the milking cows and calves and rolled them into a pit to burn.

But now it was people dying, and more still coming down with the disease. He had scrubbed himself raw when he got back to his house, drained the water, and scrubbed again. But still the stench lingered. That gut-wrenching miasma could be creeping into the homes and streets of Blessing, and they had no way to stop it.

The telephone rang his signal. Like an old man, he pushed himself to his feet and went to lift the earpiece.

"How is the list coming of those who can help?" John Solberg didn't bother with a greeting.

"Let me get it." Thorliff read him the list. "I have a question mark next to your name."

"I know. I remember Mor telling me I had the croup as a child. I don't remember it, but we don't know if it was diphtheria or not. I am going on the assumption that I am immune, since I did not die."

"I see."

Solberg continued, "Devlin is on his way over to the train after talking with Astrid and Elizabeth. I sent Boris Sidorov with him."

"Miriam and the older ones of her family are over there now, doing whatever they are asked, and Trygve and the two younger ones have been ordered not to show up."

"But Trygve helped move sick ones from the train," Reverend Solberg protested.

"I know. As did you. I am making a list of those who have been exposed and reminding all of you to be there when the train comes in. You will be first in line for the inoculations. We're going to set up the inoculations at the schoolhouse, so you needn't go into the hospital. I think Miriam will be in charge of that."

"I've told your mor not to come into town."

"As did I. She is calling to gather sheets and making more cough syrup. They are out of so many things at the hospital." Thorliff thought for a moment. "Has anyone put out a call for butchered chickens to make soup? Mor always said that chicken soup was the best food to feed the sick."

"No, but I will put someone on that, to ask the farmers, since so few of them have a telephone. Right now I am so grateful that school was already out for the summer."

Thorliff hung up, shaking his head. Good thing someone could find something to be grateful for. All he could think was *What if?* And it was all way beyond anything he could control.

He left the office and mounted the stairs to the porch, hoping for a breeze to lighten the heavy air. He didn't need to open the door to hear Roald crying, "Ma, Ma."

Inga met him. "I want to go to Grandma's to make sure she does not have sad eyes again. Roald won't quit crying."

"You cannot go to Grandma's because everyone is being asked to stay in their own house."

"But we are not sick."

"I hope not. But that is the rule, and we must obey it."

She clamped her arms across her chest. "Can I go outside at least?"

"Ja, but you have to stay in the yard and not talk to anyone." Thorliff took his son from Thelma's arms and jiggled him as he went out on the porch, where now there was a tiny breeze. "Hush, son. Ma will come back soon." Roald's eyes were red and swollen from crying, and he rubbed them again, with his nose running too. Thelma wiped his nose with a piece of muslin and rubbed some salve on his red nose and cheeks.

"Poor little one." Indomitable Thelma looked to be close to the end of her rope too.

"Inga, how about pulling Roald around the yard in your wagon?"

She glared at her little brother. "Do I have to?"

Thorliff swallowed before answering. Even so, his words were clipped sharp. "Yes, you have to."

With a snort, she stomped down the stairs.

"Where are you going?"

"To get the wagon."

Thelma handed him a bottle of milk, but Roald pushed that away and started to cry again.

Thorliff lifted a pillow from the chair on the porch and put it in the wagon for a cushion, then set Roald on top of it. Scooter jumped up to lick his face, but Roald even pushed him away, something unheard of. If anything could make Roald laugh, the little dog was always successful.

"Be gentle with Scooter," Inga ordered, leaning over to pat her dog and get her cheek kissed. She set Scooter up on the wagon and pulled them off around the corner of the house, sending a glare over her shoulder. The one-and-a-half-year-old kept on crying.

Thelma carried a tray out on the porch to set on the table. "Lemonade and cookies. Perhaps you can have a few minutes to yourself here."

Thorliff drank half a glass and held the cool surface to his face, tipped his head back against the cushion, and inhaled. The exhale brought his shoulders down somewhere toward normal. He repeated the pattern and sipped from the glass.

A pain-filled shriek jerked him to his feet. Roald! He leaped down the steps and around to the front yard. "What happened?" His son was sitting in the grass, bellowing.

"Scooter jumped out and he reached for Scooter. I grabbed for him, and the wagon fell over, and he banged his head on the wagon, and . . ." Inga gulped air.

Thorliff glared at her and scooped up his son.

Thelma charged out the front door and down the steps. "What happened?"

"I didn't mean to!" Inga looked ready to cry. He didn't need two of them.

Thorliff checked the baby's head for any bumps. Scooter yipped. Inga tried to quiet the dog.

"You have to be more careful!"

Inga burst into tears and stomped up the stairs, grabbed the screen door handle, and let the door slam behind her.

"Here, I'll take him." Thelma ignored the cries for "Ma!" and rocked back and forth, at the same time whispering mother songs.

Roald would have none of it, stiffening his body, forcing her to clamp both arms around him.

Thorliff watched his son in amazement. His easygoing, happy baby had turned into some kind of monster. He wanted his ma this bad? It wasn't as if she were with him all the time. Did babies have an inner clock and calendar to remind them that Ma had not been around for hours? Turning into days in this case but . . . He shook his head. Today a squalling child was beyond him. While he was having a hard time finding things to be thankful for these days, right now Thelma was saving his sanity. Or at least the day.

The door slammed behind Thelma. He bent over to pick up the handle of the wagon to put it away so no one could fall over it. He glanced up at the window to Inga's room. He could hear her crying. She never cried, unless you took the time she broke her arm into account.

Elizabeth was needed here. That was for sure. *Lord God, protect her please. Please protect all of us and heal the sick.* He sure hoped God was listening.

CHAPTER 17

T hank you, Thorliff." Anji stood on her front stoop and watched Thorliff hustle off on his way to the next house. And to think there was a time, when they were both young and foolish, when she might have married him.

She read the paper he had just handed her. Her heart jumped, and not from thoughts of love. Diphtheria! Yes, she certainly would keep the children at home. She vaguely remembered from somewhere that there was a cure for diphtheria—or at least a prevention measure of some sort—but she couldn't remember any more than that. She turned and went back inside.

"Ma," Melissa called from the kitchen, "we're almost out of flour."

"Ma, I'm going over to Benny's for a couple

hours, all right?" Cap in hand, Gilbert was heading for the door.

"No!"

Gilbert stopped cold and stared. "But, Ma! You *always* let me go over to Benny's!"

"Read this and come to the parlor." Anji stuffed the paper into his hand and marched on to the kitchen. "Melissa, bring the children to the parlor."

Melissa frowned, dropped the spoon she was holding, and hurried off toward the stairs.

Anji sat down in her favorite rocker by the parlor fireplace and tried to compose herself. How must she approach this? Diphtheria. She must think.

The children gathered around her, the little ones sitting on the floor. Melissa on the settee was reading the letter Gilbert had handed her.

Anji looked from child to child. "Some people on the circus train have diphtheria, and the doctors are afraid the disease will spread to the people who live in Blessing. Diphtheria is an extremely serious disease. It is painful and miserable for anyone who catches it, and some people die. Some people who recover have damaged nerves and cannot use their hands or feet the way they used to. If I am frightening you, I mean to. This disease can be deadly. You will not leave the yard at any time. None of you. Do you understand?"

Gilbert looked worried. "Then can Benny come here? Please?"

"No. You catch the disease from people who have the disease, and that person may not even know he is sick yet." She stared directly at the little ones. "If one of you catches it, you can give it to your brother or sisters before you realize you have it. That is why it is so dangerous."

"But we'll still go to church, right?"

"No. We'll go nowhere. Not until the doctors say it is safe to mingle with other people again."

Melissa shook her head. "But we'll need groceries. We need flour. And the cheese is low, and we were going to have chicken tonight. And what about the buttons for my pinafore?"

"I will go alone to the store and post office," Anji said. "But you children should never ever leave the yard. Will you promise that?"

She got solemn nods in return.

Melissa sighed. "Johnny Solberg was going to take me to see the elephants! He gets to visit the elephants. He helps Manny take care of them. What makes him so special?"

"From now on, I'm sure, he'll have to stay home. This paper came this afternoon, so the quarantine, that is, the need to stay home, is something new."

Joseph whined, "But this is summer. I want to go out to the farm, and go fishing, and—"

"No one likes this. But believe me, you don't want diphtheria. We will stay until it is safe to leave. You may go play."

Under a pall of misery, the little ones climbed to their feet and walked back to the stairs.

Gilbert took his hat and slapped it on his knee. "How long, do you know?"

"I have no idea, but I'll try to find out. Melissa, what do we need at the store besides flour, cheese, and the chicken?"

"I think maybe butter. I'll go check the potatoes and turnips." She went out to the kitchen.

Anji drew a deep breath. *Dear Lord, protect us!*

Melissa wrote out a list while Anji got her purse. With a final "Remember. Stay in the yard," she went to the store. There was a stillness in the streets, as if everyone were trying to avoid awakening someone. People talked in low tones with lots of wagging heads. She heard angry comments about the circus. This was not the friendly, lighthearted Blessing she knew.

Was there anything she could do to ease her children's sequester? When she passed Rebecca's soda shop, she smiled, turned back, and went in.

Rebecca grinned. "Hello, Anji."

"Good afternoon. I'm surprised you are

open. But since you are, I'd like a carton of strawberry ice cream, please."

She frowned. "Is that going to be enough? I'm closing as soon as the ice cream I have made is gone."

"It's for cheering up, not fattening up."

"Ah." Rebecca dipped her scoop in a bowl of water. "I'm sure it's frustrating having to stay home when school is out."

"That's what I hear. Such long faces. Do you have any idea when this will end?"

"I don't think anyone knows. I surely don't."

"But you hear everything sooner or later. Have you heard anything new?"

"Well, let's see." Rebecca scooped some pink ice cream into a container. "The doctors seem to think that once you've had the disease, you won't get it again. So your fellow teacher and swain, Mr. Devlin, has become a nurse right on the train. He says he had diphtheria as a child. Immune or not, it's a brave thing to do. And apparently he can be right there to pray the prayers for the dying, like Reverend Solberg."

"Yes, I heard he does that. And I agree he's very brave. But then, he's that sort of man. So are Thorliff and Daniel Jeffers." Anji put her money on the counter.

Rebecca handed her the ice cream. "We are so fortunate to have good people like that. Hug the children for me. In fact, I think after this is all over, I may give a free cone to each child who was good about staying home."

"What a lovely idea!" Anji said good-bye and headed home. She dropped the ice cream off and told Melissa to serve it with cookies. "I still need to go to Garrisons'."

Back on the street, her mind reverted to her conversation with Rebecca. Brave? Indeed. Useful? Constantly. She thought of the many times Thomas Devlin had helped her, something as simple as holding her coat or as difficult as getting a stuck window to open. Like Thorliff, like Daniel, like John Solberg, Thomas Devlin was a truly gentle, truly great man.

She was so lost in thought she almost walked right into a passing horse. She stopped. "Oh! I'm sorry!"

The rider was Manny. He drew his horse to a halt and tipped his hat. "G'afternoon, Miz Moen. Have you seen our elephants?"

"No, I've not been beyond the mill lately."

"No, ma'am. I don't mean where they're s'posed to be, I mean where they mighta wandered off to. They didn't get chained up right, and they walked away, looking for forage, I guess. We take them down to the river. They like to wade around in the water and eat on the willows, but they're not by the river now. Oh, and hey, please don't let your children play down on the river bottom. There's a pack of dogs down there—some pretty nasty beasts. I don't think they'd hurt a child, but you don't know. You can't trust dogs what ain't your own, especially in a pack."

"Thank you. I'll remember. The children are not supposed to go down there anyway. And I heard you have been helping with the elephants. My children are jealous. They would love to help with elephants."

He grinned. "It's more fun than you think, even the shoveling. I didn't ever think I could do it, but Mr. Devlin says I have happytude and I could. So I tried and, well, I can!"

"Happytude. Aptitude?"

"That's it! Anyhow, now I'm taking care of the elephants and even the chimp and the big cats. You know—the lion and the tiger. And the camel. I don't care for camels, but it needs tending, so I do it. It's grand!"

She laughed; the happiness in his eyes was infectious. "I can tell. If I hear anything about your elephants, I'll call the mill."

"Thank you, Miz Moen." He touched his hat brim again and rode off.

She watched him as he continued on. His bad leg would never be normal, that was for sure, but he could certainly sit a horse well. He and his horse, Joker, moved together smoothly, as one. No doubt he was good with any animals, even elephants and camels. Happytude. She smiled.

And Thomas Devlin. She smiled again,

even wider. The man was such a constant encouragement to all the children at school, the ones in his classes and everyone else as well. That was so important for growing children. And all the children loved him in return.

That was Anji's main criterion for rating any person, but a man especially. What do children and animals think of that person? True, good dogs sometimes were loyal to quite bad people. Possibly if that was their master, they were loyal more than loving. But usually, children and dogs were excellent indicators. And children and dogs—even the boardinghouse cat—all flocked to Thomas Devlin.

And what about Anji? Her dead husband's mother, Anji's spiteful and bitter mother-in-law . . . Did death break that bond? Mrs. Moen certainly didn't think so. She regularly sent small sums of money to help support her dead son's children. That was good. Anji needed those funds. But the mother-in-law insisted that if Anji so much as looked at another man, a new man, Mrs. Moen would cut off all money. Every cent of support.

As she neared Garrisons', she got angrier and angrier. The money was meant to support the children, not Anji. Whatever Anji did, the children were still Mrs. Moen's grandchildren. Shame on that angry woman. And that's what she was. Angry, as if Anji were somehow responsible for her son's death. Bitter was the best word.

Shame on you, Anji Baard Moen! Shame! The woman watched her grandchildren, the only thing she had left of her son, get on a ship and sail thousands of miles away. Of course she would be frantic. Be charitable! If you were in her shoes, would you not be just as likely to mourn and try to hang on to the children?

She did her shopping and headed back to her children. As she approached her home, her new home, she thought again warmly about how much God had blessed her. Here was a fine house with plenty of room for her and the children, a good stove, good outbuildings— good everything. Just think of all those who had brought cleaning supplies and worked all day to help to bring it back to being livable. And look. When her family needed more food, she simply put some money in her purse and went out to obtain that food without scrimping. Of course she was careful, but there was no true lack. She'd known many a time growing up when they'd had little food and scarcer money. The grocery basket she was carrying was heavy with good things. Her children had clothes to wear, a sheltering home, plenty to eat. She and her children were so blessed!

And for some strange reason, Thomas Devlin came back to mind. He did that a lot— intruded on her other thoughts. She didn't mean to think about him. He just sort of jumped into her head when she wasn't expecting it.

She loved his dry wit, that thick Irish brogue, the lilt in his voice. Did he ever feel sad or sorrowful? He must. Every human being did; but Anji had never seen it. He was just naturally pleasant. Positive in outlook.

He was industrious, and yet he still made time to be of good use to people who could not repay his kindnesses. In fact, he did not let a little thing like a potentially lethal illness keep him from helping others. What would it be like to be married to the jovial Irishman? Again she smiled. Yes, he was a priest, but he and others had assured her that in his Anglican faith a priest could marry. Indeed, he said, nearly all of them did, including the bishops. So he was, so to speak, available.

Available? Shame again, Anji Baard Moen! Listen to you! A wanton hussy!

But no, that wasn't it. He took care of what was his; he showed that plainly. Just as Thorliff and Daniel did. If she were his, he would take care of her. And likewise, Anji took care of what was hers. She had been devoted to her husband, and she was devoted to her children. Were she to marry again, she would do her best to serve him, to take care of him. In short, they would make a good pair, helping each other. And the children would have a complete home again.

Yes, she would lose the money Mrs. Moen sent. No doubt the woman would try to make the children, her grandchildren, return to

Norway. Could she do that legally? Surely not. And the money did not mean as much as having a good stable man in the family would mean.

If Mr. Devlin were to court her—several friends had mentioned that they thought that was his intent—how should she respond? Many people, especially people in Norway, would say she had to wait for the full period of mourning before even thinking about remarrying. But they were in Norway, where all the rules of life were carefully spelled out. Not here in North Dakota. Here, life was lived precariously, and a woman alone was at a severe disadvantage. Here, if you did not raise enough food to live through the winter, you starved. You maintained a good solid house and a decent woodpile or you froze. You had to stand ready to help your neighbors when tragedy struck, as they would gather to help you. She loved living here so much more than in Norway.

So what if Mr. Devlin did warm up to her? As she thought about it, how should she receive his attention? How would she respond if he chose to court her? Favorably. Yes. For sure. She would much rather have him than the approval of a demanding woman on a different continent. She would much rather have him than Mrs. Moen's money. Closeness. Love. A helpmeet in a harsh land. Mutual affection. Happiness. How she missed all that! And to go through life married to this man? She blinked at the rushing of her thoughts. Where had all that come from? *Anji, Anji,* she chided herself, *you are wasting your time and . . .* She paused and closed her eyes, feeling a smile start inside and bloom on her face. A life with Thomas Devlin? Absolutely wonderful! She looked around. If anyone was watching her, they would think she'd gone daft. *Get on home, you silly woman.*

She had nearly reached her front gate when she heard wild laughter out back. What were the children doing that was so entertaining? She left the heavy grocery basket on the steps and walked around to the back yard.

Gilbert and Annika, laughing uproariously, were patting a fuzzy baby elephant. The baby was obviously loving every moment of it, swinging its trunk to this child, to that one. Melissa and Joseph were cautiously laying their hands on the mother elephant, feeling her skin, stroking her cheek, reaching high to pat her shoulder.

And the mother elephant was tearing at Anji's newly trimmed shrubbery.

"MAN-NY!"

Devlin watched Dr. Astrid count the medicine glasses in the dispensary closet.

She turned to him. "Do you think a dozen are enough?"

"Aye, unless, of course, ye happen to have thirteen patients."

She half smiled, and that pleased him immensely. Lately, she hardly ever smiled. And her face looked so drawn.

He offered, "I raided the kitchen car on the train, and I think we have enough there. They not be marked glasses with which to measure dosage exactly, but they be about the same size. They'll serve. Use one graduated glass to measure with and the train's glasses to serve the medicine in. So I suggest ye can dismiss the needs on the train. Yer main concern is to have enough for the hospital, particularly if new patients come in."

"Not *if,* Mr. Devlin. *When.* I am terrified that the disease will spread into the town. So many of our people are vulnerable. And the children . . ." That was not mere worry or concern in her eyes. That was cold fear.

"Mayhap I can go out around town and round up some more."

"Yes, would you, please? And spoons. We are very low on spoons."

"How about rubbing alcohol? Miriam mentioned she's low on alcohol."

"We're low on everything." Dr. Astrid flopped down into a chair. "You have a good idea of our needs and what we have. And you have a better idea of what's available in the train than we do. Can you go out and find as much as you can for us? Even if we're not out of something but you think we will be, get more."

He chuckled. "An Irishman above all is a forager. We be grand at scrounging. I shall do me best."

"Take the wheelbarrow in our backyard."

"The very thing! I shall return as rapidly as I can." He walked out into the sun and fresh air, away from the smell of misery and death. Once upon a time when he was young, he was torn between choosing a life in medicine and the life of a priest. He occasionally regretted the choice he had made, but not today. He would have failed miserably as a doctor. He hadn't the heart or the stamina for it. This nursing job was bad enough. How those women could be doctors day after day after day, he could not understand.

For one thing, he had a headache. It wasn't a massive headache such as he very occasionally got, with pounding temples. Just a . . . a . . . *O God, no!* He crossed himself rapidly. What if he was getting sick? And here he was waltzing about town as if he were the king of Spain. He himself could be the person who triggered Dr. Astrid's deepest fear by spreading the pestilence out into the town. And yet they desperately needed supplies. He stood there for a moment.

It was probably just an ordinary headache, to which he was frequently prone. But what if . . . Sore throat? No. But that meant nothing—yet. What to do?

He got the wheelbarrow in the Jeffers' backyard, waved to Amelia, and trundled it down to the general store. Spoons. They had an unopened carton of spoons. No glasses, but he could try at the boardinghouse. Good idea. Rubbing alcohol? Two bottles. He bought both. He noticed they had towels, and the laundry at the hospital could not keep up with towels. He bought all they had.

His wheelbarrow was pretty much filled. Rather than risk dropping something over the side, he would return to the hospital, empty the barrow, and go back out foraging.

His headache was getting worse. Was he doing the right thing? He noticed in his ministrations on the train that diphtheria clouds the ability to make good decisions. He might be making a fatally wrong one right now.

Confusion and determination struggled with each other.

And suddenly, the worst thing in the world occurred: Anji Moen was coming across the street toward him, aiming herself straight at him with her shopping basket on her arm, smiling that glorious incandescent smile. Anji!

God knows he had not been honest with her. Never had he told her how he craved her presence or how she lit up his world simply by appearing. Never had he admitted to her that he thought about her so much. Or how bashful this mature man became in her radiant presence. He was afraid to tell her he secretly adored her, for fear she might laugh. He had remained somewhat aloof from her—as much as he could—because she sometimes seemed aloof from him.

And now she was aiming herself right at him. She stopped before him. "Good afternoon, Mr. Devlin."

"And the top of the day to yerself, Mrs. Moen." What if he was infectious? Remote chance, but a chance, no matter how unlikely. He could give her the disease, then she would give it to her delightful children, and one or more of the family might die, and it would all be because he . . . what could he do?

Get away from her! He must, for her sake. He touched the brim of his hat. "Mrs. Moen, I must . . ." *I must stop being tongue-tied. I can't think.* No! He didn't want to, but he must, for her sake. For her children.

She looked at him quizzically.

"Mrs. Moen, I cannot see you. Good-bye." He pivoted the wheelbarrow around so violently that one of the bottles of alcohol fell off. It shattered.

He glanced back. She had lost both the smile and the quizzical look. Now she appeared ready to cry.

For her sake, leave! He walked as fast as he could, his headache ringing, the wheelbarrow bumping and rattling. He parked it at the back door of the hospital and jogged to his little room on the train. He sank to sit on his bed, cradled his aching head in his hands, and wept.

CHAPTER 18

*A*h, *Devlin, me lad, sure and ye've slept under some mighty strange skies, but this one beats all.*" Thomas Devlin lay on his back studying the low ceiling above him. Bright red greeted him, and yellow trim around the sides. He knew that these train cars were painted just as gaudily inside as out. Well, some of them were. Some were also quite staid on the inside, with tasteful, muted colors. The dawn sun pouring in his window turned the red and yellow into fire and gold.

He rose, tugged his bedding into some sort of tidiness, tended to personal matters, and walked out into the passageway. He had long ago learned that sleeping in his clothes made answering an emergency during the night much easier. And those emergencies happened constantly on this beleaguered little train.

He stopped at B compartment in the fourth car, rapped quietly at the door, and stepped inside.

The middle-aged man in the bed by the window turned his head to Devlin. "I think he's dead, Padre. He won't talk to me."

Devlin knelt by the foot of the man's bed, where a boy of perhaps eleven or twelve lay. They were having to stack people two to a bed, head to foot, so many were ill. The boy did not respond to his touch. Devlin murmured, "Violet's been asking for ye, lad." No response. He spoke louder, "Michael?" He stood up. "I'll take him out to the tent, Mr. Mason. He's still breathing, so there be hope."

"No hope in this old man's heart." Mr. Mason coughed.

Best to get the vital data, for the lad's tombstone. "How old did ye say he be?"

"Twelve in August. August fourth. He looks older than he is."

"Aye, that he does. And handling a man's responsibilities too. Fine lad. Can I get anything for yerself before I go?"

The fellow wagged his head, his eyes closed, and coughed some more.

Devlin rearranged the man's covers, gathered the boy in his arms, and left. The warm, bright, welcome sun hit him in the face as he left the car and carried Michael Mason over to a tent the circus had pitched behind the mill. He stepped inside and, keeping his voice hushed, asked, "Free cot?"

Miriam gestured with a wave of her arm. "Three in that corner." She was speaking softly as well. She followed behind. "Is this boy alive?"

Devlin laid the limp body on the cot. "Nae, and I've committed a sin." He stood erect and crossed himself. "I just lied to a sick old man and told him the lad is still breathing."

Miriam knelt beside the boy's head, felt for a pulse, and held her cheek close to the open mouth. "No signs of life, but he cannot have been dead for long. He's still quite flexible. We've had two that revived after we thought they'd died, so it isn't a complete lie yet." She tucked the sheet in around the lad and stood up.

"Is that Mike?" In the quiet of the tent, the voice boomed. Manny stood in the doorway!

Devlin hurried to the boy and piloted him outside. "Ye surely saw the flyers that told ye not to come around here."

"Is that Mike?!"

"Aye."

"And his pa is sick, right?"

"Aye."

"So who's taking care of the elephants? Mike and his pa, they were the elephant keepers."

"And how would ye know that now?"

"I come round here all the time. I never seen elephants before, and they're amazing. Mike and Mr. Mason, they were showing me how they take care of them. That's amazing too. Who's taking care of them now?"

Devlin studied him. "That's a question to answer later. For now, I know not what to do with yerself. Ye've been exposed to the disease, so I cannot in good conscience send ye home, but on the other hand . . ."

"Somebody gotta take care of the elephants. Who?" Manny was getting strident.

Devlin sighed. "Let's go find out."

Manny took off toward the menagerie wagons at a run. "Slow down!" Devlin yelled, and the boy slowed from a gallop to a jog. Devlin was winded by the time they arrived at a great stout car. From one of the cars they passed, a lion roared.

"Anyone here?" Manny called. No answer. He grabbed a huge door bolt on the car's sliding door, not your average bolt a few inches long to lock a door. This one was a foot long at least and over an inch in diameter. He managed to slide it free.

"Are ye sure we not be letting something loose that should not be loose?" But Devlin might as well have saved his breath. In a wild lurch, Manny shoved the sliding door open and hopped up inside. Devlin climbed up behind him. It took a long moment for his eyes to adjust

from the bright summer sun to this gloom.
This was the elephants' home, but the three
were crowded pretty close. Wedged off in one
corner, a camel brayed. A genuine ship of the
desert. What an exotic, enchanting milieu.

"Mr. Devlin, ain't no hay here at all. This
here bin, it's supposed to be full of hay for them,
and there ain't none! They're gonna starve!
Elephants hafta have hay! They can't just graze
like the horses and goats do. And the horses and
stuff ain't been let out today either. They're still
all locked up. And there ain't no hay at all!"

"Stop!" Devlin barked it so loudly, Violet's ears flapped forward. Manny wheeled and
stared at him. "Ye're panicking, son, and panic
does nobody good. Ye cannot think when ye're
panicky. Take a deep breath. Get yer wits and
yer nerves settled, then we'll solve this problem."

Manny actually did that, sucking in a deep
breath. "What can we do? They gotta eat!"

"Aye, as do we all." Devlin spotted a milking
stool in the near darkness, dragged it nearer the
door, and sat down. "Let's think. Where might
we find fodder? Does it have to be a particular
kind of hay? Alfalfa or timothy? Indeed, does
it have to be hay? Can they eat other things?"

As Manny stared at him, his panic seemed
to subside. He bit his lip, then sat down on the
floor near Devlin's feet. He drew his knees up
and draped his arms over them. "I'm trying

to remember. Mr. Mason told about one time they turned the elephants out into a field that had some baby cottonwood trees. You know, just young ones. So Violet, she put a front leg on each side of a tree and took a step forward, and then another step forward, and another, and she rode it clear to the ground. Bent that tree clean over. Then she and the other two elephants—Fluff wasn't born yet—could reach the leaves and stripped them all off." He looked up. "Yeah. I guess they can eat most any kind of plants, but they don't eat meat. Mr. Mason said no meat."

"Good. Now let's think some more. The farmers around here don't have much hay left from winter, and the first cutting is not for a week or two yet. But there are those willow thickets down on the river. Do ye think elephants might abide willow?"

Manny brightened. "I could go cut some willow limbs and bring 'em up here, try 'em and see if the elephants like 'em."

"Excellent plan!" Devlin stood up. "Ye go do that, and meself shall make some phone calls. Is your knife sharp enough to cut willow withes?"

"Yes, sir! Grandpa Haakan, he showed me how to keep it sharp." Manny hopped down out of the car and ran off.

Devlin paused to smile. *Grandpa Haakan.* Ingeborg had told him about the lad's initial hostility and how much he was growing. Growing indeed! He even had a worthy grandpa to emulate now. He climbed down, walked over to the mill, and entered the office.

"Mr. Devlin!" Mr. Wiste stood up. "How is it going out there?"

"Top of the morning to ye, sir. Might I use yer phone?"

"You may." The man stepped aside.

Devlin rang for the operator. "Top of the morning, Gerald. Might I speak with Ingeborg Bjorklund? Thank ye." He waited. When Ingeborg answered she sounded tense, worried. No wonder. "Ingeborg, yer Manny is here with the circus and will not go home. So far he seems well and lively. How be yerself?"

She sighed. "I thought that was where he'd be. He is fascinated by the elephants. Ja, he should definitely stay there." She added, "Oh, and Freda and I are fine so far too. Thank you."

"Excellent. Now, we've a situation here that ye may be able to help with. There not be enough circus folk to properly care for the animals. I have the thought that we could turn the grazing stock out in nearby pastures. Let others tend them. 'Twould relieve the circus of some of its burden. What think ye?"

Silence for a while. Then, "Ja, I'm certain we can take care of that. With the sheep and calves, I don't have pasturage here on my farm for all of them. But the other farmers around,

I'm sure, can help. The goats, are they milking some of them?"

"Sure. But not regularly, I fear. And there be two cows, a Jersey and an Alderney. They provide the fresh milk for everyone in the circus, as I understand it."

"Alderney." She chuckled. "We call them Guernseys around here. Can you find someone to milk the cows there? Regularly, I mean."

"We can try."

"No, I have another idea. If we milk the cows and goats, we can give the people there as much milk as they need, then buy up the rest and give them the money. I can use the extra milk in the cheese house, and I'm sure they can use the money. They must be canceling so many shows."

"Ah, Ingeborg," Devlin purred, "'twould be the perfect solution. Let me talk to Mr. Stetler." *But believe me, Ingeborg, I do not want to, that liar. 'Twill be a hard thing.* He did not say that out loud.

"And you're sure Manny is all right?"

"So far, aye. He be muckle fine, that young man. He is tending the big cats and chimp as well."

"I'm sure he would love that."

Devlin continued, "Now I'm thinking about the seals. The circus has two seals. I believe they're referred to as sea lions, technically, though I've no notion of the difference.

No matter; they all eat fish. We need a source of fish."

"Oh my! The boys would love to go fishing every day and supply the seals with fish, and the girls too. Emmy is a very good fisherman. Fishergirl." She paused. "Thomas, the circus is a disaster in the middle of Blessing and could bring death. But the bright spot is the children will love helping the animals. We have to keep the bright spots in mind." Despite the upbeat note, her voice sounded so weary.

Weariness? Dread. That was what he was hearing. Dread. And he shared it. So many ill, so many dying, and it was far from over. "Aye, we must do that."

Her voice firmed up. "I will arrange to take the grazing stock and see about regular milking." She chuckled again. "And send the children out fishing. And you are going to confirm all this with Mr. Stetler, is that right?"

"That is right. Thank ye from the depths of me heart, Ingeborg." They exchanged good-byes and he hung up.

By his shoulder, Mr. Wiste said, "I could hear what she was saying. A fine plan, Mr. Devlin, but what if Mr. Stetler won't cooperate? What if he says no?"

Devlin thought about what the sheriff, Charlie Becker, had said. *"Bjorklund, I'm sworn to protect the citizens, and the citizens' lives were at stake. I didn't need any legal basis. I did it."*

There were times to use tact, and there were times to take the bull by the horns. "He'll have no choice." He headed for the door.

He would check the menagerie first. The lion roared when he passed that car. As he approached the elephants' car, Manny came leaping out, and he was jubilant. "Mr. Devlin, they love the willow! Gobbled it right up. I'm going out to cut some more."

"Splendid! And when ye've finished, might ye look in on the cats? How often do the tiger and lion eat, do ye know?"

Manny studied the ground. "I'm trying to remember. I don't know. The cat keeper—he takes care of the chimp and seals too—hasn't been by today that I see. Is he sick too?"

"I'll make sure, but if he's not been by, probably he is. Can yerself tend to them?"

"I'll have to talk to him and see what they need. And how much. Mr. Devlin, I could get sick too, right? Being around here so close to everyone."

"That is right."

"And I could die."

"Quite possible, aye."

Manny studied him. One could almost see the wheels turning. "But the animals are helpless. They need stuff—food and cleaning up after. And if there ain't nobody to do it, and I can do it, I'm bound to stay here and do it, I think. Right?"

Devlin swelled with pride. This young man was not his, would never be, but look at him! Devlin laid a hand on his shoulder. "Manasseh, lad, ye're wise and brave beyond yer years. Aye, go cut the willow." The lad—no, not a lad anymore—ran off with his crazy limping gait.

"Father Devlin?" Miriam said as she approached him. "We've three people who are asking for blessings and prayers, as they fear they are dying."

"Thank ye, lass." Devlin walked to the tent. Miriam led him to a cot with a fairly young man.

The fellow turned to look at him. "You're a real priest?"

"As real as they get." He would not tell the fellow that he was Anglican instead of Catholic, as if that were important at the moment. He would simply use the Latin, surely familiar to the man. "What be yer role with the circus?"

"I'm a clown in the first part and after intermission I'm the lion tamer. And I take care of the cats and seals."

"Excellent. We have a young man taking over yer duties with the cats and all—not with the clowning. After we perform this service, Miriam, perhaps ye will take notes as he tells ye what needs doing in regard to the animals in his care."

"You'll take care of them?" the fellow asked brightening. "Really?"

"But not as well as ye do, for we not be experienced. So yer first duty is to get well, that ye might take over again." Devlin pulled out the little vial of holy oil that hung on a cord around his neck. "And now I remind ye, as we begin, these prayers be no death sentence. I've performed it many a time on people who then got well. 'Tis a precaution and no more. Ye understand?"

"Yes, Father."

Devlin had been doing this so much of late that he could recite it in his sleep. He had to fight to keep interest, to keep inflections, to keep it from sounding like a recitation by a bored man.

This clown and cat keeper relaxed, half smiled.

Devlin finished the prayer. "Remember, sir, ye're to get well so that the animals prosper. Now tell Miriam here what ye need of the young man filling yer place." He went on to the two who had died. Two today so far, three yesterday. Were they over the hump?

And what about this young man who was the elephant keeper's son? His eyes were closed but not sunken. His muscles were not stiffening. As dead as he seemed, he apparently was still alive, barely. On impulse, Devlin prayed the prayers over him. Then laying both hands on the boy, begged for healing, not only for him, but all those ill. *Lord, help us. Please show us your mercy.*

And now he had the most difficult task of all—speaking with that Mr. Stetler.

But first, to avoid the inevitable just a wee bit longer, he stopped again by the menagerie. The goats and horses had been turned out to pasture. He heard seals barking in one of the cars. The lion roared in another.

"Patience, King of the Jungle, patience. Soon as we learn what to do, ye will be fed and cosseted like the royalty ye are."

Manny was trundling a wheelbarrow of elephant excrement down the ramp of the elephant car. He was sweating. And grinning. He lowered the barrow and stood up straight. "Mr. Devlin, I wouldn'ta guessed this part would be fun. You know, that Violet stepped aside and got out of the way so I could shovel out her place. Elephants are smart. Way smart!"

"And so be elephant keepers. Ye're doing fine. Go see Nurse Miriam. She is interviewing the cat keeper."

"Then I better go listen!" Manny ran off before Devlin could tell him not to. But then, so what? The lad had already been exposed a dozen times over. Either he would get sick or not. Going into the infirmary tent wouldn't change anything.

Here was the manager-owner's private car. *Owen Stetler* was lettered on the door. Devlin rapped briefly, paused, and went in.

Mr. Stetler turned and looked at him from a big oak rolltop desk. "Can I help you?"

"My name be Thomas Devlin."

Mr. Stetler stood up. "Devlin. Devlin. My cat keeper said he needed the services of a Father Devlin. Would that be you?"

"The very same. I just came from there, and the matter be all taken care of. I wish to discuss with ye the welfare of yer animals."

The man stiffened, frowned. "I'm not particularly a man of faith, so I have no idea what he needed from you, but I doubt it had to do with animal welfare. I mean, a priest . . ."

"This has naught to do with that."

"Uh, be seated." Mr. Stetler motioned toward a chair, so Devlin took it. Stetler sat back in his desk chair. "Now. What's going on?"

"Ye'll not be leaving anytime soon, we believe, so the local farmers are ready to take in yer grazing animals temporarily. They'll keep them milked, fed, watered. Ye'll get all the milk ye need, and the farmers will buy the rest. We've a cheese house in town, quite a good one."

"You mean disperse my stock? Those are extremely expensive animals, even the goats. Carefully trained to do tricks, you know. And the horses are worth thousands. No, I think not. They stay here."

"The pasture where ye turn them out is

eaten down already. 'Twill not support them much longer. And the elephants require hay, which ye do not have."

"No. We'll make do, but . . . no. Absolutely not."

"Mr. Stetler, I give ye this, which ye already know. Ye need us desperately. But we do not need *you*. At all. Indeed, there be a strong move afoot to pile yer sick back into the train and drive ye out of here."

"No." The man smirked and shook his head. "No, the good people of Blessing would not do that. No one with an ounce of Christian charity would do that."

"I am assured the folks of Grafton have no less Christian charity than anyone else, but they sent ye away."

Stetler lost that smirk. His face went flat. "You don't know that."

"Aye, we know that, and we know yer perfidy. Grafton not be the only town that refused ye. And ye endangered the whole of Blessing by stopping here. That we know well."

"Only for a little while, until our sick get better. And we'll take care of our animals, not you strangers."

"And whom will ye put to that task?"

"That will be my concern and mine alone. I'm in charge. No. Your people are not going to run off with my stock! That's final. Why, you could take all our milk for yourselves—in fact, all the animals. Butcher them. Sell them. What a lovely opportunity to enrich yourselves at the circus's expense! You can rob us blind and no recourse for us. The animals will not leave my control. Do you understand? And the townspeople will not interfere with their care. No. That's the end of it. Now, I believe we're done here." He stood up.

Time to play the priest card, Devlin. He stood up too. "I beg to differ. Who will care for yer sick and bury the dead? Ye toss 'Christian charity' about so free. 'Tis our charity ye need."

"I said—"

Devlin pressed forward. "And 'tis not just the priestly duties ye need. Yer stock are starving. I've seen for meself that yer hayricks are empty, yer people ill abed. And where will ye find the forage, the fish for yer seals, the people to clean up the dung? If the town withdraws, we will indeed send ye on yer way. Then when yer stock starves to death, or God forbid, yer people die, ye'll have nothing. By not trusting us, ye will lose it all, Mr. Stetler. Ye cannot afford to distrust us, not now."

Stetler wagged his head.

Devlin softened his voice as he moved toward the door. "Aye, it might well be that we are crooks and shysters who will strip ye of everything ye own. We ask that ye trust us, but if we intended to prey upon ye, 'tis exactly what we'd say. But it could also be that we be willing to risk our lives to serve our God. Ye see, Mr. Stetler, we don't do this Christian charity to serve yerself. We serve God, and He said that in serving the least of these—which be yerself, I aver—we serve Him. Nay, ye cannot trust us. But 'tis time to give us the benefit of the doubt."

Stetler looked stricken. "I don't want to lose this."

"And we don't want suffering and death if it be within us to prevent it. We will look well after yer livestock. And after yer people. Good day, sir, and God's best to ye."

He left.

CHAPTER 19

The symptoms show up anywhere from two to seven days after exposure." Astrid looked right at each of the gathered group in the hospital. "If you get a sore throat or start to cough, you have to tell me. Promise?" Coughing would be obvious but not the other symptoms. They all nodded. "We are counting on you to not try to play the hero."

She nodded to her head nurse. "Deborah, you have a schedule for us."

Looking as tired as all the others, Deborah held up a piece of paper. "We all have to get rest to stay strong, so I've moved everyone into shifts." She read off the schedule, then said, "I will post this on the bulletin board in Astrid's office. That is the only room now without at least a pallet in it. We will use the beds at the far end in the new ward. Just to remind everyone, none of us may leave the hospital, other than to work on the train. But with Thomas Devlin and Mr. Sidorov working out there . . ." She nodded to Sandra and Abigail, the two student nurses who had been inoculated. "You will be sharing the shifts. Thank you all for your dedication. We are saving lives."

"Thank you." Astrid drew in a deep breath. "Now back to work. Make sure you eat too. You have to keep your strength up to be able to help others." *O Lord, how I wish Mor were here.*

Sandy paused in the doorway. "By the way, we are out of cough syrup again."

"I'll telephone Mor and Freda." *We are about out of laudanum to mix with it too.* Was there possibly any whiskey in town? That would help cut the mucus too. Thoughts, horrible thoughts, bombarded her, clamoring to take over, fear and anger and beyond it all, a weariness not only of body but of mind and soul. *Oh, Mor, I need you. Lord, my mind says you are here in the midst of all of this, but the rest of me is screaming. No, I've not even the energy to scream but despair. Help us, Lord God. You said you would.*

Mrs. Geddick stepped in the door. "I got ten chickens. But we will need more."

"I'll call Mary Martha and have her find more. It'll take two days at least if we order them from a supplier."

"Dr. Astrid, we need you—stat." The call came from the examining room.

Please, Lord, not another trach. Get those intubation supplies here. And I thought we were well prepared for any emergency. She pushed the door open, hearing the coughing before she stepped through. A boy lay on the table, his swollen neck clamping down his ability to breathe. She used a tongue depressor and turned his head to the light. Sure enough, the telltale gray membrane covered part of his tonsils but had not grown over his esophagus. He was not *in extremis* sufficiently to warrant a trach.

She looked up at Miriam's sister Mercy, standing by his head. The dear girl had volunteered to come in and help since she had already had a mild case of diphtheria when she was younger. "I thought we were not bringing any more in from the train but treating them out there."

"I know, but they didn't think there was sufficient light out there to do a trach if we needed to."

"Let's clean him up and pack his neck in ice. Do we have a name for him?"

"No, Mr. Sidorov carried him in and rushed right out again. His English was so broken I couldn't understand him."

Astrid shook the boy's shoulder. "Can you hear me?"

He nodded, his eyes fluttering at least partway open.

"I have something here for you to drink. We'll hold you up enough to swallow. You have to swallow it, no matter how much it hurts. Do you understand?" Astrid held her hand out for the cup of warm honey, vinegar, and willow bark water. "Is the steam room ready?"

"We have three patients in there now."

"Room for another?" Astrid slid her arm under the boy's shoulders and held the cup to his swollen lips. "Drink." He slowly and slightly moved his head from side to side, the liquid draining out the side of his mouth. "Spoon it in." She shook the boy again. "You have to swallow. Now!"

While she held the patient, Mercy spooned in the concoction.

"Good for you. More." She looked to her assistant. "You might have to follow in your sister's footsteps; you're getting plenty of training already. We need to get some nourishment into him too—no telling when he last ate."

"Mrs. Geddick has the chickens cooking for broth. It will be a while."

"We are all out?"

"Sorry."

"Forgive me for being short. Clean him up and move him into the steam room." They had moved a small stove into one room and had kettles of water boiling with eucalyptus oil and menthol in them. Breathing steam was an old remedy to aid breathing, but it was helping.

If her mor ran out of herbs, they would have another mountain to climb. Were there others in Blessing who gathered herbs too? Perhaps Amelia.

Deborah stuck her head in the door. "Astrid, we need you."

Once in the hall, Astrid asked, "What now?"

"That baby girl is not going to last much longer, I'm afraid."

Astrid followed Deborah to the crib where two little ones shared the space. Gretchen was there speaking calming words to the babies. Astrid didn't need her stethoscope to tell her how bad it was. The blue lips and fingers told the story. *Lord, what can I do? Help us, help us.* She smoothed the dark hair back from the little forehead, then reached down and picked up the baby. Rocking her in her arms, she whispered more prayers. The mother was too sick to care for her little one, but surely someone could hold her. No baby should die alone in a crib.

"Let me hold her; you are needed in room one." Gretchen held out her arms.

"Thank you." If only Mor were there to help. Astrid knew her mother was praying, as were many others, but somehow her presence always brought peace into a room. And gave strength and comfort to the suffering. Right now she needed a hug from her mother as much as any of the patients did. A hug and a shoulder to cry on. She stepped into the room that was normally for one patient. A gray-haired man lay in the bed, and three other pallets took up most of the floor. Was every child on the train affected?

Abigail stood beside him. "I think his trach is plugged."

"Get me a syringe. We'll suction it out." With Abigail holding the tube in place, Astrid inserted the syringe with no needle in the tube and drew out a small glob of cloudy mucus. Squirting that into a pan, she repeated the action three times. *If only I had more supplies.* When the antitoxin and intubation supplies arrived tomorrow, they'd go around and insert as many as needed. Anything to keep the airway open until the body could fight off the infection.

"He's better."

"I see that. Get these sterilized right away." They were keeping a kettle boiling with carbolic acid in it. Had someone said they were low on that too? Astrid brushed her hair back with the back of her hand.

"When did you sleep last?" Deborah asked.

Astrid shrugged.

"Go lie down—now."

Astrid bit her lip to keep from snapping back. "What about Elizabeth? She's been out on that train for hours."

"No, she slept for three hours. She should

have slept longer, but she's eating in the kitchen right now."

"I'll stop and check with her." She looked her head nurse in the eye. "What is the body count?"

Deborah looked back at her steadily. "They had three bodies on the train when they arrived and two today, and we have lost three children, one of the mothers, and an older man they sent over this morning. Someone said he was the elephant trainer."

Together they walked toward the kitchen. "How many more are near death?"

"I wish we could tell. A child who looked like he was recovering just stopped breathing and died. A young man who had no vital signs—no pulse or breath you could detect—suddenly opened his eyes. I think he might live. It's madness, Astrid."

"Has anyone learned when the first person showed symptoms?"

"No, but it had to be at least two weeks or more."

"And Stetler, the circus owner, didn't seek any medical help?"

"He says he didn't know about it."

Astrid snorted, her fists clenched. "Would serve him right if he got it."

"Mr. Devlin mentioned hot fires of hell . . ."

"When did they give their last performance?"

"No idea." Deborah continued down the hall.

Astrid turned aside into the kitchen and stopped by Elizabeth. "Did the rest help?" If she looked as bad as Elizabeth, no wonder Deborah insisted she sleep.

"I think so. There is no way we can keep up the wash. I called on the women to bring us any that they have. We have three iron kettles on fires outside. The washing machines cannot keep up. Tonio is keeping the fires going and changing water. He's tireless, that worker."

"We should have asked Chicago to send us more help."

"Maybe they will. Dr. Deming and Vera are helping out on the train too." Elizabeth stared at the wall, shaking her head. "You realize, most places don't get a disease-laden train in the middle of the night."

Astrid gripped Elizabeth's shoulder and began rubbing, digging deep into the muscles, like her mother had taught her.

"Oh, that feels so good. How I wish Ingeborg could be here, if for no other reason than to encourage us."

"I know, makes me want to run out and hide in her lap."

Astrid was afraid she might not be able to sleep with all the chaos going on in her mind, but she was out like dropping a rock in a well.

She woke to someone shaking her shoulder. "What?"

"We're going to lose another one unless you do a trach." Miriam shrugged. "I'm sorry for waking you, but Elizabeth said her hands are shaking too much to attempt any surgery."

"She is shaking? Did you ask if she had a sore throat?" Astrid swung her feet to the floor and reached for her shoes.

"She said she thinks it is from being so exhausted."

Astrid thought while she tied her shoes. "I had that happen once, scared me silly. When I was training in Chicago." She sucked in a deep breath and got to her feet. "I'll go scrub. Bring me some coffee please. Who will be assisting?"

"Me and Gretchen. I sent Deborah to bed, along with nurse Sandra. Abigail went out on the train with Devlin."

"How long have I been sleeping?"

"Nearly five hours. We could handle all but this."

"Watch carefully and I'll talk and show you through it." Astrid leaned over the sink and started to scrub, flinching at the same time. Like everyone else, her hands were raw from all the scrubbing, in spite of repeated applications of her mother's salve. "I'm going to train you to intubate tomorrow. When did you sleep last?"

"While you were."

Astrid nodded. "Get him in surgery please

and scrub his neck with carbolic acid. We'll be ready in about five minutes."

"He's there already and prepped."

"How's that baby girl?"

"Gone. About an hour ago." Miriam turned away but not before the tears started.

Astrid closed her eyes. This should not be happening to such innocents. Not to anyone, but especially not to small children. Could it be that someday everyone would receive the antitoxin and eradicate this horrible disease?

Astrid threw the brush in the sink. "Let's go." Blinking hard, she entered the operating room. "Let's pray. Heavenly Father, guide us here, right now, that we can help save this life. Give us steady hands and bring breath back to our patient. Give us strength to get through the hours and days ahead. Please protect the people of Blessing as we strive to help these who are so ill. Breathe on them, breath of God. Amen."

She looked at Miriam as they both put on masks. "You ready? Good. Watch carefully. We need to enter the trachea between any two of the cartilaginous rings, preferably low. I choose this point just above the sternum. Make a small incision. You will sometimes hear a whistle to let you know you are in the right spot." She did exactly as she said, and Miriam sponged the site. "Now you insert this tube. Hear the breath entering and exiting?"

"Yes." Miriam heaved a sigh behind her mask. "You make it look easy."

"Actually when you have the necessary supplies, it is. The hard part is when you have to improvise."

Miriam smirked. "I see. Your tube keeping the airway open is the barrel of a hypodermic syringe. Nice improvisation, Doctor."

"Thank you. Let's move him back to the other room. Have someone sit with him until he is out of the anesthetic, and we can tell him what we had to do."

She called two others, one of them a recovering patient, to help move him to the gurney and then to the bed. While they'd been in surgery, Sandy had been scrubbing the room, supplying the bed with clean linens. At least they weren't needing blankets. While night had brought cooler temperatures, thanks to the lights, the operating room was always hot.

It was an endless process of sponging, feeding, using ice packs, dispensing what medicines they had left. The laudanum was long gone, and while two quart bottles of cough syrup had been delivered, they were running low again. The laundry kettles continued to bubble through the night. Someone brought a load of firewood. Getting the sheets dry was proving a problem at night, but the predawn breeze took care of that.

"Ingeborg is running out of honey,"

Reverend Solberg announced when he brought the last of the jars of cough syrup in. "Whoever it was who delivered it had left the jars outside the hospital with a note." He poured himself a mug of strong coffee.

Astrid held her mug out and he refilled hers as well. "What can we do for more help? I'm down to pressing patients into service."

"Keep praying for strength. The inoculations will make others immune, so that should solve part of the problem." Reverend Solberg leaned against a wall to drink his coffee.

Elizabeth entered the kitchen and plopped into a chair. "How are our people handling all this?"

"Afraid, angry, stoic—all the emotions we should expect. Hard to believe the world goes on as we fight the battle. That train . . . I don't know how we'll ever get the disease out of it. I hope you ordered gallons of carbolic acid. Does it come in barrels?"

"That train should be burned. What's happening with all the circus animals?"

"Manny has taken over seeing that the menagerie gets fed," Solberg told her. "Farmers are bringing in some leftover hay. Do you realize how much one grown elephant eats in a day? The circus has three. The owner ordered meat for the big cats, so a new family in the area, the Ericksons, butchered that runt calf they had. It wasn't gaining anyway. Stetler's anxious to leave because he's had to cancel three locations. He says this might break him. He's probably right. This is not a first-class outfit. I have a feeling he was in financial distress before the diphtheria hit them."

"Thorliff said he and the others are working to bring us what supplies they can and to keep everyone calm." Astrid shook her head. "I was on the phone with Chicago. The doctors said this is one of the worst outbreaks because people were confined in a relatively small space."

"I am praying our good North Dakota wind can blow our land clean again."

Elizabeth stared at the tabletop. "I don't even know what to pray for anymore, other than for strength to keep going, for all of us, and to protect the people of Blessing. And that we are able to contain it."

Solberg nodded. "And so we keep thanking Him for His continued presence. For His grace and mercy. That's all I know to do. He says to love the unlovely, and that we are doing. Makes me think on leprosy, but this happens so much faster. Unclean." He shook his head.

Astrid eyed him. "When did you sleep last?"

"On my way now."

"Get something to eat first."

"Yes, Doctor." Even his usually ready smile was missing. He set his mug in the sink and left.

Astrid scribbled some notes about the tracheotomy. Record keeping was important, yes, but people's lives were more so. She left her office to go stand at an eastern-facing window. The sun had yet to crest the line of trees but the sky said any moment now. Streamers of whitening clouds, the sky turning blue, birds singing, all heralded the new day. How could everything look so normal outside when death and disease inhabited the hospital and stalked her people like the worst black cloud ever seen? Had it only been two days since the train arrived? It felt like they'd been fighting this monster forever.

CHAPTER 20

Did the hours drag? Was the clock broken? Was the train late?

They moved patients in and out of the steam room, forced fluids, put ice packs on some, placed fever-reducing wet cloths on others. As much as they were able, they held the babies, small children too, in the steam room and on the wards. To contain the disease, mothers who showed no symptoms were not allowed in the hospital.

Elizabeth returned from her rounds on the train and collapsed in a chair in Astrid's office. "Only three new cases. Perhaps intubation will save them."

"Are any improving?"

"It's hard to tell, but I think so. Looks to me like people either die or start to get well within a week." She shook her head. "I guess it's that way with all sicknesses. Forget I said what I did." Tipping her head back to rest against the wall, she gave a deep sigh. "We'll inoculate the hospital staff first, then all those possibly exposed. You agree?"

"Ja, that makes good sense. But what about the circus people?"

"Before our people here in Blessing?"

Astrid rubbed her forehead. "You know people are already demanding to know how we are going to do this." She had talked with Thorliff on the telephone, their only means of communication. She didn't tell Elizabeth that Sophie was insisting the families from Blessing should come before outsiders. No matter how they did this, there would be angry people. "It all depends on how much antitoxin we receive. Hospital staff and helpers who are not immune first, all those exposed that first night, and then God help us. I wonder how long the antitoxin needs to be in the body before it can fight off the disease."

"You mean for those of us already exposed? Keep in mind that not everyone who is exposed develops diphtheria."

Astrid nodded. "I know."

Elizabeth's weakened state concerned her far more than she worried about herself. As far as they knew, neither of them had ever had it or been exposed.

"I have scrubbed my hands and arms nearly raw and worn a mask." Elizabeth held up her chapped red hands. "Even with Ingeborg's salve."

Astrid stopped and listened. "The train whistle! Thank you, Lord. Thorliff and Daniel will bring the antitoxin to the dock, and we can get started immediately. Please, God, let there be enough. Whatever enough means." Her mor had reminded her on the telephone just this morning that God was still in charge of not only all creation but here in Blessing. She wished He would make it plainer.

When they left the office, the smiles on the faces of their nurses lightened the dark of the hospital in spite of all the coughing and crying.

"I have the list of everyone here," Miriam said, "with checks by those who have either had diphtheria or been inoculated in the past. All forty of our syringes are sterilized, and I'm praying they sent more of those too. Can you think of anything else?" She looked to both of them.

"No, you've done a good job. Once we take care of everyone here, Sandra will prepare those waiting with a scrub of carbolic acid on their upper arm, and Dr. Commons and you will give the inoculations." Astrid glanced to Elizabeth, who nodded.

"And the others?"

"It all depends on how much the hospital sent us."

Miriam turned to answer a question, and Astrid looked out a window to see the rising steam from the train behind the boardinghouse, which blocked the view of the train itself.

"Can you hold this little one for a bit?" Mercy asked, coming down the hall. "I think she is not getting worse, at least."

Astrid took the child in her arms and rocked her gently. While her breathing was still difficult, Mercy might be right. "Oh, little one, please get better. We need some good news here." She laid the child down in the nearest empty crib as soon as she saw Thorliff and Daniel out the window, each with a handcart loaded with boxes and crates. They parked them and stepped back.

Astrid stared at her brother and husband. Oh, how she wanted to go out there, go home with Daniel, back to her own bed to sleep for a week. To go out to the farm, to get out of this pestilence, the sounds, the smells, the fear. But she couldn't. Miriam and Sandra went out and brought the carts back to the hospital.

"Thank you," she called from the door and opened it for the two to wheel the carts in and to the supply room. The boxes on one cart were labeled *Carbolic acid*. There were four boxes on the other cart. Once in the supply room, she peeled the envelope off the top box and slit it open. With the sheet unfolded, she read the contents. One hundred doses of antitoxin, fifty intubation kits, a box of tracheal tubes, a box of scalpels, and a few other miscellaneous supplies. She unfolded the letter behind it and read it swiftly.

Dear Drs. Elizabeth and Astrid,

I'm sorry we could not send more, but we need to keep a certain amount here for emergencies. We have ordered more delivered to you from New York, but that will take a couple more days. They said it would ship yesterday.

I suggest you use your best judgment on how to use what we could send. This must be kept cold to keep it viable. That is why we included ice and shipped it in the refrigerated car. They do not have those on all the trains, as you well know.

We are praying for all of you and are so grateful we implemented inoculations for all our nurses in training. We'll be sending three more nurses in training, along with one resident, just as soon as we can, to help take the pressure off. Please let me know if there is anything else we can do. We well know the power of praying and both have been and will continue.

Dr. Red Hawk has had a breakout on

*the reservation too. That is part of the
reason why we had no more to ship.*
                    *With heartfelt
                    prayers,
                    Nurse Korsheski*

She had signed it with her usual illegible
signature.

Astrid looked up. "Sorry, I'll read it aloud."
She did so and, when finished, folded it back
up and said, "Open the boxes. Put the crates
over in the corner for later. Let's get started. Oh,
and we need to sterilize all the syringes in the
box immediately and the other things after."
She knew she sounded like an army general
and that they already knew what needed to
be done, but she couldn't stop herself. All she
could think was *Get as many people protected as
quickly as possible.*

Using the sterilized syringes they already
had on hand, Miriam started with Elizabeth
and then Astrid.

"Do you have a sore throat, fever, or
cough?" She asked that of every person she
inoculated while the others continued caring
for their patients.

"I'm going to intubate the man in room
one as soon as the OR is set up," Astrid told
Miriam. "If we can't get that down his throat,
we'll do a tracheotomy."

"It's all scrubbed and set up ready for you."

Astrid motioned to Reverend Solberg and Tonio to carry the man in while she scrubbed.

"I thought you were sleeping," she said when Deborah showed up at the sink beside her.

"I was. Got my shot, and now I am here."

Astrid nodded toward the reverend. "John, would you scrub too? We'll immobilize him as much as we can, but we might need more muscle."

Before she had Vera start the anesthetic, she tried to explain to the man what she was going to do, but she knew he did not comprehend her. "Put him under. We'll need to block his mouth open, so he can't bite, and see if we can slide this down. And tie down his arms and legs." She tossed the belt, which had been fashioned from three saddle cinches, over his chest.

Intubation kit. This must be the latest thing in Chicago. She pulled the cardboard box open to find tubing, a rubber device to hold the mouth open, and a dose of morphine neatly labeled. "We won't need everything in this kit; for instance, the morphine. He's already under. But when you open one of these, throw nothing away. Not even the box. We don't know what we will need next."

By the time they'd finished, all of them were dripping wet. But the man could breathe. While Reverend Solberg was praying for healing and peace for the man, Astrid nearly buckled under a wave of exhaustion. She gripped the table for a moment, then headed for the scrub room to remove her apron and hair covering, along with the mask.

Back on the ward floor, she could see a group of townspeople gathering about a hundred feet in front of the hospital door. Thorliff was trying to get their attention. "Didn't he post something about us using the school for inoculations?"

"I thought so." Solberg heaved a sigh. "Fear can do terrible things to people. I'll go talk to them. Your plan is a good one, Astrid. Just get Miriam ready to go."

"She has to take a bath and get dressed in clothes that have not been in here. Trygve is waiting with them out back. We've curtained off a bathing area. Tell them an hour."

"You're going to do them before the train people?"

"Yes."

"And you can live with that?"

"Yes. These are my people and this hospital is supported by them. I pray I am doing the right thing. Well, if not the right thing, the best thing. Since we know more antitoxin will be here in two days . . ."

"How many doses have you given?"

Astrid counted down the list. "Six including you. Since you weren't sure . . ."

"I know and I appreciate that. So first we

do those who have been exposed. I will give the list to Thorliff."

"Read him the list and let him write them down. The paper may be contaminated. After those are finished, give the shot to those who run businesses here, as they are in contact with more outsiders. Then all the immediate town children. Unless this travels on the wind too, the farmers should be safe. As long as no one has come to town." She heaved a sigh.

"You are doing the best that you can. Do you want me to start telephoning people to make sure everyone goes over there?"

"Good idea. If only we had been wiser and not allowed anyone to leave the hospital after that first night."

"Hindsight is always perfect. You do your best and count on God to take care of the rest." He took the list and headed out the door.

Astrid answered the ringing telephone.

"I have Sophie on the line," Gerald said.

Astrid heaved another sigh. She seemed to be doing a lot of that. She also knew that Sophie had gotten furious with Thorliff. "Put her on." The connection clicked. "How can I help you, Sophie?"

"You would not believe what just happened. That Stetler just stormed out of here because I refused to serve him supper. I thought the train was quarantined."

"It is!"

"That man should be shot. He brought this on us all and then he comes in here like nothing is wrong. Does he have no principles at all?"

"All right, Sophie, this is what you need to do. Do you have carbolic acid?"

"Some."

"Good. Use that to scrub every surface he may have touched or breathed on. I've not asked him if he has immunity, but still, he is contaminated. Scrub, dump the water, and scrub again. Who all did he talk to?"

"Just me. The others were in the kitchen."

"Scrub the porch and steps too and slosh the wash over your walkway, just to be careful. You need to get over to the school as one who is possibly contaminated. But first come here and bring clean clothes. You can come here, wash in our special place, and get dressed to go get your inoculation. Our people here will then boil the clothes you are wearing."

"I heard to burn everything."

"Carbolic acid works the same." Astrid fought to keep the simmering rage under control and out of her voice. "Please, Sophie, I beg of you, do not tell the others about this, or we might have a lynch mob on our hands." *Lord, please, let no one be on the line for this conversation.*

"In Blessing?"

"In Blessing. I'm afraid it may have come to that." Astrid thought back to her conversation with Thorliff. Obviously, Sophie had had time to cool down. "I never dreamed we'd have something like this. And to think a circus coming to town is usually such a happy event. Do you understand what you need to do?"

"Ja, I do. Thank you."

Astrid hung up. Should she call Gerald, since he'd been the operator? Surely he didn't listen in. Surely. *Please, Lord, let this be so.* Probably it is a good thing people are not getting together.

When Reverend Solberg came back in the hospital, she told him what had happened.

He closed his eyes and took several deep breaths. "The man has no sense whatever. Thomas told me Stetler had made comments about needing to get the train going again."

"How can he? He doesn't have people for his acts. Too many of them are sick. He lost his elephant trainer, and his lion tamer is too weak to perform. Even his engineer was sick, although he's recovering nicely. And if he moves on, he spreads diphtheria to the next stop. I can't believe he had the gall—or maybe the stupidity—to break quarantine and get off the train." She sucked in a breath of her own.

John grimaced. "I'll make those telephone calls and we'll talk more. Oh, and I reminded Thorliff to make sure the residents of the apartment house are inoculated too. Some of them don't read English well enough to understand the danger."

She nodded. "Some of them do, though. They've been wonderful about helping if they had it before. Dr. Deming has quite a crew out there, and others are helping Mrs. Geddick in the kitchen. That's why Tonio has been helping in here. You emphasized to Thorliff that children came first, then the old people, and finally the others?"

John smiled. "I did, and you know Miriam will handle that well."

At least Miriam gets to see her family up close. Sometimes the need for time in her husband's arms walloped her.

Hours later, after supper and evening rounds, Astrid hid out in her office, wishing she could blot out the sounds of sickness and not just the sight. She forced herself to concentrate on a minimum of paper work, drank more coffee, and rubbed her eyes. Just for a minute, she promised herself as she swung her tired and aching feet up onto the corner of the desk and leaned back in her chair, head propped and burning eyes closed. For just a few minutes.

She jerked awake at a knock on the door. "Yes?"

"Are you all right?" Reverend Solberg.

"I am. Come on in."

"They have run out of antitoxin, but the most vulnerable are taken care of. The others will get theirs when the next shipment arrives, and then we'll move out to the nearby farms."

"Did someone think to tell my mother to get the shot?"

"Yes, Thorliff did, because she is one of the older ones." John looked just as weary as Astrid felt.

She heaved a sigh of relief that stretched into a yawn. "Pardon me, I—"

"You do not need to apologize for catching some sleep. I have something rather funny to tell you—well, not funny, but amusing."

"I need a smile."

"As do we all. Thomas heard Stetler storming on about not getting a meal at the boardinghouse, breaking quarantine, and it made him furious. So he and Mr. Sidorov grabbed Stetler, hustled him into his own quarters, locked him in, and kept the key. Those on the train who were well enough to do so applauded."

Astrid rolled her lips together to keep from laughing out loud, but the giggle snuck out anyway.

"When he yelled more, Thomas said if he didn't keep quiet, he'd call the sheriff up in Grafton and have him thrown in jail for breaking quarantine and for endangering his performers by not getting medical help at the first sign of something so contagious."

Astrid gave up and laughed. "Good for Thomas Devlin. Bless that man."

John continued, "And something you may wish to tell the circus people—indeed, everyone on the train. It might bring them comfort. We have set aside a block of plots in the cemetery just for the dead from the circus. The survivors may want to stop by Blessing someday to pay their respects to those lost, and the graves will all be in one place. They won't have to wander about seeking graves among strangers. We'll carve wooden markers until we can bring in some stone for permanent markers. And Thomas was suggesting putting a red and yellow fence around it. It sounds rather gaudy to me, but he says the maintenance crew wants to give him plenty of red and yellow paint."

"I think red and yellow is totally appropriate. Gaudy, yes, but visitors will certainly find their cemetery section easily."

John chuckled; then his face sobered. "Some of the men from the circus, assisted by Thomas, are burying the bodies that came in on the train and those who have died here. And yes, they are being careful not to contaminate anyone. Some of our people will dig more graves." His voice nearly broke. "They are having a hard time digging the small ones."

Astrid closed her eyes again, this time to squelch the tears. They shouldn't have to bury children. Innocents! When would this nightmare end?

Dear God, how can you let this keep on happening?

CHAPTER 21

"How long, O Lord, how long before we see any improvement?"

Miriam stared at her. "But, Dr. Astrid, we *have* been seeing improvement. For the last two days, we've had no deaths. And I think we're seeing a turnaround on at least two of our children here. Their throats aren't any more swollen and that awful membrane is no worse either. Out in the tent, people are still very ill but no worse. Those who have had lighter cases are eating and sleeping. Your mother's cough syrup is really bringing relief."

Astrid sighed. "I'm sorry for complaining." She cocked her head. Was that a new cough she heard, this one from the staff sleeping area? "Come with me." As they stood, she asked, "Who is sleeping right now?"

"Dr. Elizabeth, Sandy, I think Mercy . . . and Deborah." She glanced down the ward as they strode to the other ward. They stopped at the curtain and studied those sleeping. Nothing seemed amiss.

"No one has mentioned a sore throat?"

"Not to me."

"Someone coughed from here. I was sure of it. I'll check on them when they wake up. We are on day five, or is it six, since this all started?" She closed her eyes to think more clearly. "I am praying we are beyond the danger point with our people being exposed to the disease. I have to keep reminding myself that not everyone gets it so I don't go around questioning everyone and asking to see their throats."

Together they turned to go back to the main area.

The cough came again. Astrid whirled around. Elizabeth was shifting on her bed. From coughing? Had she looked any more pale than usual? If only she had not been the doctor on call that night. Elizabeth should never have gone on the train. Not with her health history. She needed sleep so desperately, would waking her make any difference in the long run? Would the antitoxin have had enough time to fight back if the disease was already started?

"I must go back out to the tent," Miriam said. "Dr. Commons is out there alone. Do you need me for anything more here?"

"No more than usual. It's time to shift patients into the steam room. Did you notice the steam condensing on the walls and running down? I've had Tonio mop that floor several times. I remember Mor holding babies and children over a steaming kettle when they had croup or congestion of any kind. She'd put a towel over her head so they had a tent. One of her folk remedy practices." Astrid rolled her eyes. "Here I am detaining you. Sorry."

"I should be back fairly soon. I have the healthier people out there spooning broth and liquids into other patients. That's a big help, even though they can't stay at it very long. I think we should let that baby's mother come take care of her now. May I tell her that? Or at least let her visit her baby?"

"Ja, that would be good." Astrid went to check the man with the tracheostomy in room one. He too was no worse. He was finally able to eat soft foods and respond to commands. Perhaps the swelling in his neck was going down. Stopping beside his bed, she checked his pulse, the motion making his eyes flutter open. A small part of a smile lit his face. She smiled and nodded.

Taking a tongue depressor from her pocket, she said softly so as not to wake the others in the room, "I would like to check your throat. Can you open your mouth, please?"

With a slight nod, he did as she asked. Even

in the poor light, she could see the membrane was receding. She felt his neck and the swollen glands along his jawline. "You are doing well. If I help you, would you like to sit up for a while?" Threading her arm behind his shoulders, she lifted him and pushed another pillow in place. "How's that?"

He nodded again and pointed to the encumbrance in his neck, the air he inhaled whistling in the tube.

"We'll take it out as soon as the swelling in your throat decreases sufficiently. You need to eat as much as you are able, and perhaps tonight or tomorrow, you can sit up and dangle your feet over the edge. You have been so ill that it will take your body time to rebuild strength."

He mouthed "Thank you" and pointed to the others in the room—his wife, who had not had as severe a case, and one of his children.

"They are on the mend also. I'll have someone bring you some soup."

Sorry I doubted, Lord, she thought as she left the room. She had awakened with a feeling of despair, but thanks to God, that was gone, at least for now. At the nurses' station, she left orders to feed the man and continued checking the other patients. One child was still unresponsive, two others barely so. They could still lose any or all of them. She picked up Ada, the unresponsive girl who appeared to be two or three, and carried her to the steam room, where she put a towel over her head and held the little one so her face was down toward the kettle to inhale the most steam. "Please, Lord God, restore health to this child. Clear the horrible—" The child convulsed once, then again, then lay flaccid in her arms.

"No, Father, do not let her die! Bring her back." She sat down in a chair and, laying the girl across her lap, compressed the girl's chest. She shuddered, wretched, and a glob of mucus flew out of her mouth and onto Astrid's apron. Another followed. Astrid wiped the girl's mouth with a square of muslin and tented them over the steam kettle again. The child was breathing far more easily.

Abigail and Mercy came in to carry another patient back to bed. "She sounds better."

Astrid described what happened. "I'll take her back to bed now."

"Why not leave her here? I'll sit with her." Abigail reached for the child. The young nurse had an affinity for small children, that was for sure.

"Then I'll help you, Mercy." Together they carried an older woman back to a fresh bed and settled her.

Mercy smiled. "Thank you. I need to give her some cough syrup and broth. She is taking both better now."

"How are you holding up?"

Mercy shrugged. "Tired, but I'm scheduled to sleep in about half an hour."

"Good."

Miriam returned from the tent and smiled at Astrid. "I set all the people still living on the train to scrubbing the cars inside and out—all the bedding, all the clothing. Manny takes the elephants down to the river now to eat the willow trees. He sure is in love with those elephants. Especially the baby, Fluff. Can you imagine that? Four hundred pounds of . . . fluff!"

Astrid laughed in spite of herself. Maybe people were getting better and that was buoying her spirits. And Fluff. The baby elephant too. "Little Ada coughed up a huge plug and Abigail is still holding her over the steam. What a difference it made in her breathing. She convulsed, and I thought she died right in my arms. I am so grateful Mor taught me about steam treatments."

"We are doing unconventional treatments here, you realize that?"

"I know, but they seem to be working. As Mor says, it's all in God's hands."

Miriam nodded. "We need to document this for Chicago. They are keeping records of all we send them, and they are using our experiences in their teaching to both their nursing students and physicians." She paused. "Although Dr. Commons seems to have a problem with much of it."

"I know. If he can't read it in a medical book, he is convinced it has no value." She didn't add *like so many other doctors*," some of whom still used blood-letting as a treatment, closed windows, heat for burns, and other outrageous practices.

With an overwhelming need to talk to her mother, Astrid glanced around the area to make sure all was being done that could be and went to the oak box on the wall. "Please ring my mother." One of the immigrant wives who could speak fair English after her classes with Amelia Jeffers was working the switchboard.

"Right away." A bit of silence and she said, "Go ahead."

"Oh, Freda, could I please talk to Mor?"

"Ja, I will get her. Are you all right?"

"As well as we can be, but no new emergencies. I just need to hear her voice." She heard the earpiece bump against the wall as it dangled. Closing her eyes, she could see the kitchen, knowing there were pots on the stove, baking bread filling the house with fragrance, and . . .

"Astrid, oh how I have wanted to talk with you."

"And I you. Did your arm get sore after the inoculation?"

"Some, but nothing to be concerned about."

"Just tell me what is going on there. It seems like I've been here for weeks, not just days."

"Freda has started another batch of cheese

today. We will send soft cheese to the hospital in the next couple of days. That should go down easy and build people up. She has gingerbread in the oven. I am making more cough syrup now that I have more honey. The Baards sent me some as soon as they heard we needed it. I ordered glycerin for the lotion, and it should be here soon. Hmm, what else? Oh, we miss Manny so. There is a big hole in our family."

"How is Clara?"

"She is getting bigger, pushing out her dresses. But also we are getting some meat on her bones. We hope and pray that she came to us early enough that she will have a healthy baby. You can feel kicking feet. She smiles and lays a hand on her big ball, as she calls it, when the baby is active. It's been so long since I was this close to a pregnant mother, I'd forgotten many of the joys. Well, the hard parts too."

"Oh, Mor, it is so good to hear your voice. This hospital is just not the same without you sitting here praying and singing. If you can think of anything else we can try to make the poor people more comfortable . . ." She went on to describe some of the patients.

"I wish I could be there. Reverend Solberg even canceled church just to be safe."

"I know. People are being so careful about doing what we ask. Symptoms can show up any day for our people here in Blessing. Keep praying for protection." Astrid sighed, weary of body and heart both.

"And God's mercy."

"They are calling me. Thank you, Mor."

"We are praying for all of you, all day and all night, prayers go up."

"Make sure you get plenty of rest, all of you. 'Bye." Astrid hung up the receiver. "Lord, protect them, please." A verse floated through her mind again. *Casting all your care upon him; for he careth for you.* Watching the suffering going on around her made trusting that verse difficult. One of these days she might have to forget battling tears and just let them drip. She glanced down at her apron. She'd not changed since she'd been in the steam room with little Ada. Before going any further, she untied and tossed her soiled apron into the wash bin, grabbed a clean one off the shelf, and returned to the ward, tying it as she went. She checked on Elizabeth, refusing to awaken her when the schedule said so, and no one argued with her.

"Have you heard anyone coughing on that ward?"

Deborah fought back a yawn. "Not that I know of, but then the roof could have fallen and unless it fell on me, I'd have slept right through it. Why?"

"I heard someone coughing in there. Let me check your throat. Say ah . . . No, you are fine." But the fear plagued her, so she checked each one as they went first to the kitchen for food and even more so, life-sustaining coffee.

When Elizabeth finally awoke, Astrid was sound asleep. However, she had left orders for the charge nurse to check Elizabeth, whether she was agreeable or not. She muttered but let Deborah peer down her throat.

Deborah frowned. "Have you been coughing?"

"Not that I know of, and other than weary, a bit stiff and sore from all of this, I am as healthy as any of the rest of you." She knew her tone was a bit sharp but was too weary to correct it.

"Sorry, but doctor's orders are that we all be checked daily since we are now in the danger zone." Deborah shrugged. "As soon as Astrid wakes up, she wants us to decide who of the train's ill can be moved out to the tent, just to be prepared for anyone coming down with it in Blessing. Oh, and we received a telephone call from a woman ready to birth her baby. I called Ingeborg and asked if she would go. I think she was delighted. Her comment? 'Ah, new life. God is so good to remind us that both life and death are part of living in this world.'"

"Leave it to Ingeborg. How I would rather be seeing a new baby born." Elizabeth wagged her head.

"Wouldn't we all?"

"How are the people of Blessing doing with all of this?"

"Thorliff says tempers have settled. Reverend Solberg's idea to set aside a section of the cemetery for the train people helped with that. Sophie settled down. I think Kaaren had a talk with her."

Elizabeth smiled. "Knowing Kaaren, that was quite a talk."

Miriam entered with a steaming mug, paused for a moment, and joined them.

Elizabeth looked at the young woman; like everyone else, she looked worn and weary. "Miriam, your family is all right?"

Miriam nodded. "Being forced to stay away from the little ones is hard, but Este went fishing and caught some fish for the seals. He was so happy. You cannot go fishing in a Chicago tenement. He loves Blessing. The three of them are working on the garden. Our mother was a garden lover, but the girls had never done that. It's their first time, and Este is teaching them from what he learned at the hospital in Chicago." Miriam fought back a yawn. "The coffee is not much help right now."

"Go to bed. I'll wake you for the meeting."

"I'll not argue." Miriam put her coffee aside and flopped down on a bed.

The rhythm continued through the night. Feed, clean, keep watch, steam, ice, cough syrup, hold the small children, sleep when one's shift to do so came around, and pray, always pray. And always, at the back of Elizabeth's mind, *We should never ever have let them come.*

Astrid awoke much later than she normally did. As soon as she got up, they called a meeting, including Reverend Solberg, Miriam, Deborah, Elizabeth, Dr. Commons, and Thomas Devlin.

She looked from helper to helper. "Let's make this as quick as we can. How many beds do you have out in the tent?"

"Well, the ones who came down first and lived through it are now recovering, so they can move back onto the train." Devlin smiled. "Though frankly, other than fighting the mosquitoes, they vow they would rather be in the tent. I cannot blame them. Fresh air and a breeze. It's quite stuffy in the circus cars. That would free up eight . . ." John looked at Devlin.

Devlin corrected, "Nine."

Nine was a start. Astrid nodded. "The main thing now is to get good food into them, and let them rest and recover. How is it going regarding day-to-day operations?"

"Miriam has them feeding each other," John said, glancing at Miriam. "She's a wonder, that woman. And Devlin's plan of farming out the cows and goats was genius. It's working perfectly. Except the camel. No one wants a camel, but someone finally took it in. Fortunately, camels can graze."

Devlin chimed in, "Manny has been such a help with the animals, along with two men who said they had had diphtheria. A big concern was cleaning the big cats' cars. Not a job to be undertaken lightly, but they all learned how to do it safely. Something akin to Daniel in the lions' den, but we suspect God did not see fit to shut the lions' mouths. I trust ye've heard the roars."

"I have."

"There will be two more buried today," Devlin added. "We lost the tightrope-walking woman during the night. Seemed to be doing well and then she was gone."

Miriam sighed. "I didn't expect that either."

"So, then, who will we move out there?"

"I have a list." Deborah read the list of five. "Possibly three more, if we can keep treating them in the steam room."

Astrid bobbed her head. "Then we'll move them after breakfast and get those beds cleaned, put the mattresses outside in the sun, and pray no one else develops symptoms. I know that would be a miracle, but we need one here. Is there anything else?"

Dr. Commons said, "Nurse Deborah and I have the supplies order ready. Any further suggestions?"

"Thank you, Dr. Commons, Deborah. I cannot begin to tell you all what a great job you are doing here. Reinforcements should arrive tomorrow, along with the supplies we already ordered. Including more of the antitoxin so we can start inoculating those outside of town. I'll ask Thorliff to be in charge of notifying them. Any questions? Comments?" Astrid looked from face to face. "Then please pray, Reverend Solberg."

"Lord God, we thank you for all the lives you have protected, for the strength you have given this group of warriors, for keeping Blessing from strife. Thank you for healing those, and we commend the spirits of those gone on to be with you. We pray that you will change the hearts of those who do not believe in you, those who are angry. Fear does terrible things to us, which is probably why you say *Fear not* so often in your Word. Thank you that you answer our prayers, that your Spirit is right here with us. You have promised over and over that you will never leave us nor forsake us. We thank you and praise your mighty name. Give us continued wisdom, strength, and grace to serve you as we are called to do. Greater love has no man than this, that he love his neighbor as himself. We are trying our best to do just that. Amen." The others echoed him. And to Astrid's surprise, so did Dr. Commons.

She smiled and nodded to him, getting an almost-nod in return. *Good, he is willing to learn.*

As they all stood to go about their duties, Elizabeth drew Astrid aside. "You better check me again. I have a sore throat, no coughing yet, but let's make sure."

Please, God, no! Astrid pointed to the examining room. Was the inoculation too late?

CHAPTER 22

A strid could barely get the words out.
"Mor, please pray and ask all the others
to pray. Elizabeth has it."

"Oh, Astrid, she did not get the antitoxin
in time? O Lord, help us!"

"He better, because I am having trouble
believing she will make it through this. She's
been near death too many times already." She
closed her eyes and leaned her forehead against
the wall. Forcing the words between clenched
teeth was nigh impossible. "I . . . I have to go
before I fall into that pit you talk about."

"And Thorliff?"

"I've not called him yet. I know he is going
to demand to come in here."

"You could ask John to call him."

Astrid sniffed again, the heaviness almost

worse than the darkness that prowled the corners and slithered like a thief along the floors. "How can I go on?"

"Only God can handle all this, but He is over, under, and all around you, but more . . ." Ingeborg choked back her own tears. "He is within us, closer than breath, part of us, and He promised He will never leave. I'll talk to John."

"He is sleeping right now. I won't wake him. I will talk to Thorliff as soon as I get myself together again." *If I ever get myself together. Is there no end to this?*

"Ask Kaaren to come to be with you, please?" She waited for her mother to blow her nose again. "Please."

"I will. But I will also go to Thorliff."

"No! He has been exposed. Please, Mor, no matter how hard that is, please do not leave home. I have to know you are safe. Please!" Who could she send to make sure Ingeborg remained at home? Take a chance and send Reverend Solberg? Miriam? Who? Mary Martha? Her mind fought to figure out who might be safe and who might have inadvertently been exposed. "Mor, promise me you will stay home!"

"I . . . I can't."

The click in her ear sounded like an anvil dropping.

Astrid clicked the prong again. "Gerald, get me Kaaren . . . fast."

"I am."

The seconds stretched like hours. *Lord God, make her answer the telephone.*

Gerald came back on the line. "I broke into a conversation—here she is."

"Astrid, what?"

"Please run to Mor and keep her from coming to Thorliff. Elizabeth has diphtheria and Thorliff has been exposed."

"Ja, I will run."

The click in her ear said Kaaren was doing as she said. Call Freda? But if Mor answered . . . Pounding the wall would only hurt her hand, a hand clenched so tight the pain of nails in her palm jerked her back to the right now. Raising her arm to set the earpiece back in the hook made her tremble. She missed the hook.

"Here, let me." Deborah spoke softly as she took the black weight from Astrid's hand and set it in place. "Come to your office. I will bring you a glass of water and a cup of coffee. We put Elizabeth in room one. Good thing we had that room ready."

"T-takk." *Lord, strength! Help me! I am the doctor here. Doctors are not supposed to disintegrate like this.* "I need to go to Elizabeth."

"Not right now. She is sleeping." She guided Astrid to her chair and waited until she sat down, then headed out the door.

Hospital sounds dimmed as she reminded herself to breathe. *O God, O God* ran through her head, joined by *Help me and please, anything to keep back the evil.* She drank the glass of water that Deborah handed her and set the glass on the desk. Focus on one thing at a time.

"I put cream and sugar in your coffee. Did you eat this morning?"

Holding the cup with both hands, Astrid inhaled the comfort of coffee steam. She drank and swallowed, following Deborah's instructions mindlessly, numbly. With another deep breath and deeper exhale, she nodded. "Thank you. I'm not sure if I ate or not."

"I'll bring you something. Just stay where you are, all right?"

Reverend Solberg entered the room, combing his graying sandy hair back with both hands. "I heard, Astrid. Have you called Ingeborg?"

"Ja, but not Thorliff." She closed her eyes and drank again. Anything to keep control of her fragile calm. Maybe the tears were all spent? If that were possible.

"I will call him. You know he will be right here to be with her?"

"I know, and short of locking him in a cell, I can think of no way to prevent it."

"Since he has already been exposed, perhaps it is best that he come."

Another ugly thought slammed her. "What about Inga and Roald?"

"How I wish we could send them to Ingeborg. It would be good comfort for all of them."

"I asked Kaaren to keep her from coming to town. I wanted to talk with Freda but . . ." She sighed again. "So much death. There's a monstrous difference between reading about something like this and being in the middle of it."

"Ja." He used the desk to hold himself up.

"There is no way to prepare for it."

His voice rumbled. "You've done all that you could. Everyone has."

She shook her head. "We should not have asked the husbands to help on the train."

"But you didn't know it was contagious."

"I should have known better. I'm a doctor."

"*Should* never did anyone any good looking back."

"Ja, easy to say."

Reverend Solberg forced a weak smile. "But hard to do in the middle of a battle. That's why we have others praying for us. God promised to deliver us from the enemies. He will not go back on His Word. He cannot."

Setting her now empty cup on the desk, Astrid stared at the door. "I'd better get back out there."

"Not yet. I'll go call Thorliff right now."

"Ja." A wave of gratitude that Daniel had had the disease as a child rolled over her. She tipped her head back and listened to the hospital sounds. People walking, pans rattling, murmurs, coughing, a child crying. All the normal sounds. She was sure that any minute Thorliff would be pounding on the doors.

Solberg returned. "He'll be here any moment. Together Devlin and I could keep him out."

"What, and tie him up? Keep him locked up? We have no jail here, remember." She headed for the front door, fully understanding that nothing she said would make any difference. But she had to make the effort. She watched him come striding down the street. She stepped outside.

"It won't work," he announced.

"Will you please listen to me for a moment? She is sleeping right now."

He clamped his arms across his chest, his jaw steel, blue eyes icy.

"We might have caught it early enough. The antitoxin might be doing its work and will help fight this off. Many survive it, as you well know."

"And her total exhaustion will not complicate things?"

Astrid shrugged. "Possibly but not definitely."

He squinted, still sending sharp icicles at her. "When can I see her?" Shaking his head, he looked around. "After all we've been through, I can't lose her." Rubbing his forehead, he stared down at the ground.

"Do you have a headache?"

"A little. Who wouldn't with all this?"

"Sore throat? Cough?"

"Don't be a doctor with me. I'd tell you if that were the case."

"Strange thing, I don't trust you at all right now."

"I had the antitoxin too, remember. And I'm strong as an ox. Always have been."

She studied his face, dark circles not just under his eyes but all around. Haggard, pale. But then he'd not had much time to be out in the sun; running a newspaper was not like farming. Reminding him wouldn't do any good.

"I am going to stay with her," he announced. "You might as well get used to the idea."

"What about your children?"

"Thelma is taking care of them. Inga keeps asking to go see Grandma. Roald seems to have gotten over the worst of wanting to see his ma. Maybe he's too young to remember long. So are you going to let me in or am I going to pick you up and move you out of the way?"

His tone sounded conversational, but Astrid had no doubt he meant every word he'd said. She inhaled slowly and stepped aside. "Stubborn, bullheaded man." She followed him. "She's in room one."

Someone had already moved a chair into the room for him. Astrid stopped in the doorway and watched her brother stare at his sleeping wife. While he reached for her hand, he did not touch it, obviously not wanting to wake her. He knew more than anyone how often she could not sleep. He didn't say a word, just watched her.

The next time Astrid stopped at the door, he was sound sleep in the chair. She tapped him on the shoulder. "The other bed is ready for you. Might as well sleep there and not fall off the chair. The clatter might awaken her."

"Takk."

For a change he did as she requested, carefully removing his boots to not dirty the linens.

Lord, please protect him. As she watched, he unconsciously scratched his right arm. Please, just a mosquito bite. But when she checked, there was no bump but a rash about the size of the palm of her hand. Dread settled on her even as she strode to the supply room for a healing ointment her mother had created and prepared. Astrid saw the bottle of honey on the shelf. Should she apply that too or scrub it with carbolic acid? She chose the carbolic and ointment, knowing there was honey in the ointment too. She thought to wait until he woke but instead went in with supplies in hand and shook his shoulder gently.

"I'm going to put this on your arm," she whispered. When he frowned at her, she added, "You've been scratching it."

He looked over to Elizabeth.

"She's still sleeping." She didn't mention

the cough. If he had not heard it, he needed the sleep as bad as his wife. He clenched his teeth at the carbolic scrub but mouthed "Thank you" when she smoothed the unguent into place.

When Solberg and Devlin checked in with her again she told them about the rash.

"Like that man with the ulcer on his leg who died?"

"I don't know. That was the first time I'd seen diphtheria as an ulcer, or I've never seen it in the early stages. Maybe he got into poison ivy or something. I'll ask him when he wakes up. He looks terrible."

"Thorliff has looked terrible for some time, but he keeps on going. I wonder when the next paper is due out."

"Why?"

"Because if it is soon, he'll be worrying about that."

"I can be of service there," Devlin offered. "Anji has already written some articles for the paper. Something to think on." Devlin rubbed his chin, nodding at the same time.

"You know the world will not stop if the Blessing paper is late or misses an edition."

"True, but since this be his livelihood . . ."

"And perhaps we can stop some of the rumors that are frightening everyone, since we can't have any meetings. Maybe an article about diphtheria, some interviews, a bit of news from elsewhere . . ." Solberg nodded as he spoke. "And maybe after some sleep Thorliff will feel restored enough to answer our questions."

"And Anji and meself will help him."

Astrid stared at them. Here she was, sure that Elizabeth was not going to be with them much longer, and these two men were planning for the future. Right now she had to get from day to day.

"I'll leave you to yourselves."

Later when she listened to Elizabeth's heart and lungs, another dread made itself known. Diphtheria could cause heart failure along with all the other problems. It seemed to attack any weak organ besides the glands that were swelling. "Elizabeth, we need to get some nourishment and liquids into you."

"What is the prognosis?" She felt her neck. "The glands are swelling. My throat is sore. I suspect I have been coughing."

"Elizabeth?" On the other bed, Thorliff turned his head to look.

She glanced over to the other bed. "Why is Thorliff here?"

"Because I insisted." He sat up and swung his legs over the side.

Astrid snorted. "*Demanded* is more like it."

"Why didn't you wake me?" he asked Astrid, accusation lacing his voice.

"I needed to examine Elizabeth first."

Elizabeth's voice sounded raspy. "Can you

please help me sit up, Thorliff? Then if you would go to the kitchen and bring me some soup and a glass of water."

"Get supper for yourself too while you are there. Mrs. Geddick will give you a tray."

"Is it that late?"

"Nearly. Since you are here, you might as well make yourself useful." She watched his inner argument fly across his face. When she smiled at him, good humor won, and he smiled to his wife.

"I'll get my boots on and be right back."

As soon as he left the room, Elizabeth stared into Astrid's eyes. "You know and I know that there is only a slim chance that I will be able to overcome this. What does my heart sound like? And no hedging here."

"Weak and erratic."

"Check to see if the membrane is growing."

Astrid took another tongue depressor from the bag in her apron pocket. "Possibly on your tonsils."

"Then I will gargle with salt water like Ingeborg says, eat honey by the spoonful, do everything you tell me, and we'll all keep praying." She closed her eyes and one tear trickled down her cheek. "I want to hold my children." She held Astrid's hand in a vise grip. "Lord, please protect my babies." Looking back up at Astrid, she asked, her words halting, "Do you think it would be better for them to not see me again or come over and we can talk through the window at least?"

Astrid puffed out a breath of air, shaking her head at the same time. "One side of me says Inga needs to come, but not Roald. He won't remember anyway. He is too little. Should I ask Mor or John?"

"Let me think on it, but it must be soon, like before dark."

"I agree. One more thing, there is a rash on Thorliff's arm that he was scratching in his sleep. Not a mosquito bite."

Elizabeth shut her eyes again. "My fault."

"How can it be your fault? He's not exhibiting other symptoms." She cut off the *yet* that threatened.

"I let him come help when the call came in."

"But both Thorliff and Daniel would have been there in spite of us. Where help is needed, they are there. You know that." She squeezed Elizabeth's hand. "Maybe he got into some poison ivy."

"Sure, he grows it behind the newspaper office." She was silent again. "Don't tell him."

"I won't have to. He's not dumb or blind, you know. I have a feeling he won't leave until you are out of the woods. At least the other times you were home. Well, not for Roald's birth, but you recuperated at home."

"I am so tired, Astrid, so very tired."

Mrs. Geddick herself entered with a laden

tray, and Thorliff came in right behind her. Mrs. Geddick announced, "We need more chickens."

Astrid nodded. "Daniel is working on that. Thank you, Mrs. Geddick."

"Yes, thank you." Thorliff took the tray and carried it to the bedside table.

Astrid forced brightness into her voice. "Oh, look! She sent you some raspberry juice too. And beef stew. Mrs. Geddick made the stew for those who can swallow well. I don't know how she can stand the chicken soup, she's made so much of it. Here's some cheese too and a slice of fresh bread with butter and jam."

Astrid backed away. They didn't need her. Thorliff knew how to take care of his wife.

"Before you leave, Astrid." Elizabeth sounded so frail. "I want Thelma or someone to bring Inga over so I can talk with her through the window."

"Roald?"

"No," Thorliff said. "He won't remember, and it might make him cry for you even worse. Yes, I know what's been going on, but we can't take chances. I'm just praying we were not contagious yet when we went home the next day."

Astrid watched Thorliff, who was studying his wife. "Please call, Astrid, while I make sure she eats and drinks plenty." He tried to smile, but the pain did not leave his eyes.

When Astrid returned, Elizabeth was

asleep and Thorliff sat watching her, holding her hand. "Daniel is bringing Inga so Thelma can stay with Roald."

"She could come on her own."

"I know, but I think this is better. She loves Onkel Daniel."

"Inga loves everybody. She's like Mor."

"True."

Elizabeth woke and heaved a sigh. "How long until she is here? I want to be in the chair to watch her come. Astrid, please bring me an apron to cover this gown." She pushed herself upright and swung her legs over the edge of the bed. "How does my hair look?"

"Good. A bit like you had a nap, but . . ."

Astrid handed her a clean apron and tied it for her in the back.

Thorliff carried the chair over to the window and set it down so she could rest her elbows on the sill. "Shame we can't open the window."

"I don't want to take any chances. If I have to cough . . ."

He helped her get settled, and Astrid finger-combed some tendrils into the bun.

"There they come. She's dragging Daniel."

"Ma!" Inga waved, dropped his hand, and ran to stand under the window. "We sure are missing you. Roald fusses. I want to go out to the farm to see Grandma, but most I want you to come home." Her words fell over each other, then got up and ran on again. She was speaking plenty loud enough for Elizabeth to hear her through the glass.

"I need something to stand on so I can see you better. 'Member when I stood on Benny's wagon and it tipped over when we were trying to get to know Manny? He sure was mean at first. Did you know he is taking care of the elephants? He even rode Olive. Just think, riding on an elephant. I sure hope I can too."

"How about I let you stand on my knee?" Daniel asked, smiling at those inside.

"But you are standing on them."

Daniel knelt on one knee and bent the other. "You can hold on to me."

"Don't wobble or we might both fall over." She stood up on his knee and gripped the windowsill. "Now I can see you good. Did you have a good nap?"

"I did. How is Scooter?"

"He barked at the elephants. You should have seen him tear up and down by the fence. Violet flapped her ears at him and kept walking, but the little one went on the other side of her. They sure can walk fast. I watched Manny take them down to the river to eat. He walked by our fence just 'cause I asked him to."

"When did you talk with Manny?"

"We didn't talk close. He won't come near anyone." She grabbed for Daniel's head when she wobbled.

"Easy there. Don't go jumping around."

She stared down at him. "I did not jump. I just jiggled."

Astrid had to laugh. That was Inga all right. Be careful that what you said was accurate. She caught her husband's eye, and he winked at her. Even this was better than just on the telephone. "Thank you," she mouthed.

"Ma, when are you coming home?"

"I'll be there as soon as my germs can't make you or anyone else sick."

"There is a sickroom at our house, you know."

"I know, but I need to stay here, where Dr. Astrid and the nurses can take care of me."

Inga looked at her, no more joy on her face. "Did you get the dip, dip-ria."

"Diphtheria. Possibly."

Astrid closed her eyes. Inga was too smart for her own good. What other child would have picked up on a slip like that?

"From all the people you been taking care of?"

"I hope you get to ride on the elephant."

"Me too. When is the circus train going to leave? I wish we could see the circus. Pa won't let me even go look at the lion, but I heard him roar. Pa, can we go fishing tomorrow for the sea lions? Emmy said they catch fish for them every day. I haven't seen her forever either." She huffed her disgust and down she went.

Astrid could hear her giggling and Daniel

laughing. Someday maybe they would have a little girl or several girls and boys as well.

Elizabeth reached up for Thorliff's hand and laid her cheek against it.

Inga and Daniel got her back up on his knee.

"We'll come back tomorrow. I know, we'll bring the wheelbarrow, or I could bring Roald in the wagon, then Onkel Daniel won't have dents in his leg." She sobered again. "Thelma and me, we pray for you and all the sick people every night and I pray during the day too."

"Thank you." Elizabeth blew her daughter a kiss. "And I'm sending you a hug too."

Inga blew a kiss back and then one for her pa. "I drew you a picture, but I forgot to bring it. I'll bring it tomorrow."

"Good. And I'll put it on the wall so I can see it."

Dear God, please don't rip this family apart. Please.

CHAPTER 23

By morning the rash had deteriorated to a suppurating wound as the bacteria ate through the epidermis and into the next layer of tissue.

Thorliff stared at it, then at Astrid. "Not like poison ivy or anything I've ever seen."

"We've seen it here, on one of the men from the train, but that had ulcerated clear down to the bone. Let me check your glands." She palpated his jawline and more in his neck. "Swollen. Is your throat sore yet?"

"More scratchy but nothing to be concerned about." He started to roll his sleeve back down but stopped at her command.

"I have bad news, I'm afraid. All this points to diphtheria for you too, just starting differently than the others."

He stared at her, then shook his head. "I-I thought I was beyond the danger point."

She wagged her head. "'Fraid not." Was she getting calloused or just detached? She refused to acknowledge that this patient sitting on the examining table was her brother. He was a patient who had to be treated for a disease.

"But I'm not even old or young. I thought those were the primary victims. Astrid, this can't be."

"The positive side is that you are healthy, you do not live in squalor, and you've not been cooped up with folks getting sicker and sicker around you to the point of dying. Many victims, most actually, live through this and become immune. Now, we pray not only for healing, but for a light case, and we are starting treatment at the very first sign. Now, please, just do what we tell you and—"

"Will my being with Elizabeth make her any worse?"

"No, but perhaps we should not tell her right away. She feels so guilty already that she asked you to help the night the train arrived."

"The night we should have sent them on their way." He shook his head. "Charlie Becker was so much smarter than we were. He saved Grafton, and we let the demon into Blessing."

"As Reverend Solberg says, the past is past. You can't change it, so don't waste your time dwelling there."

"Ja, well right now . . . What about Inga and Roald? They've been with me."

"We'll have to watch them carefully. They did not have contact with the ill here like you did. That spot on your arm—you might have had a bit of a scratch or some such for the bacteria to invade."

"What will you do?"

"Scrub it with carbolic acid, apply poultices, honey, like treating a boil or some other infection. Make sure you get lots of sleep, all the things we are doing for the others here."

"I really didn't think it would get me."

"As soon as we treat it, you can go back to Elizabeth. Make sure she gets fluids, food, and all we can do for her."

"Let's get on with it."

"I'll send in Sandra. Just wait here."

"Astrid, can you call Devlin and ask him to come by? We have to get the paper out."

"He should be here anytime." She left the examining room, gave instructions, and returned to her office, closing the door behind her. How would she tell her mother this news? And Andrew?

Later that morning, when the train arrived, Daniel and the new intern pushed the handcarts with supplies over to the hospital, accompanied by three student nurses. Astrid met them at the door.

"Welcome. You have no idea how much we

appreciate your coming. Thank you, Daniel."
She smiled at her husband, wishing she could
go home with him and sleep for a week or at
least a day in her own bed. His smile in return
said he felt so too.

"I am Dr. Astrid Bjorklund." She beckoned them in. "And I know you must be Dr.
Johnson." He smiled and shook her hand. As
she nodded to the others, each of them said
her name.

"Rose Kendricks."

"Ethel Brand."

"Alice Williams."

"Now, since we are under quarantine,
once you are here, you will not be allowed to
leave. We take turns sleeping in the other ward.
I'm sorry to say we have to share beds, unless
you choose to sleep on a pallet on the floor."
She watched their faces, trying to gauge their
responses. "I hope they prepared you for the
siege we are under."

While Reverend Solberg and Dr. Johnson
wheeled the boxes into the supply room, she
showed the nurses where to put their suitcases.

"Dr. Astrid!"

"Excuse me. You will find aprons in the
supply room on the shelf." Wiping the perspi-
ration from her forehead, she headed down the
ward to where Vera was holding a convulsing
child. "Suction his throat and bring him into
the steam room." She placed her stethoscope

on the boy's chest. "Heart rate up. Come on, son, hold on a while longer. We thought you were improving." He lay limp in Vera's arms.

"He's not breathing." Vera carried the child into the steam room, and together they held him over the steaming kettle. "There, he is now." Astrid tented a towel over their heads. Hot as it was in the hospital, this room made them drip immediately. But it helped, if nothing else, to help the sick relax as the airways cleared even the smallest amounts.

Astrid heard Miriam taking over introducing the newcomers to the rest of the staff and the way of the hospital. "We also have a tent full of folks from the circus train that we are taking care of."

"The train that brought diphtheria to your town? Correct?" the resident asked.

"Yes. They briefed you in Chicago?"

"Yes, but none of us have worked with diphtheria."

"I know you must be tired from your trip, but people here are exhausted too. Our head nurse is sleeping now. We all do whatever needs to be done. Most of our patients need close to full-time care. Dr. Commons is healthy, but our other full-time doctor has contracted the disease and is getting worse by the minute. So, Dr. Johnson, if you will scrub and work with Dr. Bjorklund." Miriam paused. "I hope you brought a uniform. All we have are regular nurses' aprons."

"I did. Where do I change?"

"The bathroom would be all right." She pointed in the direction. "I will assign each of you to two patients to start. Dinner will be in an hour, but we try to feed around the clock for those who have so much trouble swallowing."

Astrid headed for room one, Time to check Elizabeth again. Both of them were sleeping, Thorliff in the chair by her bed. His neck was now visibly swollen. She carefully unwrapped the dressing on his arm. It was worse too. Much worse. She wrapped it in clean bandaging. "Thorliff, please go lie down on the other bed."

"I can help you." The rasp in his voice startled him. He laid his hand on his throat and blinked. "Getting worse, right?"

She nodded. "You have to drink. Fill your glass from that pitcher and keep drinking. I can work more if you will move to the other bed. Our new staff members arrived a bit ago. I'll be right back." Back to the kitchen for broth in a cup and a spoon.

When Dr. Johnson joined her in room one, he asked, "Why are you not using a straw?"

"We have run out of them, and patients with diphtheria are not able to suck in the liquid due to the swelling in the throat."

He nodded. "We did bring a box of straws. They are in the supply room."

"Thank you." She shook Elizabeth gently. "Time to get more into you." She set the cup and spoon on the bedside stand. "Let's get you sitting up."

Elizabeth nodded, but as soon as she tried to move, the cough wracked her so hard the bed shook.

Astrid motioned to the young man to assist with getting the pillow in place.

Thorliff swung his feet up on the bed, watching them as he sipped.

With Elizabeth propped up, Astrid wiped her face with a warm cloth and introduced her helper.

"Thank you for coming."

He had to lean down to hear her. "You are welcome." Automatically he took her wrist and counted for her pulse, then looked at Astrid, eyes slightly widened. She nodded back.

"If you would please check her heart and lungs, then her throat after she drinks some." She held the cup to Elizabeth's mouth. She swallowed several times before she started coughing again. "I have the cough syrup right here, but you need some broth first."

"Sorry. How is Thorliff?"

"Drink."

"Steam room?"

"After this."

It took both her and Dr. Johnson to help Elizabeth to the steam room, but they quickly got her settled in a chair near the steaming kettle.

344

"Can you sit by yourself?"

She shrugged before tipping her head back on the cushion, her eyes drifting closed. "I can't . . . cough . . . anything up."

"I know. Doctor, will you please go ask Miriam for the cough syrup." Returning to Elizabeth, she continued. "I should just carry a bottle in my pocket, much as we go through."

"It . . . helps." A pause, then, "Thorliff?"

"Neck worse, running a temp, and the ulcer is still there. We'll keep treating it." She would not tell Elizabeth that the ulcer was out of control, not responding to treatment.

After they put Elizabeth back to bed, she beckoned Astrid closer. "So tired. You take care of Thorliff." With pauses between words, she was even harder to understand, the weak voice fading in and out.

"Of course."

"After." But she drifted off to sleep before Astrid could ask her what she meant.

That evening after supper and the patients were readied for the night or the next round of nursing, Astrid left instructions to be awakened if any emergencies occurred and gratefully sank into bed. She needed to tell . . . But that thought didn't even get finished.

Deborah woke her with a touch and a whisper. "Astrid, come quick. Elizabeth."

Astrid didn't bother to put her shoes on, just dashed to room one.

Thorliff was holding his wife's hand, tears streaming down his face. He smoothed her hair back and kissed her, then turned to Astrid. "She's gone. I was watching her, and she gasped once and quit breathing. She could still breathe. Why did she die?"

Astrid dropped her stethoscope back around her neck. "I am sure her heart gave out." She mopped the tears streaming down her own face and stroked Elizabeth's cheek. "I think she knew it was coming."

"How could she?"

"Sometimes people just know. All I know is she is out of pain and home in heaven."

She came around the bed and put her arms around her older brother. "I'm sorry, Thorliff, I'm so sorry."

He sobbed on her shoulder. "How do I tell Inga? Roald won't understand, but Inga knows about heaven. After all, Far is there." He stared at Astrid. "I can't even tell her, can I? Through the window? If only I could send her out to Mor. Is it safe to do that yet?" He coughed so hard and long he couldn't catch his breath. "Astrid, I *have* to get well." He gasped between words.

"I'll get the cough syrup." She turned to see Deborah and the others in the doorway, tears streaming down their faces too.

"I'll get it," Deborah said. "We should have wakened Reverend Solberg. I'll do it now."

Astrid shrugged and handed her brother

the glass of water. "Here, drink this. That will help and . . ." Her voice trailed off as a fresh wave of tears caught her. When it came, she poured the syrup into the cup on the stand and handed it to Thorliff. "Drink this slowly, and let it coat your throat."

She turned to the bed of her dear sister-in-law, feeling they were really closer than sisters with all they had been through together. Ignoring her burning eyes, she gently pulled the sheet over Elizabeth, telling her good-bye as she did so.

"I'm so sorry," Reverend Solberg whispered as he came into the room. "Thorliff, Astrid, I would like to read the prayers over her and for you before you move her."

Astrid nodded and looked to Thorliff, who had moved to the chair and taken his wife's hand again. "Do you want to be alone with her for a while?" Thorliff shook his head.

After folding back the sheet from Elizabeth's face, the reverend opened his book and made the sign of the cross on her forehead. "Our Lord God is welcoming you home, we know, but we are bereft," he said, his voice cracking on some of the words. "Please, Lord, may thy grace and peace surround us all, and the comfort only thou canst give." He closed his book. "I know there are no words to convey my sorrow, but we do know God is right here with us. He promised to never leave us, and

He has not for a moment left Elizabeth alone either. Heaven is as close as the last breath she breathed."

Thorliff tried to clear his throat and instead started coughing. When the spasm passed, he propped his head, his elbows on his knees. Wiping his eyes with his fingers, he shook his head slowly as if it were too heavy to move. "Who will tell my children?"

"Thelma will. You know how they love and trust her."

"How can we even have a funeral?"

"We can't now. The burial will have to be tomorrow."

"Ja. Is there a coffin? She has to have a coffin."

"Ja, there will be."

"If there is not one, we will build it." Solberg laid his hand on Thorliff's shoulder.

"We will take care of everything, and when this is all over, we will have a celebration of life for Elizabeth."

Had someone made coffins for all the circus people who had died? The thought wandered through Astrid's mind, chased by more tears. "I will call Mor first thing in the morning."

"That's not very far away."

"I didn't check the time she died."

"I did," Deborah said. "It was 3:04 a.m."

"I . . . I think I better go to bed." Thorliff sounded woozy.

Astrid helped him to his feet. "The cough syrup has a bit of laudanum in it to help control the coughing. It will help you sleep too." After he flopped on the bed, she pulled the sheet up. "I am going to open the window so you get some fresh air. God bless." She kissed his forehead and stared down at him. He still had not really recovered from grieving for Far. This would be much worse.

CHAPTER 24

O God, no, not Elizabeth." Perhaps the practice of keening was not so bad. She fought to suck in a breath of air.

"Mor! Are you there?" Astrid's voice shouting through the dropped earpiece.

Ingeborg sank down on the chair Clara had just scooted against the back of her knees.

"Mor!"

Ingeborg swallowed, fighting to answer. She picked up the dreaded black thing and answered. "I am here. Sorry I dropped you. I have to go to Inga."

"No! You cannot!" Astrid broke all doctor ethics and screamed into the telephone. Her voice dropped. "Please, Mor. Stay home. We don't know if the antitoxin has worked enough in you yet."

"But my babies."

"I know." Astrid's voice was laced with tears too. "Who is with you?"

"Freda and Clara, making breakfast. No, they are both right beside me. How is Thorliff?"

"Sleeping. I gave him extra cough syrup."

"Is he worse?" Ingeborg forced the words through the tears. As the silence stretched, she added, "Tell me!"

"Ja, he is worse. If only . . ." The last was a whisper.

"Does Thelma know yet?"

"No. I am calling her next. Thomas Devlin and Reverend Solberg built the coffin sometime after four this morning, or they are in the process. They will bury her. Mor, we cannot even have a funeral."

Ingeborg's mothering instincts kicked back in. "Oh, Astrid, you are having to carry so much." And now the hospital would be all her responsibility. *O Lord, keep her safe, be her strong right arm.* She felt a hand on either shoulder. Who would be standing by Astrid? And she couldn't even go home to Daniel. *Only you, Lord God. O God, hold her!* "We are all praying." That sounded inadequate, but she knew it wasn't.

"I know that most likely is what is keeping me both sane and healthy." A pause. "Mor, I cannot catch this."

"You have the antitoxin at work, and you are strong in our Lord."

"At least we have more nurses, and Dr. Kenneth Johnson, another resident, arrived yesterday. He is sleeping right now. He and Dr. Commons are a wonderful help."

"Are you eating right and sleeping?"

"Ja, I am. I have to be careful, I know. So many deaths. So many."

Ingeborg heard her daughter blow her nose and sniff again. *O Lord.* That was all she could seem to pray.

"I was afraid Elizabeth would die after Inga was born, but with Roald she recovered fairly quickly for her. But she had no strength to fight with. She knew it. I think I envy her. She is free of this horror. Promise me you will stay home."

"I promise, much against my heart's cries. Take care of Thorliff. We can't lose Thorliff too. Do you want me to call Thelma? Kaaren?"

"I'd appreciate it if you would call Kaaren. Right now I am glad Elizabeth's folks do not have a telephone. I will have to send a telegram, but at least I won't have to talk with them."

"Ja, it's easier."

"I love you, Mor. When this is over . . ."

"We will recover, all of Blessing, and you will come out here, and we will be together." *Please, Lord.* "'Bye." She listened for Astrid's answer and, with a shaking hand, set the earpiece back. Freda hugged her from one side and Clara the other.

"You come out on the porch, and we will have our coffee and breakfast out there. The birds are singing, the men are about done milking, and . . ."

"Where is Emmy?"

"I heard her moving around. She'll be down soon."

Ingeborg allowed herself to be led out to the porch to sit on the cushioned settee. Freda sat beside her, still holding her hand. Her head wagging, too heavy to hold still, she let the back cushion help her. Eyes closed, she listened to the songs of the morning, birds singing, a rooster crowing, Patches scratching, his leg thumping on the wooden floor, a thrush heralded from the garden, a cow bellered, sheep bleated. Life went on in spite of the tragedies, the sorrows. She felt a small body sit beside her and lean against her shoulder.

"Inga needs us."

"Ja, she does, but we have to stay here. I promised Astrid we would not go into town."

Clara bumped the door open with her hip and set the tray on the table. She beckoned Emmy to follow her.

Emmy kissed Ingeborg's cheek and slid off the cushion. "Be right back."

Freda handed Ingeborg a steaming cup and took one herself. Together they cupped their hands around the warmth, welcome even though the air was only slightly chilly, thanks to the shade. "The strawberries are ripening. I will pick some for dinner."

"There are enough?"

"Emmy and I will see. I put out the stakes with fluttering strips of one of the raggedy dish towels yesterday. Should have earlier. Those robins and the blackbirds do like strawberries."

"Life goes on."

"It does. I will bake cookies for Inga. And I will take them to the back porch. Thelma can pick them up there."

"We will bake gingerbread men."

The screen door swung open, and Clara carried the tray half propped on her shelf, as she had started calling her middle. Emmy followed her with a basket of biscuits and the jam. Clara handed out the plates, and after she and Emmy sat down with theirs, Ingeborg nodded to Emmy to say the grace.

Emmy closed her eyes. "Dear Jesus, thank you for our food. Please take care of Inga. And help Grandma have happy eyes again. Amen."

"Thank you, Clara, this looks so good."

Clara nodded with a smile and passed the biscuits.

They ate in a gentle silence, broken only with words like *Pass the biscuits, jam,* and other meal things. Ingeborg felt the comfort float in on the slight breeze and take up residence in her bleeding heart.

Patches leaped off the porch, barking his friend and family welcome. Kaaren leaned over to pat him, then waved to Ingeborg. Panting, she climbed the steps. Ingeborg met her with an embrace that lasted as they cried together.

Clara went for the coffeepot and another cup.

Freda started to stand up, but Kaaren waved her to stay where she was. "I'll sit in the rocker."

When they were seated, Ingeborg blew out a sigh. "So much. Too much."

"It could be so much worse. So far most of our people are safe." Kaaren, ever practical.

"All but those involved with the train. And now Thorliff has it too."

"He is going to make it. I didn't have that confidence with Elizabeth, but I believe this."

"I so pray you are right. Surely we are all running out of tears."

"Our doctors have been so wise to slap a quarantine on the town before the disease got further away."

"If everyone does what they say." Freda added to the conversation. "Thank you, Clara. You are taking good care of us this morning."

Kaaren sighed. "I so look forward to church again, to meeting with the others, to having a wonderful Sunday dinner after church. To banishing this fear, catching up on all the news that does not have to do with diphtheria and death. It is important to think ahead."

"To be praying together, singing . . ." Ingeborg stopped and her eyes filled again. "Elizabeth will not be playing the organ anymore. Nothing will ever be the same again. O Lord, my Inga."

"We will take strawberries in with the cookies. She loves strawberries."

Anji stood at the kitchen sink, staring out at her two boys fighting over a shovel and the hole they were digging. Her children fighting, another hiding out in her bedroom, and Thomas had literally run from her when they nearly bumped into each other on the street. What had happened? Granted, he was working both with the patients in the hospital and with the people from the train and therefore under quarantine. But still, he needn't be rude like that. She had seen the white tent out behind the mill, only because she had walked beyond the train that seemed to have taken up residence in Blessing. And why had she walked that far?

How she hated it when she asked herself questions she didn't want to answer.

"I'm going to tell Ma!" Joseph stormed toward the house, and Gilbert resumed digging, not appearing in the least sorry he had made his little brother cry.

Anji had had enough! She met Joseph at the door and pointed at the steps down from the back porch. "Sit." He did. "Now stay there." She stomped past him and out to where Gilbert was digging furiously.

"Give me that shovel."

He jerked to attention, his eyes wide. She never spoke to her children like that, and he knew it. He handed her the shovel. "Now, get out of that hole." Since it was up to his knees, he had to step high, never taking his eyes off her. When he stood in front of her, staring at his feet, she waited. And waited.

"I . . . I'm sorry."

"You are sorry for what?"

He glanced over at his younger brother, who was no longer crying. He was staring at their mother, eyes wide. "For not sharing with Joseph."

"That is right, young man. So what do you say?"

"I'm sorry." He looked up at her, worry creasing his forehead.

"Not to me." She pointed at the huddled figure trying to disappear into the wooden step. "Him."

"But, Ma . . ."

"Do not 'but Ma' me." She stared into his eyes until he quit studying his bare feet and went to Joseph and muttered.

"Louder. I want to hear it!"

"I'm sorry."

"And?"

He looked at her over his shoulder already tanned from the sun and from running around in overalls with straps over his shoulders. "You can have the shovel." He pointed to the shovel handle in his mother's hand.

"We can take turns," Joseph offered.

Anji shook her head. "Both of you boys go put your shoes on, and I will show you where you can dig. We are going to plant more in our garden." When they ran upstairs, she carried the shovel over to the garden and slammed it into the edge of the plot they had already planted. The best place for weeds to grow. While they dug, she and Melissa would pull weeds. As soon as Annika woke from her nap, she could help too. This wasn't what she'd planned to do today, but it was better than standing at the window trying to understand Thomas Devlin. Perhaps she had been reading him wrong. After all, had he really treated her any differently than he treated everyone?

She crossed the grass to stand under Melissa's window. "Lissa, can you hear me?" Her daughter's face appeared between the two lacy curtains. "Come on down and help me. Bring the basket from the pantry too." She waited.

"All right."

Both boys leaped down the steps and ran across to join her in the garden.

"Tie your shoes." She set the shovel blade into the weeds, pushed down on it with her foot, and turned over the shovel of soil. Repeating the action three more times, she handed the shovel to Gilbert. "Now you dig just like this clear down even with the far edge. Joseph, you break up the clods and pull out the weeds. Stack the weeds in the next row." Gilbert turned a clump and Joseph squatted down and dug it into it, just like she'd said. "Good. I'll be weeding the lettuce and carrots. We need a space about three rows apart." She nodded to the rest of the garden.

"Lissa, do you want to use the hoe or pull the weeds close to the plants?"

Sweat first trickled down her back, then her face and neck. She should have donned her straw hat. "Looks good, boys. Keep it up." Hoeing a garden wasn't the easiest job she could think of, especially not on a hot June day. She wiped her face with her apron. What to do about Thomas? She slaughtered the weeds that dared to grow in the rows of vegetables. The lettuce was ready. She should have picked that earlier in the day. Now it would wilt too fast.

"Hurry up," Gilbert ordered. "You're too slow."

"Then let me shovel for a while."

"Here!" Gilbert handed his brother the shovel handle and wiped his forehead with the back of his arm. He glanced at his mother and shrugged.

Anji shook her head. She looked around. They had dug three rows, she had hoed three, and Lissa's basket was full again. What were they doing out here at the hottest part of the day? "We'll come back to this after supper, when it is cooler. I think we need some of that lemonade from the icebox and cookies."

"And play dominoes?"

"Lissa, you help me in the kitchen, and boys, you set up the game."

"Ma?" Annika stood on the porch, rubbing her eyes.

"Coming." They stopped at the pan of sun-warmed water on the bench by the house. "Wash first."

They were well into their domino game and had refills on the lemonade, the cookie plate with not even a crumb when the telephone rang. She counted the rings and got to her feet. "I'll be back, but just skip my plays."

"I heard you all outside," Rebecca said after their greetings. "Benny wanted to come over so bad."

"He could have joined in the argument between the boys. I decided to work it out of them, but we didn't last long. Too hot out there."

"I know. I might close the soda shop since hardly anyone comes to buy sodas. If you want some ice cream, it is in the freezer."

"Business will pick up as soon as the quarantine is lifted."

"I know, and I am so grateful no one else has come down with it, but it seems like forever."

"I know." Anji wiped her neck and face again. The house was only a bit cooler than outside. Since there was no breeze inside, the back porch was the best place to be.

"Have you heard from Mr. Devlin?"

"No."

"He's in quarantine, you know."

Anji dropped her voice. "But what if he has it?"

"Oh, my right foot. Surely Astrid would tell you if he was in the hospital."

"I don't think Astrid has much time to make phone calls, not after the news this morning."

"I can't believe Elizabeth is really gone. And poor Thorliff. He lost his wife and now he has it too." She stared up at the wall to keep from crying. And here she'd been fretting about Thomas acting so strange. Such a petty thing when friends were suffering and dying. Just four blocks away. How could she be so shallow? She, who knew what the grief of losing a mate felt like? "Have you heard how Ingeborg is doing?"

"No, not many phone calls going through either. Gerald says maybe people are afraid they'll get it through the phone lines."

Anji glanced down to see Gilbert waiting to talk with her. "Hold on a minute. What, son?"

"Can we have more cookies? Er, may we?"

"Of course. I need to go, Becca. If you hear anything, please let me know." She hung up and returned to the kitchen. How could she help Thorliff? Of course she was praying. Everyone was. But there must be something more. *Please don't let him die too*. Just the thought twisted and squeezed her heart.

CHAPTER 25

Eh, Devlin, a sorry mess ye've made of yer life.
Thomas Devlin stared at the gaudy ceiling of his little cabin aboard the train. He was going to have to get up now. And then he would wander the aisles of this accursed train, carrying out the dead, cajoling the living, changing bedding, managing bedpans, and doing all the other tasks more fitting for devotees of Florence Nightingale than a humble priest.

Priest? A priest without a parish, a cleric without a church. If he were any sort of priest at all, he would be serving a flock somewhere, not wandering about in this alien land. He should give up the silly notion of being a priest, throw away his clerical collar, and find good work as a carpenter or craftsman. Or even a teacher. 'Twas not so hard. You had only to know more about a subject than your pupils did, and you could pass something on to them.

This headache had persisted for several days, and still it raged, worse than ever. He'd never had a headache this persistent or this fierce. Surely any hour now the sore throat would begin, and he would fall to diphtheria, giving lie to the notion that surviving the disease conferred immunity. He completed the necessaries and walked next door to the kitchen car for breakfast.

The cook grinned as he entered. "Dobry den, Mizzer Devlin!"

"And the top of the morning to yerself." Devlin settled on a stool at the long table.

The cook plopped a plate of eggs and sausages in front of him. The fellow did not know English, but he did indeed know good food well seasoned. Devlin paused to thank God, crossed himself, and dug in.

Far from making the priesthood his life's work, he had failed. True, it was not his fault exactly, but that unfortunate tangle with the Archbishop of Canterbury had left him little choice save to emigrate. He should not have insisted so strongly upon his position when the bishop said otherwise. But he had, and he was banished. Well, not officially, but *de facto*. And he was still convinced he had been right and the archbishop wrong. Sadly, no one on this side of the water seemed to want a priest such as himself.

Carpentry? He had been paid very little for his work as a carpenter and woodcarver in Blessing, but then no one else was paid much either. And some of the supervisors even worked without pay. Still, that could hardly be called success. Master woodcarver Grinling Gibbons had earned fat pay and worldwide renown; Thomas Devlin got a free meal at Ingeborg Bjorklund's occasionally.

He had quite enjoyed teaching, but school was out, the children sequestered until this hideous plague abated. It was, in a sense, seasonal work. However, if he managed to find a position as a schoolmaster, he could work as a harvester during summer.

But what truly plunged his sorry heart into the depths was Anji. One way or another he could support himself in this town, but there was Anji. The look on her face when last he saw her said it all. She was not about to have anything to do with a worthless slug such as himself.

And he didn't blame her.

He finished breakfast, thanked the cook profusely, and started in on his rounds. For the first time since he'd come to the train, he had not found one person dead by the time he reached the far end of the train. He went outside to the tent. Glorious day today, shimmering opaline sky, the slightest whiff of a breeze. And it was quite warm already.

No other medical people were in the tent. As Devlin moved from cot to cot, speaking with this patient and that, his spirits lifted. No overnight deaths here either. He would check with Dr. Elizabeth or Dr. Astrid, of course, but it appeared to him that four or five of those in the tent could go back to their quarters. And the ill who were still on the train would be up and about soon. Perhaps the worst was over for the train's denizens. Now if the populace of Blessing all escaped, the crisis would be done. What a wonderful thing that would be.

He left the tent, staying in the shadow of the mill as much as possible to avoid the heat, and entered the back door of the hospital.

There was coughing, of course, much coughing. And yet, he immediately felt a heavy stillness. Unnatural quiet. Something was massively, hideously wrong here. One of the things that had swayed him toward the priesthood was his ability to sense the spirit of a place. The spirit of this place was the most oppressive he'd ever known. He rapped quietly on Dr. Astrid's office door and pushed it open. Her chair sat vacant. The heavy silence in this room was so palpable it whispered in his ear.

He stepped back into the hall and closed the door. The student nurse who wore her hair in a bun was approaching. He asked her, "Who died?"

She looked at him for a moment as if to say,

Don't you know? "Dr. Elizabeth." She continued on.

He stood stunned. Just stood there. The pillars of the hospital could not fall ill. They could not! They got pregnant, perhaps, but not sick. Surely the young lady was wrong. She had just arrived, she did not know all the people here yet. She must have . . . Dr. Elizabeth. *Dear God in heaven* . . . Slowly, painfully he crossed himself. Dr. Elizabeth.

Where . . . ?

He entered room one. Not Thorliff also! The man was sleeping fitfully on the side bed. He coughed in his sleep. Yes, Thorliff. The other bed, where patients lie, was empty, stripped of its bedding. The children leapt to mind. What about the children?

Devlin hastened to the kitchen. There was Dr. Astrid seated at the table. Nurse Deborah sat across from her, clasping Astrid's hands in hers. Should he intervene? Yes.

He flopped into a chair beside Dr. Astrid and covered the women's hands with his. "Words and platitudes will not serve here. Has she received the appropriate rites?"

"Yes." Astrid's voice was stricken.

"Has she a proper coffin?"

"John was going to make one."

"I shall go assist him." He squeezed their hands in his. "Me very deepest condolences, lady."

He left the hospital, the scene of death and misery, for the first time since he'd destroyed his relationship with Anji. That headache was pounding his skull with rubber mallets.

Where would John build a coffin? The outbuilding behind the Jeffers' home? He ran to that shed, trying to escape the enormity of this nightmare. No one there.

More to the point, *how* would John build a coffin? The man knew a little something about woodcraft, but not enough to make a solid coffin in a day, and with this heat they would have to bury her soon.

Trygve had built himself quite a nice shop behind his new house. Devlin jogged to that building, sweating profusely. He heard the clatter of falling lumber even before he got there.

The door stood open. Inside, John Solberg, in shirtsleeves, had just dropped a pile of boards. Devlin stepped in beside him and knelt to scoop up the boards.

Tears were running down John's face.

They said nothing. Devlin helped him put the boards on a side bench. He snatched up a couple of sawhorses stacked in the corner and set them out. John chose one of the boards and laid it on the sawhorses as Devlin picked out another. Devlin paused long enough to strip off his shirt. It was soaked now. John did as well. Did Trygve have a carpenter's rule? He did, right there on the shelf. Devlin unfolded it open and measured. Devlin measured to his chin, about the height Dr. Elizabeth had stood. He measured and marked a board with a pencil stub. Solberg nodded.

There were no boards broad enough to build a bottom of one piece, and there was no time to glue up an appropriate bottom board. So Devlin cut three one-by-two cross pieces. Solberg drilled holes and set the screws as Devlin held it all in place. They flipped it over so that the cross braces were on the bottom.

Devlin calculated briefly—this particular job was not new for him—and drew two angled lines. They measured, truing them up. Solberg began sawing as Devlin began to shape the sides. An hour later they had a box, more specifically an anthropoid irregular hexagon. He had learned that as he was finding information for the geometry class he had taught. Quite highbrow, knowing what an anthropoid irregular hexagon was, and completely useless.

Solberg started measuring for the lid, but Devlin was not interested in building lids. He had set himself to a different task. He spent some minutes digging through the odd lumber to choose exactly the right piece of wood. He sawed the right length, braced it into clamps, and rapidly sketched guidelines on its face.

What kind of wood chisels did Trygve own? And adzes? A hand adze would make it go faster. In a drawer he found good chisels, even a veiner. He chose what he needed, honed them on the whetstone and strop in the corner, and set to work.

Almost two hours later when Solberg finished the lid and hinged it into place, Devlin had his own masterpiece close to completion. Solberg watched in silence as Devlin put the finishing touches on the feathered wings at the top of a pole, the two snakes intertwined around it. Devlin laid the bas relief caduceus on the coffin lid. Perfect.

They paused briefly to admire it. Solberg whispered, "Thank you."

Devlin held the carving in place on the lid as Solberg drilled and screwed it down tight from the back.

The reverend walked over to the side and shook out his shirt. "I'll go tell Astrid this is ready."

Devlin nodded and tugged into his own shirt. He was still wet with sweat. He stepped outside into exquisite heat. In the depths of winter, when your spit freezes before it reaches the ground, you forget about the heat of summer. He walked to the hospital and continued on beyond it. He walked past the mill, past the tent, past the train. Past responsibilities that he was supposed to be shouldering right now. He continued down to the river shore.

Peace.

Manny was not there with his elephants

just now, but their tracks and droppings were everywhere. The streamside willows all looked mangled and shaved. The cattails were growing nicely, with fresh green spears—the ones on the far shore, that is. On this shore they had become elephant fodder.

He heard a rustle off to the side. And another. The dogs! He knew a little something about dog packs. These mangy curs were stalking him! He opened his pocket knife and cut himself a stout willow withe from the mangled grove. He slapped it a couple times into the open palm of his left hand. Good. Good! Let the straggly beasts try something now!

He turned quickly and started walking firmly toward the nearest dog, the alpha bitch. She snarled and wheeled away. He turned immediately toward another mutt. The dog disappeared beyond the mangled remains of the willow thicket. Devlin walked back to the train without being challenged or stalked.

But what if he had been a defenseless child?

His weapon was still in his hand when he was passing the train and Stetler was stepping down out of his personal car. The man stopped and froze, wide-eyed, staring at the branch in Devlin's hand.

A thousand thoughts raced about in Devlin's mind, chasing each other through his brain. How imbued with the spirit of Jesus

Christ was he, really? His seminary training never mentioned situations like this.

Stetler eyed him warily. Most of his attention was on the switch. "Mr. Devlin."

"Mr. Stetler."

"What are your intentions?"

"I do not know. Meself has just come from building a sturdy coffin for one of the two founding doctors of this hospital where ye brought yer pestilence. Ye might say, mixed feelings."

"A doctor . . ." He drew a deep breath and licked his lips. "I was coming to find you. I need your help, Mr. Devlin. Our train engineer respects you. I need you to convince him it is now safe to travel. We have to get back on our schedule, and he is afraid to go."

"The quarantine has not been lifted, sir, and many of yer people be yet too weak to travel, let alone perform. Some will never perform again if their limbs be affected, as diphtheria sometimes does. How will ye assemble a show worth the price of admission? How can we let ye go to bring death to some other town?"

"I must!" The man looked desperate. "We have no money, Devlin, no income! The very survival of this circus depends upon bringing in money to keep going. Do you realize how much the elephants eat, just the elephants?"

"Aye, a whole willow thicket, for starters. Ye have no elephant trainer, no—"

"I know he is weak, but he is on the mend. Mr. Devlin, please. I need you!"

A moment ago a thousand thoughts had raced through his head. Now ten thousand thoughts did. He wanted to wreak godly vengeance upon this pitiless man. Jesus said, "Love your enemies." He wanted Stetler to pay somehow for the death of a splendid physician who was such a boon to this community. Jesus said, God "sendeth rain on the just and on the unjust."

"Frankly, sir, if ye leave now, I do not see how ye can make it."

"That's my concern." His voice softened. "Devlin, we're at the end of our rope. We can't make it if we don't get going. We lost so much, but . . ."

He threw away the stick. It thudded against the rail ties. "The stick was for a dog pack, not yerself. I shall speak to yer engineer. Where is he?"

"At the ice cream parlor."

"Eh, breaking quarantine. Perfect."

He turned his back on Mr. Stetler and took his time walking over to Rebecca's soda shop. Halfway there he stopped in midstride. The headache was gone. Sometime in the last few hours, it had evaporated. He still felt weary, but that headache had left. Curious. He continued.

The engineer was sitting off in the corner at one of those delicate little wrought-iron tables.

The treat in his ice cream dish was only half eaten. He looked up as Devlin came over and sat down across from him.

Devlin smiled. "How ye going, Mr. Ranson?"

Mr. Ranson smiled wanly. "How did you know I was here?"

"Where else would a refugee come if there be no tavern in town?"

The man laughed bitterly. "Refugee. Yes, I am that. Did Mr. Stetler send you?"

"He did. He seems to think he must have ye to run the train."

"He's right. I'm the only one can do it."

Devlin walked over to the counter, ordered a dish of strawberry ice cream, and returned to sit down across from Mr. Ranson. "Just how old might that locomotive be, anyway?"

"Older than the transcontinental railroad. Older than the war. During the War of Secession, it ferried Southern troops to the battlefront."

Devlin called upon his history knowledge, which, regarding the United States, was scant. He could list the complete royal succession in England, however. With exact dates. "Let's see. That war ended in 1865, correct?"

Ranson nodded. He stared at nothing. "Our little old locomotive is a relic, Mr. Devlin. That big bonnet on the stack. Wood-fired. Four two four. The boiler is about rusted through. Not many can operate those old ones anymore. Especially not this one. She's downright cranky."

"Then me hat's off to ye."

His ice cream arrived. Rebecca smiled wanly at him and left. She looked so sad. Obviously, she knew. No doubt the whole town knew by now.

Devlin dipped into his ice cream, surprised at how hungry he was. No surprise. Breakfast had been hours ago. "I cannot imagine that Mr. Stetler can put together a decent show, since so many people have died, and so many are weak from illness."

"Most of us, we did two or three jobs, you know. Like me. I'm the engineer, but I'm also a clown. Can you picture me in a big red rubber nose?"

Devlin laughed. "And the lion tamer told me he be a clown first, then changes to his new role."

"Sam. Good man, Sam. And that new kid is really good with animals."

"Manny."

"Manny. And there's another young man from town, a Johnny."

"Johnny Solberg. The reverend's lad." Devlin paused. "I was with his father less than an hour ago. John and I built a coffin. For Dr. Elizabeth. She just died."

"Doct—" Ranson stared at him. "At the hospital? Now you see why I'm not going back. If the doctors themselves are victims . . ."

"The crisis is nearly past, as we see it. No one from the train has died lately. No new cases. The old cases be getting better. 'Twill be a long haul, of course, getting one's strength back, but the worst be behind us, for which I praise God."

Ranson studied him closely. "You think the train is safe?"

"As I understand it, two to seven days after exposure and ye're home on the pig's back. The local folk who were not innoculated—who did not receive the antitoxin—be still in a modicum of danger. Yerselves, the circus, most likely be past it."

"I'm scared, Devlin."

"Ye need be no longer, I should think."

"I really do love running that locomotive. Making her behave when she hates to."

Devlin grinned. "'Twould be quite a kick. And ye keep her in such fine shape. The paint is fresh, no rust that shows. Did ye build a whole new flywheel? It looks so."

"You noticed! No, I found that in a scrap yard. I told you the engine's old, didn't I?"

Devlin lapsed into silence. Sometimes silence did great things in a conversation.

Ranson asked, "Are you sure it's all right to be on the train?"

"No, ye can never say 'I'm sure' about something like that. But everything points to it being safe again, aye."

"I might go back. I really do love to mess with that old locomotive." He picked up his spoon and scooped some ice cream. He studied it for a moment and popped it into his mouth.

"I trow ye have some time. 'Twill take at least a day to gather in all yer elephants and goats and horses. And the blessed camel."

He cackled. "Mr. Kabrhel—he's our Slovak cook—says the townspeople, the farmers, have been true to their word. They give us all the milk we need and buy the rest. Honest people. And giving."

"Godly people, aye. Easy people to get attached to." *Anji.*

Mr. Ranson scraped the last from his dish. "Think I'll go tell Mr. Stetler I'm back on."

"He'll deeply appreciate it. Ask him for a raise."

Mr. Ranson cackled again. "I just might!" He rose to go. Devlin stood, they shook hands, and Devlin sat down again.

What did he just do? Stetler had no business leaving, yet he had to leave. Most of the town would say good riddance, especially all those children who were homebound. And Devlin had just cajoled the engineer into helping a man who was his enemy. Enemy? No, not exactly, but a man whom Devlin did not—could not—respect. And that sort of person is even harder to forgive than a true, fierce enemy.

He finished his ice cream and headed back

toward the hospital a little bit refreshed, a little bit ready to resume his duties, and a whole lot grateful that the headache was gone.

"Mr. Devlin! Yoo-hoo!" Little Maxine, the girl who was a part-time postal helper, flagged him down from the post office door. "You've a letter, sir."

"A letter? Indeed. Thankee."

He accepted the envelope and studied it a moment. She went back inside.

From the Diocese of Michigan. What had the Diocese of Michigan to do with him? He wandered over to the bench in front of the general store, sat down, and slit it open with his pocket knife.

It was not from the diocese. Rather the diocese had forwarded it to him from a parish named St. Patrick on the Lake, a letter within a letter. He opened the envelope from the parish and read the two-page letter. Read it again. Read it again.

And his soul descended into turmoil again. It was their search committee. They were asking him to come to their church and sit down with them. He would preach for two weeks, meet with the vestry, and conduct a question-and-answer session with the congregation in a parish meeting. With all that, both he and the parish would decide if this was a good fit for both them and him. If the fit seemed good, he would become the rector of St. Patrick on the Lake.

A parish of his own. But Anji was here, not on Lake Michigan somewhere. He was trained in the priesthood. This was what he had prepared for. But Anji . . . why must life be so terribly complex?

He stood up, confused and heavy-hearted. A parish. Anji. A parish. Anji. But he had destroyed the relationship with Anji. Or had he?

CHAPTER 26

*L*ord, how do I get through this day? All I want
is to hide in some dark place and cry my eyes
out. I don't want to deal with any more death or
sickness or . . . Astrid dried her eyes again, and
again, and again. Would they never stop? She
sat at her desk with the door closed, wishing
she had a lock to put on it.

A knock. Miriam's voice. "Astrid, Reverend
Solberg and Father Devlin are here with the
coffin. Do you want me to release the body?"

Astrid sniffed again. "No, give me a minute, and I'll be right there." Should she take
Thorliff to the storage room to see the body
one more time? No. What good would it do?
They had wrapped her in sheeting. All that was
needed was for them to place her in the box.
Fighting the strain of doing what she knew she

must do, she used her arms against the top of the desk to help get her upright. Out in the hall, she looked around. Where was all her staff? Was there another emergency no one had told her about? But when she turned the corner to the storage room, everyone was lined up, most with tears trickling down their faces.

"We'd salute if we were military," Miriam said. "But at least we can see her onto the wagon, if that is all right with you."

Astrid nodded. What fine people worked in this little hospital! She opened the door and, after sucking in one more deep breath, entered the dimly lit room. All the others followed her in and lined the way to the door. The men had set the coffin on sawhorses by the cot. Sorrow hung in the room like the densest fog. Glancing at the open door that provided the light, she saw Trygve and Daniel standing just outside the door, bareheaded, hats in their hands. If only she could go to her Daniel.

"We lined it with a quilt," Reverend Solberg said, his voice catching on the words.

Astrid nodded and picked up one corner of the sheet under the wrapped body. Devlin took one corner, Solberg another, and Deborah stepped forward to take the fourth. On three they lifted and settled the body in the coffin.

Astrid folded the quilt over her dearest friend, sister, mentor. "I know this is only a leftover husk of our Elizabeth, but even so, we honor you, dear friend."

"Let us pray." Reverend Solberg bowed his head. "Lord God, into your hands we commend our dearest Elizabeth. We rest in the assurance that we will see her again and that you are God and you do not make mistakes. Please comfort Thorliff, her children, and all the family. Give them and all of us your peace. We thank you that you sent your Son to the cross, that we might know for sure that we have an eternal home with you. Please bring healing to all our people and keep us steadfast in this battle against the enemy." He paused. "Amen."

Everyone echoed the amen. The two men set the coffin lid in place and nailed it down. Astrid laid a hand on the carving and nodded her thanks to Father Devlin. It must have been he who did this. He was the carver, not John. If only they could all go to the burial at least. She started to take hold of one of the boards under the coffin to move it to the wagon, but Miriam nudged her aside.

"Please let us." Miriam, Deborah, Mrs. Geddick, and Dr. Johnson assisted Devlin and Solberg as they moved the coffin to the wagon bed just outside the door and slid it into place. The shriek of wood against wood echoed the cries of their hearts.

"We are going along," Trygve said. "We will walk."

Astrid started to order them not to and instead nodded. She watched as John and Devlin climbed up to the wagon seat and clucked the horse forward. Turning back into the room, she looked to the new nurses. "Please scrub this room down. The mops, pails, and carbolic acid are in the storage closet. Try not to disturb Mr. Bjorklund. Miriam, show them where that is, please."

"We know, Dr. Bjorklund," Rose Kendricks said. "We'll take care of it."

"I have coffee made if anyone wants." Mrs. Geddick took Astrid's arm and patted it. "You come. You did not eat today. I fix you a plate."

"Ja, I will. I need to wash my hands first." Coffee. Would coffee help this time? At least Thorliff was asleep. She had decided to not waken him. He would probably be furious with her at some point, but right now her responsibility was to help him survive this scourge.

When she sat down at the table where the others were sitting, Mrs. Geddick set a plate in front of her.

"Now, you eat. You must stay strong." She laid a hand on Astrid's shoulder and gently squeezed, then looked up at the others. "Please eat. Dr. Elizabeth would want you to."

Someone started passing the stew around, and obediently they all helped themselves. Finally someone asked the question they were all thinking. "How are we going to manage?"

"We got through it when she was so ill, and we will again. As my mor would say, 'God will provide. The Lord gives and the Lord takes away, blessed . . .'" She was forced to clear her throat. "'Blessed be the name of the Lord.'" Several of them finished the verse with her.

"I wish Ingeborg were here," Deborah said. "Not being here must be so terribly hard on her."

"Ja, it is. And that she can't hold and comfort Inga. That is tearing her up the most, I think."

"Poor little Inga. Roald is so small he won't remember, but Inga can't have her pa or her grandma to comfort her."

"Ja, thank God for Thelma."

Astrid dutifully ate what was on the plate, not even registering what she had swallowed. Now the hospital depended on her alone.

As the others returned to sleeping or treating patients, she went to room one first. A barrage of coughing met her from the hallway. Thorliff's dull eyes opened when she picked up his wrist. He coughed again and a glob of ugly hit the sheet. She cleaned that up and dropped the muslin square in the pail by his bed. "Good. Time for the steam room for you. I'll ask Dr. Johnson to come help me move you there."

His eyebrows rose.

"A resident from Chicago. He and three nurses arrived on the train yesterday," she explained. "Or was it the day before? I'd have to check the notes." All the while she talked, she probed his swollen neck and picked up a cloth to dip in the pan of water they kept by his side to help sponge him cooler. "Sure wish this heat would break. We need a good thunderstorm to clear it all away." *Please, Lord, keep him from remembering his wife died.*

She leaned closer as he tried to talk, but only guttural noises could be heard. "Look at me. The diphtheria is affecting your vocal cords now too, so don't even try to talk. If you need something, tap my hand." She watched him shake his head, barely. "I'm going to get you some syrup and water before we move you, so I'll be right back."

She met Dr. Johnson in the hall. "Would you please help me move Thorliff into the steam room? We'll use the wheelchair." She pointed down the hall and stopped in the supply room to pour some cough syrup into a cup, then fetched a cup of water, answering a question from one of the new student nurses. Both of their resident student nurses were sleeping, thankfully.

Back in Thorliff's room, she held the cup to his mouth and watched to see if he was swallowing. His Adam's apple was barely visible within all the swelling, but it moved. Was it time to intubate him? She turned to Dr. Johnson beside her. "Have you looked in his throat?"

"Earlier."

"Please check again and tell me if you see any differences." She'd looked several hours earlier, and the membrane had spread overnight, but not quite to the danger zone yet. She watched his face and hands. Mrs. Korsheski in Chicago had said this young man was the best they had of the current three in residency.

"The same, as near as I can tell."

"Good. That's what I thought too." She wiped Thorliff's face with the cool cloth again. "When he returns from the steam room, pack him with cool cloths and ice around his neck."

"Yes, Doctor."

"Help us if you can, Thorliff. We're moving you into the steam room."

He blinked his eyes.

Between the three of them, they got him transferred to the chair, into the steam room, and parked near the stove.

"I know it is unbearably hot in here, but breathe as deeply as you can and cough as much as you can."

"Might ice wrapped in a cloth and applied to his head and the back of his neck make him more comfortable in here?"

"Good idea. I'll go make an ice pack. You stay with him."

Outside the door, she leaned against the wall and inhaled as deeply as she could of what seemed like cold air compared to the air inside that room. She waved to Vera. "Please change Thorliff's bed and replenish the supplies in there. How long since you've slept?"

"Too long it seems, but I'm due soon." She wiped her forehead with the edge of her apron. "Maybe we should all be wearing ice packs."

"If you can figure a way, let's do it." She moved on down the ward, talking with the nurses, making suggestions, trying to keep her thoughts away from Thorliff—and Elizabeth. Questions regarding what if this or that, like who will take the children if Thorliff dies too and what else could she do to prevent the disease from getting worse and what was going on in the outside world? Now, that one, that one she could dwell on.

When John Solberg and Father Devlin returned, she invited them into her office and ordered that coffee be brought in. "Did you have any dinner?"

They looked at each other and then her and shook their heads. "Then let's go to the dining room. It's cooler in there anyway. This box has no windows, even though there is an air vent into the roof." She remembered tripping over it when they were fighting to save the hospital from setting on fire when the grain elevator exploded. They sat down at one of the small tables in front of a window and put in an order when Mrs. Geddick came to see them, coffeepot in hand.

"You not eat?" She looked at the two men aghast. "I fix that right now."

"Don't bother to tell her you are not hungry. She'll probably bring you more food that way." She looked across the table at the two men. They had obviously cleaned up, but no amount of scrubbing would remove the sorrow from their faces. Astrid shut her eyes and shook her head. "Did anyone else show up?"

"A few, but they stayed far away. I think everyone in this town is so terrified of the disease, they are willing to follow the instructions." Reverend Solberg rubbed his forehead.

"Headache?"

"Not really. Even my skin feels heavy, full of sorrow. I didn't count the number of graves in the circus section of the cemetery. I am just praying no more have to be dug for our people. Thanks to your quick thinking, Astrid . . ."

"Not mine, Elizabeth's. She blamed herself for not sending that train on its way."

"They did not ask," Devlin reminded her. "They just showed up on yer doorstep with litters of sick people. I cannot picture either of ye doing any differently. If anyone be blamed, 'tis Stetler."

"Ja, and he was desperate too. But laying or trying to lay blame does no good at all. That train should be on its way soon. Thank you, Mrs. Geddick." John looked at the full plate before him. "Looks good as always."

"I will bring cake soon." She wiped her hands on her apron, shaking her head. "Such a sad day."

Astrid watched her return to the kitchen. She huffed and shook her head. "I didn't notify the hospital in Chicago. I better go do that. Dr. Johnson talked with them earlier. Excuse me, please." She paused. "And thank you for taking care of . . . of . . ." She turned and left before she started crying again.

Later that night after Dr. Johnson had just come on to relieve her, Astrid answered the demanding telephone. "Dr. Astrid, I have an emergency call for you."

"Thanks, Lucy, put it through. Dr. Bjorklund speaking."

"Doctor, my wife is going to have her baby tonight, she says. She's pacing something awful. Can you come?"

"Is she one of our patients?"

"Ja. She's been seeing you. Mabel Stavenger."

"Yes, of course." Astrid's mind whirled. "I cannot leave the hospital right now, but I will send a midwife with years of experience to help her. You probably know Ingeborg Bjorklund."

"Of course." He told her how to get there. "Tell her to please hurry."

"I will. In the meantime keep walking with Mabel. That's the best thing you can do to help. Good night." She hung up and clicked the earpiece again. "Please connect me to Ingeborg's." She waited, her foot tapping until her mor's sleepy voice answered.

"Mor, how quickly can you get out on a birthing call?"

"Really?"

"Ja. Mr. Stavenger just called. It has to be the son. His folks are too old to be having children."

"I brought that young man into the world. I know where the place is. I'm going to take Clara with me, let her see how babies are born. Freda will hitch up the buggy. 'Bye."

Astrid stared at the telephone as she hung up. Leave it to her mor. She knew everyone within a twenty-mile radius.

"If only Manny were here to hitch up the buggy." Ingeborg went to the foot of the stairs. "Freda! Freda!"

"Ja."

"I need to go help a baby into this world. Could you hitch up the buggy?"

"Where's the horse?"

"In the near pasture. Rattle a can of oats, and they'll all come."

Within a minute, Freda, wearing a robe and

shoes, clumped down the stairs. "You want me to go with you?"

"I'm going to take Clara. Soon as I get my clothes on and the bag, I'll come help you."

"I'll go get the horse." Emmy appeared right behind Freda and darted out the door.

Ingeborg woke Clara and both of them dressed swiftly. Ingeborg lit a lantern and they headed for the barn. Emmy had the horse tied to the hitching rail, and Freda was throwing the harness over its back. They finished adjusting the harness, backed the horse into the shafts, and while Clara held the lantern in the shed where the buggy was kept, they hitched in the lines. Ingeborg helped Clara up into the buggy, then got in herself and, making sure her medical bag was safe, flipped the reins, hupped the horse, and they were on their way.

"Be careful!" Freda called to them.

She set the horse to a trot down the lane and headed west. "You said you've never seen a baby born, right?"

"Good thing we have a moon. I've gone on birthing calls when it was so dark the horse could hardly see, and they can see in the dark. I used to do this all the time, you know. In fact, I brought this baby's pa into the world." *Thank you, Lord. You have given me a gift tonight.*

Soon they saw a lantern hanging on a post by a lane going north. They turned in and young Stavenger leaped down the steps and reached up to help Ingeborg down. "Thank you for coming. Felt like you would never get here."

"I'm sure it did." Ingeborg reached back in for her bag. "You needn't show me the way. Help Clara down and then you can tie my horse." She knew she needed to give him quiet instructions for something definite to do to help him calm down. Inside she was chuckling. "When did the contractions start?" She didn't wait for an answer but climbed the three stairs to the porch and stepped into the kitchen.

"In here," called a wavery female voice.

Ingeborg felt Clara right behind her. "Could you please make sure there is water on the stove to heat. You might have to start the fire. We need to sterilize our instruments, so start a small kettle too."

Clara nodded, and Ingeborg went on into the bedroom. "Hello, Mabel," she said to the young woman who was pacing back and forth. "How are you progressing? And when you saw Dr. Bjorklund, she told you what to expect, right?"

"I remember when my youngest . . ." She panted and stopped pacing to catch her breath. "Dr. Elizabeth told me all what to do, but Walter is a bit worried."

A bit was an understatement. They should probably have instructions for expectant fathers, besides the ones for the mothers. But then they did not usually come along for the pre-birth appointments.

"How about you lie back down on the bed and let's see how far you are dilated."

Mabel sat down on the edge of the bed. "I lost one baby a year or so ago, but this time all has been well." She hauled herself onto the bed with her arms, then froze and panted again. "I think they are getting closer together."

Ingeborg checked and smiled at the young almost-mother. "You are right, you're getting close. Let's get you up and walking again. The water hasn't broken?"

"No, ma'am. Is that Walt out in the kitchen?"

"No, I brought a helper, Clara, who lives with me. She is due in August, we think." Once she had Mabel on her feet again, they walked and chatted. Clara appeared in the doorway, and Ingeborg pointed to her black bag. "The birthing things are wrapped in a cloth all together and they must be boiled." Clara nodded, fetched the bundle, and looked at Ingeborg, who nodded. "That is what we need. Boil the cloth too and see if there is a cookie pan or a tray or even a large plate to bring them when we need them."

"Good thing I like to walk." Mabel grabbed Ingeborg's arm. "Uff da. It's getting harder."

"While you walk, I'm going to get the bed ready. I see you have sheets and towels ready. You followed the doctor's instructions well."

"The baby things are in that cradle my pa made for us."

Clara was sitting in the room with them when the water broke and leaked down on the floor. She looked wide-eyed at Ingeborg.

"Just part of birthing. The baby grows in a sack of water. The sack is called the placenta. When the water breaks, you know the sack has broken, and it has to break for the baby to leave. It won't be long now. Mabel, you keep walking while I clean this up."

Clara shook her head and grabbed a cloth to kneel on the floor with an oof and a grunt.

"I know just what you feel like," Mabel said. "Scrubbing floors got a bit difficult there to the end." After a couple of slowing passages crossing the room, Mabel doubled over with a groan.

"Let's get you in bed and ready. This could go fast. I'm going to call Walt in now so he can help."

Within minutes she had Walt with his back to the headboard on the bed and legs spread with a sheet over them, his wife cradled against him. His face was white in the lamplight.

"Now, you hang on to him, and when I say push, Walt, she is going to push against you, so be prepared and hang on for dear life." Ingeborg checked on her patient again. "Easy now, no hurry. Breathe. Clara, you come over here now. See that tiny patch of wet hair? It's the baby's head. This is called crowning." She looked over the tented legs at Mabel. "On the next contraction, you push. Walt, be ready."

Mabel groaned, her face all scrunched.

"Breathe." Ingeborg spoke softly but the order was there. "Good, good, Mabel. Soon. Be ready for one more and give it all you've got." Ingeborg watched for the start. "Now, push! Keep pushing. We have a head. Clara, see? We put our hands under the baby's head, like this. The neck is so weak, it will flop. Here, you do it. Now, Mabel, rest and breathe and push!"

The baby slipped out and right into Clara's waiting hands.

Wide-eyed, Clara grinned and stared at Ingeborg.

"Ja, you helped. Mabel, Walt, you have a baby boy." Ingeborg took the baby and, as the cord went flaccid, laid him belly down on his mother's chest. "You two get acquainted while I show Clara what to do. Now soon as I cut the cord, I am going to massage her belly to slow the blood loss. You can take this baby over to that basin and wash him all clean. Make sure you keep his face out of the water. The cloth is right by the basin." Ingeborg tied off and cut the cord, then handed the baby to Clara, who stared down at the infant, tears trickling down her face.

"Ja, I know. There is nothing more astounding than bringing a baby into this world."

Ingeborg sniffed and, mopping her own tears, looked to Mabel, who touched her baby's head with one finger.

She looked up to Ingeborg. "Thank you." She smiled up at Walt. "You were a big help." She flinched, then continued, "How are your hands?"

"Not bleeding but almost." He watched Clara come over with the baby all wrapped up in a blanket. "Now you be careful."

Clara grinned at him and looked down at the little red-faced boy in her arms. She nodded.

Back out in the buggy, Ingeborg looked toward the sun just over the horizon. "That baby came right quick. Ah, how I love seeing new life like this, bringing a baby into the world. There's nothing finer. Especially today. God called Elizabeth home, but He sent another life. Thanks be to God." She patted Clara's arm. "Hear that rooster? I love the songs of morning. Let's get on home. Freda will have breakfast ready. Now you know what is going to happen to you soon. And we will rejoice." She returned Clara's smile. *Dear Lord, let it be so.*

CHAPTER 27

I didn't think the summer was going to be like this." Melissa sat staring out the window, her chin cupped in her hands.

"I'm glad you're only suffering from boredom. Many are suffering from diphtheria." Anji realized that her edges were getting a little frazzled too. She should not have reacted so sharply. "I'm sorry. I shouldn't be so testy. This summer is not my cup of tea either."

She felt rejected. She certainly was disappointed. And in a way, she was disgusted with herself. She thought she was fairly good at reading people's intentions. How could she so horribly, woefully, have misread Thomas Devlin's? She really did think he cared about her. Hardly! He didn't just politely rebuff her. He ran away! Shoved his wheelbarrow away down the street at a jog! She couldn't get over it. It ate at her.

She got up from her rocker and started for the kitchen. Perhaps if she got busy with something, she could shake this lethargy and get her mind off him. Her telephone jangled her rings, so she continued over to the wall and picked it up.

Melissa instantly appeared at her elbow. "Is it Linnea?" she asked in a hoarse whisper loud enough to be heard in Grafton.

"No, it's Ingeborg." She shooed the girl off. "It's so good to hear your voice, Ingeborg. It's so good to hear any adult voice."

Ingeborg laughed sadly. "I suspect the quarantine will end soon. There have been no new cases on the train, and the antitoxin is surely taking effect by now. Anji, Thorliff is very ill and getting worse. He insists the paper must get out on time, but he simply cannot. You know."

"Oh. My. Do I know. No matter how sick they are . . . yes."

"He trusts Devlin. And he trusts you. Always has. So I am asking you and Thomas to go down to the office and get the paper out."

"Mr. Devlin . . . me . . . uh, I don't think we could work together very well, Ingeborg. I'm flattered you thought of me, but—"

"You worked together very well teaching in the school, and you've helped with the paper before. John mentioned that frequently. In fact, he thought he saw the beginning of a romance sparking."

"I really don't think . . ." Oh dear! How could she explain this? *God, give me the words!*

"I'm not asking for myself, Anji. It's for Thorliff. It would ease his mind so much. Oh, and Dr. Astrid agrees that Mr. Devlin is not contagious. It's safe."

For Thorliff. How could she say no to that? "But I've never done anything like that. I can write, but I can't typeset or—"

"Mr. Devlin helps Thorliff often, and he can do that sort of thing. But it will take at least two, he says. He cannot get all the jobs done in time by himself."

"I cannot leave my children alone."

"Freda will stay with them while you do this."

"I guess I can try." *And when he kicks me out, I'll just come home.* "I have to go, Ingeborg. Someone is knocking at the door." They said good-bye and she hurried to the door.

"Maybe it's Linnea!" Melissa looked hopeful.

Anji swung the door open and gasped. "Freda!"

The woman marched grimly by her into the house.

"But . . . but . . . you had to leave Ingeborg's fifteen minutes ago to get here now, but she just . . ." Anji wagged her head. "She really is desperate. I'll go to the newspaper office."

So Ingeborg was so convinced Anji could do this that she sent Freda even before she picked up the telephone. Poor Ingeborg. She didn't understand. Oh well. For Thorliff.

When she arrived at the newspaper office she did not bother to knock; she just stepped inside. Thomas Devlin was already there, putting oil on some mysterious part of the press. Obviously he was doing this for Thorliff also. *Very well. Let's get this over with.*

She pasted on a smile. "Mr. Devlin."

"Mrs. Moen." He seemed to be forcing his smile also. How long did it take to print a newspaper? However long, it would be too long.

"Are all the articles written?"

"Not yet." He set his oil can aside and crossed to the desk. He laid his hand on a stack of notebook pages. "These have not been written up yet, but the facts are there. There be about half a dozen, and none of them need go on the front page. If ye can handle that, I'll set the second page. We'll leave the masthead as it is, aye? Thorliff be publisher still, even if he lies abed."

"Yes, of course." She sat down at the desk and leafed through the notes. "Stavenger. I used to know a Walter Stavenger. Why yes. This must be he. A baby boy." That was nice. Walter was always a good boy and a good playmate.

He'd no doubt be a fine father. She would start with that one. She rolled a sheet of paper into the typewriter and began. When she finished each one, she handed it to Devlin.

The final article, for the front page, was the hardest of all. Did she know enough about Elizabeth's life to write a good article? She would do her best. Halfway through she mopped her eyes. And then again at the end. She pulled the page out of the typewriter and closed her eyes for a moment to settle herself.

She glanced up at the clock. Two hours had passed! But she had finished her task.

She stood up, stretched, and walked over to Mr. Devlin with the completed articles. He was putting together the last corner of page three. "Will we have room for all these?"

"Aye, and to spare. I am making the margins a bit wider, just to take up space. We'll do fine at four pages. 'Tis what it usually runs anyway." He handed her some papers. "I printed these off immediately after I set the type. If ye could, go over the first two pages here and circle the errors."

"Certainly." She took the proof sheets over to the desk and reached for a pencil. This job was not going as badly as she had feared. They had their work. They kept their distance. And she was so glad now that she had consented to do this. For Thorliff. The press made very loud sounds, and Mr. Devlin brought the next page over. She tucked it in behind the first two.

There were not many errors at all. Should she circle double spaces between words? No, that no doubt was to make both margins come out even. "Is *boardinghouse* capitalized?"

"Thorliff capitalized it when it mentions Blessing Boardinghouse. Otherwise, no."

"Thank you." She finished the first page. Now what? Ah. She simply carried it over and placed it beside him, glad for the chance to move around a little. She would not do well to just sit all day. How Gerald could work the switchboard for hours at a time amazed her.

By the time she finished proofing the first three pages, Thomas was running off the last page. He brought it over to her.

"My, that was fast."

"Mostly advertisements, ye'll notice, and they come as a block. Ye just drop the block in place. Thanks be to God for advertisements. And the only obituary is on the first page."

Elizabeth Bjorklund. And she felt sad all over again.

He made his corrections as she proofed the final page. But now they were going to have to work together more closely because it was time to print. She dreaded it, but she'd see this to the end. For Thorliff.

He described to her how the press operated, explaining in greater detail than she was interested in. She inserted paper as he had showed her. They cranked the press down. Pages one and four were on top, two and three on the back side. He folded the sheet in half. One newspaper. He unfolded it and laid it out flat again. "Let the ink dry before folding, but ye see how 'tis done. We keep this one and the next two for archives."

He looked at the final proof. "Ah, good. All four pages be right side up. Thorliff almost printed a paper once with page three upside down." He strung a wire across the room and hooked it into an eye in the opposite wall. He hung their brand-new newspaper on the wire. So that was how they dried the ink.

She put another sheet in the press. As he cranked the press down, she strung a second wire she had seen coiled on the wall. "How many clotheslines will we need?"

"Those two should do it." He hung up their newspapers as she slid a sheet into the press.

They fell quickly into a rhythm, and it went faster than she would have guessed. When they filled one clothesline, they started on the next.

She ached to ask him why he had run away from her, but she didn't dare be so bold. She wanted to know why she was rejected. Do people who are rejected ever find out the truth of why they were rejected? Probably not. The second line was filling up.

"If ye would, remove the pages from that

first line, folding them as ye go. Then fold them again, in half, with the masthead up. They be dry enough and then some."

She did so. This was actually fun. For one thing, it got her out of the house a while and into adult company. That was a much bigger blessing than she would have guessed. No whining children's voices, no arguing. Also, it was easier than she had anticipated. She had pictured herself not knowing enough about printing a newspaper to be of much use. With a tiny bit of pride, she noted that she was doing quite well. Too, it was an important job, putting the paper out. This issue especially had news everyone in the area should know. And Elizabeth's death hit her yet again.

She stacked the papers twenty to a pile. When she ran out of room on the folding table she doubled up the stacks. Now they were forty to a pile. It gave her a very good feeling to be this productive. Look at the stacks! She went back to feeding paper into the press.

Lemuel, who always picked up the finished papers to deliver, showed up at three. He broke into a grin. "I heard Thorliff was sick, and I figgered there wouldn't be no paper today. But you did it."

Devlin pulled the last of them down from the line. "There's a fine reason they be ready. Mrs. Moen here went to it with a will, caught on instantly to all the jobs I asked of her, and was a splendid helpmeet. I could not have done it without her."

Her mouth fell open. This is the man who had rejected her! And listen to him. Her mind was completely confused now. She helped them bundle and carry out the papers with her thoughts still in a muddle. Talk about mixed messages. She could not read this fellow to save her life. What was going on in his head? What was going on in hers? The fruit of hard work rolled away.

Thomas clapped his hands together. "Finished. Now we celebrate, aye? I shall proceed forthwith to Rebecca's for ice cream. Mrs. Moen, would ye please join me?"

Anji had been trying to figure out an appropriate way to say good-bye and go home. This caught her completely off guard. "Why, I suppose . . . uh . . . yes. Thank you."

They strolled off to Rebecca's.

"And how be yer wee ones faring?"

She might as well be honest, so she told him. The two little ones squabbled a lot—he chuckled knowingly—and Melissa really missed her best friend, Linnea Bjorklund. Even with five in the house, there was only so much cooking and sewing you could do, and even Melissa, who would rather read than anything, was starting to get bored.

"Take heart, milady. This quarantine should be lifted shortly."

"But I am so glad the doctors were wise

enough to impose it. No one from town has fallen ill, except, of course, those who worked directly with the circus people. Imagine if any of our children got sick."

"Aye, we be blessed. And see, we also be at Rebecca's front door." He opened it for her and entered behind her.

Anji stood a moment at the counter, undecided. What flavor? She loved them all. Finally she picked chocolate.

Mr. Devlin bobbed his head. "A fine choice. I shall have the same, please." He ushered her to a table and held her chair. It had been a long time since she had been treated so royally.

He sat down across from her. "Thank ye from the bottom of me heart for yer help this day. Thorliff was so certain the paper could not be put to bed without him. Dr. Astrid assures me that when the papers arrive at the hospital, she will straightway take one to him. Reassuring him thus should help him greatly as he battles this disease. Ease his mind."

Anji's mind needed easing too. What was going on between them? And what was going to go on between them, if anything? "I can see how important it is to ease his mind. Yes."

The ice cream arrived. Anji skimmed half a spoonful off the top. That first taste was always the most delicious of all. "I feel just a little bit guilty, enjoying this while my children cannot. I will take a container home to them."

They ate in silence for a few minutes.

Then Mr. Devlin cleared his throat. "I must apologize, Mrs. Moen. Ye may recall the time that ye approached me and I hastened away. I ask yer forgiveness for being so abrupt."

Now her brain really was in a muddle. What could she say? She couldn't even think! "Uh, er, of course I accept your apology. Uh . . ." How lame! *Say something intelligent, Anji Baard Moen!* Instead, "Why did you, may I ask?" sort of burst out of her.

He wagged his head. "A fine mixup. One of the first symptoms of diphtheria is usually a headache, and I was suffering a bad one. I feared greatly that I had contracted diphtheria from the patients around me, for I was living aboard the train as a nurse. I had the disease as a tad, but I thought the doctors must be wrong and ye can indeed suffer the ailment twice in yer life. Later I learned that the headache was caused by fumes from the kitchen car. So I was not contagious after all."

A most happy tidal wave of relief washed over her. She was not rejected! All those miserable, sad, and sorry thoughts had been for nothing. "Mr. Devlin, I am so very pleased that you do not dislike me, and of course, that you are not ill. Everyone associated with the hospital has been so careful to not bring it into the community. I'm grateful for that too."

A real smile, not just a polite one, broke

on his face too. "About this *Mr. Devlin* ye use so freely. Might we address each other by the first name again? I suggest we've earned the privilege, having put a newspaper to bed all by ourselves and doing it without one of those splendid new linotype machines. I've counseled Thorliff frequently on the wisdom of buying that labor-saving device."·

"Oh, I agree. Yes." She smiled and nodded. "I believe he feels the machine would be too costly. I've known Thorliff a long, long time. He is entirely too practical." Yes, she knew him well. She would not mention to Mr. Devlin—that is, to Thomas—that once upon a time they had almost married.

"The very thing." He glanced out the window. "'Tis getting late, and I shall be helping me patients with their dinner."

"I must get back as well." She stood up. Her heart was singing happy songs.

He insisted on buying the container of ice cream for her children. "Tell them Mr. Devlin is proud that they be obeying so well." And they left. They shook hands as they parted on her doorstep. She was a happy, happy, happy woman.

Devlin was a happy, happy, happy man. She had accepted his apology! His social clumsiness was not a relationship destroyer after

all, though he was certain it was a relationship strainer and she was just too polite to say
so. As he approached the train, he saw them
starting to load the goats, so he walked down
to the animal cars.

Manny was there, expertly herding the crit-
ters. The lad was certainly good with animals.

And it startled him that Johnny Solberg
was there as well. Had the quarantine been
lifted? Despite that Johnny had two good legs
and Manny only one, he was not doing the job
half as well as Manny. The last of the goats
clambered up the ramp, and Manny disappeared inside.

He came back out and grinned. "Evening,
Mr. Devlin! Johnny, the camel is next."

The cat handler called from the next car
back. "Can somebody help me here a few minutes?"

"I'll do it." Johnny slogged off. The lad
appeared quite tired.

Devlin pointed. "Manny, lad, ye best get
yer horse, Joker, out of the corral there before
they accidentally load him too."

"He's going too, Mr. Devlin. Mr. Stetler
says I can take him even if he can't do tricks."

"Going too." Alarms went off in Devlin's
head. He kept them from reaching his face.

"Yes, sir. I'm joining the circus."

"I see." In fact, Devlin saw quite a lot. He
well knew that if you oppose a boy's dreams,

he locks on to those dreams more solidly. This would require extreme diplomacy. "Well, then, I want to toast yer new life. Let us do so with some ice cream."

Ice cream? Or more smelly work? You could see the tussle, the choice to be made, but only for a moment. "Yes, sir, I'd like that. Do they happen to have chocolate?"

"They do indeed." Devlin led the way toward Rebecca's shop. He should be helping to serve dinners, but this was far more important. "When be ye leaving? Do ye know yet?"

"Tomorrow, Mr. Stetler says, or the day after. The engineer has to get the locomotive to run. So far it ain't."

"I've heard from Mr. Ranson himself that the engine be a persnickety beast."

Manny cackled. "Sure 'nuff. And pulling all them cars takes a lot of power. Why, just the elephants have to be ten tons at least. One of the clowns was telling me that if they have to go up a steep hill, they leave half the train behind and pull the front half up. Then they go till they find a siding—a town or a water stop—to put the first half while they go back and pull the other half up. Takes a long time. And it gobbles a lot of wood. You can't imagine how much wood it eats."

"I should think. Too bad Mr. Stetler will not spend some money on a decent engine."

"Yeah. Coal fired. Mr. Ranson says coal

takes up a lot less space in the tender than wood, and they could go lots farther on a tender load of coal. And out here on the prairies coal is sometimes cheaper."

They arrived at Rebecca's and went inside. She looked surprised to see him again so soon, but she didn't say anything.

Manny chose chocolate, Devlin ordered the same, and they each took a chair.

Devlin grinned. "I be muckle happy ye've found yerself a paying job!"

Manny licked his lips. "Well, it ain't paying, at least not yet. Mr. Stetler says if I do good and prove my worth, then he'll pay me. Maybe the end of the season or next spring. They go south to winter over, so's it's warmer, then come north."

"Well, sure, and he'll pay ye sometime. After he pays the rest of his crew. They've not seen any money lately either."

"That's what Mr. Ranson says."

Devlin wagged his head. "Mr. Ranson ought to be paid the very most, for the whole train depends upon him."

"Ain't that the truth!"

Rebecca set their ice cream in front of them. Manny dug right in.

Devlin had just eaten a serving of ice cream, but there was always room for a little more. "I be glad the horses and cows be fattened up again. They were looking so poorly when they arrived."

Manny nodded. "Yeah, they was clear out of feed when they got here. Nothing left at all. That's why they wanted to put them out to graze right away. Out of water too."

"I hope things get better for them quickly. I wouldn't want to see Joker suffer like that. He's a beautiful horse."

Manny was obviously going to say something, but he stopped. He ate in silence.

Perhaps Devlin was getting through to him. "Ye were doing so splendidly with school. I assume they have some sort of school aboard the train—so many tykes of various ages."

"Some circuses do. Don't know if this one does."

"I hope so. A good education is the only defense a man has that he won't be fleeced by some shyster. To be able to read and understand contracts, for example."

"Johnny heard some of the folks on board had contracts, but it don't do any good. They still ain't getting paid. So why bother? Johnny works with the other animals too. He don't like the camel. But we like Mr. Mason a lot. He never beat his boy. Not like my pa."

Ingeborg said Manny had come a long way. How true. "If you have a contract, you can take the person to court, and the judge will make him pay what he owes. That's about the only advantage I see, but 'tis a beauty."

"Sure would be." Manny stared at his

empty dish. "Dr. Elizabeth was such a great lady."

"She was that. We all be grieving."

"And crazy little Inga. She's been such a good friend." He looked across the table to Devlin. "Her and Benny, they made me want to learn to walk again."

"Aye, and baby Roald. Thorliff is going to have a hard time this winter without the children's mother to help."

"Grandma Ingeborg."

"She not be getting younger. Astrid is worried. Ingeborg is not frail, but she not be as strong and spry as Astrid remembers. No, they'll need more help than what Ingeborg can offer."

"I grew up in Kentucky. Never felt a winter as fierce as this place gets."

Devlin sat quiet. Let the lad's thoughts work.

Manny looked up at him. "They really need me on the train, Mr. Devlin. But Grandma needs me too. I don't know what to do."

Devlin nodded slowly. "I wager ye never wanted to run away to sea."

"Work on a boat? It'd be interesting, though."

"It is. And hard. The boat is how I came to America, working me passage over. There be a truism aboard ship: 'One hand for the ship and one hand for yerself.' That is, ye work for the ship, but ye must always keep yerself safe as well. When I have a hard choice, I try to remember that saying. If I must do one of two things, and one is better for me, that should be the choice."

Manny nodded. "I see. If both choices need me, which one is better for me. Prob'ly staying here would be, you think?"

"Probably better for Joker too. I don't like the way those animals were so starved."

Manny bobbed his head. "Me either, Mr. Devlin. It really upset me the way all those animals didn't have no feed at all. And those poor elephants. And with Grandma getting old . . . I'm staying. She needs me."

"A wise decision, Manny."

They walked back to the train talking and joking. Manny seemed in a happy frame of mind. The decision must have been weighing more heavily on him than Devlin had guessed. At the train, he brought his saddle down out of the car while Devlin caught up his horse. They took it down to Thorliff's and tied it out behind the house. Manny waved to a face in the window as they left.

"I'm gonna help 'em load, then I'll go back to the farm. Can I go back to the farm?"

"Aye, but I can help them load here. Ye should go see Mrs. Geddick in the hospital kitchen. Tell her you want to wash up thoroughly in order to go back to the farm. She'll know what ye should do. No dirt, no germs."

"Yes, sir." Manny went off to the hospital's back door.

Near the horse car, Johnny Solberg sat off to the side on a steamer trunk, his elbows on his knees and his head in both hands.

"Ye don't look well, son." Devlin knelt beside him.

"Got a headache. It will go away. I think I'm catching a cold."

"Ah. Sore throat, eh?"

"Yeah."

Devlin thought about all this a moment. "Did ye get that shot they gave everyone?"

"What shot? They gave them that already?" He raised his head. "You mean the shot everyone was going to get so they wouldn't get sick? Far was inside the hospital and didn't come home, so I just stayed here and helped Manny with the animals. If I didn't, I woulda had to stay home like all the rest of the children had to. And I didn't want to do that."

Devlin stood. "Come with me."

"I gotta help load."

"This is more important." Devlin assumed his schoolmaster voice. "Come with me."

Johnny stood up and started walking.

Devlin guided him to the hospital and led him inside with a heavy, heavy heart.

No, Dr. Astrid, this impossible nightmare is not over yet. And now I am certain it is striking the heart of John Solberg's family.

CHAPTER 28

They were gathered in Dr. Astrid's office: the good doctor, Nurse Deborah, Devlin, and John Solberg. He wondered idly just how sturdy this hospital building was. Sure, and his heart just now was heavy enough to go through the floor. And his heart's burden was nothing compared to poor Astrid's. He had never seen her looking so weary, drawn, and pale. What a horrible toll life was taking on her.

"I really am not thinking clearly anymore," she said. "Is it time to lift the quarantine?" She looked at Devlin. "Has anyone died on the train in the last few days?"

"No." He was not ready to mention Johnny Solberg. He could not. Not right now. Besides, there was no definite diagnosis yet.

"No one in the town other than those

immediately associated with the hospital."
Solberg looked at Deborah. "And everyone received the antitoxin?"

"As far as we know. We still don't have any for the outlying farmers, but that should arrive from New York today. I have already assembled teams that will go out on the major roads, inoculating as they go. By tomorrow night we should have just about everyone in the area."

Solberg smiled. "Remarkably efficient, Nurse. Thank you."

She dipped her head, a silent *You're welcome.*

Astrid looked at Devlin. "Will you prepare flyers, the way you and Thorliff did before, to post around town?"

"They be all ready, lady. I printed them up in anticipation. No dates, of course, but the general announcement."

She didn't smile, but almost. "Wonderful. Are we agreed that the quarantine can be lifted?"

Solberg suggested, "Perhaps the teams you set up, Deborah, could distribute the flyers around town."

"Or," Devlin cut in, "give a few sheaves of flyers to the first children ye come upon and let them distribute to the rest, adjuring them, of course, to get the older folks as well as the school families. Methinks ye'll have a willing army of soldiers who think they've been pent up far too long."

Solberg laughed out loud and Deborah giggled.

Astrid really did smile, wanly, but the corners of her mouth turned up. "And Inga can take a flyer out to Mor and to her friends. Oh, she will love that! Yes. Let's do that. Are there any other matters we should tackle?"

No one had any. They got up and left the office.

"John? If ye may." Devlin caught up to him and fell in step.

"I was headed for Thorliff's office to get the flyers."

"As am I. Too, I've several matters to discuss."

"Discuss away. I'm all ears."

Ye are jovial now, John, with the lifting of quarantine, but ye'll not be in another minute or two. Devlin's heart, if anything, got heavier. "I turned your Johnny over to Miriam to take a look at him. She be an excellent nurse and thorough. He has a headache, and I thought they ought to examine him."

John paused, then picked up the pace again. "He gets headaches now and then. He always has. And he got the shot."

"No. He did not."

John stopped dead and stared at him.

"He be in love with the elephants, as are

we all. He has been helping Manny care for the circus menagerie. They are loading their grazing stock."

They resumed their walk to the newspaper office.

"The whole time? He's been out with the train the whole time? I have not been home in days, so I assumed he was home with his mother."

"And no doubt she assumed he was here with you. And ye recall we did not have enough antitoxin to inoculate all the circus folk. We missed him."

John marched on, and Devlin could see the anger building in him. "He knows better! He's a good boy, nearly a man. He wouldn't deliberately mislead both of us."

"Manny told me he lost his little brother to the croup back in Kentucky and that the whole family had it. From his description, 'twas probably diphtheria. If so, Manny would be immune." *And if Johnny saw Manny staying well, the exuberance of youth would make him feel invincible as well. That is how boys that age are.* Devlin, of course, did not say that aloud. John would figure it out on his own.

They entered the office and Devlin handed John a sheaf of flyers.

He looked at them. "I'm going back to the hospital. I'll distribute these in that direction."

"And I shall go in the other direction."

Devlin watched his friend head off down the street.

Distributing the flyers did not take long. He dropped some at Anji's, and the children were off like a shot, eager to serve the community and get out of the yard. He dropped some at the boardinghouse, and Sophie snatched them up eagerly to take elsewhere. He had three left when he knocked on the door at the Bjorklunds'.

Thelma opened it. "Hello, Mr. Devlin." She looked stricken. "I've been waiting for your knock."

"I be muckle pleased to inform ye, madame, that our Thorliff still be here and under the best of care."

"Oh, praise God!"

"And the quarantine is lifted. I've a task for yer little Inga."

Inga popped into the doorway behind Thelma's skirts. "Did you just say my name?"

"I did indeed." Devlin dropped down to one knee. Inga was growing. He had to look up into her eyes. "Yer onerous sequestration be ended." Her face screwed up as she mulled the words. He continued, "Might ye take these to yer grandmum Ingeborg, please? And others in that neighborhood."

She looked at him for a moment, then looked up at Thelma. "It's over? It's over now?"

Thelma nodded, smiling.

Without a word, Inga snatched the flyers

and ran away toward her grandmother's, faster than one would think a little girl could run.

Tears were running down Thelma's cheeks. "I'm so glad it's over."

Devlin stood up and took her hands in his. "The sick still need prayer, of course, but we think the worst be behind us. Farewell, lady." He turned and walked back toward the hospital. John would need a friend just now.

John was coming out the front doors as Devlin was approaching them. His shoulders were sagging.

Devlin invited, "Shall we take a walk?"

"I'd like that." He fell in beside Devlin, and they strolled out across a field lush with new grass. "The diagnosis isn't positive yet. I have to go tell his mother." They strolled on. "I talked to Johnny. He knows very well what he did was wrong. He was certain that because Manny was not sick, he would not be either. Devlin, he *knew*. He knew about the quarantine, he knew about spreading germs, and he knew he was doing wrong! I am so angry I could tan his hind end from here to Christmas!"

"'Tis not anger, John," Devlin said quietly. "'Tis fear."

They strolled on.

John nodded. "You are so right." He heaved a monstrous sigh. "You said you wanted to discuss things. Let's discuss your matters and put mine aside."

"By circuitous means, I received a letter from a parish in Michigan—St. Patrick on the Lake. Their search committee wants me to consider serving there."

John wheeled, opened his mouth, and closed it again. They strolled on. "Well." He stared at the ground. "A long ways away."

"Nicer climate in winter. Or possibly not."

"You've wanted a parish of your own."

"'Tis dangerous, John, to ask God for something. Ye might get it."

He nodded. "Do you want to go?"

"This is where I be confused. Aye, I want to go. 'Tis a dream of mine. And no, I desperately do not."

"Why not?" John stopped. "Time to turn back, I suppose." They reversed their steps and started back toward town at that leisurely pace.

"The friendships I've forged here. They be the best I've ever had, and yerself foremost, I assure ye. The people here are matchless. 'Tis a growing town, heady, lively, a fine place to live. I doubt I'll find this elsewhere."

John walked along silently. "And Anji Moen. What about her?"

"Ye see? That be what I treasure most about ye, John. Ye know me better than I know meself."

"So what will you do about her? I know there's a spark there. What are your intentions?"

Devlin thought. He tried to frame those thoughts. They remained like a will-o'-the-wisp, out there somewhere, but nothing you could grasp. "I don't know. For the life of me, I do not know." They strolled on. "Never have I felt before about a woman the way I feel about Anji. And yet . . ." He shrugged. "I don't know."

John was still studying the ground. "Perhaps, Thomas . . . perhaps you should discuss this with Anji. Bare your souls, in a way. Be honest. What the two of you learn about each other should go a long way toward shaping your decision."

"Aye. I shall do so. What about you, John? Have ye any feelings on it?"

"Certainly. I don't want to see you leave. Especially not now with Johnny in peril and Thorliff on the edge of death." He studied Devlin instead of the ground, met his eye squarely. "And for selfish reasons, I want you to stay. When we were building Elizabeth's coffin, there was a mutual respect, a bond, a togetherness that few men find. I don't want to lose that."

"Nor do I. And yet, I was trained for the formal ministry. It has long been me calling."

They strolled on in silence, each of them pondering imponderables. John turned aside toward home, and Devlin carried his own heavy heart over to Anji's.

He knocked at her door.

She opened and her face brightened. "Oh, come in, Thomas. Welcome! You're just in time for supper."

"'Tis that late? I did not mean to call so late."

She laughed. "This time of year, the sun stays up forever. Come in. Please come in. The children, all four of them, are over at Linnea's, but they will be home soon. And I have chicken potpie prepared and waiting. I was even able to use the first of the fresh peas. You will stay, won't you?"

"If ye don't mind a fellow barging in, aye. I would be much pleased."

"Come into the kitchen, please. I'm in the middle of making bread."

He followed her into the kitchen. This was a roomy house and pleasant, a perfect place to raise children. Were they to marry . . . no! He put that aside. Too premature.

"Coffee? It's made."

"Thankee." He looked around at a cozy room, at a huge cooking range with two warmers and an oven large enough to hold a very large turkey. The gingham curtains reminded him of his own mum's kitchen.

She waved an arm. "Have a seat. You cannot imagine how happy I am that all this is behind us. Well, about behind us. Poor Thorliff. He's going to be a long time getting over this, and I don't just mean the illness."

"I've been mulling important matters lately, and I'd like to have a serious discussion with ye. The both of us being brutally honest. 'Tis why I came by."

"Brutally honest?" She paused from drizzling melted butter over four pale loaves to study him.

The kitchen door burst open. "Mom, we're home!" A churning mass of children poured in.

She smiled. "Obviously. Wash up. The potpie is ready."

They stopped and singsonged, "Good evening, Mr. Devlin." They ran off, a whirlwind come and gone.

He wagged his head. "Youth is wasted on the young."

She brought a stack of dishes off the shelf. He got up, took them from her, and started setting the table. She pulled open the drawer to show him where the flatware was kept and went back to her bread. She brought out a big iron pot of potpie and carefully set her risen bread in the oven. She moved smoothly, almost affectionately. No, not almost. *Affectionately* was the right word. She obviously enjoyed cooking and being a mother. And he knew from observation that she enjoyed teaching school just as much.

With a maximum of noise and bustle, the children came in and settled themselves at the table. Anji sat down at one end, Devlin at the other. "Mr. Devlin? Would you do the honors?"

"With pleasure." He bowed his head. "Father in heaven, we thank ye for the abundance ye bestow upon us, of which this food, and these friends, be part. Please bless this food to its intended use, bless the hands that prepared it, and keep us ever mindful of the needs of others." He deliberately did not cross himself, his usual habit, because no one else there did.

He watched from afar, so to speak, observing Anji and her brood. They were children well raised, and the love was palpable. Everything he saw was positive. She had mentioned the little ones argued a lot. Of course they did. They were that age, and they had been closely confined. It was healthy.

Afterward even the youngest, four-year-old Annika, carried plates to the counter and helped tidy the table.

"It has been a long and exciting day. Time for bed." Anji looked at Melissa. "Would you read their bedtime story tonight, please?"

"Sure." The children left. Anji took off her apron, went to the foot of the stairs, and called, "And don't forget to wash behind your ears!"

She came into the kitchen. "More coffee?"

Devlin raised a hand. "No, thankee. I'm fine."

"The porch is pleasant this time of evening. Shall we sit there?" She led the way and they settled into wicker chairs. The view from there was interesting even though flat. Very flat. Cattle with calves in the fields beyond, sheep with lambs, and new green everywhere.

Best get right to it. Don't become tongue-tied now, Devlin. "Ye have been much on me mind of late, but I be not certain how to proceed. Ye see, I have never courted a lady, because never before did I find a lady I cared to court. I have done so now."

He forced himself to look at her. She was even brighter than before. He couldn't explain how she seemed brighter, but she did.

"But there be a kink in the plowline, a major one. So I've some questions for ye. For one, the most important, would yerself be amenable to me courting ye?"

She purred, "Oh yes, Thomas. Most amenable."

His heart gave a happy little jump. "A question quite as important: Would ye be willing to leave Blessing if it all came to that?"

The brightness slipped behind a cloud. "I . . . you see . . ."

"Take yer time, eh. Not something to jump upon but to sneak up on."

She giggled. And sobered. "The question really is, would I leave everything and go somewhere else with you. Right?"

"Correct. I phrased it poorly. Let me explain. Of late I learned I must consider becoming rector of a parish in Michigan. 'Tis a bolt from the blue. I'd not have thought I would receive such an offer, but I have. I do not want to leave here, but a parish be me long-time calling. I be greatly torn."

She sat back in her chair and gazed out across the distance. "Is it certain you will go there?"

"By no means. I am to have a visit there and we—the parish and I—are to decide if we are well matched. There be a specific way of doing it, of calling a new rector to a parish. Committees, and letters of intent, all manner of formalities. In the end I may not like the people or the area at all. Or they may run me out on a rail the moment I preach."

"So no decision has to be made instantly."

"No, but I want to know how the decision, either way, would affect our relationship—or potential relationship, if ye will." He could not read her face. "And what yerself decides will greatly influence me own decision."

"We're being honest, you said. I grew up here, Thomas. These people are my own. I left once, but now that I'm back I don't want to leave again. I want my children to grow up here. These people, my friends and family, are my cushion. We all take care of one another. Should I die, they would raise my children."

He nodded. "And we have all been reminded fiercely how fragile life is."

"Yes." She looked at him with sad eyes. "When are you going to—you said Michigan?"

"Shortly."

"And the decision is to be made after that."

"Aye."

She sighed. "I don't know. I'm sorry, Thomas. I just don't know. I will think about it and pray about it. But at this moment, I do not see a happy outcome for me either way."

And neither did Devlin.

CHAPTER 29

Astrid, Miriam, and Deborah stood at the window watching the circus train slowly, slowly begin to move, thick smoke billowing. Westward bound. "Thank God we are seeing the last of that carrier of pestilence."

"Do you think they'll be able to perform?" Miriam asked. "Does that man realize how weak some of his people still are?"

"I have no idea." Astrid banished the wish that Stetler had caught diphtheria too. After all, vengeance did belong to God, not her. A good thing. She turned and looked out over their ward. For the first time in who knew how long, they had empty beds. Surely she could send some of her people back to their homes, and life could return to normal. She did an interior snort. Whatever *normal* meant. The next instant she was blinking tears. Elizabeth was gone. Life would never be the same. She blew her nose and realized the other two were doing the same.

"Let's get this place cleaned up and get Thorliff better."

"Will you send the temporary help back to Chicago now?" Deborah asked.

"Ja, I think so. I would be happy to keep Dr. Johnson here for a time longer, but . . ." She watched those on duty going about scrubbing beds.

Miriam inhaled a breath of the cool morning air coming in the window. "Can I tell my family they can go home? After they scrub up, of course?"

Astrid smiled. "Ja, and you. I know Trygve will be happy." She nudged the woman beside her. "And I know you will appreciate your own bed. In fact, you take a couple of extra days off, get some rest, enjoy your family."

"Thank you. You mean right now?"

"Ja, right now."

Miriam had her cap and apron off before Astrid could change her mind and headed out to pass on the news.

Deborah watched her go. "That was a generous thing to do."

"I let her go first because of her family."

"I figured. How about I tell Vera the same?"

"Go ahead and redo the schedule. I'm going to go work with Thorliff and check on Johnny."

She entered Johnny's room first.

He looked horribly droopy. "Can I go home now?"

"Not yet. We'd better keep you here, just in case. Let me see your throat again." His throat was inflamed, but if the membrane was growing on his tonsils, she couldn't see it yet. "I can't let you go back home until we know for sure."

After turning the boy over to Deborah and her nurses, Astrid scrubbed again, this time with carbolic acid, and headed for Thorliff's room. The others might get a reprieve, but she would be staying on here at the hospital, not that she'd done more than dream of home. She dissolved into another round of tears, so she let them come. So much. So much.

Once she had herself back together, she went into Thorliff's room, his coughing meeting her at the door. Was the swelling down in his neck? "Thorliff, I'm taking your temperature. Can you hear me?" He nodded and opened his mouth. When she read the thermometer, she laid a hand on his shoulder. "Thorliff, your temp has remained down, as it was earlier this morning. That is good news."

He turned his head and stared at her. "She's gone," he croaked. He started to say something else and instead started coughing.

"Yes. John and Thomas buried her."

A tear leaked out the edge of his eye and

trailed into his hair. "I . . . I . . ." Another coughing fit wracked him.

"Don't try to talk. That just makes the coughing worse."

He closed his eyes and turned his face away.

She checked to see if there was cough syrup in the cup on the bed table and held it to his lips. "Drink this." *Please, Thorliff, cooperate.* She held it to his mouth. When he didn't open his mouth at all, she said firmly, "You will take it from a spoon, and then we will move you to the steam room." The medicine done, she went to find Dr. Johnson to help her move Thorliff.

"Two men want to talk with you," Sandra said, pointing to the door.

"Go get Dr. Johnson and help him move Thorliff to the steam room, please." When Sandra nodded, Astrid went to the door. Two men indeed. Daniel and Trygve! She smiled at her husband, wishing she could leave with him. His return smile made her wish that even more. She asked, "What can I do for you gentlemen?"

Her husband asked, "How is Thorliff? Please, I hope you have some good news for us."

Other than the train leaving? Now was not a time to be flippant. "He is no worse. He still is running a temperature, but not much above normal. The swelling seems to be diminished too. Not a lot but . . ."

Daniel nodded. "Now that the quarantine is lifted, send for us when you need something."

"I shall." She walked down the hall and watched them leave. *I need to go home! I need to have a normal life again.* But they couldn't cure that.

She looked up to see Reverend Solberg with Mary Martha trotting at his side. *Lord God, help us. I'm glad I can give someone good news.* She held open the screen door and beckoned the Solbergs inside.

"Astrid, are you sure?" Mary Martha held her handkerchief to her leaking eyes.

"No, we are not sure, but we must act as if we know. Be ready to do all we can if it appears. That is why I am keeping him here. Come, he's in room two."

Johnny lay sleeping. His eyes fluttered open when they spoke his name. "Ma, Pa . . ." He reached for them with a smile, but the smile vanished, and he sniffed. "I'm so sorry. I didn't mean to miss the shots. I didn't know about it."

"You would have if you'd been home where you were supposed to be," his mother said in a tone of voice that mothers so often use.

Astrid closed the door and went to check on Thorliff in the steam room. The nurse was making sure his head stayed upright so that he could inhale all the steam possible. Both were drenched in steam and sweat. "Make sure he gets broth and ice packs after this. After the broth, another dose of cough syrup."

Thorliff did not open his eyes, but the sound of difficult breathing seemed to fill the room. "Let me know when you have him back in his room." She went down to the telephone and asked for her mother's home.

There was no answer. "Try Thorliff's house. She may be there."

Moments later, her mor picked up the phone at Bjorklunds'. "Oh, Astrid, I just heard about Johnny," Ingeborg said. "All I know to do is pray, and I know we all have been. We just thought we were safe."

"I'm glad you are there with Inga. She needs all the solace she can get."

"She is cranky, but look at what she's lost! What can I tell her about her far?"

"He is no worse and his temperature seems stable. I wish Inga could come see him, but not yet. His condition would frighten her."

"Oh, thank you, Lord. We praise your mighty name. Oh yes, Astrid, that is good news. And Clara and I got to welcome a new baby into this world. We are making strawberry jam, and I will take that and fresh berries to Emmy. Oh, Astrid, such great news. Tell John we are all praying for Johnny and for them. I need to go. See you soon."

Astrid smiled at the click she heard in her ear. *Thank you for my mor.* She hung up and headed for the back of the hospital, where there just might be a breeze in the shade. What if she had them wheel Thorliff out there? Perhaps tomorrow, if he continued to improve.

On her late evening rounds, Astrid checked Johnny's throat again. Her heart sank. He had diphtheria. The membrane proved it. She sighed.

John sat up on his cot along the wall. "He has it, doesn't he?" John Solberg almost had his pastoral self back in place. Only his eyes showed he was now a grieving father too.

Astrid nodded. "It's for sure now."

"I will telephone Mary Martha and tell her. We decided we would take turns here at the bedside."

"I'm sure someone would gladly stay with him through the night."

"This won't be the crisis night though, will it? Seems it usually takes a few days to get to that point."

"Remember . . ." Astrid paused. Did they dare let these two dear people go back and forth to home and expose the other children to possible danger? She knew she might be erring on the side of caution, but when was too much? She had yet to go home. Could she now? Could she leave Dr. Johnson in charge and go home? The thought made her ache. But John was right. Tonight was not the danger night, nor tomorrow. But what about Thorliff? Was he really beyond the danger point?

"We will bring in an extra bed if you both want to stay."

John smiled wanly. "Thank you, Astrid. Have you seen Thomas?"

"Not since he brought Johnny in. He'll be in soon, I am sure." She left the room still pondering. Sleep here or go home? She'd be waking Dr. Johnson in an hour. By then she would have decided.

On her way past, the telephone jangled. She picked it up. "Dr. Bjorklund."

"Your mor."

"Thank you. Put her through." No wonder the telephone operators knew everything going on before the others. All they had to do was leave the line open. "Yes, Mor. Did you enjoy your visit with Inga?"

"I am still here. She has a cough and a slight temperature. I don't want to bring her over there, just in case. I don't see any sign of a sore throat."

Please, God, no more. Was that fear she heard in her mor's voice? "What about Roald?"

"He seems fine yet."

"Good. If you see any change, bring her right over." No choice, she was staying here.

The next morning, she checked Thorliff first thing. He seemed to be improving, almost imperceptibly, but even so, he was better. The membrane was fighting a losing battle.

On the other hand, Johnny was getting sicker. When she mentioned intubation or a tracheotomy if it went that far, John and Mary

Martha agreed. Do whatever she could to help their son. Knowing too much about the disease made it even harder for John. She knew that but also knew there was nothing she could do to help him.

The day dragged on. She knew it was only a day, but it seemed like weeks. No one else came in with suspicious symptoms, including Inga. But the Solbergs took up their own vigil with Johnny. They changed cooling cloths, fetched their own ice, in reality took over the care of their son. Both of them now vowed to remain at the hospital around the clock. When one was caring for the boy, the other was praying.

"You have to get some sleep," Astrid said on her way to bed herself. "Both of you."

"We are." John laid a hand on her arm. "You do the same."

"He is putting up a good fight."

"Thank God for that." John asked, "Shall I take him to the steam room again?"

"Ja, that seems to help him the most. Make sure you get some more broth in him." She shrugged. "Sorry, I know you knew that, and you are doing all you can too." She laid a hand on his arm and squeezed, wishing there were some way she could pour all her strength into this man who strengthened so many others. "Call me in when you need me."

He nodded. "Sleep, Astrid. You need that too."

At her bed, Astrid took off her shoes. *Lord, tell me when it is time to protect that airway.* A sense of peace made her certain God had indeed heard her. *Lord, please keep Johnny alive.*

The next thing she knew, the sounds of morning awakened her. She sat up and swung her feet over the edge, then looked up when Dr. Johnson stuck his head through the curtain gap.

"Oh, excuse me, but I think we need to intubate Johnny. The membrane . . ."

"Go prep and I'll be right there. Tell whoever is on to get the OR ready."

"I already did that."

"Thank you." She slammed her feet into her shoes and twisted her hair into a bun as she headed for the scrub sink. John and Mary Martha stood on either side of the gurney, their hands on their son, so struggling to breathe.

Nurse Abigail was pushing the gurney. "Deborah is preparing the anesthetic."

"Good, thank you." Turning to the Solbergs she nodded and set to scrubbing. "You might as well wait in his room. It's more comfortable there. This won't take long." She couldn't look at them again. Feeling herself submerge into being a doctor, she inhaled a deep breath. Apron, hat in place, she held dripping hands up and entered the operating room, already hot from the lit lamps. Gowned and ready, Dr. Johnson was prepping the boy's neck. He could no longer be Johnny to her. He had to be a patient.

"Ready."

She looked to Deborah. "Give him another minute. Let's pray." Astrid inhaled and exhaled. "Father God, we plead your mercy on us and this young man. You alone are the true healer, but we are fighting in your battle. Give us strength and wisdom beyond our ways. We thank you and praise you. Amen." She opened her eyes. "Ready?"

At both of their nods, she picked up the tube. As if they'd been working together for years, Dr. Kenneth firmly clamped the boy's head. Easing the narrow tube up into the nostril and threading it through the inflamed tissues, Astrid could already feel the sweat dripping down her back and face. *Patience,* she ordered herself. All had to be done by feel, so she closed her eyes, the better to sense when to increase the pressure. "Done." She looked to Deborah. "Thank you." To her assisting doctor, "Thank you and please stay with him."

At his nod, she left the room and met with the Solbergs waiting right outside the door. "He did well. The tube is in. In just a few minutes, Dr. Johnson will wheel him out."

"Thank you, Astrid."

Did she do right? Would a trach have been better? Would that narrow tube actually give him enough air? Such thoughts bombarded her mind as she tossed her apron and cap into the laundry, scrubbed, and rubbed her mother's lotion into

her hands and arms, clear to her shoulders. *Lord,
like Mor keeps reminding me, I have to trust you,
but* . . . Arms propped on the edge of the sink,
head heavy, she waited, praying for that sense
of peace she'd felt the night before. *I've done all
I can, Lord. He is in your hands. Please, please,
leave him here with his family.*

"Your mor and Inga are in the examining room," one of the nurses said. She raised
both hands quickly, so Astrid's face must have
betrayed her thoughts. "No, no. Ingeborg wants
you to check Inga, just in case."

Astrid donned a clean apron and tucked
stray hairs back into the bun. *Smile. You know
Inga will see any sorrow.* She need not know
about Johnny right now. Did she dare let her
stand in the doorway to her pa's room?

Ingeborg sat in the chair, holding Inga
on her lap as the little girl fought to catch her
breath after a spasm of coughing.

Astrid forced a smile and leaned over to put
an arm around Inga's shoulders. "Not feeling
too good, are you?"

Inga looked up at her through eyes of misery. "Hurts."

"I know. I'm going to put you up on the
table, where I can see your throat better." She
slid her arms around the little girl and lifted her
to the examining table. "Open wide for me."
Inga did as she was told. "Can you say ah?"

Astrid checked carefully. While the throat

was red, most likely from coughing, her tonsils were somewhat swollen but no gray membrane—anywhere. Breathing a sigh of relief, she checked the neck. Glands were a little swollen, but that was to be expected.

"Clear?" Ingeborg stood beside her.

"Ja, most likely croup. Keep dosing her with cough syrup without laudanum but extra honey, steam, and—"

"Drink lots of fluids." Ingeborg picked up the mantra. "Thank you, Lord. That's what I thought, but my eyesight isn't what it used to be, and I just wanted reassurance." Ingeborg took Inga's hand and squeezed it. "Good thing we don't have far to walk."

"You want Dr. Johnson to carry her?"

Inga jerked upright, coughing again. When she could breathe again, she shook her head. "Can I see Pa?"

Astrid debated. "I'm sure he wants to see you too, but he is still very, very sick. He doesn't look too good."

"He is not going to die?"

"No, he is getting better."

Inga leaned into her grandmother. "Let's go home now."

"Can you walk that far?"

"I walked here." That was Inga, always practical. "Can I have ice cream?"

"Ja. Thelma can go get some."

"Soda." Inga coughed again. "Strawberry."

She looked to Astrid. "Will you come too, Tante Astrid?"

"Oh, how I wish."

Then she asked, "Is Johnny going to die?"

So she knew about Johnny Solberg. "I pray not." *Please, Lord, don't let her ask any more questions.* "Here, let me help you down." Surprised that Inga had not said anything about her ma, Astrid saw them out the door and waved good-bye.

Oh to be out in the fresh air, walking on the ground rather than a floor, no sounds of coughing. She turned back and closed her portal to the world. She could hear Thorliff coughing from here. But he was better. Her heart sang. Inga did not have diphtheria, Thorliff was better, and barring unforeseen complications, there was more hope for Johnny too.

And strawberries. Fresh strawberries. This was the season. How she would love to go pick strawberries.

She'd just finished breakfast when Daniel appeared in the doorway.

"What are you . . . ooh!" She grinned up at him, this dear thoughtful man. "Fresh strawberries!"

"Ma sent them over. She remembered how you like these." He handed her the bowl.

Astrid popped one in her mouth and closed her eyes in bliss. "You have no idea how much I wanted to go pick strawberries."

Love leaked out of his eyes and washed over her. "How are your patients?" he asked softly, never taking his eyes off her.

"Thorliff is improving slowly. Inga does not have diphtheria, and I have a better feeling about Johnny. He's not out of the woods yet, but he's not worse."

"Good. I'll get out of here then before you kick me out. Thank you for lifting the curfew. Blessing is coming back to life."

"Thank you, and thank Amelia for me too. Such a good gift to start this day." She watched him turn and walk from the room, waving at Mrs. Geddick. Did that woman never sleep?

Anji crossed the dew-bathed grass to sit on the bench set by the garden. This and the swing on the porch had become her favorite places to ponder. How could she miss Thomas already? He'd not been gone that long. He'd said he had to spend two weeks at the church that was interested in having him. Two weeks did not include the travel time. The town was somewhere east of Chicago, she believed. He probably wasn't even there yet.

Yet she felt like a cloud sat right on her. At their parting, she had agreed to think about whether she loved him and if so, how much. He said that he thought he loved her. Apparently his emotions were even more tangled up than hers. She had loved before, but he had not.

What if he really did need to leave Blessing? Did he have to agree to accept the call? If they wanted him, that is. How could anyone not want him?

Questions, questions, and no answers.

She heard the children in the house, the sounds floating out through the open window to her. The curfew was lifted. She would telephone Ingeborg and ask if they could come out to the farm to see the new calves and to see Emmy. She wondered if Benny might like to go too. She stood and stretched. When one needed wisdom, one talked with Ingeborg. Freda answered the ring.

"Good morning, can I talk with Ingeborg?"

"If you call Thorliff's, you can. She is helping with Inga, who has the croup, but not diphtheria."

"Oh, I see. I thought to bring the children out to play on the farm and—and talk with her."

"Call her there." That was Freda, abrupt as always.

"I will, takk." She had just turned to announce to her children that there would be no farm trip today when her ring sounded.

Sophie was calling. "Sure, put her through. Good morning, Sophie."

"We need to celebrate the lifting of the quarantine. How about you and the children come here for coffee? They can play while we catch up. We're taking cookies out of the oven right now. Rebecca is coming, and Penny. They can't stay long, so hurry up."

"You mean right now?"

"Ja, right now."

"We are on our way out the door." She hung up. "Melissa, please comb Annika's hair. Joseph, you have jam on your face. Hurry, we are invited to Sophie's for coffee."

Benny was waiting for them in his wheeled cart outside on the street. "Ma is coming in a minute."

When they'd all arrived, the children happily playing out in the yard, the women made themselves comfortable on the porch, Sophie dropping into her chair with a grin. "I have so missed all of you . . ." She flung her arms out. "Everybody."

"At least you could go to the boarding-house."

"Ja, and I watched everyone who came in like a starving hawk. Only I was looking for sickness. If anyone had coughed, I'd have banished him. I don't even trust the train bringing in people and supplies. Not that many stopped once they knew we were under quarantine. I am sure that if we got ahold of that crook, Stetler . . ." She glowered, then made an effort to regain her happy mood. "But like Reverend Solberg says, 'That is in the past and you can't change the past.' I do hope we've learned some lessons." She slapped the arm of the chair. "There I've done it again. Sorry." Blinking, she looked to the others. "I still cannot believe she has gone."

"I am so tired of the tears," Anji whispered, wiping the tears away.

"We all are. So let's cry and get it over with. I have learned that the tears give up eventually, and now we are gathered to be grateful we can finally do this again. Ingeborg said for us all to have a good time—she is taking care of croupy Inga—and to rejoice that it is not diphtheria." She shuddered. "I hate even saying the word. Like it might come creeping back out of some corner where it is hiding."

The others murmured agreement, sighed, and nodded.

Rebecca shook her shoulders and looked to Anji. "Tell us the latest installment."

"Becca!"

"We all need a touch of romance to lighten things up."

"Here you go, ladies." Helga, Sophie's sister-in-law and her lifesaver, as she referred to her, set a tray of cookies and glasses on the table. "Strawberry swizzle, first of the season. Help yourselves, and I'll be right back with the children's."

"Then sit down and join us," Sophie told her firmly. "Anything else that needs doing can wait." She turned to Anji. "So? You can drink and talk too."

Oh, how good it felt to laugh. Anji reached for a glass of swizzle, putting off an answer. She could feel her face heating up. Then, like reciting a lesson, she said, "Mr. Devlin . . ." Rebecca shook her head. "All right, *Thomas* received a letter from an Anglican parish, St. Patrick's on the Water, or something like that, in Michigan. They asked him to come visit and interview with them, possibly to become their pastor. Priest."

"Michigan? That's far away." Sophie stared at her. "You can't go to Michigan! You finally came back to Blessing."

"Thanks, Sophie. That is part of the problem."

"Do you love him?" Sophie gave her the piercing look that made even carousing drummers at her boardinghouse settle down.

Anji twisted her napkin, smoothed it out on her knee, and looked up to see all eyes staring at her. "I . . . I don't know. I mean, I care for him a great deal, but do I love him enough to change my life around all over again? I did that before . . ." She shook her head. "I can't see myself as a minister's wife. I don't really want to leave Blessing and my family again." She smiled at Rebecca. "But . . ."

"Aha. I knew it." Sophie bobbed her head. "I left Blessing all those years ago, and I was never so glad as to get back." She cocked her head. "Of course, my husband dying out on that fishing boat was awful. But I am grateful I could come home." She passed the cookie plate to Rebecca. "But if you love the man and this is what God wants for you, I guess we could wave good-bye to you. Devlin is a fine man and I, for one, hope he decides to stay here. Where he belongs."

"Yay, Sophie." Rebecca raised her glass. "You said it better than I could have."

"I was hoping to talk with Ingeborg today, but I will later. She always helps me think right."

"She helps all of us think right. Between her and my mor, we have much to live up to."

"I wish Astrid were here." Rebecca nibbled on her cookie. "She sure needs time away from that hospital. We never get to have our girls-together parties anymore. Did we outgrow them?" She looked out over the children to see her little son, Mark, chewing on a twig. "Be right back." She charged down the steps, grabbed him up, and took away his toy. He looked at her, his face starting to wrinkle up in the beginnings of a righteous howl. "Benny, could you give your brother a ride in your wagon for a bit?"

He smiled up at her. "Sure, come on."

"I'll pull." Joseph ran over to the wagon.

"Me too." And the children made her little son smile again.

"Thank you, all."

"A squall averted." Sophie grinned at Rebecca as she came back up the stairs. "You sure move fast for one of our advanced age."

Grateful the attention was off her, Anji sipped from her glass. *What am I going to do? I have no idea.* Thomas said he'd write . . .

The telephone jangling caught their attention. Sophie rose to answer it, shaking her head. "There better not be a crisis at the boardinghouse. I am fresh out of prepared-for-another-crisis." She returned a short time later. "That was Astrid. Thorliff is indeed better, but now the big concern is what she thinks is a partial paralysis on his right side. It is affecting his arm the most. Ingeborg is going to be giving lessons on how to help him regain his strength. She is hoping some of us can come to help." She stared at Anji.

Maybe there is something more I can do for Thorliff after all. Anji nodded back. "When?"

CHAPTER 30

*What has gotten into you? Thorliff Bjork-
lund, you do not seem to be even trying!*
"How is it going, Anji?" Ingeborg asked,
stopping beside her in room one. Together
they studied the man, breathing hard from the
exercises, but unwilling to even look at them.
The never-ending cough struck him again. But
when he tried to raise his right arm, it would
go no higher than a couple of inches off the
bed. His groan shredded Anji's heart. At least
his eyes looked a little more alive, even if it was
now anger that sparked them. She followed
Ingeborg out of the room.

"This is the second round today. It's been
a week now. Shouldn't we see some improvement?"

"There is slight improvement, more with

his leg than his arm. I'm beginning to wonder if this has affected his brain too. It would make sense, since the brain controls the motor functions. As soon as he can walk with a cane, I think we can move him home. That might help his mind too."

Anji flinched when they heard him coughing again. "He can sit on the edge of the bed, so at least he has full use of his left side." Her heart ached to see this man, usually so vital and pleasant, now barely civil.

"That cough is typical for a long time after diphtheria, so I read in one of Astrid's medical books. All we can do there is give him cough syrup with plenty of honey to soothe his throat. And keep up with the massage and movements. They will help strengthen him."

"I will be back tomorrow then, if you are sure I am helping."

"You are." Ingeborg walked out the door of the hospital with her. "How I love summer. The strawberries are slowing down, but the raspberries will be ready soon."

Anji stopped at the post office to see about the mail. A letter in her box. She pulled it out, fully expecting her mother-in-law's flowing penmanship. Instead, the handwriting was very masculine. Thomas wrote to her! She was beginning to think he'd forgotten. Without waiting to get home, she worked her fingernail under the edge and pulled out his letter.

Dear Anji,

As you no doubt have realized, I arrived here safely and have been made to feel very welcome. The town is smaller than Blessing, a hamlet, really, and my parish duties will include a second church, seven miles away. The people are mostly fishermen or farmers, mostly dairy and some orchards, and friendly. They have been without a priest for nearly a year and are very appreciative that I came to meet them.

It has been so long since I preached a homily, that is, a sermon, I wasn't sure I would remember how. I have met most of the families in the larger church, and the rectory, as they call the house where their priest has lived, is right next door. It is a good-sized house that is in need of some work. The former priest had been ailing for some time.

This next Sunday I will preach at both churches, first here in the morning and the other one in the afternoon.

I was so grateful to hear from John that Johnny lives. I know I asked you to write, but I will be home before it could get here. I will not make my final decision regarding this call until you and I can talk again.

Sincerely,
Thomas Devlin

Anji stared at the sheet in her hand. Rather a businesslike letter. She had no idea if he was excited about going there or would rather be in Blessing—with her. Tomorrow was Sunday, so he should be back by Wednesday or Thursday. That meant she would have to make up her mind what she wanted to do.

What she wanted to do was stay right here in Blessing, and after a time of courting, after all, that is what he asked her agreement for, marry Thomas Devlin and live happily ever after in this house she now called home. She wanted her children to call him Pa, and maybe they would even have a baby of their own. Turning into the gate, she shut it behind her and grinned when she heard her youngest's voice.

"Ma! You finally came home!" Annika charged to greet her, hugged her hard, then grinned up at her. "Did you bring ice cream?"

"Sorry, not today. Were you good for Mercy?"

"Ma, I am always good." She swung her mother's hand as they mounted the steps. "We baked cookies to go with ice cream."

"Where is everyone?"

"Joseph is with Benny, Lissa is upstairs reading, and I don't know where Gilbert is. I could have his ice cream."

"You don't give up, do you. Sure smells good in here." She removed her straw hat and hooked it on the coat tree.

At the supper table that evening, she looked to the other end and in her mind could see Thomas sitting there, like he had the one time. How easy it was to see him everywhere.

But Thorliff needs you. It wasn't the first time that thought had come to rest in her mind. *You can't leave Blessing. He needs you desperately, even though he does not realize his need. But I've just realized how much I love Thomas. Oh, how I hope he will remain in Blessing. I don't want to pick my children up and move again. Lord, how am I going to know what you want me to do?*

"Ma, are you all right?" Melissa asked, staring at her intently.

Anji jerked her mind back to the moment. "Sorry. Now, where were we?"

"I said grace." Gilbert wrinkled his forehead, always her worrier.

"And we passed you the food." Annika pointed to the bowls beside her.

"And I want to eat too," Joseph added from her right side.

Anji shook her head. "Just a lot on my mind." She dished up the chicken and rice and passed it on to her son. "Now, did you get those rows weeded in the garden?"

They all nodded. "We planted the rest of the beans. We sure are going to have a lot of beans." Gilbert dug into the food piled high on his plate.

"We'll can and then dry some too. The way you are all growing, we'll use a lot of beans. How about tomorrow, when I get back from the hospital, we pick up Inga and go see Grandma Ingeborg."

"Can Benny come too?"

"Why not?"

On Monday, when she was massaging Thorliff's arm and hand, she straightened his fingers one at a time. "All right, now push back. Harder. Come on, push."

"I am pushing!"

"I know. Now flex. Good again. Push." She glanced from his fingers to his face and returned a smile for his glare. "Your mor assured me she can see improvement. So we will keep working. You know you could use your left hand to do the same things I am doing with your fingers. Will you do that?"

"I already am."

"Good." She stepped back. "Now sit up straight and swing your legs over the edge of the bed." She watched him struggle with the right arm not responding and a horribly weakened body, but he sat up, using his left leg to push the other over the edge. How much easier it would be to assist him.

"It would help to have a bar to pull up on." He looked up at the ceiling. "Put a hook up there, ropes down, knotted to a bar. Tell Trygve I want to see him."

Out on the back porch at Ingeborg's, after the children all headed for the barn and the calves, Anji told her what had happened.

Ingeborg nodded, her smile widening. "Of course, perfect. And did you tell Trygve?"

"I did. I imagine it will be in place by tomorrow." Anji leaned back against the cushions of the wicker chair. "I have a problem and I need your advice."

"I hope I have some."

"Thomas wrote about the church in Michigan. He said he would not tell them his decision until he and I talked. I know he is going to ask me to marry him and move to that place."

"Do you love him?"

"I do, but . . ."

"But?"

"I want him to stay here. He can teach school and build things, and there is always lots of work here in the summer. My home and family are here. I don't want to uproot my children again."

Ingeborg studied her. "His calling is to be a parish priest. What is yours?"

"I . . ." She paused. "I think Thorliff will need help both to get well and to handle the paper. I can do those things for him. You know how I loved him and he loved me. Who better to help him now?"

A herd of noisy children swarmed up. "Ma, come see the calves and the baby kittens and the lambs and . . ." Joseph's words tumbled over each other. "And there are baby pigs too, and the mama is really grouchy." Annika came running up beside him.

"You didn't try to catch her babies, did you?"

Annika shook her head, setting her pigtails to bouncing. "No, Inga said no. Emmy did too. Benny laughed when I fell in the mud puddle." She lifted her pinafore skirt. "Stinky, like the pigs."

"How did you happen to fall in a puddle?"

Joseph said breathlessly, "The mama pig jumped at us and banged into the fence!"

Annika completed it. "And I runned."

"I see. You all sit on the steps. Freda has lemonade and cookies." Ingeborg started to rise, but Anji laid a hand on her arm. "I'll help."

The noisy, happy gang had their treat, then swarmed off again.

Ingeborg watched them. "They do enjoy this area. Are there farms in that part of Michigan?"

"Thomas mentioned that it was rural. I assume so. But not like here. There are none like here."

The silence between them started to grow heavy. Not unpleasant. Just heavy. *Calling* kept going through Anji's head. Thomas's calling, and hers.

Ingeborg stared off into the distance. "That Thomas is a wonder worker with children. Manny told me he had intended to run away and join the circus, but Mr. Devlin changed his mind."

"I knew Manny loved working with the animals. He was going to do that?"

Ingeborg nodded. "And he explained to me why he didn't. Mr. Devlin showed him that if you have two choices that can't be compromised, you go with the one that is best for you personally. Manny decided it would be best for him to finish school, and he didn't want Joker to get scrawny like the circus horses were. That's a brief summary. Manny's explanation took ten minutes." She turned and looked at her. "Two men, Thorliff and Thomas, are tugging at your heart. Which choice would work out best for Anji Baard?"

When Thomas Devlin stepped off the train on Thursday morning, his gaze found hers as if by a magnet. She felt that smile clear to her toes. He greeted Reverend Solberg and the others but strode directly to Anji. Fedora pushed back on his head, he stopped in front of her, a sparkle dancing in his eyes when she held out her hand.

"Welcome home," she said properly. He did not let go of her hand but tucked it into the crook of his arm. "I be in bad need of one of Rebecca's sodas. Will ye join me for one?"

As they drank their sodas and caught each other up on the news, a drum beat behind her eyes. *Remain in Blessing. Remain in Blessing.*

"So you really liked it there?" She fiddled with the straw in her empty soda glass.

"I do. The people are good there. I like the hills and ah, the trees. Magnificent trees. But most of all, I do believe God is calling me there." He covered her hand that lay on the table with his. "I want ye there with me, Anji."

The silence between them stretched tighter and tighter, so tight it began to hum.

"Anji, do ye love me?"

She looked across at him. "I think so, but Thomas, I . . . Yes. I do. But I also believe God is calling me to remain here. My children are so happy here. He brought me home again. Oh, how I wish—"

"Wish?"

"That you would stay here."

"I struggled with that too, ye know. But methinks I have learned a mite or two about the necessity of minding the business God has given me. I am certain again that me calling be the priesthood, and that has to be the most important part of me life. I want to serve Him with all my heart and soul. He brought me here for a time, but now He is saying St. Patrick on the Lake is where I need to be." He took both of her hands in his and leaned his elbows on the table. "So marry me and come with me."

Anji closed her eyes, feeling a tear meander down her cheek. "I . . . I can't."

Again, another stretch of silence, this one heavy with sorrow. Thomas squeezed her hands. "Aye, lass. I pray ye all happiness and peace. I am grateful for our time together and . . . give me best to yer children. I'll be leaving then on tomorrow's train."

"So soon?"

"It be best." He lifted her hands and kissed the back of each. "Go with God." He pushed his chair back, rose, and headed out the door.

Anji laid her face on the table and wept.

CHAPTER 31

W e cannot let Devlin go without a proper blessing." John Solberg nodded rather emphatically as he spoke.

"You are right, but what do you want to do?" Ingeborg, Kaaren, and Mary Martha all looked to him from their chairs on Ingeborg's porch. "If you want a meal after a church service, you take care of the service, and we will organize the food. The men will get the tables set up. But please, we need more than three days to do this." Ingeborg gave him a pleading look.

"He planned on just getting on the train and waving good-bye." John shrugged and shook his head.

"I am not surprised." Ingeborg shrugged. "He has no idea how important he has become to all of us in Blessing."

"He has agreed to wait until Monday to leave."

"Three days is what we have then." The women swapped headshakes and eye rolls. Kaaren sucked in a deep breath. "I am very grateful we have telephone service again. Ingeborg, you get the manpower going, and we'll do the calling. We will put up some signs for those who have no phones."

"Since we can't get anything printed, what if we send some of the older children around with an invitation saying to bring whatever you want for the meal and a baseball game will start after that. Devlin can umpire one more game before he leaves." John glanced to his wife and smiled when she nodded.

"I'll get the paper." Ingeborg had learned that she could have the odd pieces left from the printing press, so she always had a stack of paper for letters and for the children when they were playing school on a rainy day. She set the stack on the table and passed out pencils. "If we all print the same, we can get enough done in half an hour. Emmy will help too. Her printing is very legible."

"So the runners can go out later this afternoon?"

"Ja, we'll get this done."

As John roughed out a flyer, Ingeborg called Emmy in from the garden to help. And they all started printing out the invitations, or whatever they should be called. "I'll have Manny ride out to the farms when he comes in. Joker needs a good ride."

As soon as the papers were ready, the women divided up the telephone list, and Ingeborg called the construction office. "Good morning, Daniel. We need men on Sunday to put up the picnic tables, as we are having a good-bye blessing, dinner, and ball game for Thomas Devlin."

"I'll take care of that, but I tell you, I hate to see him leave."

"As do we all. And in such a short order."

"But you ladies will manage as you always do, and the men are always up for a ball game. Anything else you need?"

"Not at the moment. Takk." Ingeborg hung up and smiled at Emmy, who had the papers in a basket. Mary Martha had a stack to give to Melissa Moen and Linnea.

"Everyone will know by this evening. I'll start calling as soon as I get home." Mary Martha smiled at her husband. "Never underestimate the power of women in action."

"Especially the women of Blessing." Kaaren took her list to call and waved as she went out the door.

By the time the church bells tolled for the Sunday service, all the sawhorses had tops covered by tablecloths with rocks and bricks to hold them in place in case the light breeze picked up speed. The coffeepots were heating up on the stove in the church basement, and as people arrived for church, they set their covered dishes on the tables. Dish towels kept off the flies, and as the piano prelude flowed out the windows, people filed in to the church until it was full and then others sat on the benches outside the open windows.

Wearing his Sunday vestments and still in his office, Reverend Solberg nodded to Thomas Devlin. "You are prepared to say a few words?"

"Ye expect this Irishman to be sayin' only a few words?"

"I always have great expectations."

"That ye do."

"And you'll sit in the front row?"

Devlin shook his head. "If ye insist."

"Then let's go in and celebrate the time you have been with us." The two men walked out of the office to the left of the altar and took their places. Jonathan Gould was at the piano, Joshua Landsverk with his guitar, and two of the immigrants playing a fiddle and concertina. Gould paused, and at his nod, the congregation rose and joined in singing "Holy, Holy, Holy." Everyone sang with gusto in their different languages. Grace Knutson Gould signed the words in the front, and those who could not hear sang along with others by using their hands.

When the hymn ended, the amen was in perfect harmony, with all the parts.

Reverend Solberg stood in front of the congregation. "Welcome to our Lord's house on this Sunday He has given us as another gift. I believe heaven will sound like all of us together. Please be seated for the Scriptures. Garth Wiste will read the Old Testament lesson."

Garth strode to the front and read the story of God calling Abraham to a far land. "And behold, I will always be with thee."

"The Psalm for today is the twenty-third, and we will say it together. Please speak in the language you learned it. For those who want to read it, you'll find it in the back of the hymnal." When the rustling stopped, Solberg began, "'The Lord is my Shepherd . . .'" Many spoke in Norwegian, the Sidorovs in Russian, Devlin in Gaelic, and several other languages could be heard.

Again, they sang the amen.

Ingeborg felt goosebumps rise on her arms. She looked to Thorliff, who sat rigidly in front of her with Inga on one side and Astrid on his other side, holding Roald on her lap, with Daniel beside her. Since Thorliff's wife had died, church was nearly impossible for him, she well knew. *O Lord God, help him through this service. All I could do for months after Haakan died was cry through the hymns and often the sermon too. He fights so hard against the tears.* Her beloved husband, Haakan, had gone home to heaven two summers before. Thorliff reminded her of his far, Roald, who brought her as his new bride from Norway in 1880. Roald would never have allowed himself to cry. Straight, nearly frozen, were her son's shoulders. She wanted to reach over and rub his neck and upper back but knew better. He was barricading the door against his feelings for all he was worth. She was just grateful he was strong enough to be out of the hospital and sitting up in church.

"Our New Testament lesson for today will be read by Daniel Jeffers from Matthew 28:18–20."

"'And Jesus came and spake unto them, saying, All power is given unto me in heaven and in earth,'" Daniel started. "'Go ye therefore, and teach all nations, baptizing them in the name of the Father, and of the Son, and of the Holy Ghost: Teaching them to observe all things whatsoever I have commanded you: and, lo, I am with you always, even unto the end of the world. Amen.'"

Reverend Solberg moved to the pulpit and opened his Bible. "Our gospel today is Matthew 6:33. This is Jesus speaking to his disciples and not just the twelve. 'But seek ye first the kingdom of God, and his righteousness; and all these things shall be added unto you.'"

When he finished reading the verse, Reverend Solberg closed his Bible and looked down at

Thomas Devlin from the raised pulpit. "Today we honor a man God sent to us for a time and a season, Thomas Devlin. I met him the day he led his limping horse into town, and we became the kind of friends that only our God can put together. This Lutheran pastor and this Anglican priest have more in common than we ever knew, and our many hours of prayer, discussion, laughter, and service have blessed all of us.

"Thomas Devlin has ministered to many here because he can speak several languages and because he has the heart of a servant. He has prayed for people, helped me bury those who died, taught our children at the school, and taught woodworking skills to young men at the Deaf School. I was hoping God was going to leave him here with us, but he has now been called to a parish again and, sadly, not one near here. So today we will bless him and send him out as the apostles sent out Paul and Barnabas and Timothy.

"God calls all of us out into places we might not have chosen on our own. He has brought many of you here to Blessing for a livelihood, to become members of this family here, for all of us to grow in grace and the love and knowledge of God. We have been through fires, blizzards, floods, sickness, the struggles of growth, and the blessings He pours out on all as we care for one another. We have all generations here now, the original pioneers, their grown children, and now their children are growing, some starting school already. And all of you who came because we had work to offer you." He smiled around at all the families, so many sitting together in what had unofficially become their pews.

"We have lost those we love, and sometimes God has led us to the brink and then given us the gift of more time together." He cleared his throat as he looked out over the congregation, many of whom wiped their eyes or could not look at him. Solberg nodded. "And all of this has brought us closer together in this family of God. I thank Him daily for all of you, all of us, for the privilege of being your pastor for all of these years.

"Our Lord God reminds us over and over of how much He loves us and desires us to trust Him to teach us and guide us. He promises that no matter what happens in our lives, He will never leave us nor forsake us. He asks us to praise Him and thank Him for everything He gives us, even the hard and difficult things. We say, 'Lord, I trust you,' and then we try to figure out and plan by ourselves. Then we get in trouble and like Peter sinking in the lake cry out, 'Lord, help me.'

"Lord, help me! Three small words." He paused and gazed around, catching his parishioners' eyes around the entire room. "Lord, help me!" He spoke each word distinctly. "Lord God, help us all, as we learn to trust you and believe your Word." He paused.

"Lord, help me as I have to bid farewell to a friend. Yes, I pray we will see each other again. After all, it isn't the other side of the world, and we can write letters and perhaps even make telephone calls eventually. Ah, the blessings of so many modern conveniences. And above all, we can continue to pray for each other and our congregations. Help us, Lord."

He motioned to Devlin. "I have asked this Irish friend to speak a few words, and then I will say a blessing over him, and we will continue with the offering and a hymn, and together we will pronounce the benediction. Thomas, I give you our pulpit."

Devlin rose. "I be honored, John, but can I speak from the front here?"

"Whatever you wish, but you are passing up an amazing opportunity. I don't loan out my pulpit often." A chuckle ran over the congregation as Solberg sat down.

Thomas Devlin stood looking over the congregation smiling and nodding. "I am honored to have been with you these nearly two years. I had no idea when me and me horse limped into town what our God had in mind. All I had was some woodworking tools and a couple of dollars left in me pocket. Within a few hours, me horse was freed of the bolt that had caught in his shoe—this Irishman had no knowledge of horses—and the poor beast was put out to pasture and recovered well. I was put to work, given a place to live, and welcomed to dwell among you. Like me horse, meself found healing here in Blessing. This town be named so perfect. Blessing. I had no idea where me Father was going to put me to work, nor who He had in mind for me to help in some way. Blessing, a town that welcomes the stranger, puts him back together and, in this case, sends him on his way. Ye all have a place in me heart, and me thanks ye from the bottoms of me shoes that someone here added new soles to."

He smiled. "Thank ye every one and may our Lord continue to bless ye and prosper ye. And may we all, all be remembering that prayer of St. Peter. Lord, help me. May we remember to say it before we sink too far. We dwell under the shadow of His mighty wing and cling to His mighty hand. Amen."

He choked on the amen.

Solberg rose and stepped down to the floor, hymn book in one hand, and laid the other on Devlin's shoulder. "Thomas Devlin, fellow servant of our Lord God, may you go forth to serve your new parish with all wisdom and love, depending solely on His mighty Word and seeking His will moment by moment. May you be a blessing there and far more than you have been here with us. I thank our God for the privilege of friendship and teaching, as He said, iron sharpening iron. Let us pray." When the rustling stopped, he continued. "Thank you, Most High God, our heavenly Father, for the blessings you pour out upon us, and your promises to continue to protect us all, near and far, this congregation and the one that will be blessed by this man you have commissioned and sent forth. Lord God, we praise you and thank you. Amen."

The two men clasped each other in a mighty hug. Devlin sat down and Reverend Solberg nodded to the musicians. Four men walked forward to receive the carved wooden offering plates that Thomas Devlin and his woodworking students at the Deaf School had turned from a local seasoned oak tree and presented to the congregation months earlier. As they moved down the aisles, the musicians played "'Tis So Sweet to Trust in Jesus." Everyone rose to sing the offering hymn when the men came forward. "Let us pray together the prayer Jesus taught us to pray. 'Our Father . . .'" The congregation joined in and at the amen, the musicians moved into the doxology. Thomas joined John again, and together they raised their hands and prayed. "The Lord bless thee and keep thee. The Lord lift up his countenance upon thee and give thee His peace. In the name of the Father, and of the Son, and of the Holy

Spirit." They both made the sign of the cross as they did so.

The musicians began the hymn "Blest Be the Tie That Binds" as the two friends sang and strode down the aisle. At the amen, Reverend Solberg said, "Go in peace and serve the Lord." Everyone said amen. Jonathan Gould signaled his fellow musicians, and they played a medley of Irish tunes as the congregation rose, greeted each other, and filed out.

Thomas Devlin took a handkerchief out of his pocket and mopped his eyes. "Blessed for sure. Thank ye, my friend."

As the congregation reached them, both men greeted and shook hands.

"Do you have to leave?" Inga asked when she and Emmy took their turn, Ingeborg right behind them.

"I do, but I will never forget either one of ye."

"I don't like people to leave." Inga buried her face in her grandma's skirt, then sighed and turned to reach for her pa's right hand. Together they walked out the door, Thorliff using Haakan's cane, with Inga and Emmy on either side of him and Ingeborg carrying his son.

As folks gathered outside in their normal groups, the women getting the tables ready, someone whistled when all was prepared, and together they sang the table prayer.

Solberg nodded and announced, "Since today we honor Thomas Devlin, he will be at the front of the line and then will be the umpire behind the plate for our ball game. Thorliff will umpire first base and Lars will be behind the pitcher. Our teams will be announced after dinner. The diamond is all set at the school, and we have made sure to bat out away from the windows of both school and church. Let's eat."

"Must I truly be first?"

"Ye do!" John pointed to the head of the line.

"Then ye have to be second and Ingeborg third."

"Mighty bossy for a man who's leaving town."

"Ja, you Norwegians taught this wandering Irishman how to do that." With everyone laughing, the lines formed on either side of the long table, and people filled their plates.

Plate in one hand, fork in the other, Devlin wandered around visiting with people. When he came to Thorliff, he asked, "Did ye agree to umpire?"

Thorliff nodded. "Ja, I would rather play, bat the leather off the ball, but not yet." He lifted his weak right arm.

"I be right proud of you, son."

Thorliff tightened his jaw and inhaled as if running out of air. "Enough, please."

"Pa, Roald is eating dirt."

Thorliff rolled his eyes, and while unable to return the laughter from around him, he reached for his toddling son.

"Let me take him, please?" Ingeborg asked softly.

Thorliff nodded. "Be my guest." He set his empty plate down and rose to his feet. "You want some coffee?"

"Please and thank you."

Inga leaned against her grandma. "Pa has sad eyes."

"Ja, he does, but someday his happy eyes will be back." She snatched a leaf out of Roald's fat little fist and hugged Inga close with her other arm. "Let's see if we can keep him on the blanket, all right?"

Inga heaved a sigh and shook her head. "Roald will eat anything."

"You want to go get him a cookie?"

"Me too?"

"I'll watch Roald, Grandma, if you want to go visiting," Emmy offered.

"How about you go with Inga and bring us a plate with cake and cookies on it to go with the coffee Thorliff is bringing."

"Okay." Emmy smiled. "I'll take Roald for a swing later."

"Takk." Ingeborg watched the two girls, who were best friends, run off.

Astrid swooped over and picked up Roald,

making him giggle. "You getting in trouble again, Roally?"

"At the rate he is going, he is always going to be in trouble of one kind or another." Ingeborg smiled up at her son, who held out a cup of coffee. "Takk." She shifted back to Astrid. "I'm glad to see you here."

"No emergencies at the hospital, so I left Dr. Johnson in charge. He can handle most anything. I sure will hate to see him go."

"When does he leave?"

Astrid sat down on the blanket, one hand locked in Roald's suspender. "Another week. He asked if he can come back here when he finishes his residency."

"Really? I thought he was a city boy."

"He thought so too. If only we could afford him. I think the hospital would rather send us interns than pay a full-time staff member. I don't know. We have to do more talking."

Daniel and his mother joined them on the blanket, and Roald made a beeline for him. Ever since Elizabeth's death, Astrid and Daniel had spent more time with both Inga and Roald, helping take some of the pressure off Thelma, the Bjorklund housekeeper, since Thorliff spent so much time in his printshop.

Daniel lifted Roald up in the air and made him giggle even more. "How about washing this guy's face?"

Inga and Emmy brought back plates of

dessert, just in time for Inga to advise, "Roald does not like to have his face washed."

"Hands either," Emmy added as she passed the plate around.

"Five minutes to game time," Reverend Solberg announced. "I'll read off the teams as soon as everyone gets to the diamond."

"You sure you want to do this?" Daniel asked Thorliff.

"Ja, you going to play?"

"He better. His name is on the list." Astrid elbowed her husband. "No rest for the weary, you know."

"I thought that was for the wicked."

"I was trying to be nice."

"Onkel Daniel isn't wicked." Inga looked at Astrid like she needed scolding.

Ingeborg and Astrid exchanged headshakes.

"You tell 'em, Inga." He handed Roald back to Astrid. "Let's go play ball."

Ingeborg watched the two men walk off. Maybe a baseball game would help Thorliff think of something else for a change. Grief could eat one up if you allowed it. Losing his pa was hard enough, but losing Elizabeth along with good use of his right arm had hit her son horribly hard.

While the men headed for the field, the women gathered up their blankets and moved over to watch. Ingeborg showed the girls where to spread the blanket under the cottonwood tree that Inga had fallen out of. Since she broke her arm, others had fallen from the big tree also, causing various scrapes and bruises. She remembered the day they had planted the sapling to grow up and help shade the schoolhouse. Now there were other trees getting of shade size too. The whole town looked like it had been in place a long time as the trees had grown. Trees made a town feel more welcoming. Main Street used to be dusty in the summer, muddy in the spring, puddles when it rained, and frozen solid in the winter. The early pictures they had did not look welcoming.

"Where did you go, Mor?" Astrid asked.

"Sometimes I just get lost in memories." She smiled and grabbed Roald's suspenders again. "I have a feeling this young man needs a diaper change."

"I'll take care of him."

"Batter up!" called Devlin from behind home plate. "Blue team first. Rebecca promised free sodas to the winning team."

"I sure am going to miss Devlin," Ingeborg said with a sigh.

"Not as much as John will, and we have yet to find a schoolteacher for the high school, let alone the woodworking program at the Deaf School." Amelia Jeffers still taught English to anyone who wanted to come. She always had a big class but had started a new one on reading. Many of the immigrants could now converse in English, albeit with heavy accents, but they needed to be able to read too and know their numbers.

By the time the five-inning game finished, with blue winning by one run, Roald had slept for an hour, some of the spectators were hoarse from cheering their team, and all the players were dripping wet. Devlin announced the winning team and handed out tickets to be redeemed at the soda shop in the future. The ice cream makers who had been cranking the ice cream earlier announced the flavors, and everyone lined up for their bowl of ice cream. Big jugs of lemonade had been hauled over from the boardinghouse.

"What a celebration," Ingeborg said as she accepted the bowl of ice cream Inga brought her. "Takk."

"I got you strawberry 'cause I know you like that best."

"What kind are you going to get?"

"Strawberry, with chocolate syrup."

Devlin brought his dish over and sank down on the blanket. "I sure am going to miss this place and all of ye."

Ingeborg watched his face as he watched Anji Moen help dish out the ice cream. Leaving her behind would undoubtedly be the hardest thing of all for him. Being turned down when in love was never easy either.

EPILOGUE

Anji watched Thorliff fight a losing battle with his typewriter. "I can do that for you, you know. Just tell me what you want to say, and I'll type it."

"No!" Thorliff turned from the typewriter and his painfully learned left-handed typing. After more than four months of therapy, he could use his right arm and hand, but his fingers were stiff, clumsy, and terribly weak. "How many times do you suppose you've said 'The more you use your hand the better it will become?' Well, I'm trying. And nothing's happening. But your doing it for me isn't going to make it happen either, so stop offering." His clipped words grated. They stung. The dark circles around his eyes had grown larger in these last months, rather than diminishing.

"Sorry." She could do clipped too. All right, she understood he was frustrated. But she was only trying to help get the paper out on time, this time. The hours were speeding by, and he could be setting type, which he did adequately one-handed. "Do you want me to start setting?"

"No!" He used the back of his hand to kick the carriage back. He blew out a breath. "Look, Anji, I'm sorry I blew up. You have been and are a big help!" His tone slammed like the carriage. "I appreciate it. But I *have* to do this myself." He scrubbed his left hand over his hair, smearing ink on his forehead. "I sure wish Devlin had stayed here."

Yeah, well, so do I! Keeping her mouth shut took a major miracle. "So it's all right if Thomas Devlin helps you, but not Anji Moen." Sarcasm bit.

"I didn't mean it that way." He leaned forward to look at his page. "Stop taking me wrong."

"How many months have we been having this discussion, Thorliff? You can't manage, but you don't want me to help." Anji caught herself. She truly believed God had assigned her this calling. But right now! She sucked in a deep breath. "Sorry." A calling was not necessarily an easy thing.

He yanked the paper out of the carriage. "Proofread this for me and then I'll get it set. If nothing more goes wrong, we'll get this printed yet tonight."

Or die trying? She didn't say that, but she couldn't hold back the "You're welcome." She hoped the ice dripping from her tone caused bleeding. He had resented her from the first time his mother showed her how to move his right leg, shoulder, arm, and lastly the hand. The hand that would rather become a claw. With both her and Ingeborg working with him, he had finally been able to walk with barely a limp, but the arm and the hand were as stubborn as his manly pride. Why was it so hard for a man to accept help? Especially help from a woman?

Ten o'clock had come and gone by the time they had the paper printed, folded, and bundled, ready for Lemuel to distribute in the morning. Her hands ached, her shoulders, back, and clear down to her feet. If she felt this beat, what about him? *"Serves you right"* itched to be said.

Under normal circumstances, even when she and Thomas had filled in while Thorliff was still bedridden and until he got on that train, the job should have been done by five. There were weeks without a paper in Blessing, but when he was finally able to oversee the press with Anji doing the labor, things had gone more smoothly. Several times they had been forced to skip a week, taking two weeks for an edition, especially when he decided he should be able to do it himself again. She had written most of the news, almost like dictation, but when he decided he would type too . . . She would rather teach school any day.

At the sink she scrubbed the ink off her hands and watched him struggle through cleaning both of his hands. He refused her help there too, so she had stopped offering. If only he were not so stubborn, stubborn and proud, life could be so much easier for him.

And for her. She damped the stove, he blew out the lamps, and they shrugged into their coats. Wrapping her scarf over her head and around her neck, she tucked the ends in her coat.

"Winter is coming early." Stepping into the cold, she tried to ignore the bite of the November wind.

He paused. "Anji? Thank you."

The shock of those simple words took her breath away more than the wind. Especially after *this* miserable evening. "You are welcome."

She stopped at the gate, then turned to watch him mount the steps, one foot on a riser, the weak foot up beside, then one up again. Halting, using the hand rail on the left. She always made sure he got into the house since the night he had slept in the newspaper office because he was too tired to make it to the house. She only knew that because Thelma had told her.

Wind scudded the clouds in front of the moon that lit her way. While some snow still hid in the shadows, most of the first snowfall of the year had melted. Replaying this paper production in her mind and not any closer to answers to questions she wasn't clear on either, she hurried up her walk. Grateful that Mercy had set a lamp in the window to light her way, she opened the front door and stepped inside to warmth.

"I'm home."

Mercy rose from the rocking chair near the heat vent from the coal furnace. A textbook slid from her lap to the floor. She yawned and stretched. "I must have dozed off."

"Mercy, I'm thinking that on the nights we put the paper out, you should plan on staying here, especially now that winter has blown in."

"If you'd like. I usually make breakfast when Miriam works the night shift, but the others can do that." She bent over to pick up her book and yawned again. "Starting next week?"

"Good, then you can go to bed when you want to." Anji dug in her purse and pulled out a quarter. "Thank you again." She walked Mercy to the door and watched her leave, then took her place in the rocker. The warm air reminded her she needed to stoke the furnace and damper it down for the night. Tomorrow she would teach Norwegian again at the high school. But instead of moving immediately, she rocked and enjoyed the heat, her thoughts turning heavy.

She and Thorliff never used to fight like this. She should be able to ignore his anger and impatience, but sometimes she almost walked out on him. Perhaps that would make more of an impact than staying silent or slipping into sarcasm. Or better for her so she didn't have to live with *"You shouldn't have said that"* or *"You should have said . . ."* *Lord, I just don't know how to handle this. I've been so happy to be back in Blessing, and I truly felt . . .* She paused. Felt. Did she no longer feel that helping Thorliff was what God had called her to do? *Had* was another stumbling word. *Anji Moen, you do not give up because something is difficult. If you learned nothing else from your mor, you know better.* But sometimes knowing better and slogging through created an interior war.

She blew out a sigh that tried to turn into a cough. "Lord, I want to do your will, but sometimes figuring it out is terribly hard. I want my family to be happy and healthy. I want to help Thorliff. Oh, how I miss Thomas." Her mouth dropped open. That one had snuck up on her. She blew out another sigh.

And a vivid thought struck unexpectedly. Is a calling always forever? Or can it be for a season? A purpose?

She would say, and Ingeborg agreed with her, that Thorliff still needed her, but maybe he did not. He clearly resented any help she offered. What if her calling here in Blessing had ended?

He paid her a small sum to work on the paper, but that was different. That was a job, not a calling. Or was it all part of the same package?

Eyes closed, she remembered when they were young, feeling so grown up—so in love. She couldn't be near him without feeling little zings and sizzles. She knew he had felt the same way, both in wonderment at the glory that was their love. Now there were no such feelings. She wanted to at least remain friends, but at times she wondered if that was even possible. It certainly was not probable, as short and snappy as he always was. And always with her, not with others. At least that's the way it seemed to her.

Lord, it seems to me that you called me to stay here and help bring Thorliff back to health. Could that calling be complete?

Her mind floated instantly to Thomas Devlin.

Thomas had written to her only once in the months since he'd left, although to be fair, it sounded as if he was very busy with two churches in his parish. His letter was pleasant. He told how the congregation had given him a horse and buggy, and he had no idea whatever how to care for a horse. He was taking horse-care lessons from the parish boys.

Working at odd hours, he was restoring his manse or rectory, as he called the house. He had mentioned the necessary repairs. No surprise there. She knew he was a master carpenter and woodworker. In his spare time he was carving gargoyles for the larger of the two churches. Gargoyles? He stated strongly that he missed life in Blessing but made no mention of love. Had his feelings toward her cooled, or was he simply the usual, practical Thomas?

He did seem to write to John Solberg regularly, so if he became ill or had a problem, John would find out first and tell Anji. What a curious relationship. But what if he had met someone else to spend his life with? Would John hear about that? Maybe not.

Her children asked after Thomas often. Even little Annika asked God to bless Mr. Devlin in her prayers at night. Perhaps moving from Blessing would not be as hard on them as she'd feared . . . if she could be with Thomas. They could come home to visit. They could write letters. But . . .

But! How could one little word have such heavy jobs to do?

The old saw said that absence makes the heart grow fonder, but sometimes it went the other way. Especially for practical people.

If Thomas were to find someone new, it would be because the old flame had flickered out. Absence can do that. And by doing nothing, Anji would be partly to blame.

Was there a future for Anji with Thorliff? She knew she could not simply sit on her hands when he struggled with something. She would keep trying to help him. It was the way she was. And he would probably keep resenting it, a constant source of friction. Too, it would take him years to get over Elizabeth, if at all. What if he never did?

Thomas.

Thorliff.

Thomas.

Thorliff.

Lord God, I want to walk in your will, like Ingeborg says. "Wait on the Lord . . ." from Psalm 27 was one of her favorite verses. She also said she'd been learning that all her life.

"I will wait. I will trust." Anji spoke into the silence. Sometimes silence was a comfort, other times . . . But tonight, the silence did not feel heavy but full of peace. Tears burned the back of her throat and nose and trickled down her cheeks. Sniffing didn't stop them, so she pulled out the handkerchief she kept tucked into her sleeve and blew her nose. Mopped her eyes and tipped her head against the back of the chair. *Thank you.* She nodded along with the rocker. *Thank you.*

During the week she wrote the articles Thorliff asked her to, taught her classes at the high school for two days, made sure her children did their homework, had supper one night with Rebecca and family, attended church on Sunday, in short did all the normal things of her daily life. Another snowstorm blanketed the area, the temperatures fell, and everyone admitted that winter was truly settling in.

Thorliff taught at the high school, filling in for the loss of Thomas Devlin, and spent far more time at the office because everything took him so long to accomplish.

One day, when sun turned the snow to eye-blinding glitter, the two left school at the same time. "Anji, could you please come to the office?"

She mentally ran through her list of things she needed to do at home. "To work on the paper, you mean?" The thought of another session like the last one made her stomach clench.

"No, I think we need to have a talk."

Relief warmed even her nose. "I need to go home and stoke the furnace and start supper. Then I'll leave a note for the children. Lissa can manage for a while."

"Good. Thank you."

Puzzled was all she could think as she went about her chores. What could he want to talk about? Maybe fire her from the newspaper? While she appreciated the money, she could do without the misery of putting the paper out. Confusion roiled her mind into all kinds of scenarios. He was giving up the paper. He was having a relapse and didn't want anyone to know. As she went out the door, *dread* was the only word that even began to cover her tumultuous fears and feelings. The last place she wanted to go was to the newspaper office.

When she stepped into the warmth of the building, she realized he had built the fire to heat the office, while the printing room door was closed. She inhaled the fragrance of coffee and saw a platter of gingerbread with applesauce on the counter. Thelma had been at work. She removed her gloves and stuffed them into her pockets, then hung her coat, hat, and scarf on the coatrack by the door. Was she stalling? Most likely. Although the coffee and gingerbread—no, that was Thelma. *Keep your thoughts under control. Be gracious and do not let him upset you. Be calm. Smile. Lord, help me.* The uneven clatter of the typewriter did nothing to calm her.

"Would you please bring the tray in with you?" he called.

Thorliff asking for help? "Of course." Anji picked up the tray and set it on the corner of the desk. "Shall I pour?"

"Ja, coffee sounds mighty good." He flexed his fingers and glared at the typewriter.

Anji ignored his glare while at the same

time felt sorry he had to work so hard at making his hand work. She poured the coffee and set cup and plate beside the typewriter. Then, pulling the other chair up to the front of the desk, she set her cup and plate in place. The actions helped quiet the thoughts rampaging through her mind. She inhaled the fragrance before taking a sip to see how hot it was. "At least this hasn't been sitting on the stove here and turning to mud." Humor might help.

He worked his right hand with his left, an almost flinch twitching his eyebrows. "The cold is making it worse, I think."

"Probably." She started to suggest putting his hand in warm water and clamped a stop on her mouth. *Do not set him off again with unasked for help.* The papers scattered across the desk made her hands itch to fix. Thorliff used to be so fastidious, with pages stacked neatly, books on the shelves, pencils in the cup he kept for them.

He heaved a sigh and picked up his cup with his left hand, stretching the other around it. "Thank you for coming."

"You are welcome." Formal might be best.

"I have been talking with John . . ."

Her eyes widened and she hid behind a forkful of gingerbread and applesauce.

"He mentioned that he had a letter from Thomas Devlin."

"Ja, I know they have been corresponding."

Thorliff stared into his mug of coffee. "I thought perhaps you and Devlin were interested in each other."

"We were good friends."

"I thought it more than that. Elizabeth . . ." His voice cracked. A pause that felt long, though it might not have been. "She mentioned that she thought . . ." He inhaled, his fingers clenching the mug. "She had the impression that Thomas was courting you." He cleared his throat. "And then he received the call to that parish in Michigan."

Anji waited. It was a good thing the applesauce helped the gingerbread slide down her throat.

"Did he ask you to marry him?"

"Ja."

"So why didn't you?"

"I . . . I didn't want to leave Blessing. My children are so happy to be here, and I felt like I had come home again. After all, I grew up here and . . ." She forced herself to look up, to find him watching her.

"And?"

"And after all that happened last summer, I felt that God was telling me to stay here."

"To take care of me?"

"To help you regain your strength, and I knew you would need help with the newspaper. Between Astrid and Ingeborg, they needed help too."

"Anji, you changed your life for me years ago."

"I loved you."

"And I loved you, but you ordered me to get on with my new life and not come back here for you. I thought you would wait for me. I thought I was getting an education for us."

"I believed you needed freedom to do all you dreamed of doing. It seemed the best thing at the time." The two of them stared at each other. No spark that danced like it did those years ago when all they wanted was to be together, to . . . Only—only sadness. Or acceptance?

Thorliff leaned back in his chair, slowly shaking his head. "And now you . . . Anji, I am grateful for the help you have given me." His head continued to move from side to side. The silence and the air both felt heavy, as always overlaid with the odors of ink and paper.

Anji left the last piece of gingerbread on the plate and set it back on the desk. A thought floated through her mind. *A calling might not be forever.* She watched as he massaged the right hand with his left. Could God be releasing her from . . . from helping Thorliff? What if all the past was in the past? A memory of Thomas at her kitchen table for supper, laughing with her children. Promising the boys that he would teach them how to use a carving knife. Smiling at her and her heart feeling both a leap and a laugh.

"I have learned that one of the immigrants

worked once on a newspaper. He can set type too, although in Dutch. He has learned to speak English well enough from Amelia to tell me that he is now learning to read and write English too."

"So you are saying I am fired?" She hoped she made it sound like a joke.

He didn't look at her. "I am going to cut back to every other week for now."

She stared at him in surprise. "Good for you." Then glanced up at the clock on the wall above the door. "I need to get home."

"Thank you . . . for everything."

Walking home, Anji kicked away a clump of snow and ice. A crow scolded her from the bare branches of the maple tree in front of the boardinghouse. When it flew away, she felt like she could fly too, as she watched the black wings beat against the unseen air. Freedom, that crow was free. And now she was too. "Thank you, Lord. I believe I have learned one of your lessons today. You have freed me. I don't know what is going to happen next, but tonight I will write a letter. If Thomas Devlin is to be in my life, that too will be if you will it. One step at a time."

That night after the children were in bed, she sat down at the desk in the parlor and pulled out paper and pen. She hushed the voice that whispered *But what if he has changed his mind?*

with a firm admonition. *God is in control. I can only go forward.*

> *Dear Thomas,*
> *I know Reverend Solberg has kept you abreast of all the news of Blessing, not that there is that much. Everyone here misses you, including Thorliff. He told me he wishes you were still here to help with the newspaper. His right hand is not working as well as it should, or rather will, according to Ingeborg. I too wish you were here.*
> *I have been doing a great deal of thinking and praying . . .*

Her pen paused. She almost wrote *I truly believe my calling here is completed.* But she caught her hand before the words poured out. That would be a matter for later, if and when they sat talking face to face.

She continued.

> *I have realized that sometimes in life, or maybe mostly in life, we can only go forward. We cannot go back. If that is still your desire, I would be overjoyed to go forward with you.*
> *With love and basking in the streams of God's mercy,*
> *Anji*

She read it through again. *Yes, in this life, we cannot go back.*

Lauraine Snelling is the award-winning author of over 70 books, fiction and nonfiction, for adults and young adults. Her books have sold over 4 million copies. Besides writing books and articles, she teaches at writers' conferences across the country. She and her husband make their home in Tehachapi, California.

Don't Miss the Beginning of the Story!

Visit laurainesnelling.com to learn more.

Miriam intended to complete her nursing training in Blessing, North Dakota, and then return home. But her growing attachment to Trygve Knutson soon has her questioning a future she always considered set in stone.

To Everything a Season
SONG OF BLESSING #1

After she is called home due to a family emergency, will nurse-in-training Miriam Hastings find a way to support her loved ones and return to Blessing, North Dakota—and the man who is never far from her thoughts?

A Harvest of Hope
SONG OF BLESSING #2

◈ BETHANYHOUSE